Simply Learning, Simply Best!

Simply Learning, Simply Best!

新托福100+

iBT單字

倍斯特編輯部◎著

《三大學習特色》

破解字彙密碼、準確猜測上下文字義、
強化不熟悉主題的應答力

1. 「字首、字根、字尾」學習法：迅速於腦海中建構單字藍圖，輕鬆記憶1萬單！
2. 「語境記憶法」：秒提升由上下文推測文意的能力，表現超乎水平的實力。
3. 「主題式記憶法」：擴充知識面及廣度，增進初次閱讀各類型文章時，片刻就理解未知訊息的能力。

Editor's Preface

編 者 序

❶「字首、字根和字尾」學習法

新托福考試中尤其在聽力跟閱讀測驗中，主題極為廣泛會需要一定量的單字才能聽懂或理解文意，其中最快速累積字彙量和最常使用的就是「字首、字根和字尾」學習法。考生能在累積相當字彙後使用此學習法串起更多的字彙，迅速增加字彙量。考試的閱讀文本和題目中，同、反義詞的轉換也是影響得分的關鍵之一，在閱讀中更可以使用此學習法憑藉字首等迅速了解字彙是否是「否定」字義等等，了解單字是哪個領域的字彙。此外，書籍中規劃了324組必會的學習詞組，能快速累加學習到的字彙，在備考上更為無往不利。

❷「語境」學習法

在閱讀中不太可能每個字都懂，學術閱讀中更充滿著許多專有名詞等，但卻不需要每個字都懂才能答對或理解文意。例如：雖然看不懂專有名詞，但專有名詞後會有同位語以更簡單的子句等等去解釋該專有名詞的概念。而書籍中雖無文法介紹，但規劃了vocabulary in

context的學習法，其實意思近似於同位語等的概念，都是用閱讀技能強化學習跟答題。語境學習法則是強化推測文章中單字的能力，即the ability to make an inference，因為在很多時候透過推測段落文意就能答對新托福或英語測驗中的單字題。考生可以使用書中的練習累積更多同反義字並強化自己閱讀推測文意的能力，讓自己答題上能表現出超乎自己水平的實力。

❸ 主題式學習法

新托福考試中主題廣泛，常常是我們不熟悉的主題，書籍中規劃了主題式學習法，考生可以藉由閱讀更多主題的文章拓寬自己的知識面，降低自己遇到不熟悉文章時的答題表現以及閱讀時間不夠的問題。此外，考生更可以多聽音檔，累積更多高階字彙與提升自己寫作水平。

倍斯特編輯部 敬上

使｜用｜說｜明

INSTRUCTIONS

- 精選例句，例句均中英對照便於學習，背誦例句能大幅提升英文寫作能力。

- 每個字首／字根／字尾均搭配精選四組單字，可倍速擴充字彙量和相似詞。
- 除此之外，更可以靈活運用於記憶書中未列出的字彙，短時間內累積數千字彙量。

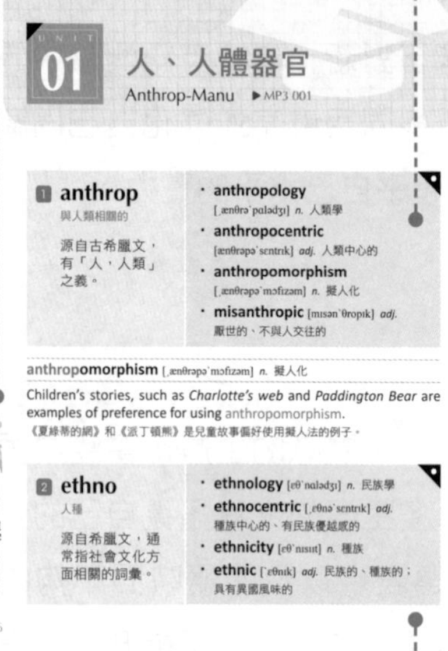

UNIT 01 人、人體器官

Anthrop-Manu ▶MP3 001

1 anthrop
與人類相關的

源自古希臘文，有「人，人類」之義。

- **anthropology** [ˌænθrəˋpɑlədʒɪ] *n.* 人類學
- **anthropocentric** [ænθrəpəˋsɛntrɪk] *adj.* 人類中心的
- **anthropomorphism** [ˌænθrəpəˋmɔfɪzəm] *n.* 擬人化
- **misanthropic** [mɪsənˋθrɑpɪk] *adj.* 厭世的、不與人交往的

anthropomorphism [ˌænθrəpəˋmɔfɪzəm] *n.* 擬人化

Children's stories, such as *Charlotte's web* and *Paddington Bear* are examples of preference for using anthropomorphism.
《夏綠蒂的網》和《派丁頓熊》是兒童故事偏好使用擬人法的例子。

2 ethno
人種

源自希臘文，通常指社會文化方面相關的詞彙。

- **ethnology** [ɛθˋnɑlədʒɪ] *n.* 民族學
- **ethnocentric** [ˌɛθnəˋsɛntrɪk] *adj.* 種族中心的、有民族優越感的
- **ethnicity** [ɛθˋnɪsɪtɪ] *n.* 種族
- **ethnic** [ˋɛθnɪk] *adj.* 民族的、種族的；具有異國風味的

IBT單字100+ 16

ethnology [ɛθˋnɑlədʒɪ] *n.* 民族學

Ethnology is a study which focuses on human societies and cultures.
民族學是一門專精於人類社會與文化的學問。

3 vir
男、男性的

源自於拉丁文男性、男人的意思，於英文衍生為人類的意思。

- **virilescent** [ˌvɪrɪˋlɛsənt] *adj.* 擁有男性特質的
- **virilization** [ˌvɪrɪlaɪˋzeʃən] *n.* 男性化、變成男人的過程
- **virility** [vɪˋrɪlɪtɪ] *n.* 陽剛氣息、男性魅力
- **virile** [ˋvɪrəl] *adj.* 有男子氣概的、陽剛的

virilescent [ˌvɪrɪˋlɛsənt] *adj.* 擁有男性特質的

The strict and unreasonable female principal Agatha in the fiction *Matilda* is a very virilescent character.
小說《瑪蒂達》中，嚴格又不講理的女校長阿格莎是一個非常陽剛的角色。

4 fem
女、女性的、陰性的

源自於拉丁文，具有「女性的」或「非男性的」意思。

- **femininity** [ˌfɛməˋnɪnətɪ] *n.* 女性氣質、女人味
- **feminism** [ˋfɛmənɪzəm] *n.* 女權主義
- **feminine** [ˋfɛmənɪn] *adj.* 女性氣質的
- **female** [ˋfimel] *n.* 女性、雌性 *adj.* 女性的、雌性的

femininity [ˌfɛməˋnɪnətɪ] *n.* 女性氣質、女人味

In *The Danish Girl*, artist Einar first found his femininity when his wife asked him to dress like a woman and to be her painting model.
電影《丹麥女孩》中的藝術家艾納在妻子要求他裝扮成女人以當她的繪畫模特兒時，第一次發現他的女性特質。

PART 01 字首、字根、字尾記憶法
PART 02 語境記憶
PART 03 主題式記憶：神秘事件

17

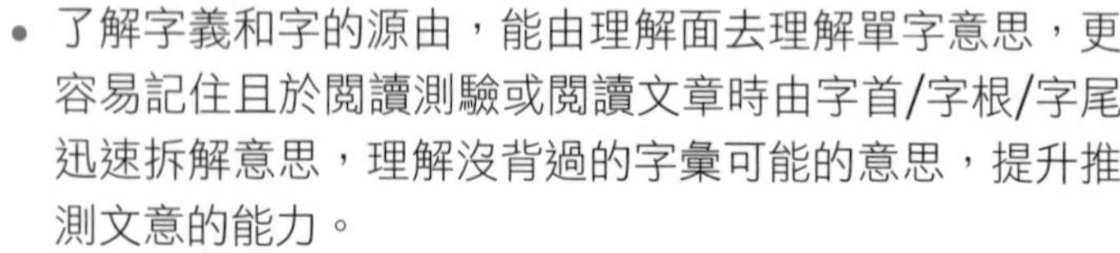

- 了解字義和字的源由，能由理解面去理解單字意思，更容易記住且於閱讀測驗或閱讀文章時由字首/字根/字尾迅速拆解意思，理解沒背過的字彙可能的意思，提升推測文意的能力。

- 例句中英對照，便於翻閱和學習。
- 除了作對題目外，每個選項的字彙均為常考字，有要將其列入背誦字彙表中。

- 由測驗題理解同義詞意思，提升閱讀上下文推測文意和理解力，並記憶相關詞組的同、反義字，提升應試水平。

UNIT 01 精選必考字彙

Vocabulary in Context

❶ The newly elected administration has launched an aggressive ________________ for federal counterterrorism in hopes of solidifying national security.
Planning is in the closest meaning to this word.
A. transaction　B. prejudice
C. strategy　D. disconnection

❷ The research findings about hypnosis healing remain inconclusive and ________________; therefore, the curing method still has a long way to go.
Debatable is in the closest meaning to this word.
A. potential　B. anxious
C. magnificent　D. controversial

❸ Animal rights groups ________________ to take more drastic measures unless the cosmetic manufactures stopped inhumane animal tests.
Announced is in the closest meaning to this word.
A. claimed　B. unraveled
C. surrendered　D. liberated

❹ The Internet ________________ among adolescents brought about serious academic and personality problems and has gradually aroused social attention.
Dependence is in the closest meaning to this word.
A. governance　B. addiction
C. retreat　D. provocation

❶ 新上任的內閣已經推動積極的國家反恐策略，為的是希望鞏固國家安全。
Planning 的意思最接近於這個字。
A. 交易　B. 偏見
C. 策略　D. 中斷

❷ 有關於催眠治療的研究發現依舊是未定且有爭議的；因此，這種治療方式仍有待努力。
Debatable 的意思最接近於這個字。
A. 有潛力的　B. 焦慮的
C. 壯麗的　D. 有爭議的

❸ 動物權益團體宣稱，除非化妝品製造廠商停止不人道的動物實驗，否則將採取更激烈的手段。
Announced 的意思最接近於這個字。
A. 宣稱　B. 闡明
C. 投降　D. 解放

❹ 青少年的網路成癮導致嚴重的課業及人格問題，並且逐漸地引發社會關切。
Dependence 的意思最接近於這個字。
A. 管理　B. 上癮
C. 撤退　D. 挑釁

答案 ❶C ❷D ❸A ❹B

使 | 用 | 說 | 明

INSTRUCTIONS

- 精選有趣的主題，若是寫TPO感到累，也可讀讀鬼屋等有趣的閱讀小文章，活絡思緒。

01 UNIT The Loch Ness Monster
尼斯湖水怪

MP3 028

The Loch Ness Monster is an aquatic creature said to live in Loch Ness, a lake in the Scottish Highlands. The earliest mention of "Nessie," another name for it, can be dated back to AD 565. The modern legends of the Monster have started since 1933. However, it became famous only when the so-called "Surgeon's Photograph," taken by a London doctor, Robert Wilson, was published in 1934. The picture was the first photo that clearly captured a dinosaur-like creature with a long "head and neck."

尼斯湖水怪據說是住在蘇格蘭高地尼斯湖的海洋生物。小尼斯，它的另一個名字，最早被提及的時間可追溯到西元 565 年。水怪現代的傳說則從 1933 年開始。然而，它是在由倫敦醫生羅勃．威爾遜所拍攝所謂的「外科醫生的照片」在 1934 年出版後才出名的。這個照片是第一張很清晰地顯示出具有長的頭部和頸部像恐龍般生物的照片。

字彙加油站

aquatic *adj.* 水生的；水棲的	surgeon *n.* 外科醫生

2 MP3 029

Specialized and amateur investigators kept launching expeditions, using sonar and underwater photography to search in the deep lake and tried to explore the truth about it. Over the years, a variety of explanations have been made to account for sightings of the Monster. The giant long-necked creature could probably be an eel, a bird, an elephant, or a resident animal. Nevertheless, nothing conclusive was found. The famous 1934 photo was later proven to be fake, and most scientists claimed it was impossible for a dinosaur-like creature to have survived for millions of years. With the complicated formations of the water areas there, till today, scientists still can't be sure if the monster actually exists.

專業和業餘的調查學者，不停地發動探險，並使用聲納和海底攝影術到深湖去搜尋它。多年以來，有各式各樣的說明來解說被目擊到的水怪。這隻巨大的長頸生物很可能是鰻魚、鳥、大象，或是當地的生物，然而，沒有得到具體的證實。後來，1934 年著名的照片被證實是假造的，而大部分的科學家們宣稱像恐龍般的生物要存活數百萬年是不可能的。由於尼斯湖地形複雜，直到今日，科學家們仍舊無法確定水怪是否存在。

字彙加油站

amateur *adj.* 業餘的；外行的	investigator *n.* 調查者；研究者
launch *v.* 開辦；發起	expedition *n.* 遠征；探險
conclusive *adj.* 決定性的；最終的	survive *v.* 由……生還；活下來

285

- 精選字彙，段落中的字彙均為常考字，也可以將未列出的字彙列在筆記本上，考前複習衝刺用。

- 由各主題的短段落擴充知識面，提升應試時閱讀不同主題的應對能力。
- 聆聽MP3強化聽力和學習成果，並記憶每個段落中所遇到的不熟悉的字彙。

CONTENTS

目 錄

1 PART 字根・字首・字尾記憶法・

2 PART 語境記憶

CONTENTS

3 PART 主題式記憶：神秘事件

CONTENTS

字根

共八大主題包含人、人體器官、心理感覺、行為動作、性質狀態、實務器具、顏色溫度、方位、動植物與自然界。

字首

共四大主題，包含空間方位與程度、否定、使成為、除去、取消。

字尾

共兩大主題，包含名詞字尾和形容詞字尾。

PART 01

·字根·字首·
·字尾記憶法·

人、人體器官

Anthrop-Manu ▶MP3 001

1 anthrop

與人類相關的

源自古希臘文，有「人，人類」之義。

- **anthropology** [ˌænθrə`pɑlədʒɪ] *n.* 人類學
- **anthropocentric** [ænθrəpə`sɛntrɪk] *adj.* 人類中心的
- **anthropomorphism** [ˌænθrəpə`mɔfɪzəm] *n.* 擬人化
- **misanthropic** [mɪsən`θropɪk] *adj.* 厭世的、不與人交往的

anthropomorphism [ˌænθrəpə`mɔfɪzəm] *n.* 擬人化

Children's stories, such as *Charlotte's web* and *Paddington Bear* are examples of preference for using anthropomorphism.

《夏綠蒂的網》和《派丁頓熊》是兒童故事偏好使用擬人法的例子。

2 ethno

人種

源自希臘文，通常指社會文化方面相關的詞彙。

- **ethnology** [ɛθ`nɑlədʒɪ] *n.* 民族學
- **ethnocentric** [ˌɛθnə`sɛntrɪk] *adj.* 種族中心的、有民族優越感的
- **ethnicity** [ɛθ`nɪsɪɪt] *n.* 種族
- **ethnic** [`ɛθnɪk] *adj.* 民族的、種族的；具有異國風味的

ethnology [εθˋnɑlədʒɪ] *n.* 民族學

Ethnology is a study which focuses on human societies and cultures.
民族學是一門專精於人類社會與文化的學問。

3 vir 男，男性的 源自於拉丁文男性、男人的意思，於英文衍生為人類的意思。	▪ **virilescent** [ˌvɪrɪˋlεsənt] *adj.* 擁有男性特質的 ▪ **virilization** [ˌvɪrılaɪˋzeʃən] *n.* 男性化，變成男人的過程 ▪ **virility** [vɪˋrɪlɪtɪ] *n.* 陽剛氣息、男性魅力 ▪ **virile** [ˋvɪrəl] *adj.* 有男子氣概的、陽剛的

virilescent [ˌvɪrɪˋlεsənt] *adj.* 擁有男性特質的

The strict and unreasonable female principal Agatha in the fiction *Matilda* is a very virilescent character.
小說《瑪蒂達》中，嚴格又不講理的女校長阿格莎是一個非常陽剛的角色。

4 fem 女，女性的，陰性的 源自於拉丁文，具有「女性的」或「非男性的」意思。	▪ **femininity** [ˌfεməˋnɪnətɪ] *n.* 女性氣質、女人味 ▪ **feminism** [ˋfεmənɪzəm] *n.* 女權主義 ▪ **feminine** [ˋfεmənɪn] *adj.* 女性氣質的 ▪ **female** [ˋfimel] *n.* 女性、雌性 *adj.* 女性的、雌性的

femininity [ˌfεməˋnɪnətɪ] *n.* 女性氣質、女人味

In *The Danish Girl*, artist Einar first found his femininity when his wife asked him to dress like a woman and to be her painting model.
電影《丹麥女孩》中的藝術家艾納在妻子要求他裝扮成女人以當她的繪畫模特兒時，第一次發現他的女性特質。

5 **pater-, patri-**

父，祖

源自於拉丁文，「父親」的意思。

- **patriarchy** [ˋpetrɪɑrkɪ] *n.* 父權社會（patri 父；arch 首腦，長）
- **expatriate** [ɪksˋpætrɪət] *n.* 僑民、旅居國外者（ex 外；patri 祖國）
- **patriot** [ˋpætrɪət] *n.* 愛國者
- **paternal** [pəˋtɝnəl] *adj.* 父親的、如父親般的

patriarchy [ˋpetrɪɑrkɪ] *n.* 父權社會（patri 父；arch 首腦，長）

Most of the Aboriginal tribes in Taiwan are patriarchy, but a few of them are matriarchy.

臺灣原住民大多是父系社會，但有少數是母系社會。

6 **mater, matr**

母

源自於拉丁文，「母親」的意思。

- **maternity** [məˋtɝnətɪ] *n.* 母親身分
- **matriarchy** [ˋmetrɪɑrkɪ] *n.* 母系社會、母權社會
- **matriarch** [ˋmetrɪɑrk] *n.* 女族長、女首領
- **maternal** [məˋtɝnəl] *adj.* 母親（般）的；母系的

maternity [məˋtɝnətɪ] *n.* 母親身分

Judgement of the real maternity of a child is one of the most famous stories about King Solomon’s wisdom.

判定誰是孩子真正的母親，是有關所羅門王的智慧中最有名的故事之一。

7 her, heir
繼承人

源自於拉丁文，代表取走剩下之物的人。

- **inherit** [ɪn`hɛrɪt] *v.* 繼承
- **heritable** [`hɛrɪtəbəl] *adj.* 可遺傳的、可繼承的
- **heredity** [hə`rɛdətɪ] *n.* 遺傳
- **heir / heiress** [ɛr], [`ɛrəs] *n.* 繼承人、女繼承人

inherit [ɪn`hɛrɪt] *v.* 繼承

The lonely wealthy businessman decided to let his sole pet inherit his large amount of heritage after his death.
這位孤單的富商決定死後要讓他唯一的寵物繼承巨額的財產。

8 capit
頭

源自於拉丁文「頭、首、第一」的意思。

- **recapitulate** [͵rɪkə`pɪtjʊlet] *v.* 概括（re-再）
- **per capita** [pɚ `kæpɪtə] *ph.* 平均每人（的）（per- 每一）
- **decapitate** [dɪ`kæpətet] *v.* 把…砍頭；去除首領（de-去除）
- **capital** [`kæpɪtəl] *n.* 首都；柱頭；大寫

recapitulate [͵rɪkə`pɪtjʊlet] *v.* 概括（re-再）

You have to recapitulate your findings and main ideas in the abstract of a thesis so that readers can have a general picture before reading the content.
你必須在論文的摘要中概括你的發現和主旨，如此讀者才能在閱讀全文前有大略的了解。

9 barb

鬍鬚

拉丁文「鬍鬚」、或「像鬍鬚形狀的突起物」。

- **barbule** [`barbjul] *n.* 羽毛上的羽小支
- **barber** [`barbɚ] *n.* （專為男性服務的）理髮師
- **barb** [barb] *n.* （箭或魚鉤的）倒刺；帶刺的話語

barbule [`barbjul] *n.* 羽毛上的羽小支

Shifts, barbs, and barbules can form various kinds of feathers of birds.

羽軸、羽支和羽小支可以組合成各式各樣的鳥類羽毛。

10 dent

牙齒

源自拉丁文，「牙齒」的意思。

- **dentures** [`dɛntʃɚ] *n.* 假牙
- **indent** [ɪn`dɛnt] *v.* 縮排、在…邊緣留下空間（in-裡面，dent 於此有牙齒般大小的空間，合起來有往裡縮一點空間的意思。）
- **dentist** [`dɛntɪst] *n.* 牙醫
- **dental** [`dɛntəl] *n.* 牙齒的

dentures [`dɛntʃɚ] *n.* 假牙

Catherine needs a new pair of dentures because the old ones are overused.

凱薩琳需要一副新的假牙因為舊的已經使用太久了。

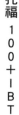

11 chiro

手

源自於希臘文，「手」或和手有關的意思。

- **chirography** [kaɪˋragrəfɪ] *n.* 手寫體、筆跡（和電腦字體相對）
- **chiromancy** [ˋkaɪrəmænsɪ] *n.* 手相術（mancy-占卜）
- **chiropractor** [ˋkaɪrə͵præktɚ] *n.* 指壓按摩師
- **chiropractic** [ˋkaɪrəˋpræktə] *n.* 脊椎指壓療法（practic(al)-有「做」的意思）

chirography [kaɪˋragrəfɪ] *n.* 手寫體、筆跡（和電腦字體相對）

Her beautiful chirography is derived from her long term practice since childhood.

她漂亮的字是來自從小長期的練習。

12 manu, mani

手

拉丁文「手」的意思。

- **manufacture** [mænjʊˋfæktʃɚ] *v.* 製造、大批生產
- **manuscript** [ˋmænjʊskrɪpt] *n.* 手稿、原稿（script-書寫）
- **manual** [ˋmænjʊəl] *adj.* 手做的；手動的
- **manipulate** [məˋnɪpjʊlet] *v.* 操控、玩弄、掌握（pulate 源自拉丁文，pulu- 充滿、完全）

manufacture [mænjʊˋfæktʃɚ] *v.* 製造、大批生產

Once the medicine is proved effective, it will be manufactured on a large scale immediately.

只要藥物證明有效，其將會馬上被大量生產。

UNIT 02 人、人體器官

Cord-Sen ▶ MP3 002

13 cord, cordi, cour

心

源自於拉丁文「心臟」的意思，衍伸出和「心靈」有關之意。

- **cordial** [\`kɔrdɪəl] *adj.* 誠摯的、友好的（al-和…相關的特質因此合起來有溫暖的特質；cordially *adv.*）
- **accordingly** [ə\`kɔrdɪŋlɪ] *adv.* 依照、做相對應地；因此
- **accordance** [ə\`kɔrdəns] *n.* 依照（ac-朝向，ance-名詞結尾，合起來有朝向內心，衍生為依心裡想法的意思。）

cordial [\`kɔrdɪəl] *adj.* 誠摯的、友好的（al-和…相關的特質因此合起來有溫暖的特質；cordially *adv.*）

I've never thought that I could receive such warm and cordial welcomes in foreign countries. 我從沒想過能在國外受到如此溫暖且友好的歡迎。

14 corp

身體

從拉丁文、法文演化而來，跟人類身體有關。

- **corporeal** [kɔr\`porɪəl] *adj.* 身體的；物質有形的
- **corpulent** [\`kɔrpjʊlənt] *adj.* 肥胖的（ulent-拉丁字尾，大量的）
- **corpse** [kɔrps] *n.* （人的）屍體
- **corporal** [\`kɔrpəəl] *adj.* 肉身的、身體的

corporeal [kɔr`porɪəl] *adj.* 身體的；物質有形的

In many religions, spiritual improvement is more important than corporeal stuff.

許多宗教信仰裡，心靈上的進步比物質的東西還重要。

15 **carn, carni**

肉

源自拉丁文「肉體」、「肉」意思。

- **carnivore** [`karnɪvɔr] *n.* 肉食動物
- **carnival** [`karnɪvəl] *n.* 嘉年華（val-源自義大利文；-levare 提升、展現，整個字原有展現肉體之意）
- **carnal** [`karnəl] *adj.* 肉慾的；性慾的
- **carnage** [`karnɪdʒ] *n.* 大屠殺（-age 過程。全字有取肉過程之意）

carnivore [`karnɪvɔr] *n.* 肉食動物

Carnivores, herbivores, and omnivores are conducive to balancing the natural food chain.

肉食動物、草食動物和雜食動物有助於平衡自然食物鏈。

16 **neur (o)**

神經

源自於古希臘文，代表「神經、神經系統」。

- **neurology** [ˌnjʊ`ralədʒɪ] *n.* 神經（病）學
- **neurosis** [ˌnjʊ`rosɪs] *n.* 精神官能症、精神病【複】neuroses
- **neurotic** [njʊ`ratɪk] *adj.* 神經質的、神經過於敏感的
- **neuron** [`njʊran] *n.* 神經元、神經細胞

neurology [ˌnjʊ`ralədʒɪ] *n.* 神經（病）學

Neurology is a branch of medicine and biology, and it is a study about our brain and nerve system.

神經學是醫學和生物學的一支，它是一門關於我們大腦和神經的學問。

17 face, fici

臉；面

源自拉丁文，「臉」、「面容」的意思。

- **deface** [dɪ`fes] *v.* 破壞…外觀
- **efface** [ɪ`fes] *v.* 消除、塗抹掉、擦掉
- **surface** [`sɝfɪs] *n.* 表面、外層
- **superficial** [ˏsupɚ`fɪʃəl] *adj.* 膚淺的、表面上的

deface [dɪ`fes] *v.* 破壞…外觀

Graffiti is not allowed in this region because it will deface the walls.
這塊區域不可以亂塗鴉，因為這會破壞牆壁的外觀。

18 ped, pede

足

拉丁文「腳」、「足」的意思，通常衍生為雙腳的運動如「走、跑」等。

- **centipede** [`sɛntəpid] *n.* 蜈蚣（俗稱百足蟲；cent-百）
- **pedestrian** [pə`dɛstrɪən] *n.* 行人（即用腳走路之人）
- **pedal** [`pɛdəl] *n.* 踏板 *adj.* 腳踏的 *v.* 騎、踩踏板（前進）
- **impede** [ɪm`pid] *v.* 阻止、妨礙（im-否定。否定足部，延伸為妨礙之意）

centipede [`sɛntəpid] *n.* 蜈蚣（俗稱百足蟲；cent-百）

Most centipedes like wet places such as bathrooms in the city, but few of them are really poisonous.
大部分的蜈蚣喜歡潮濕的環境，如都市中的浴室，但很少真正有劇毒。

19 gen

生

源自於傳到拉丁文的希臘文，有「源頭」、「創新」、「繁殖」等意思。

- **generate** [`dʒɛnəret] *v.* 造成、產生、引起
- **generation** [dʒɛnə`reʃən] *n.* 一代、同輩人；產生
- **genetic** [dʒə`nɛtɪk] *adj.* 基因的、遺傳的
- **genesis** [`dʒɛnəsɪs] *n.* 起源、創新（Genesis-《聖經》中的〈創世紀〉篇）

generate [`dʒɛnəret] *v.* 造成、產生、引起

A small new step could generate a huge change in the end. You never know!

小小一步創新可能最後會產生巨大的轉變。你永遠無法預測！

20 par

生

於自希臘文，「帶來」、「產生」、「生產」之意。

- **viviparous** [vaɪ`vɪpərəs] *adj.* 胎生的（vivi-活生生的，胎生的定義是寶寶在母體內已經有生命的）
- **parturition** [ˌpɑrtjʊ`rɪʃən] *n.* 分娩、生產
- **parental** [pə`rɛntəl] *adj.* 父母的、父（母）親的
- **parentage** [`pɛrəntɪdʒ] *n.* 家世、出生

viviparous [vaɪ`vɪpərəs] *adj.* 胎生的（vivi-活生生的，胎生的定義是寶寶在母體內已經有生命的）

Most mammals are viviparous animals.

大部分的哺乳類都是胎生動物。

21 nat, nasc 生 拉丁文「出生」、「生產」的意思。	▪ **nascent** [ˋnæsənt] *adj.* 新生的、剛萌芽的、剛開始發展的 ▪ **nationwide** [ˋneʃənwaɪd] *adj. adv.* 全國性的（地） ▪ **native** [ˋnetɪv] *adj.* 土生土長的、與生俱來的；原住民的 ▪ **innate** [ɪˋnet] *adj.* 天生的、原有的

nascent [ˋnæsənt] *adj.* 新生的、剛萌芽的、剛開始發展的

Look at those nascent green leaves on the branches!
看樹枝上新生的綠葉！

22 vit, vita 生命 拉丁文「生命」或「生活」的意思。	▪ **revitalize** [rɪˋvaɪtəlaɪz] *v.* 復興、使…獲得生機 ▪ **vital** [ˋvaɪtəl] *adj.* 生命的、生氣勃勃的；非常重要的 ▪ **vitality** [vaɪˋtælətɪ] *n.* 生命力、活力 ▪ **curriculum vitae** [kʌˋrɪkjʊləm ˋvɪtaɪ] *n.* 簡歷、履歷（=CV）

revitalize [rɪˋvaɪtəlaɪz] *v.* 復興、使…獲得生機

Revitalizing the national economy should be the top priority of the new elected president.
振興國家經濟應該是新當選總統的首要任務。

23 **juven-**

年輕

源自拉丁文，「青年」、「年輕的」等意思。

- **rejuvenate** [rɪˋdʒuvənet] *v.* 使年輕、使…恢復活力
- **juvenility** [dʒuvəˋnɪlətɪ] *n.* 不成熟；青少年期（juvenile *adj.*）
- **juvenescent** [dʒuvəˋnɛsənt] *adj.* 年輕的；變年輕的

rejuvenate [rɪˋdʒuvənet] *v.* 使年輕、使…恢復活力

Enough rest, regular exercise, balanced diet as well as a relaxed mind can rejuvenate any person who is tortured by heavy works.

充足的睡眠、固定的運動和均衡飲食，加上輕鬆的心境會使一個飽受繁重工作的人恢復活力。

24 **sen, seni**

老

拉丁文「年老的」、「年長的」或「老年」的意思。

- **senile** [ˋsinaɪl] *adj.* 老化的、老態龍鍾的
- **senior** [ˋsinɪɚ] *adj.* 年長的、經歷較多的
- **seniority** [sinˋjɔrətɪ] *n.* 資歷、排行較長
- **senate** [ˋsɛnɪt] *n.* 參議院（從法文傳來的拉丁文，原指「長老聚集的地方」，現指美、澳等國會一部份）

senile [ˋsinaɪl] *adj.* 老化的、老態龍鍾的

What all senile parents want is just more care and some caring actions from their children.

所有年邁的父母們所要的，不過是他們子女多一點的關心和關懷的舉動。

人、人體器官－心理感覺

Morb-Cur ▶MP3 003

25 morb

病

拉丁文「疾病」的意思。

- **morbid** [`mɔrbɪd] *adj.* 病態的、病態般著迷的
- **morbidly** [`mɔrbɪdlɪ] *adv.* 病態地
- **morbidity** [mɔr`bɪdətɪ] *n.* 病態、發病率
- **morbific** [mɔr`bɪfɪk] *adj.* 引起疾病的

morbid [`mɔrbɪd] *adj.* 病態的、病態般著迷的

His imaginary paintings are full of morbid interest of death and love.
他奇幻的作品充滿了對死亡和愛的病態般興趣。

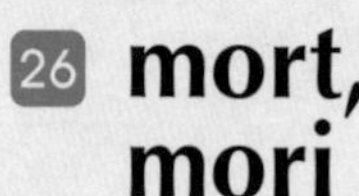

26 mort, mori

死

拉丁文字根，跟「死亡」、「瀕死」等狀態。

- **moribund** [`morɪbʌnd] *adj.* 垂死的、奄奄一息的；無生氣的、停滯不前的
- **mortality** [mɔr`tælətɪ] *n.* 必死性；死亡率
- **mortal** [`mɔrtəl] *adj.* 會死的；致命的
- **immortal** [ɪ`mɔrtəl] *adj.* 永生的、不朽的

moribund [`morɪbʌnd] *adj.* 垂死的、奄奄一息的；無生氣的、停滯不前的

He has to send his moribund grandfather into the hospice for the rest of his life.　他必須將垂死的祖父送進安寧病房以度餘生。

27 am, amor, amat

愛

拉丁字源，「愛」、「愛情」或「喜愛」的意思。

- **enamor** [ɪ`næmɚr] *v.* 迷上、使迷戀
- **amorous** [`amərəs] *adj.* 示愛的、情色的
- **amatory** [`æmətorɪ] *adj.* 戀愛的；性愛的
- **amateur** [`æmətʃʊɚ] *n.* 業餘愛好者 *adj.* 業餘愛好的（eur- 源自法文「…者」）

enamor [ɪ`næmɚr] *v.* 迷上、使迷戀

At her first visit, she was enamored by the beauty of North England.
在她第一次拜訪，她就迷上了北英格蘭的美。

28 phil

愛

源自希臘文，有「愛」的意思，另有「對…特別偏愛、瘋狂喜愛」之意，多用在學術或專業用語。

- **bibliophile** [`bɪblɪəfaɪl] *n.* 愛書者；圖書收藏家（biblio-書）
- **philology** [fɪ`lalədʒɪ] *n.* 語言學
- **philosopher** [fɪ`lasəfɚ] *n.* 哲學家（希臘文，愛智者之意）
- **philharmonic** [ˌfɪlhar`manɪk] *adj.* 愛好音樂的（harmonic-和音樂、旋律有關的）

bibliophile [`bɪblɪəfaɪl] *n.* 愛書者；圖書收藏家（biblio-書）

Miss Jong is an ancient book bibliophile; therefore, she is a regular at book auctions.
鍾小姐是古書收藏家，因此她也是圖書拍賣會的常客。

29 mis (o)

恨

希臘文「憎恨」、「厭惡」或「鄙視」的意思。

- **misogamy** [mɪˋsɑgəmɪ] *n.* 厭惡婚姻、恐婚（gamy- 希臘文，婚姻、結合）
- **misogyny** [mɪˋsɑdʒənɪ] *n.* 厭女（症）（gyn(o)-希臘文，女性）
- **misanthrope** [ˋmɪzənθrop] *n.* 厭惡人類者，遁世者
- **misandrist** [mɪˋsændrɪst] *n.* 厭惡男性者（andr-希臘文，男性）

misogamy [mɪˋsɑgəmɪ] *n.* 厭惡婚姻、恐婚（gamy- 希臘文，婚姻、結合）

The failure of her parents' marriage only deepens her misogamy.
她父母婚姻失敗只更加深她的恐婚症。

30 dol, dolor

悲

源自於拉丁文，「哀傷」、「疼痛」、「悲傷」之意。

- **dolorous** [ˋdolərəs] *adj.* 憂傷的、極度傷感的
- **indolent** [ˋɪndələnt] *adj.* 懶散的；【醫】無痛的（in-否定；整個字意思由「脫離痛苦」之意轉化而來）
- **doleful** [ˋdolfʊl] *adj.* 悲傷的、哀傷的
- **condole** [kənˋdol] *v.* 弔唁

dolorous [ˋdolərəs] *adj.* 憂傷的、極度傷感的

Many Russian folk tales have a dolorous atmosphere.
許多俄國民間故事有著憂傷的氣氛。

31 **mir**
驚奇

拉丁文字源，有「驚嘆」、「驚奇」的意思。

- **mirage** [mɪrɑʒ] *n.* 海市蜃樓、幻景；妄想
- **miraculous** [mɪ`rækjʊləs] *adj.* 如奇蹟般的、不可思議的（miracle- 奇蹟）
- **admirable** [`ædmərəbəl] *adj.* 令人欽佩的、值得讚賞的
- **admire** [əd`maɪə] *v.* 欣賞、欽佩、讚賞（ad-傾向、對於）

mirage [mɪrɑʒ] *n.* 海市蜃樓、幻景；妄想

Winning the lottery for a better life is just a mirage.
中樂透然後過好生活不過是妄想。

32 **sper, spair**
希望

源自拉丁文，「希望」的意思，為其變體。

- **prosperous** [`prɑspərəs] *adj.* 繁榮的、富裕的
- **prosper** [`prɑspə] *v.* 成功；經濟繁榮（pro- 正面的，贊成的）
- **desperate** [`dɛspərət] *adj.* （絕望所以）拚命的、冒險的；非常需要的；非常嚴重的
- **despair** [dɪ`spɛr] *n. v.* 絕望、失去希望（de-沒有）

prosperous [`prɑspərəs] *adj.* 繁榮的、富裕的

It is amazing to realize that the ghetto is actually very near to the prosperous area of this big city.
我很驚訝地了解到，貧民區其實離大城市繁榮的地區很近。

33 cred

相信

拉丁文「相信」、「信仰」、「信心」或「信任」的意思。

- **credibility** [krɛdəˋbɪlətɪ] *n.* 可信度、可靠性
- **incredible** [ɪnˋkrɛdəbəl] *adj.* 難以置信的
- **discredit** [dɪsˋkrɛdɪt] *n.* 喪失信譽 *v.* 使信譽受損
- **creditor** [ˋkrɛdɪtɚ] *n.* 債主、債權人

credibility [krɛdəˋbɪlətɪ] *n.* 可信度、可靠性

The credibility of politicians seems lower nowadays.
現在政治人物的可信度似乎較低了。

34 latry

崇拜

希臘文「崇拜」或「極其投入」的意思，通常接在崇拜對象的後面。

- **idolatry** [aɪˋdɑlətrɪ] *n.* 偶像崇拜
- **Mariolatry** [ˌmɛrɪˋɑlətrɪ] *n.* 聖母瑪利亞崇拜
- **herolatry** [hɪrəˋrɑlətrɪ] *n.* 英雄崇拜
- **bardolatry** [bɑrˋdɑlətrɪ] *n.* 莎士比亞崇拜（bard-詩人）

idolatry [aɪˋdɑlətrɪ] *n.* 偶像崇拜

True idolatry is not blind because it is after doing some serious thinking.
真正的偶像崇拜不是盲目的，是因為幾經思考之後才相信的。

35 **sent, sens**

感覺

源自拉丁文「感覺」，也指源自身體感官的感受。

- **sensational** [sɛn`seʃənəl] *adj.* 聳動的、引起轟動的
- **sentimental** [sɛntə`mɛntəl] *adj.* 多愁善感的、感情用事的；感傷的
- **sensation** [sɛn`seʃən] *n.* 感覺、知覺；轟動的事件
- **resentment** [rɪ`zɛntmənt] *n.* 憤怒、不滿、厭惡

sensational [sɛn`seʃənəl] *adj.* 聳動的、引起轟動的

The social responsibility of a journalist is not writing sensational gossip but reporting ignored humane issues for instance.

記者的社會責任不是撰寫八卦新聞，而是報導被忽視的人道議題。

36 **cur**

關心

拉丁文「關心、關照或特別注意」之意，衍生為「治療、照顧」。

- **insecure** [͵ɪnsə`kjʊɚ] *adj.* 缺乏把握的、不安全的、沒有自信心的（in- 否定，se- 不須、沒有；secure- 不需關心）
- **curiosity** [kjʊrɪ`ɑsətɪ] *n.* 好奇心（形容詞 curious 在拉丁原文中有「仔細的、注意的」意思）
- **curable** [`kjʊrəbəl] *adj.* 可治癒的
- **accurate** [`ækjʊrət] *adj.* 準確的、精確的（拉丁文原意指「小心做事或完成」）

insecure [͵ɪnsə`kjʊɚ] *adj.* 缺乏把握的、不安全的、沒有自信心的（in- 否定，se- 不須、沒有；secure- 不需關心）

People who feel insecure and are very dependent on others need autonomy.

沒有安全感且非常依賴別人的人最需要的是自主性。

UNIT 04

心理感覺—行為動作

Sci-Port ▶ MP3 004

37 sci

知

拉丁文「知道」、「學習」的意思，也衍生為「知識」之意。

- **prescient** [`prɛsɪənt] *adj.* 預知的
- **scientific** [saɪən`tɪfɪk] *adj.* 科學的、用科學方法的、有科學根據的
- **conscientious** [ˌkɑnʃɪ`ɛnʃəs] *adj.* 盡責的、認真的；有良心意識的（con- 一起、scienc- 科學、準則）
- **consciousness** [`kɑnʃəsnɪs] *n.* 意識、感覺、知覺、神智（清醒）

prescient [`prɛsɪənt] *adj.* 預知的、有先見之明的

It is not a bad thing to accept the prescient warnings from elder people because they usually have more experience.

接受長者的事先警告不是件壞事，因為他們通常比較有經驗。

38 cogn (i)

知

源自於拉丁文，「學習」、「認知」的意思。

- **incognito** [ɪn`kɑgnɪˌto] *adj. adv.* 隱姓埋名的（地）
- **recognize** [`rɛkəgnaɪz] *v.* 識別、認出
- **cognitive** [`kɑgnətɪv] *adj.* 感知的
- **cognition** [kɑg`nɪʃən] *n.* 認知、認識

incognito [ɪn`kɑgnɪˌto] *adj. adv.* 隱姓埋名的（地）

The famous actress enjoyed her freedom by going abroad incognito for a break.
著名的女演員隱姓埋名出國享受她的自由假期。

39 memor
記憶

拉丁文「回憶」、「記憶」或「回想」的意思。

- **commemorate** [kə`mɛməret] *v.* 紀念、緬懷
- **memorize** [`mɛməraɪz] *v.* 記住；熟記
- **memorial** [mɛ`morɪəl] *adj.* 紀念性的、悼念的 *n.* 紀念物、紀念碑
- **memoir** [`mɛmwɑ] *n.* 回憶錄、自傳

commemorate [kə`mɛməret] *v.* 紀念、緬懷

The British government released a Peter Rabbit coin to commemorate the 150th birthday of its author, Beatrix Potter.
英國政府發行一款彼得兔的硬幣以紀念其作者碧雅翠絲・波特女士的 150 年冥誕。

40 mne
記憶

源自希臘文，「記憶」、「記得」的意思，也表示對於過去與現在的時間性有所察覺。

- **mnemonic** [nɪ`mɑnɪk] *n.* （幫助記憶的）順口溜、詩歌 *adj.* 有助記憶的
- **amnesty** [`æmnɛstɪ] *n.* 特赦、赦免
- **amnesia** [æm`niʒɪə] *n.* 失憶症、健忘症

mnemonic [nɪ`mɑnɪk] *n.* （幫助記憶的）順口溜、詩歌 *adj.* 有助記憶的

The creative teacher revealed that the secret to writing so many mnemonics like him is to be imaginative.
富有創意的老師説出讓他寫出這麼多順口溜的祕密就是要有聯想力。

41 vol

意志、意願

拉丁文「自由意志」、「自由選擇」的意思，或有「個人希望、期望」的涵義。

- **malevolence** [mə`lɛvələns] *n.* 惡毒、惡意（male- 邪惡）
- **volunteer** [͵vɔlən`tɪɚ] *n.* 志願者、志工 *v.* 自願做、主動做
- **voluntary** [`vɔlənterɪ] *adj.* 自願的；公益的
- **benevolent** [bɪ`nɛvələnt] *adj.* 仁慈的、和藹的；慈善的（bene-好的，benevol- 好心的）

malevolence [mə`lɛvələns] *n.* 惡毒、惡意（male- 邪惡）

His hatred creates a layer of malevolence around him, and therefore no one wants to be close to him.

他的恨意在他身邊建造出一層惡意，因此沒有人想靠近他。

42 dox, dogma

意見

源自於希臘文「相信」，衍生為「相信是對的想法」、「信條」、「律令」等。

- **dogma** [`dɔgmə] *n.* （宗教或政治的）信條、教條
- **dogmatic** [dɔg`mætɪk] *adj.* 教條的、固執己見的
- **orthodox** [`ɔrθədɑks] *adj.* 正統的、傳統的

dogma [`dɔgmə] *n.* （宗教或政治的）信條、教條

Dogma is actually a set of beliefs from certain people, so it should be flexible as the time passes by.

信條其實不過是某群人信仰的總和，所以其實應該要隨著時間更有彈性。

43 cept

拿

源自拉丁文，有「獲取」、「攫取」、「解受」或「抓住」的意思，通常會用在比較抽象的字詞中。

- **conception** [kən`sɛpʃən] *n.* 概念、觀念、看法（con- 一起，concept- 一起抓住，指統一的一個大略想法）
- **susceptible** [sə`sɛptɪbəl] *adj.* 能被理解的；易受感動的（sus-靠近，拉丁文 suscept = take up for 支持）
- **perception** [pɚ`sɛpʃən] *n.* 洞察力、感知；看法、見解（per- 完全，percept- 完全接受）

conception [kən`sɛpʃən] *n.* 概念、觀念、看法（con- 一起，concept- 一起抓住，指統一的一個大略想法）

They decided not to go into a relationship due to their different conceptions of life. Friends can last longer and being more stable.
他們由於對於生活的觀念不同決定不要進入關係。朋友可以持續更久更穩定。

44 emp, empt

拿

拉丁文「拿取」、「購買」或「選擇」的意思。

- **peremptory** [pə`remptərɪ] *adj.* 武斷的、霸道的、不容置喙的（per- 完全，perempt- 完全奪走）
- **preempt** [prɪ`ɛmpt] *v.* 先發制人、搶先行動（pre- 先）
- **exempt** [ɪg`zɛmpt] *v.* 豁免、免除 *adj.* 豁免的、免除義務的
- **exemplify** [ɪg`zɛmpləfaɪ] *v.* 舉例說明、作為典範

peremptory [pə`remptərɪ] *adj.* 武斷的、霸道的、不容置喙的（per- 完全，perempt- 完全奪走）

Her peremptory attitude does not help her business at all.
她霸道的態度無濟於她的事業。

45 fer

拿

拉丁文「擁有」、「持有」或是「生產」、「帶來」的意思。

- **fertility** [fɚ`tɪlətɪ] *n.* 土地的肥沃度、生產力；繁殖能力
- **referendum** [rɛfə`rɛdən] *n.* 公民投票（拉丁文，被提及的東西）
- **offering** [`ofɚiŋ] *n.* 禮物；供品、（教會）捐獻；產品
- **confer** [kən`fɝ] *v.* 賦予、授予

fertility [fɚ`tɪlətɪ] *n.* 土地的肥沃度、生產力；繁殖能力

This riverside park is just developed by the government, so its fertility cannot afford a small forest.

這座河濱公園是政府新開發的，所以這裡的土地肥沃度無法培育出一片小森林。

46 hibit

拿

源自拉丁文，有「擁有」、「容易掌握」或「居住」的意思。

- **inhibited** [ɪn`hɪbɪtɪd] *adj.* 約束的、拘謹的、受限的
- **prohibition** [ˌproə`bɪʃən] *n.* 禁止、禁令（pro-事先；prohibit，拉丁文，阻止）
- **inhibit** [ɪn`hɪbɪt] *v.* 限制、約束；抑制
- **exhibition** [ˌeksə`bɪʃən] *n.* 展覽

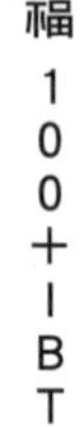

inhibited [ɪn`hɪbɪtɪd] *adj.* 約束的、拘謹的、受限的

He felt inhibited during the presentation because he thought he was not well-prepared.

他在報告中感覺放不開，因為他覺得自己沒有準備好。

47 lat (e)

拿

拉丁文「擁有」、「具有」的意思。

- **dilatory** [`dɪlətərɪ] *adj.* 緩慢的；拖延的
- **relate** [rɪ`let] *v.* 有聯繫、找到關聯
- **correlate** [`kɔrəlet] *v.* 相關、相互有關
- **collate** [kə`let] *v.* 整理；核對

dilatory [`dɪlətərɪ] *adj.* 緩慢的；拖延的

Proponents are not very happy with government's dilatory legislation to protect animals.

擁護者不是很滿意政府拖延立法保護動物。

48 port

拿

源自於拉丁文，「攜帶」、「擁有」或「帶來」的意思。

- **deport** [dɪ`pɔrt] *v.* 遣返、驅逐出境
- **supportive** [sə`pɔrtɪv] *adj.* 支持的
- **import** [ɪm`pɔrt] *v.* 進口、輸入、引進
- **export** [ɪk`spɔrt] *v.* 出口、輸出

deport [dɪ`pɔrt] *v.* 遣返、驅逐出境

That foreigner was deported due to his illegal staying.

那名外國人因非法居留而被遣返。

行為動作

Pel-Scend ▶ MP3 005

49 pel

推

拉丁文「推開」、「打擊」或是「趕走」的意思。

- **compel** [kəm`pɛl] *v.* 強迫、逼迫；激發
- **expel** [ɪk`spɛl] *v.* 驅逐、開除
- **propel** [prə`pɛl] *v.* 推進、推動
- **repel** [rɪ`pɛl] *v.* 排斥；擊退、逐回

compel [kəm`pɛl] *v.* 強迫、逼迫；激發

Adversity can compel a person's greatest potential.

逆境能激發一個人最大的潛能。

50 trud, trus

推

拉丁文「刺」、「推」和「推擠」的意思，通常用於動詞，改成形容詞或名詞時會變成。

- **extrude** [ɪk`strud] *v.* 擠壓；壓製
- **intrude** [ɪn`trud] *v.* 闖入、入侵
- **intrusive** [ɪn`trusɪv] *adj.* 打擾的、侵擾的
- **protrude** [prə`trud] *v.* 突出

extrude [ɪk`strud] *v.* 擠壓；壓製

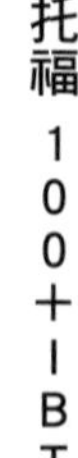

The strongest thread invented so far is the extruded spider silk.
至今發明最強韌的線是由蜘蛛絲壓製成的線。

51 tract
拉

源自於拉丁文「拖拉」、「拖放到一起」或「引出」的意思。

- **distraction** [dɪ`strækʃən] *n.* 令人分心的事物；心煩意亂（dis- 分離；disctract- 分心）
- **tractor** [`træktɚ] *n.* 牽引機、拖拉機
- **extract** [ɪk`strækt] *v.* 取出、萃取、拔出；壓榨
- **abstraction** [əb`strækʃən] *n.* 抽象、抽象概念（拉丁文，脫離現實）

distraction [dɪ`strækʃən] *n.* 令人分心的事物；心煩意亂

Experts warn that smartphones have become a distraction of the close relationship.
專家警告智慧型手機已成為親密關係不緊密的原因。

52 tort
扭

拉丁文「彎曲」、「扭曲」或「旋轉」的意思。

- **contort** [kən`tɔrt] *v.* 扭曲、變形
- **distort** [dɪ`stɔrt] *v.* 使變形、歪曲
- **torture** [`tɔrtʃɚ] *n. v.* 虐待、折磨、煎熬
- **retort** [rɪ`tɔrt] *v.* 反駁、回嘴

contort [kən`tɔrt] *v.* 扭曲、變形

The reason why villains usually don't look pretty is that their faces were contorted by hatred or jealousy.
反派角色通常不太好看的原因是因為他們的臉因仇恨或嫉妒扭曲了。

53 **miss**

投，送

源自於拉丁文，「傳送」、「放出」或「投送」的意思。多用在名詞。

- **emission** [ɪ`mɪʃən] *n.* 散發、排放；排放物
- **transmission** [trænz`mɪʃən] *n.* 傳遞、播送、傳送
- **missionary** [`mɪʃənɛrɪ] *n.* 傳教士
- **dismissal** [dɪs`mɪsəl] *n.* 解雇、解聘；請退

emission [ɪ`mɪʃən] *n.* 散發、排放；排放物

Long term emission of polluted water from the factories has already destroyed the ecology of the river.

長期從工廠排放出來的汙水已經破壞河流的生態。

54 **mit**

投，送

與 miss 同源，同樣具有「傳送、放出或投送」的意思。多用於動詞中。

- **intermittent** [ɪntɚ`mɪtənt] *adj.* 間歇的、斷續的（inter- 之間）
- **submit** [səb`mɪt] *v.* 投交、提交；屈服
- **vomit** [`vamɪt] *v.* 嘔吐
- **emit** [ɪ`mɪt] *v.* 散發、射出（光、氣體或聲音）

intermittent [ɪntɚ`mɪtənt] *adj.* 間歇的、斷續的（inter- 之間）

The weather is great for hiking and a picnic. With intermittent sunshine, it will not be too warm, and it is not very windy!

這天氣十分適合健行和野餐，斷續的陽光不會太熱，而且風也沒有很大！

55 pon

放置

拉丁文「擺放」、「建立」的意思，特別強調物體間的位置關係。

- **component** [kəm`ponənt] *n.* 成分、零件
- **opponent** [ə`ponənt] *n.* 對手；反對者
- **proponent** [prə`ponənt] *n.* 支持者、擁護者；提倡者（pro- 支持）
- **postpone** [po`spon] *v.* 拖延、延期、延後

component [kəm`ponənt] *n.* 成分、零件（com- 一起；compon 放在一起，組成成分）

Every person is an important component of the society, so a well-functioning community needs everyone's involvement.

每個人都是社會中重要的組成成分，因此一個完善的社區需要每個人的投入。

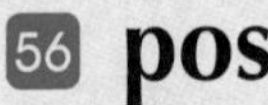

56 pos

放置

pon 的同源拉丁字根，一樣是「擺放」和「建立」的意思。

- **juxtapose** [ˏdʒʌkstə`poz] *v.* 並列（對照）
- **propose** [prə`poz] *v.* 提出建議；求婚
- **depose** [dɪ`poz] *v.* 罷免、使下台
- **composition** [kɑmpə`zɪʃən] *n.* 作文；音樂作品；構圖

juxtapose [ˏdʒʌkstə`poz] *v.* 並列（對照）

Juxtaposing the traditional and the modern buildings makes this area a popular tourist destination.

傳統與現代建築的並列使這個區域成為受歡迎的觀光景點。

57 text

編織

拉丁文「編織」的意思，衍生為「組織、建造」之意。

- **texture** [`tɛkstʃɚ] *n.* 質感、質地；作品特色
- **textual** [`tɛkstʃʊəl] *adj.* 文本的、正文的、文章文字的
- **textile** [`tɛkstaɪl] *n.* 紡織品
- **pretext** [`prɪtɛkst] *n.* 藉口、託詞

texture [`tɛkstʃɚ] *n.* 質感、質地；作品特色

He likes to wear clothes with a natural texture and believes it is healthier not to put on artificial fabrics.

他喜歡穿有自然質感的衣服，而且相信不穿人造纖維衣物比較健康。

58 lev

舉，升

源自拉丁動詞「提升」、「舉起」或「重量輕」的意思。

- **alleviate** [ə`livɪet] *v.* 減輕、緩解
- **elevate** [`ɛlɪvet] *v.* 抬高、上升；提升、改進
- **elevation** [ˌɛlə`veʃən] *n.* 晉升、提拔；海拔高度
- **lever** [`livɚ] *n.* 把手；把柄 *v.* 撬開、用槓桿操縱

alleviate [ə`livɪet] *v.* 減輕、緩解

Many western medicines can only alleviate symptoms immediately, not really cure the illness.

許多西藥只能迅速減輕症狀，但不是真正治療疾病。

59 **tain**
握，持

源自拉丁文，「持有」、「緊握」等意思。

- **abstain** [əb`sten] *v.* 戒除（abs- 遠離）
- **detain** [dɪ`ten] *v.* 居留、扣押、留下；耽擱、拖延
- **retain** [rɪ`ten] *v.* 保持、保有；保存、容納
- **sustain** [sə`sten] *v.* 維持、使持續

abstain [əb`sten] *v.* 戒除（abs- 遠離）

He promised to abstain from smoking for their future baby.
他答應為了將到來的孩子戒菸。

60 **scend**
攀，爬

源自於拉丁文，「攀爬、往上」的意思。

- **transcendent** [tran`sɛndənt] *adj.* 傑出的、卓越的；超出一切的
- **transcend** [tran`sɛnd] *v.* 超越、越界、超出
- **descendant** [dɪ`sɛndənt] *n.* 子孫、後代（de-往下）
- **ascend** [ə`sɛnd] *v.* 攀登、登上

transcendent [tran`sɛndənt] *adj.* 傑出的、卓越的；超出一切的

Two years of studying abroad was a transcendent experience for a university student.
在國外求學兩年對一個大學生來說是個無與倫比的經驗。

UNIT 06 行為動作

Scrib-Err ▶ MP3 006

61 scrib, script

寫

源自於拉丁文，有英文「write」之意，有書寫、抄寫的含意。

- **descriptive** [dɪˋskrɪptɪv] *adj.* 描述性的；描寫的、描繪的
- **transcript** [tranˋskraɪb] *n.* 成績單、文字記錄
- **prescribe** [prɪˋskraɪb] *v.* 開藥
- **ascribe** [əˋskraɪb] *v.* 認為是…所創作；歸咎於

descriptive [dɪˋskrɪptɪv] *adj.* 描述性的；描寫的、描繪的

The analyst does not judge the situation for the employers; she just provides a descriptive passage for them to understand.

分析師不直接為雇主判斷情況，而是給予描述性的篇章讓他們理解。

62 pict

畫

源自拉丁文，「繪畫、描繪」或「圖畫」的意思。

- **picturesque** [ˌpɪktʃəˋrɛsk] *adj.* 美麗如畫的
- **picture** [ˋpɪktʃɚ] *v.* 以圖片呈現；想像、設想
- **pictorial** [pɪkˋtɔrɪəl] *adj.* 圖畫的、照片的
- **depict** [dɪˋpɪkt] *v.* 描繪、描述

picturesque [ˌpɪktʃə`rɛsk] *adj.* 美麗如畫的

He likes to visit his grandparents who live in a picturesque countryside.
他喜歡去拜訪住在美麗鄉村的祖父母。

63 **ras, raz** 擦，刮 源自於拉丁文，「刮去、擦」或「搓揉」的意思。	▪ **abrasion** [ə`breʒən] *n.* 磨損、擦傷（處） ▪ **razor** [`rezɚ] *n.* 刮鬍刀 ▪ **erase** [ɪ`rez] *v.* 抹去、擦掉 ▪ **abrasive** [ə`bresɪv] *n.* （擦洗用）磨料 *adj.* 粗礪的、清潔用磨料的

abrasion [ə`breʒən] *n.* 磨損、擦傷（處）

He can't tolerate any abrasion on his precious car.
他無法忍受他的寶貝車子有一點刮傷。

64 **dit** 給 拉丁文字源，有「給予、提供」等意思。	▪ **rendition** [rɛn`dɪʃən] *n.* 表演、表現、呈現 ▪ **extradite** [`ɛkstrədaɪt] *v.* 引渡 ▪ **edition** [ə`dɪʃən] *n.* 版本；第…版／期 ▪ **edit** [`ɛdɪt] *v.* 編輯；剪輯（e=ex 出，edit 原指提供出版的意思）

rendition [rɛn`dɪʃən] *n.* 表演、表現、呈現

After listening to all the editions of this song, the original singer's rendition is still his favorite.
聽過這首歌所有的版本之後，原唱者的表演還是他的最愛。

65 **capt** 抓 拉丁文「抓住」、「緊握」或「被俘虜」的意思。	▪ **captivate** [`kæptɪvet] *v.* 著迷、吸引 ▪ **capture** [`kæptʃɚ] *v.* 俘虜、捕捉、獲得 ▪ **captivity** [kæp`tɪvətɪ] *n.* 囚禁、束縛、困住 ▪ **captive** [`kæptɪv] *n.* 俘虜 *adj.* 被俘的

captivate [`kæptɪvet] *v.* 著迷、吸引

His cuteness and humor plus great dancing skills captivate many young women.
他的可愛和幽默加上一級棒的舞姿吸引了許多年輕女性。

66 **ambul** 走 源自拉丁文「漫遊、流浪」的意思，衍生為「行走、移動」。	▪ **perambulate** [pə`ræmbjʊlet] *v.* 徘徊、漫步（per- 穿越） ▪ **perambulator** [pə`ræmbjʊletɚ] *n.* 嬰兒車、手推車 ▪ **ambulatory** [`æmbjʊlətərɪ] *adj.* 能走動的、不需臥床的；可移動的 ▪ **ambulance** [`æmbjʊləns] *n.* 救護車

perambulate [pə`ræmbjʊlet] *v.* 徘徊、漫步（per- 穿越）

She enjoys perambulating along the lake on the weekends.
她週末喜歡在湖邊享受漫步。

67 **cede**

走

源自於拉丁文，「行動中」、「走動」或「離開」的意思。

- **unprecedented** [ʌn`prɛsɪdəntɪd] *adj.* 史無前例的；空前的
- **precedent** [`prɛsɪdənt] *n.* 先例、前例；慣例
- **precede** [prɪ`sid] *v.* 在…之前、先於
- **concede** [kən`sid] *v.* 讓步、讓與；認輸、承認錯誤

unprecedented [ʌn`prɛsɪdəntɪd] *adj.* 史無前例的；空前的

Malala's achievement is unprecedented in Pakistan.

馬拉拉的成就在巴基斯坦是史無前例的。

68 **it**

走

拉丁文「走」、「離開」或「旅行」的意思。

- **circuit** [`sɝkɪt] *n.* 環形（道路）；巡迴
- **exit** [`ɛksɪt] *n.* 出口 *v.* 離開
- **itinerant** [ɪ`tɪnərənt] *adj.* 移動的、巡迴的
- **transit** [`trænsɪt] *n.* 運輸、運送

circuit [`sɝkɪt] *n.* 環形（道路）；巡迴

He decided to start a lecture circuit about a close relationship for communities all around the country.

他決定踏上全國各社區，進行關於親密關係的巡迴演講。

69 gress

走

源自於拉丁文，有「走動」、「四處移動」或「採取行動」的意思。

- **regress** [rɪˋgrɛs] *v.* 退化、倒退
- **progressive** [prəˋgrɛsɪv] *adj.* 漸進的、逐漸的
- **digress** [daɪˋgrɛs] *v.* 離題、篇題
- **aggression** [əˋgrɛʃən] *n.* 攻擊；侵犯

regress [rɪˋgrɛs] *v.* 退化、倒退

Not learning anything means you're regressing when everyone is progressing.

不學習就是在每個人進步時你退步了。

70 vad

走

源自拉丁文，「走入」、「走進」的意思。

- **pervade** [pɚˋved] *v.* 滲透、充滿、瀰漫
- **invader** [ɪnˋvedɚ] *n.* 入侵者
- **invade** [ɪnˋved] *v.* 入侵、侵略；蜂擁而至
- **evade** [ɪˋved] *v.* 逃避、躲開

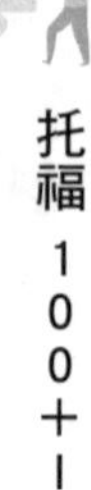

pervade [pɚˋved] *v.* 滲透、充滿、瀰漫

She just finished cooking the lunch, so the smell of garlic pervaded the kitchen.

她剛煮完午飯，所以整個廚房充滿大蒜的味道。

71 vag, vaga

漫走

拉丁文「漫步」、「四處移動」或「居無定所」的意思。

- **vagrant** [`vegrənt] *n.* 無業遊民、流浪者
- **vague** [veg] *adj.* 含糊的、不清楚的
- **vagabond** [`vægəbɑnd] *n.* 流浪者 *adj.* 流浪的、無家的 *v.* 流浪
- **extravagant** [ɪk`strævəgənt] *adj.* 奢侈的、浪費的；過度不切實際的

vagrant [`vegrənt] *n.* 無業遊民、流浪者

She prepared a meal for vagrants around this area and tried to think of a solution for them.

她為附近的遊民準備了一餐並試著想辦法幫他們解決問題。

72 err

漫步

源自於拉丁文，「漫步」、「流浪」的意思，衍生為「偏離」。

- **aberration** [ˏabə`reʃən] *n.* 反常行為、異常現象（ab- 脫離）
- **errant** [`ɛrənt] *adj.* 出軌的、離家犯錯的
- **erratic** [ɪ`rætɪk] *adj.* 不規則的、無法預測的
- **unerring** [ʌn`ɛrɪŋ] *adj.* 萬無一失的、永不出錯的

aberration [ˏabə`reʃən] *n.* 反常行為、異常現象（ab- 脫離）

The doctor advised the relatives watch James carefully because he suspected his violent behavior might not be a temporary aberration.

醫生囑咐詹姆士的親屬好好看緊他，因為他懷疑他的暴力行為可能不是一時反常。

UNIT 07

行為動作

Cur-Audi ▶ MP3 007

73 cur

跑

源自於拉丁文「跑動」的意思。

- **currency** [`kʌrənsɪ] *n.* 流通貨幣；流行、通用
- **curriculum** [kə`rɪkjʊləm] *n.* 課程（古代指戰車競速的意思，為貴
- **族課程）**
- **incur** [ɪn`kɝ] *v.* 招致、承受、自食惡果
- **recur** [rɪ`kɝ] *v.* 反覆發生；再發生、再出現

currency [`kʌrənsɪ] *n.* 流通貨幣；流行、通用

The Euro became a widely used currency around the world since the establishment of the European Union.

歐元自歐盟成立後變成一項廣泛使用於全球的貨幣。

74 salt, sali

跳

源自於拉丁文，「飛躍」、「跳躍」、「往前彈跳」的意思。

- **saltatorial** [sæltə`torɪəl] *adj.* （動物）會跳躍的、跳躍的
- **saltatory** [`sæltətorɪ] *adj.* 跳躍式的
- **saltation** [sæl`teʃən] *n.* 大躍進、突然改變；大幅度跳躍
- **salient** [`selɪənt] *adj.* 突出的、顯著的

saltatorial [sæltə`torɪəl] *adj.* （動物）會跳躍的、跳躍的

Rabbits are not saltatorial animals in zoology because they do not hop like grasshoppers.

兔子在動物學中不算是會跳躍的動物，因為牠們不像蚱蜢那樣可以高高跳起。

75 sist

站立

拉丁文「站立」、「留下」或「立定」的意思。

- **insistent** [ɪn`sɪstənt] *adj.* 堅持的、堅決的
- **irresistible** [ɪrɪ`zɪstəbəl] *adj.* 無法抗拒的
- **persistence** [pɚ`sɪstəns] *n.* 堅持、執意；持久性
- **subsist** [səb`sɪst] *v.* 勉強度日、維持生計

insistent [ɪn`sɪstənt] *adj.* 堅持的、堅決的

He is very insistent that desserts are served before the main course for better digestion.

他非常堅持為了更好的消化，甜點要在主菜之前上。

76 sta

站立

與 sist 同源，同樣有「站立」、「留下」或「立定」的意思。

- **stature** [`stætʃɚ] *n.* 身高；聲望
- **statue** [`stætʃu] *n.* 雕像、雕塑
- **stance** [stæns] *n.* 立場、公開觀點
- **status** [`stetəs] *n.* 身分、地位；尊重程度

stature [`stætʃɚ] *n.* 身高；聲望

Her short stature becomes her mark and makes her easy to notice in this group.

她矮小的身高變成她的標誌，讓她在這團體中很容易被注意到。

77 ven	
來 源自於拉丁文，「過來」、「來臨」的意思。	▪ **intervene** [ɪntɚ`vin] *v.* 干涉、阻撓；調停 ▪ **preventive** [prɪ`vɛntɪv] *adj.* 預防的 ▪ **convene** [kən`vin] *v.* 召開（會議）、集合 ▪ **advent** [`ædvənt] *n.* 來臨、到來、出現

intervene [ɪntɚ`vin] *v.* 干涉、阻撓；調停

It is difficult for outsiders to intervene in the argument between a couple because they are the only people who know what really happened.

外人很難去干涉情侶間的爭執，因為只有他們才知道真正發生了什麼事。

78 sid	
坐 源自於拉丁文「坐下」的意思，衍生為「穩定狀態」。	▪ **insidious** [ɪn`sɪdɪəs] *adj.* 潛藏的、潛害的（in- 裡面的） ▪ **preside** [prɪ`zaɪd] *v.* 主持、掌管（pre- 在…前面，原指「坐在前面」） ▪ **residential** [rɛzɪ`dɛnʃəl] *adj.* 居住的、住宅的 ▪ **subside** [səb`saɪd] *v.* 趨於平緩、平息

insidious [ɪn`sɪdɪəs] *adj.* 潛藏的、潛害的（in- 裡面的）

Hepatitis is an insidious disease which has almost no symptoms in the early stage.

肝炎是種潛伏性病症，在初期時幾乎沒有症狀。

79 sed

坐

與 sid 同源，拉丁文「坐下」的意思，衍生為「穩定狀態」。

- **sedentary** [`sɛdəntərɪ] *adj.* 久坐的、缺乏運動的
- **sediment** [`sɛdɪmənt] *n.* 沉澱物、沉積物
- **supersede** [ˌsupɚ`sid] *v.* 取代、代替（super- 在…之上）
- **sedate** [sɪ`det] *adj.* 平靜的、平穩的

sedentary [`sɛdəntərɪ] *adj.* 久坐的、缺乏運動的

A sedentary lifestyle seems common for office workers, yet it is very unhealthy.

缺乏運動的生活方式似乎是上班族的一般現象，但卻非常不健康。

80 sess

坐

與 sid 同源，拉丁文「坐下」的意思，衍生為「穩定狀態」或「有」的意思。

- **repossess** [ˌripə`zɛs] *v.* 收回、重新擁有（房產）
- **dispossess** [dɪspə`zɛs] *v.* 剝奪、奪走（possess- 擁有）
- **obsessive** [əb`sɛsɪv] *adj.* 念念不忘的、無法擺脫的；迷戀的
- **assess** [ə`sɛs] *v.* 評估、評價

repossess [ˌripə`zɛs] *v.* 收回、重新擁有（房產）

The family repossessed their old house after paying off all their debts.

這家人付清所有的債務後，重新收回他們的舊家。

81 **cub, cumb**

躺

拉丁文「平躺」、「躺下」或「躺著睡著」的意思。

- **incubate** [`ɪŋkjʊbet] *v.* 孵、孵化
- **cubicle** [`kjubɪkəl] *n.* 小房間、小隔間（拉丁文原指躺下，衍生為房間）
- **incubus** [`ɪŋkjʊbəs] *n.* 夢魘（文言用法）
- **incumbent** [ɪn`kʌmbənt] *adj.* 在職的；須履行的（in- 在…之上）

incubate [`ɪŋkjʊbet] *v.* 孵、孵化

Male penguins are responsible for incubating eggs, while the female ones search for food.

公企鵝在母企鵝去尋找食物時負責孵蛋。

82 **dorm**

睡

源自於拉丁文，「睡」、「睡著」的意思。

- **dormancy** [`dɔrmənsɪ] *n.* 冬眠、休眠
- **dormer** [`dɔrmɚ] *n.* 屋頂窗、老虎窗（斜屋頂上突出的天窗）
- **dormitory** [`dɔrmətorɪ] *n.* （學校）宿舍（-tory 指「…地方」）
- **dormant** [`dɔrmənt] *adj.* 蟄伏的、休眠的、沉睡的

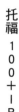

dormancy [`dɔrmənsɪ] *n.* 冬眠、休眠

Many insects need a period of dormancy during the winter.

許多昆蟲冬天時需要冬眠。

83 somn

睡

源自於拉丁文「睡著」或是「做夢」的意思，通常用在比較學術或文雅的詞中。

- **hypersomnia** [ˌhaɪpɚˋsɑmnɪə] *n.* 嗜睡症（hyper- 希臘文，超過）
- **insomnia** [ɪnˋsɑmnɪə] *n.* 失眠（in- 無法）
- **somnolent** [ˋsɑmnələnt] *adj.* 催眠的、令人昏昏欲睡的
- **somnambulism** [sɑmˋnæmbjʊlɪzəm] *n.* 夢遊症（ambul- 走）

hypersomnia [ˌhaɪpɚˋsɑmnɪə] *n.* 嗜睡症（hyper- 希臘文，超過）

Sleeping too long every day and feeling tired all the time may be hypersomnia, and it could also be a symptom of depression.

每天都睡很久又很累，可能是嗜睡症，也是憂鬱症的徵兆之一。

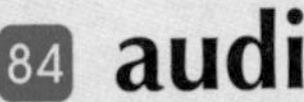

84 audi

聽

拉丁文「聆聽」的意思，衍生到和「聽覺」有關的詞彙。

- **audible** [ˋɔdəbəl] *adj.* 可聽到的
- **auditorium** [ɔdɪˋtɔrɪəm] *n.* 聽眾席、觀眾席；（美）音樂廳、禮堂
- **auditory** [ˋɔdɪtorɪ] *adj.* 聽覺的
- **audit** [ˋɔdɪt] *v.* 旁聽；審計（舊時審查帳目是由口述的）

audible [ˋɔdəbəl] *adj.* 可聽到的

The wall between these two rooms is not very thick, so every movement that makes sounds is audible.

這兩個房間的隔牆沒有很厚，所以任何會發出聲音的動作都聽得一清二楚。

行為動作

Habit-Mens ▶MP3 008

85 habit
居住

源自於拉丁文，「居住」、「生活」的意思。

- **cohabitation** [koˌhæbɪˋteʃən] *n.* 同居；共存
- **habitable** [ˋhæbɪtəbəl] *adj.* 適合居住的
- **inhabit** [ɪnˋhæbɪt] *v.* 居住於、佔領
- **habitat** [ˋhæbɪˌtæt] *n.* 棲息地、生長地

cohabitation [koˌhæbɪˋteʃən] *n.* 同居；共存

In countries where marriage is invalid for homosexual couples, they can only choose cohabitation.

在同志結婚不被認可的國家裡，他們最多只能選擇同居。

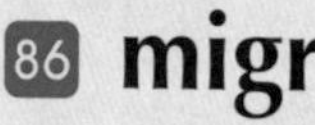

86 migr
遷移

源自於拉丁文，「遷徙」、「搬移」或「移動」的意思。

- **emigrant** [ˋɛmɪgrənt] *n.* （移居國外的）移民
- **immigrate** [ˋɪmɪˌgret] *v.* 移入（國外）、移民
- **migrate** [maɪˋgret] *v.* 遷移、遷徙、移居
- **migration** [maɪˋgreʃən] *n.* 遷移、遷徙

emigrant [ˋɛmɪgrənt] *n.* （移居國外的）移民

Many countries, when encountering economic recession, will try to

reduce emigrant workers to protect their local citizens.
許多國家遭逢經濟衰退時，會試圖減少移民工作者以保護當地居民。

87 **oper**
工作

源自於拉丁文「工作」、「運作」的意思。

- **inoperable** [ɪn`ɑpərəbəl] *adj.* 不宜動手術的；行不通的、無法操作的
- **operative** [`ɑpərətɪv] *adj.* 有效的、實施中的 *n.* 技工
- **operational** [ɑpə`reʃənəl] *adj.* 工作上（中）的、運作中的、實行上的
- **co-operation** [ko͵ɑpə`reʃən] *n.* 合作

inoperable [ɪn`ɑpərəbəl] *adj.* 不宜動手術的；行不通的、無法操作的

The idea he presents in this model is really great, but in reality it is inoperable.
他在這個模型中呈現的概念十分地好，但是現實中是行不通的。

88 **pend**
懸掛

拉丁文「懸掛」、「有重量」或「使…下垂」的意思。

- **pendulum** [`pɛndʒʊləm] *n.* 鐘擺；搖擺不定的局面或觀點
- **pendant** [`pɛndənt] *n.* 垂飾、有垂飾的項鍊 *adj.* 下垂的、懸垂的
- **dependent** [dɪ`pɛndənt] *adj.* 依賴的、需要照顧的；取決於
- **appendix** [ə`pɛndɪks] *n.* 盲腸；附錄（append- 掛在／加在後面）

pendulum [`pɛndʒʊləm] *n.* 鐘擺；搖擺不定的局面或觀點

The pendulum between total forbiddance and continuous development of nuclear power is never settled in the governmental policy.
政府政策總是在全面禁止和繼續發展核能這兩個選項中擺盪。

89 pens

懸掛

與 pend 同源，有「懸掛、有重量」或「使…下垂」的意思。

- **pensive** [`pɛnsɪv] *adj.* 沉思的
- **suspense** [sə`spɛns] *n.* 懸念；焦慮、擔心
- **dispensable** [dɪ`spɛnsəbəl] *adj.* 非必要的、非強制的（dis- 不用的；dispense- 不用的重量，衍生為「省去」）
- **compensation** [ˌkɑmpɛn`seʃən] *n.* 補償金、賠償（物）（com- 一起；compensate- 一起秤重，衍生為「補償」）

pensive [`pɛnsɪv] *adj.* 沉思的

He was a pensive boy in school days, and now he has become a warm philosophy teacher.

在校時他曾是個愛沉思的男孩，現在他變成一個溫暖的哲學老師。

90 flic

打擊

拉丁文「擊倒」、「摧毀」或「損壞／害」的意思。

- **affliction** [ə`flɪkʃən] *n.* 痛苦、苦惱
- **inflict** [ɪn`flɪkt] *v.* 使遭受、承受（不愉快的事）
- **conflict** [`kɑnflɪkt] *n.* 衝突、紛爭 *v.* 衝突、牴觸
- **afflict** [ə`flɪkt] *v.* 使痛苦、折磨

affliction [ə`flɪkʃən] *n.* 痛苦、苦惱

Searching for doctor's or friends' support is helpful to remove the afflictions in your mind, but you can only do it when you are open to yourself.

尋求醫生或朋友的支持對於去除心中的苦惱是很有幫助的，但只有你對自己誠實才能真正做到。

91 **clud**
關閉

源自於拉丁文，「關閉、封合」的意思。

- **occlude** [ə`klud] *v.* 阻擋、阻攔、覆蓋
- **preclude** [prɪ`klud] *v.* 防止、杜絕
- **exclude** [ɪk`sklud] *v.* 阻止、排除、不包括
- **conclude** [kən`klud] *v.* 結束、斷定、做出決定

occlude [ə`klud] *v.* 阻擋、阻攔、覆蓋

To prevent little children from walking into the small chink between the two buildings, they occluded the entrance with a wooden board.
為了避免小孩走入兩棟大樓間的小縫，他們用木板將其入口擋住。

92 **tect**
遮掩

源自於拉丁文「遮掩」、「掩蓋」的意思。

- **undetectable** [ʌndɪ`tɛktəbəl] *adj.* 無法察覺的、探測不到的
- **protective** [prə`tɛktɪv] *adj.* 防護的、對…呵護的
- **detection** [dɪ`tɛkʃən] *n.* 察覺、發現、偵破
- **detect** [dɪ`tɛkt] *v.* 發現、察覺；測出（原拉丁字義為揭開）

undetectable [ʌndɪ`tɛktəbəl] *adj.* 無法察覺的、探測不到的

With the improvement of technology, astronomers are able to explore the space in universe that was undetectable before.
隨著科學進步，天文學家現在可以探索以前無法探測的宇宙空間。

93 **fic**

製造

拉丁文「製作」、「建造」、「造成」或「形成」的意思。

- **artificial** [ɑrtɪ`fɪʃəl] *adj.* 人工的、人造的；虛假的
- **fiction** [`fɪkʃən] *n.* 小說；虛構的事、謊言
- **unification** [ˌjunɪfə`keʃən] *n.* 統一、合併
- **proficient** [prə`fɪʃənt] *adj.* 精通的、熟練的

artificial [ɑrtɪ`fɪʃəl] *adj.* 人工的、人造的；虛假的

We can only decorate the room with artificial flowers because we don't have a garden.

我們只能用假花裝飾房間，因為我們沒有花園。

94 **greg**

聚集

源自於拉丁文，「群集」、「聚集」或「一起」的意思。

- **gregarious** [grɪ`gɛrɪəs] *adj.* 群居的、愛交際的
- **segregate** [`sɛgrɪˌget] *v.* （種族）隔離、分隔
- **congregation** [kɑŋgrɪ`geʃən] *n.* 信眾；集合
- **aggregate** [`ægrɪˌget] *v.* 使聚集 *n.* 具集體、總數 *adj.* 合計的

gregarious [grɪ`gɛrɪəs] *adj.* 群居的、愛交際的

It is said that people who have a gregarious nature are suitable for jobs related to sales.

據說有愛交際天性的人適合銷售相關的工作。

95 damn, demn

傷害

源自於拉丁文，「傷害」、「損失」或「值得責罵」的意思。

- **indemnify** [ɪn`dɛmnɪfaɪ] *v.* 賠償損失、保障
- **damning** [`dæmɪŋ] *adj.* 譴責的、（證據）確鑿的
- **condemnation** [ˌkɑndəm`neʃən] *n.* 指責、譴責、聲討
- **condemn** [kən`dɛm] *v.* 指責、譴責

indemnify [ɪn`dɛmnɪfaɪ] *v.* 賠償損失、保障

In the terms and conditions, it states clearly that the insurance indemnifies the travellers against belonging loss.

在條款和條件中有清楚說明，保險有包含保障旅客的隨身物品損失。

96 mens

測量

源自於拉丁文「測量」的意思，和空間大小有關。

- **immensity** [ɪ`mɛnsətɪ] *n.* 巨大、廣大、大量
- **dimension** [daɪ`mɛnʃən] *n.* 空間、維度、層面
- **immense** [ɪ`mɛns] *adj.* 巨大的、無限的
- **commensurate** [kə`mɛnʒərət] *adj.* 相稱的、相當的

immensity [ɪ`mɛnsətɪ] *n.* 巨大、廣大、大量

The researchers did not expect the immensity of data.

研究人員沒有預料到如此大量的資料。

UNIT 09

行為動作—性質狀態

Pol(y)-Misc ▶MP3 009

97 pol (y)

賣

源自於希臘文，常出現於單字後半，「販賣」、「交易」等意思。

- **oligopoly** [ˌalɪ`gapəlɪ] *n.* 寡頭壟斷（oligo-少數）
- **duopoly** [dju`apəlɪ] *n.* 雙寡頭壟斷
- **monopolize** [mə`napəlaɪz] *v.* 壟斷、包辦、專售
- **monopoly** [mə`napəli] *n.* 壟斷、專賣

oligopoly [ˌalɪ`gapəlɪ] *n.* 寡頭壟斷（oligo-少數）

TV broadcasting is no longer limited in control of government's oligopoly.

電視播映已經不在市政府寡頭壟斷的控制下了。

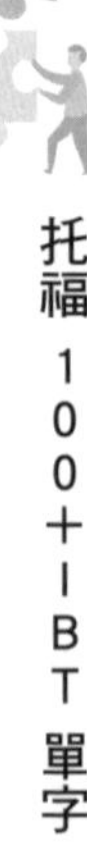

98 pute

思考

源自於拉丁文，「思考」、「考慮」或「推想」的意思。

- **putative** [`pjutətɪv] *adj.* 認定的、假定存在的
- **dispute** [dɪ`spjut] *n.* 紛爭、爭執 *v.* 爭議、對…有異議
- **computing** [kəm`pjutɪŋ] *n.* 電腦學、資訊處理技術
- **computerize** [kəm`pjutəˌraɪz] *v.* 電腦化、用電腦處理

putative [`pjutətɪv] *adj.* 認定的、假定存在的

Atlantis is a putative land which sunk into the ocean before any other civilizations contacted it.
亞特蘭提斯是一個被認定存在的陸地，在其他文明抵達前就沉沒到海底了。

99 fid
相信

源自於拉丁文，帶有「相信」、「信任」或「忠貞」的含意。

- **perfidious** [pɚ`fɪdɪəs] *adj.* 背信的、不忠貞的
- **fidelity** [fɪ`dɛlɪtɪ] *n.* 忠誠、忠貞
- **confidential** [kɑnfɪ`dɛnʃəl] *adj.* 機密的、祕密的
- **confidant** [kɑnfɪ`dænt] *n.* 知己、密友

perfidious [pɚ`fɪdɪəs] *adj.* 背信的、不忠貞的（per- 超過，perfid- 超過忠實的限制）

The electors are already tired of the perfidious candidates who never fulfill their campaign promises.
選民已經厭煩那些永遠不實現競選承諾的背信候選人。

100 reg
治理

拉丁文「指導」、「治理」或「統治」的意思。

- **regal** [`rɪgəl] *adj.* 帝王般（莊嚴）的
- **regent** [`rɪdʒənt] *n.* 攝政王
- **regime** [re`ʒim] *n.* 政府、政體；體系
- **regulator** [`rɛgjʊˌletər] *n.* 管理者、監管者；調節器

regal [`rɪgəl] *adj.* 帝王般（莊嚴）的

Regal clothes for men are out-of-date in the current fashion world.
如帝王般莊嚴的男性服飾已經在流行界退潮流了。

101 **ori** 升起 拉丁文「太陽升起」的含意，衍生為「源頭」、「東方」等意思。	▪ **disorientate** [dɪs`ɔrɪɛn͵tet] *v.* 使迷失、使失去方向 ▪ **aboriginal** [abə`rɪdʒɪnəl] *adj.* 土生土長的、原住民的（ab-從） ▪ **oriental** [ɔrɪ`ɛntəl] *adj.* 東方的 ▪ **originate** [ə`rɪdʒə͵net] *v.* 起源、始於、開始於

disorientate [dɪs`ɔrɪɛn͵tet] *v.* 使迷失、使失去方向

We were totally disorientated when the heavy fog suddenly came.
突然起濃霧時我們完全迷失方向。

102 **cid** 墜落 源自於拉丁文「墜落」、「掉落」，後衍生為「降臨」。	▪ **incidence** [`ɪnsɪdəns] *n.* 事件、發生率 ▪ **recidivist** [rɪ`sɪdəvɪst] *n.* 慣犯、累犯 ▪ **coincidence** [ko`ɪnsədəns] *n.* 巧合、碰巧、偶而機遇（coincide- 同時發生） ▪ **incidental** [ɪnsə`dɛntəl] *adj.* 附帶的、伴隨的

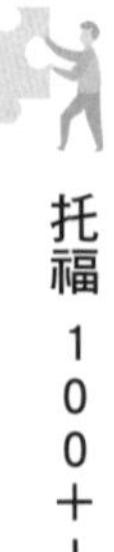

incidence [`ɪnsɪdəns] *n.* 事件、發生率（in- 臨、面對，incident- 降臨發生的事）

The local government wishes to decrease the incidence of the queries of parking place by revising the current policy.
地方政府希望藉由修改現行政策來降低停車糾紛的發生率。

103 **merg**

沉，浸

源自於拉丁文，「沉沒」、「潛入」或「跳進」的意思。

- **emergence** [ɪˋmɚdʒəns] *n.* 嶄露、出現
- **merge** [mɝdʒ] *v.* 合併、融合
- **merger** [mɝdʒɚ] *n.* 合併
- **submerge** [səbˋmɝdʒ] *v.* 沉入水中、浸泡

emergence [ɪˋmɚdʒəns] *n.* 嶄露、出現

We need more translation experts for the emergence of markets in South East Asia.

我們需要更多翻譯人才以面對東南亞的新興市場。

104 **clin**

傾

原和拉丁文「床」有關，後延伸為「依靠」、「傾斜」的意思。

- **recline** [rɪˋklaɪn] *v.* 使斜倚、使向後靠
- **inclined** [ɪnˋklaɪnd] *adj.* 傾向於的
- **incline** [ɪnˋklaɪn] *v.* 使傾向於
- **cling** [klɪŋ] *v.* 依附、緊貼著、緊抓住；堅持

recline [rɪˋklaɪn] *v.* 使斜倚、使向後靠

She made herself a cup of coffee and reclined on the sofa to enjoy her weekend afternoon.

她為自己沖泡一杯咖啡並斜倚在沙發上，享受她的週末午後。

105 **vert** 轉 源自於拉丁文，有「凹折」、「反轉」的意思。	▪ **avert** [ə`vɝt] *v.* 轉移；防止 ▪ **obvert** [əb`vɝt] *v.* 轉到對立立場、轉到反面 ▪ **invert** [ɪn`vɝt] *v.* 顛倒、使倒置 ▪ **convert** [kən`vɝt] *v.* 轉變、改變；改信

avert [ə`vɝt] *v.* 轉移；防止

The psychologist suggests the public avert their eye from sad but meaningless local news to more positive information.

心理學家建議大眾將視線從悲傷但無意義的地方新聞轉移到更正面的資訊。

106 **flu** 流 源自於拉丁文，含有「流動」、「流暢」的意思。	▪ **confluence** [`kɑn,fluəns] *n.* 合流點；匯合、集合 ▪ **effluent** [`ɛfluənt] *n.* 汙水、廢水 ▪ **fluency** [`fluənsɪ] *n.* 流利 ▪ **fluid** [`fluɪd] *n.* 流體、液體 *adj.* 流暢的；不固定的、易變的

confluence [`kɑn,fluəns] *n.* 合流點；匯合、集合

She decided to move from her old house because it was on an island standing at the confluence of two rivers.

她決定搬離她的舊家，因為舊家是在兩條河流匯合點的島嶼上。

107 **fus**

混合

從拉丁文轉成法文後才傳到英文的字根，有「傾倒」、「融化」或「混合」的意思。

- **confusing** [kən`fjuzɪŋ] *adj.* 含糊不清的、令人困惑的
- **diffuse** [dɪ`fjuz] *v.* 傳播、擴散 *adj.* 擴散的、分散的
- **fuse** [fjuz] *v.* 融合、結合、融化 *n.* 保險絲
- **fusion** [`fjuʒən] *n.* 融合、結合、合併

confusing [kən`fjuzɪŋ] *adj.* 含糊不清的、令人困惑的

"The explanation in this manual is so confusing. Can you help me sort them out, please?"

「這手冊裡的說明好含糊不清，你能幫我理出個頭緒嗎？」

108 **misc**

混雜

源自於拉丁文，有「混合」、「混雜」等意思。

- **immiscible** [ɪ`mɪsəbəl] *adj.* 不能混合的、不相容的
- **miscellaneous** [ˌmɪsə`lenɪəs] *adj.* 各式各樣的、混雜的
- **miscellany** [mɪ`sɛlənɪ] *n.* 混合物、大雜燴；合集
- **promiscuous** [prə`mɪskjʊəs] *adj.* 淫亂的、濫交的

immiscible [ɪ`mɪsəbəl] *adj.* 不能混合的、不相容的

Oil and water are immiscible in natural condition, but detergent makes this possible.

油水在自然情況下無法混合，但洗潔精卻讓這個變成可行的。

性質狀態—實務器具

Mut-Cart ▶MP3 010

109 **mut**

變化

來自拉丁文「變化」、「改變」或「可轉變的」的意思。

- **immutable** [ɪ`mjutəbəl] *adj.* 永不改變的
- **commute** [kə`mjut] *v.* 變成、折換、減刑；通勤
- **mutation** [mju`teʃən] *n.* 突變、異變
- **transmute** [tranz`mjut] *v.* 完全改變（成另一種物品）

immutable [ɪ`mjutəbəl] *adj.* 永不改變的

Nothing is immutable in the universe and that is why there are always surprises.

這宇宙中沒有永不改變的事，所以才總會有驚喜。

110 **luc**

光

源自於拉丁文，「光線」、「陽光」或「光明」的意思。

- **elucidate** [ɪ`lusɪˌdet] *v.* 闡明、解釋
- **lucid** [`lusɪd] *adj.* 清晰明瞭的、頭腦清楚的
- **translucent** [træns`lusənt] *adj.* 半透明的
- **pellucid** [pɪ`lusɪd] *adj.* 乾淨明亮的；明瞭的（pel=per-通過）

elucidate [ɪ`lusɪˌdet] *v.* 闡明、解釋（e=ex- 出來，elucide- 將…清楚弄出來）

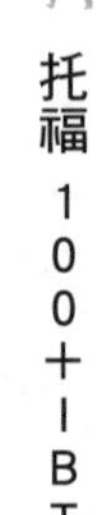

Scientists cannot totally elucidate global climate changes due to their complexity.
科學家因其複雜性還不能完全闡明全球氣候變遷。

111 lumin
光
拉丁文「陽光」、「火炬」或「燈光」的意思，與 意義相近。

- **luminescence** [ˌluməˋnɛsəns] *n.* 弱光、冷光
- **luminous** [ˋlumɪnəs] *adj.* 發光的、夜光的
- **illumination** [ɪˌlumɪˋneʃən] *n.* 光、照明、燈飾
- **illuminate** [ɪˋlumɪnet] *v.* 照亮；闡明

luminescence [ˌluməˋnɛsəns] *n.* 弱光、冷光（escence- 表示一種狀態）

Luminescence of fireflies carries various meanings from mating to warning.
螢火蟲的冷光帶有許多含意，從求偶到警示都有。

112 son
聲音
源自於拉丁文，指「被聽到的聲音」或「噪音」。

- **resonant** [ˋrɛzənənt] *adj.* 響亮的、共鳴的、回響的
- **sonar** [ˋsonɑr] *n.* 聲納
- **supersonic** [supɚˋsɑnɪk] *adj.* 超音速的
- **consonance** [ˋkɑnsənəns] *n.* 和諧、一致同意；和音

resonant [ˋrɛzənənt] *adj.* 響亮的、共鳴的、回響的

He missed the days when he could hear the resonant voice of his nanny to wake him up in the morning.
他想念過往可以在早晨聽到保母喚醒他的宏亮聲音。

113 vac (u)

空

源自於拉丁文，有「空洞」或「將…淨空」的意思。

- **vacuous** [`vækjʊəs] *adj.* 空洞的、無知的
- **vacuum** [`vækjum] *n.* 真空、空白；真空吸塵器
- **vacancy** [`vekənsɪ] *n.* 空缺、空位
- **evacuate** [ɪ`vækjʊet] *v.* 撤離、疏散

vacuous [`vækjʊəs] *adj.* 空洞的、無知的

She could only hide her sadness of losing her parents with a vacuous smile.

她僅能以一個空洞的微笑隱藏她失去父母的悲傷。

114 nihil

空無

源自拉丁文「什麼都沒有」的意思。

- **annihilate** [ə`naɪəlet] *v.* 徹底摧毀、徹底擊敗
- **annihilation** [əˌnaɪə`leʃən] *n.* 全毀；一敗塗地
- **nihilism** [`naɪəlɪzəm] *n.* 虛無主義
- **nihilistic** [naɪə`lɪstɪk] *adj.* 虛無的

annihilate [ə`naɪəlet] *v.* 徹底摧毀、徹底擊敗

The little town near the seashore in Japan was annihilated by the tsunami.

日本沿海的小鎮被海嘯完全摧毀。

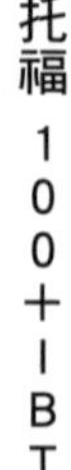

115 **plic**
摺疊，重

源自於拉丁文 plicare，「折疊」、「重複」的意思。

- **duplicate** [\`djupləkət] *adj.* 複製的、一模一樣的 *n.* 複製品、副本 *v.* 複製、拷貝（du- 二，duplic- 折兩折）
- **explicit** [ɪk\`splɪsɪt] *adj.* 清楚明白的、不含糊的
- **implicit** [ɪm\`plɪsɪt] *adj.* 含蓄的、隱晦的
- **replicate** [\`rɛplɪket] *v.* 重複、複製、再生

duplicate [\`djupləkət] *adj.* 複製的、一模一樣的 *n.* 複製品、副本 *v.* 複製、拷貝（du- 二，duplic- 折兩折）

The landlord asked the blacksmith to make a duplicate of the key for the new tenant.

房東請鎖匠打一把鑰匙給新來的房客。

116 **ver (i)**
真實

拉丁文「真實的」、「誠實的」或「事實」的意思。

- **veracity** [və\`ræsətɪ] *n.* 真實性、誠實
- **verdict** [\`vɝdɪkt] *n.* 依事實做出的決定、判決（dict-說）
- **verify** [\`vɛrɪfaɪ] *v.* 證實、證明
- **veritable** [\`vɛrɪtəbəl] *adj.* 不折不扣的、名副其實的

veracity [və\`ræsətɪ] *n.* 真實性、誠實

New evidence destabilized the veracity of witness's testimony.

新證據動搖了證人證詞的真實性。

117 fals, fall

假，錯

源自於拉丁文，「欺騙」、「不實」或「錯誤的」。

- **fallacious** [fə`leʃəs] *adj.* 謬誤的
- **fallacy** [`fæləsɪ] *n.* 謬見、謬論
- **falsely** [`fɔlslɪ] *adv.* 錯誤地
- **falsify** [`fɔlsə,faɪ] *v.* 竄改、偽造；證實為錯

fallacious [fə`leʃəs] *adj.* 謬誤的

He has to rewrite his dissertation because all his argument is based on a fallacious theory.

他必須重寫他的論文，因為他的論證都建立在謬誤的理論基礎上。

118 grav

重

源自於拉丁文，表示「沉重的」、「有重量的」。

- **aggravate** [`ægrə,vet] *v.* 加劇、加重、使更嚴重、惡化
- **grave** [grev] *adj.* 重大的、嚴重的
- **gravity** [`grævətɪ] *n.* 重力；嚴重性
- **gravitate** [`grævɪ,tet] *v.* 受吸引而轉向⋯

aggravate [`ægrə,vet] *v.* 加劇、加重、使更嚴重、惡化

The roadside construction aggravates the traffic congestion of this narrow road.

路旁的建設使這條窄路的交通壅塞更加惡化了。

119 val

強

源自於拉丁文，「強壯」、「有力」或「健康的」意思。

- **convalesce** [͵kɑnvə`lɛs] *v.* 康復；療養（至恢復）
- **valor** [`vælɚ] *n.* 英勇、勇敢
- **valiant** [`væljənt] *adj.* 英勇的、勇猛的、大膽的
- **prevalent** [`prɛvələnt] *adj.* （古）強勢的、有力的；流行的、普遍的

convalesce [͵kɑnvə`lɛs] *v.* 康復；療養（至恢復）

He has to spend longer time for convalescing after the major operation because of his age.

因為他年紀較大，大手術後必須花較多的時間康復。

120 cart

紙

源自於希臘文「地圖」，後傳到拉丁文衍生為紙片的意思。

- **cartridge paper** [`kɑrtrɪdʒ `pepɚ] *n.* 厚繪圖紙
- **carton** [`kɑrtən] *n.* 硬紙盒
- **cartographer** [kɑr`tɑgrəfɚ] *n.* 繪製地圖者
- **cartogram** [`kɑrtə͵græm] *n.* 統計地圖、單一主題地圖

cartridge paper [`kɑrtrɪdʒ `pepɚ] *n.* 厚繪圖紙

If you wish to participate in the illustration competition, please draw or paint your work on a cartridge paper and hand it in.

若你想要參加插畫比賽，請繪製於厚繪圖紙上並繳交作品。

UNIT 11 實務器具—顏色溫度

Fil-Blanc ▶MP3 011

121 fil
線

源自於拉丁文「絲線」、「線狀物」等細長的意思。

- **filigree** [`fɪləgri] *n.* 金屬絲飾品
- **profile** [`profaɪl] *n.* 輪廓、側影；略傳、簡介
- **filament** [`fɪləmənt] *n.* 細絲、長絲；鎢絲
- **defile** [dɪ`faɪl] *n.* 山中狹路

filigree [`fɪləgri] *n.* 金屬絲飾品

His vintage silver filigree earrings are stunning and shine in the handicraft exhibition. 他復古的銀絲耳環十分令人驚艷，並在手工藝展上發光。

122 fib (r)
纖維

源自於拉丁文「纖維」或「纖維狀的」意思。

- **fibrosis** [faɪ`brosɪs] *n.* 纖維化
- **fibrous** [`faɪbrəs] *adj.* 纖維構成的、纖維狀的
- **fiber optics** [`faɪbɚ `ɑptɪks] *n.* 光纖
- **fiber** [`faɪbɚ] *n.* 纖維、纖維組織

fibrosis [faɪ`brosɪs] *n.* 纖維化

Pulmonary fibrosis is an incurable symptom. The medicine can only stop the situation from worsening.

肺部纖維化是無法治癒的症狀，藥物只能防止情況惡化。

123 bibli (o)

書

源自於希臘文「書籍」的意思，也和聖經（Bible）有關。

- **bibliotherapy** [`bɪblɪo͵θɛrəpɪ] *n.* 讀書療法
- **bibliography** [͵bɪblɪ`ɑgrəfɪ] *n.* 參考書目、文獻資料目錄
- **bibliolater** [bɪblɪ`ɑlətɚ] *n.* 熱情愛書者
- **biblical** [`bɪblɪkəl] *adj.* 有關聖經的

bibliotherapy [`bɪblɪo͵θɛrəpɪ] *n.* 讀書療法

The study shows that bibliotherapy is able to help children overcome their negative emotions.

研究顯示書目療法可以幫助孩童克服他們的負面情緒。

124 mur

牆

源自於拉丁文「圍牆」、「牆壁」的意思。

- **extramural** [͵ɛkstrə`mjʊrəl] *adj.* 校外的、機構或城鎮外面的；（大學）為非在校生設的
- **intramural** [͵ɪntrə`mjurəl] *adj.* 內部的、校內的
- **immure** [ɪ`mjur] *v.* 監禁、幽禁（常以被動態使用）
- **mural** [`mjurə] *n.* 壁畫、壁上藝術 *adj.* 牆壁的

extramural [͵ɛkstrə`mjʊrəl] *adj.* 校外的、機構或城鎮外面的；（大學）為非在校生設的

Academia Sinica subsidizes certain amount of funds for extramural researchers annually.

中研院每年補助固定額度經費給院外研究者。

125 clin

床

源自於拉丁文「床」的意思，衍生為「傾斜」等意思。

- **clinician** [klɪ`nɪʃən] *n.* 臨床醫師
- **decline** [dɪ`klaɪn] *v.* 減少、降低、衰弱
- **clinical** [klɪnəkəl] *adj.* 臨床的、門診的
- **clinic** [klɪnɪk] *n.* 診所

clinician [klɪ`nɪʃən] *n.* 臨床醫師

He suddenly decided to join Doctors Without Borders after being a clinician for ten years.

在成為一位臨床醫師十年後他突然決定要加入無國界醫生組織。

126 lib(e)r

天平

源自於拉丁文，衍生為「平衡」的意思。

- **disequilibrium** [dɪs͵ikwə`lɪbrɪəm] *n.* 不平衡、失去平衡
- **deliberate** [də`lɪbərɪt] *adj.* 蓄意的；謹慎的
- **equilibrium** [͵ikwə`lɪbrɪəm] *n.* 平衡、均衡；平靜、安寧
- **librate** [`lɪ͵bret] *v.* 保持平衡、（月球或其他星體）震盪

disequilibrium [dɪs͵ikwə`lɪbrɪəm] *n.* 不平衡、失去平衡

The disequilibrium between supply and demand in the vegetable and fruits market makes the price easily rise and fall quickly.

蔬果市場的供需失衡使價錢容易快速升降。

127 **rub**

紅

源自於拉丁文「紅色」，亦指「帶有紅色的」意思。

- **rubricate** [\`rubrə͵ket] *v.* 以紅色標記
- **ruby** [\`rubɪ] *n.* 紅寶石
- **rubric** [\`rubrɪk] *adj.* （古）書中用紅色強調的標題；標題；指示、說明
- **rubicund** [\`rubɪkənd] *adj.* 臉色紅潤的

rubricate [\`rubrə͵ket] *v.* 以紅色標記

Archaeologists found an ancient textbook rubricated with red ink.

考古學家發現一本古老的教科書，有用紅色墨水標記的痕跡。

128 **verd**

綠

源自於拉丁文「綠色」或「帶點黃的綠色」。

- **verdancy** [\`vɝdənsɪ] *n.* 翠綠
- **verdant** [\`vɝdənt] *adj.* 翠綠的、草木青翠的、蓊鬱的
- **verdigris** [\`vɝdɪgrɪs] *n.* 銅綠、銅鏽
- **verdure** [\`vɝdʒɚ] *n.* 翠綠的草木；青綠

verdancy [\`vɝdənsɪ] *n.* 翠綠

The musician likes to hike on the hills and admires the verdancy of the forest which brings him tranquillity.

音樂家喜歡到小山丘健行，欣賞森林的翠綠和其帶來的平靜。

129 vir 綠 源自於拉丁文「綠色」的意思，也和草木有關。	▪ **virescence** [vɪ`rɛsəns] *n.* 呈綠色；綠化、變綠 ▪ **viridescent** [ˌvɪrɪ`dɛsənt] *adj.* 帶綠色的、淡綠的 ▪ **viridian** [və`rɪdɪən] *n.* 鉻綠、藍綠 *adj.* 藍綠色的 ▪ **viridity** [və`rɪdətɪ] *n.* 青綠、草綠

virescence [vɪ`rɛsəns] *n.* 呈綠色；綠化、變綠

One of the goals in urban renewal plan is the virescence of central city.

都市更新計畫中的其中一個目標為市中心的綠化。

130 negr, nigr 黑 拉丁文中「黑色」的意思，有時和膚色有關。	▪ **denigrate** [`dɛnəˌgret] *v.* 抹黑、詆毀 ▪ **negroid** [`nigrɔɪd] *adj.* 具有黑人特質的 ▪ **negrophobia** [ˌnigrə`fobɪə] *n.* 黑人恐懼症（phobia-恐懼症） ▪ **nigrescent** [ˌnaɪ`grɛsənt] *adj.* 發黑的、帶黑色的

denigrate [`dɛnəˌgret] *v.* 抹黑、詆毀

Winning the election by denigrating the opponents is not respectable at all.

藉由詆毀對手贏得的選舉一點也不值得尊敬。

131 **scot**

黑

源自於希臘文「黑暗的」的意思，在醫學上也有「盲」的意思。

- **scotomatous** [skə`tomətəs] *adj.* 盲點的
- **scotopia** [sko`topɪə] *n.* 夜視力
- **scotomize** [`skotəmaɪz] *v.* 視而不見
- **scotoma** [skə`tomə] *n.* （醫）盲點、黑點

scotomatous [skə`tomətəs] *adj.* 盲點的

With a glance of the sun, you can create a temporary scotomatous phenomenon.

只要瞥一眼太陽你就能製造出暫時的盲點現象。

132 **blanc**

白

源自於古法文「白色」的意思。

- **blancmange** [blə`mɑnʒ] *n.* 牛奶凍
- **carte blanche** [kɑrt `blɑnʃ] *n.* 全權委任、完全自由
- **Mont Blanc** [ˌmon`blɑŋk] *n.* 白朗峰
- **blanch** [blæntʃ] *v.* 變白、變蒼白

blancmange [blə`mɑnʒ] *n.* 牛奶凍

You can make the delicious blancmange yourself.

你可以自己做美味的甜點牛奶凍。

UNIT 12 顏色溫度—動植物與自然界

Alb-Zoo ▶ MP3 012

133 **alb**

白

源自於拉丁文「白色」、「蒼白」的意思。

- **albescent** [ˌæl`besənt] *adj.* 變白的、帶白色的
- **albinism** [`ælbəˌnɪzəm] *n.* 白化症
- **albino** [æl`bɪˌno] *n.* 白化症患者、白化變種
- **alb** [ælb] *n.* 天主教白麻布衣

albescent [ˌæl`besənt] *adj.* 變白的、帶白色的

I was amazed by the suddenly albescent landscape outside my window in the morning. There must have been snow last night.

早晨我對窗外突然變白的景色感到吃驚，昨晚一定下了一場雪。

134 **frig**

冷

拉丁文「寒冷」、「冷凍」或「冷酷」的意思。

- **frigidity** [`frɪdʒɪdətɪ] *n.* 寒冷；冷淡
- **refrigerate** [rɪ`frɪdʒəˌret] *v.* 冷藏、保鮮
- **refrigerator** [rɪ`frɪdʒəˌretə] *n.* 冰箱（簡稱 fridge）
- **frigid** [`frɪdʒɪd] *adj.* 寒冷的；冷淡的

frigidity [`frɪdʒɪdətɪ] *n.* 寒冷；冷淡

He could sense the frigidity in the environment on his first day of

work.
他第一天來上班就感受到這環境中的冷淡氛圍。

135 **gel**
冷

源自拉丁文「冷凍」、「結霜」或「凝結」的意思。後衍生為動物膠 的縮寫。

- **gelatinous** [dʒə`lætənəs] *adj.* 動物膠的；膠狀的
- **gelation** [dʒə`leʃən] *n.* 凍結、凝膠化
- **gelid** [`jɛlɪd] *adj.* 極寒的、冰冷的
- **regelate** [`rɛdʒə,let] *v.* 重新凝結、重新結冰

gelatinous [dʒə`lætənəs] *adj.* 動物膠的；膠狀的

She likes to eat gelatinous agar, known as kanten in Japan, made by her grandmother.
她喜歡外婆做的石花凍，也就是日本的寒天。

136 **ferv**
熱

源自拉丁文「煮沸」的意思，衍生為「燙的」、「熱的」或「熱心」的意思。

- **effervesce** [,ɛfɚ`vɛs] *v.* 起泡、冒泡；興奮、歡騰
- **fervor** [`fɝvɚ] *n.* 熱誠、熱心
- **fervid** [`fɝvɪd] *adj.* 熱情的、熱心的；熾熱的
- **fervent** [`fɝvənt] *adj.* 熱情的、熱烈的；強烈的

effervesce [,ɛfɚ`vɛs] *v.* 起泡、冒泡；興奮、歡騰

The effervescing mud pond in Yanchao, Kaohsiung is actually a ready-to-erupt mud volcano.
在高雄燕巢的冒泡泥池塘，其實是即將噴發的泥火山。

137 levo

左

源自拉丁文「左邊」或「向左」的意思，多用在學術名詞中。

- **levorotary** [ˌlivo`rotətorɪ] *adj.* 左旋的、逆時針旋轉的
- **levorotation** [ˌlivoro`teʃən] *n.* 左旋
- **levodopa** [ˌlivə`dopə] *n.* 左旋多巴

levorotary [ˌlivo`rotətorɪ] *adj.* 左旋的、逆時針旋轉的

Due to the effect of Coriolis force, depressions like typhoons in North hemisphere are levorotary.

因為科氏力的影響，北半球的低氣壓如颱風都是左旋的。

138 sinistr

左

拉丁文「左手邊」的意思，在傳統中左邊有代表邪惡的意思。

- **sinistrous** [`sɪnɪstrəs] *adj.* 笨拙的；不吉利的
- **sinistrorse** [`sɪnɪˌstrɔrs] *adj.* 向左旋轉的、左捲的
- **sinistral** [`sɪnɪstrəl] *adj.* 左邊的、左撇子的
- **sinister** [`sɪnɪstɚ] *adj.* 不祥的、凶兆的；邪惡的

sinistrous [`sɪnɪstrəs] *adj.* 笨拙的；不吉利的

Then dean saw the sinistrous smile of that naughty child. Something bad was going to happen.

然後校長瞥見那頑皮小孩不吉利的笑容，有什麼壞事要發生了。

139 dext(e)r

右

拉丁文「右手邊」的意思，傳統中有「幸運」或「靈活」、「能幹」的涵義。

- **dexter** [`dɛkstɚ] *adj.* 右側的；幸運的
- **dexterity** [dɛk`stɛrətɪ] *n.* 嫻熟、靈巧、敏捷
- **dextrad** [`dɛkstræd] *adv.* 向右（-ad-向）
- **dextral** [`dɛkstrəl] *adj.* 右邊的、右撇子的

dexter [`dɛkstɚ] *adj.* 右側的；幸運的

According to Fengshui, doors setting on dexter or sinister side of the facade can bring different luck for a company.

根據風水，門開在正面的右邊或左邊會為公司帶來不同的運氣。

140 medi

中

源自於拉丁文「中間」的意思，衍生為「不偏袒」或「不突出」的意思。

- **mediocre** [ˌmidɪ`okɚ] *adj.* 中等的、普通的、平庸的
- **intermediate** [ˌɪntɚ`midɪət] *adj.* 中間的、居中的
- **mediate** [`midɪet] *v.* 調停、調解、斡旋
- **medieval** [ˌmɛd`ivəl] *adj.* 中世紀的

mediocre [ˌmidɪ`okɚ] *adj.* 中等的、普通的、平庸的

His mediocre performance cannot help him gain the scholarship.

他平庸的表現無法讓他拿到獎學金。

141 ext(e)r

外

拉丁文「外部」、「外面」或「超越」的意思。

- **exterior** [ɪk`stirɪɚ] *adj.* 外部的、外表的 *n.* 外部、外面
- **external** [ɪk`stɝnəl] *adj.* 外面的、來自外部的
- **externals** [ɪk`stɝnəls] *n.* 外表、外觀、外在
- **extrovert** [`ɛkstrəvɚt] *n.* 性格外向的人 *adj.* 外向的

exterior [ɪk`stirɪɚ] *adj.* 外部的、外表的 *n.* 外部、外面

The exterior of the building is painted white and blue, making it look like the Greek style.

大樓的外部被漆成白藍相間，看起來很有希臘風。

142 dors

背，背後

源自於拉丁文「背部」或「背後」的意思。

- **dorsal** [`dɔrsəl] *adj.* （動物）背部的、背側的
- **dorsum** [`dɔrsəm] *n.* 器官背面
- **endorse** [ɪn`dɔrs] *v.* 背書、公開贊同、支持、廣告代言
- **endorsement** [ɪn`dɔrsmənt] *n.* 支持、認可、代言

dorsal [`dɔrsəl] *adj.* （動物）背部的、背側的

Fishermen cut the dorsal fin of sharks and let them die in the ocean.

漁夫割去鯊魚的背鰭後任牠們在海裡死去。

143 **alt**

高

源自拉丁文「高度」的意思，衍生為「高的」或「提高」的意思。

- **altocumulus** [ˌælto`kjumjʊləs] *n.* 高積雲
- **exaltation** [ɛgzɔl`teʃən] *n.* 晉升、提拔；興高彩烈
- **exalt** [ɪg`zɔlt] *v.* 晉升、提拔；讚揚
- **altitude** [`æltɪtjud] *n.* 高度、海拔

altocumulus [ˌælto`kjumjʊləs] *n.* 高積雲

One Chinese proverb says that the appearance of fishscale like altocumulus is able to be used as weather forecast.

某一中國古諺說魚鱗般的高積雲能用來做天氣預報。

144 **zoo**

動物

源自希臘文「動物」的意思，也衍生為「生命」、「生命體」。

- **zoogenic** [ˌzoə`dʒɛnɪk] *adj.* 源自動物的、動物生成的
- **zoological** [ˌzuə`lɑdʒɪkəl] *adj.* 動物的、動物學的
- **zoologist** [zu`ɑlədʒɪst] *n.* 動物學家
- **zoology** [zu`ɑlədʒɪ] *n.* 動物學

zoogenic [ˌzoə`dʒɛnɪk] *adj.* 源自動物的、動物生成的

A vegan is a person who does not eat or use any zoogenic products.

一個全素主義者就是不吃也不用動物製品的人。

動植物與自然界

Avi-Botan ▶MP3 013

145 avi

鳥

源自拉丁文「鳥群」的意思，也含有「飛翔」之意。

- **aviation** [evɪ`eʃən] *n.* 飛行；航空（學）
- **aviculture** [`evɪˌkʌltʃɚ] *n.* 鳥類飼養
- **aviary** [`evɪərɪ] *n.* 鳥舍、大鳥籠
- **avian** [`evɪən] *adj.* 鳥類的、禽類的

aviation [evɪ`eʃən] *n.* 飛行；航空（學）

After the serious terrorist attack happened, the aviation security became stricter.

嚴重的恐怖攻擊事件發生後，飛航安全變得更加嚴謹了。

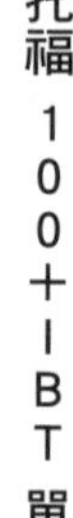

146 ornith

鳥

源自希臘文「鳥類」的意思。

- **ornithic** [ɔr`nɪθɪk] *adj.* 鳥類的
- **ornithophobia** [ˌɔrnɪθɔ`fobɪə] *n.* 鳥類恐懼症
- **ornithology** [ˌɔrnɪ`θɑlədʒɪ] *n.* 鳥類學
- **ornithoid** [`ɔrnɪθɔɪd] *adj.* 鳥形狀的、結構似鳥的

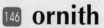

ornithic [ɔr`nɪθɪk] *adj.* 鳥類的

The team found a suspected ornithic fossil at the South East China.

這個小組在中國東南方發現疑似鳥類的化石。

147 pisc
魚

源自拉丁文，和「魚類」有關的。

- **piscivorous** [pɪˋsɪvərəs] *adj.* 吃魚維生的
- **piscine** [ˋpɪsaɪn] *n.* （法）浴池 *adj.* 魚的
- **piscatorial** [ˌpɪskəˋtorɪəl] *adj.* 漁民的、漁業的、捕魚的
- **piscary** [ˋpɪskərɪ] *n.* 捕魚權

piscivorous [pɪˋsɪvərəs] *adj.* 吃魚維生的

Colorful kingfishers mostly live in tropical places and are piscivorous birds.
色彩鮮艷的翠鳥大部分生長在熱帶地區，是吃魚維生的鳥類。

148 brut
獸

源自於拉丁文「野獸」，衍生為「愚笨」或「野蠻」的意思。

- **brutalize** [ˋbrutəlaɪz] *v.* 殘忍對待
- **brutish** [ˋbrutɪʃ] *adj.* 野蠻的
- **brutal** [ˋbrutəl] *adj.* 野蠻的、殘忍的；不顧他人感受的
- **brute** [brut] *n.* 殘忍的人、野獸

brutalize [ˋbrutəlaɪz] *v.* 殘忍對待

The newly released prisoners revealed that they were brutalized in the prison.
新釋放的囚犯透露他們在監獄中被殘忍對待。

149 **porc, pork**

豬

源自於拉丁文「豬豕」的意思。

- **porcupine** [`pɔrkjʊpaɪn] *n.* 豪豬
- **porky** [`pɔrkɪ] *adj.* 肥胖的
- **porker** [`pɔrkɚ] *n.* 食用豬；肥胖的人
- **porcine** [`porsaɪn] *n.* 豬的、像豬的

porcupine [`pɔrkjʊpaɪn] *n.* 豪豬

Porcupines are rodents and are different from hedgehogs in size and order.

豪豬是嚙齒科的動物，而且在體型科目上都和刺蝟不一樣。

150 **cani**

狗

源自於拉丁文「犬」、「狗類」的意思。

- **canicular** [kə`nɪkulər] *adj.* 天狼星的
- **canine tooth** [`kenaɪn `tuθ] *n.* 犬齒
- **canine** [`kenaɪn] *n.* 犬隻 *adj.* 犬的、狗的

canicular [kə`nɪkulər] *adj.* 天狼星的

Sirius, the so called Dog Star in ancient times, rises at dawn around midsummer, and these days are called canicular days when is usually pretty hot.

古代所謂的狗星─天狼星在仲夏左右從清晨時分開始東昇，而這幾日就被稱為是天狼星日，通常會是很熱的時候。

151 **vacc, bov, bu**

牛

vacc, bov 源自於拉丁文關於乳牛、牛隻的意思，而 bu 則是源自於希臘文。

- **bucolic** [bju`kalɪk] *adj.* 鄉村的、田園的
- **bugle** [`bjugəl] *n.* 號角、喇叭（古代號角由牛角製成）
- **bovine** [`bovaɪn] *adj.* 牛屬的；遲鈍的、愚笨的
- **vaccine** [`væksin] *n.* 疫苗（早期疫苗使用牛痘的病毒來對抗天花）

bucolic [bju`kalɪk] *adj.* 鄉村的、田園的

The bucolic scene of farmers with cattle on the field can no longer be seen in Taiwanese countryside.

農夫和水牛一起在田地上的田園景象已不見於台灣的鄉村了。

152 **caval**

馬

拉丁文「馬匹」的意思，後來與「騎士」相關的意思連結。

- **cavalcade** [ˌkævəl`ked] *n.* （遊行的）馬隊、車隊、騎兵隊
- **cavalier** [ˌkævə`lɪɚ] *n.* （古）騎士、護花使者 *adj.* 傲慢的、目空一切的；輕率的
- **cavalry** [`kævəlrɪ] *n.* 騎兵部隊；裝甲部隊
- **cavalryman** [`kævəlrɪˌmɛn] *n.* 騎兵

cavalcade [ˌkævəl`ked] *n.* （遊行的）馬隊、車隊、騎兵隊

When a cavalcade passed through the avenue, little boys watched it with admiration.

當一隊遊行車隊經過大道時，小男孩都欽佩地看著。

153 chival

馬

源自於法文 chevalier「騎馬的人」，衍生為騎士。

- **chivalric** [ʃɪˋvælrɪk] *adj.* 騎士的
- **chivalrous** [ˋʃɪvəlrəs] *adj.* 有騎士風度的、體貼有禮的
- **chivalrously** [ˋʃɪvəlrəslɪ] *adv.* 俠義地；如騎士一般地、彬彬有禮地
- **chivalry** [ˋʃɪvəlrɪ] *n.* 騎士制度；騎士精神、騎士風度

chivalric [ʃɪˋvælrɪk] *adj.* 騎士的

She loved to read chivalric romance in her childhood and wished to find a partner similar to the main male characters.

她小時候很喜歡看騎士小說，並希望能找到一個像小說中男主角的伴侶。

154 equi, eque

馬

源自於拉丁文「馬」的意思。

- **equerry** [ɪˋkwɛrɪ] *n.* （古）馬官；英國皇室侍從
- **equestrian** [ɪˋkwɛstrɪən] *adj.* 騎馬的、馬術的 *n.* 馬術師、騎馬者
- **equine** [ˋikwaɪn] *n.* 馬科動物 *adj.* 馬的、似馬的
- **equitation** [ˌɛkwɪˋteʃən] *n.* 騎術、馬術

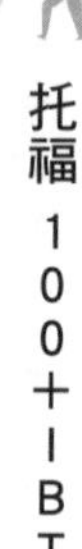

equerry [ɪˋkwɛrɪ] *n.* （古）馬官；英國皇室侍從

She heard many interesting stories from her grandfather, who was an equerry of the Royal family.

她從曾是皇家侍從的爺爺口中聽到許多有趣的故事。

155 **ophi (o)**

蛇

源自於希臘文「蛇類」或「像蛇的」意思。

- **ophidian** [o`fɪdɪən] *n.* 蛇類 *adj.* 蛇的
- **ophiolatry** [,ɑfɪ`ɑlətrɪ] *n.* 蛇類崇拜
- **ophiology** [,ɑfɪ`ɑlədʒɪ] *n.* 蛇類學

ophiolatry [,ɑfɪ`ɑlətrɪ] *n.* 蛇類崇拜

Paiwan tribe is known for its ophiolatry and the totem of hundred-pacer can be seen everywhere in the tribe.

排灣族以蛇類崇拜著名，百步蛇圖騰部落內到處可見。

156 **botan**

植物

從希臘文傳到拉丁文，原意為「藥草」、「草地」後衍生為「植物」之意。

- **ethnobotany** [,ɛθno`bɑtənɪ] *n.* 民族植物學
- **botanist** [`bɑtənɪst] *n.* 植物學家
- **botanical** [bə`tænɪkəl] *adj.* 植物（學）的
- **botany** [`bɑtənɪ] *n.* 植物學

ethnobotany [,ɛθno`bɑtənɪ] *n.* 民族植物學

The Native American scholar hopes to use his knowledge of ethnobotany to understand the wisdom of his ancestors.

這名美洲原住民學者希望利用他民族植物學的知識來了解祖先的智慧。

UNIT 14 動植物與自然界—空間方位與程度

Anth-Ante ▶MP3 014

157 anth

花

源自於希臘文「花朵」、「開花」的意思。

- **amaranth** [ˋæmə͵rænθ] *n.* 傳説的不凋花；莧菜；紫紅色
- **anther** [ˋænθɚ] *n.* 花藥、花粉囊
- **anthesis** [ænˋθisɪs] *n.* 開花期 anthemion [ænˋθimɪən] *n.* 花狀平紋（金銀花花瓣或細長的葉子紋路）

amaranth [ˋæmə͵rænθ] *n.* 傳説的不凋花；莧菜；紫紅色

Her bright amaranth dress catches the attention of everyone in the party.

她亮麗的紫紅色洋裝引起宴會中所有人的注目。

158 herb

草

拉丁文「綠色植物」或「草」的意思，後特別指「藥草」。

- **herbivorous** [hɚˋbɪvərəs] *adj.* 草食的
- **herbalism** [ˋhɝbəlɪzəm] *n.* 藥草學
- **herbage** [ˋhɝbɪdʒ] *n.* 牧草、草本
- **herbal** [ˋhɝbəl] *adj.* 藥草的，草本的

herbivorous [hɚˋbɪvərəs] *adj.* 草食的

Pandas are not herbivorous bears. They eat not only bamboo and grass but also insects.
熊貓不是草食性的熊，牠們除了吃竹子和草外，還會吃昆蟲。

159 **dendr**
樹

希臘文「樹木」或「似樹木形狀」的意思。

- **dendrology** [dɛn`drɑlədʒɪ] *n.* 樹木學
- **dendrite** [`dɛndraɪt] *n.* （神經）樹突；樹枝狀結晶
- **dendritic** [dɛn`drɪtɪk] *adj.* 樹枝狀的
- **dendriform** [`dɛndrə,fɔrm] *adj.* 樹狀的

dendrology [dɛn`drɑlədʒɪ] *n.* 樹木學

The old man living in the forest never studies dendrology but has wealthier knowledge than many experts.
住在森林中的老先生沒學過樹木學，但卻有比許多專家更豐富的相關知識。

160 **radi (c)**
根

源自於拉丁文「根部」的意思。

- **deracinate** [dɪ`ræsɪnet] *v.* 迫使離鄉背井、流離失所
- **eradicate** [ɪ`rædɪket] *v.* 根除、滅絕、連根拔除
- **radicle** [`rædɪkəl] *n.* 胚根；根狀部
- **radish** [`rædɪʃ] *n.* 小蘿蔔、櫻桃蘿蔔

deracinate [dɪ`ræsɪnet] *v.* 迫使離鄉背井、流離失所

Refugees are forced to deracinate and now face a difficult dilemma of where to go.
難民被迫流離失所，現在正面臨不知何去何從的困境。

161 **foli**

葉

源自於拉丁文中植物的「葉子」。

- **defoliate** [di`folɪet] *v.* 除葉、使落葉
- **foliar** [`folɪɚ] *adj.* 葉子的
- **foliate** [`folɪət] *adj.* 葉狀的、葉飾的
- **foliage** [`folɪɪdʒ] *n.* 樹葉（總稱）

defoliate [di`folɪet] *v.* 除葉、使落葉

Before transplanting a tree, it needs to be defoliated so that it will not wither for lack of water.

移植一棵樹之前必須先將其除葉，才不會讓樹木在之後因水分不夠枯死。

162 **fruct**

果實

遠自於拉丁文「果實」，「可以享受的食物」的意思。

- **fructify** [`frʌktɪfaɪ] *v.* 使結果、使有成果
- **fructose** [`frʌktoz] *n.* 果糖
- **fructiferous** [frʌk`tɪfərəs] *adj.* 結果實的
- **fructuous** [`frʌktʃʊəs] *adj.* 多果實的、多產的

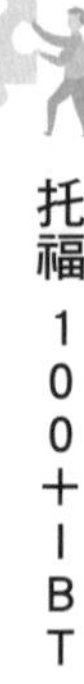

fructify [`frʌktɪfaɪ] *v.* 使結果、使有成果

The teacher wishes to fructify her students not only with the marks but also with their creativity and critical thinking.

那名老師希望不只能培養學生成績的成果，還有在創意及批判性思考上亦有成果出來。

163 **vent**

風

拉丁文「空氣」或「風」的意思。

- **vent** [vɛnt] *n.* 排氣口、通風口 *v.* 發洩（情緒）
- **ventiduct** [`vɛntɪdʌkt] *n.* 通風管
- **ventilate** [`vɛntɪlet] *v.* 使空氣流通；提出、説出
- **ventilator** [`vɛntɪˌletɚ] *n.* 通風設備、人工呼吸器

ventiduct [`vɛntɪdʌkt] *n.* 通風管

The female staff could not believe she had to hide into the ventiduct to prevent dangers like in the movie.

女職員不敢相信她居然要像電影裡面一樣躲進通風管裡以避開危險。

164 **aqu**

水

源自拉丁文「水」或「含水溶液」的意思。

- **aqueous** [`ekwɪəs] *adj.* （含）水的、似水的
- **aquatic** [ə`kwætɪk] *adj.* 水上的、水中的；水生的、水棲的
- **aquarium** [ə`kwɛrɪəm] *n.* 水族箱；水族館
- **aquaculture** [`ækwəkʌltʃɚ] *n.* 養殖漁業

aqueous [`ekwɪəs] *adj.* （含）水的、似水的

Whether an aqueous solution is conductive depends on the ions inside.

一個水溶液是否導電關鍵在於裡面的離子。

165 ign

火

源自於拉丁文「火」或「燃燒」的意思。

- **ignescent** [ɪg`nɛsənt] *adj.* 火爆的、敲擊而冒火的
- **igneous** [`ɪgnɪəs] *adj.* 火成的；似火的
- **ignitable** [ɪg`naɪtəbəl] *adj.* 可燃的、易起火的
- **ignite** [ɪg`naɪt] *v.* 點燃、使燃燒、爆炸

ignescent [ɪg`nɛsənt] *adj.* 火爆的、敲擊而冒火的

On the first day of life to experience in an uninhabited island, he tried to search for ignescent stones before sunset.

在第一天體驗荒島求生時，他試圖在天黑之前尋找可生火的石頭。

166 glaci

冰

源自於拉丁文「冰」的意思。

- **deglaciation** [ˌdiglesɪ`eʃən] *n.* 冰消期、冰河消退
- **glaciate** [`gleʃɪet] *v.* 被冰覆蓋、受冰川作用、被冰凍
- **glacial** [`gleʃəl] *adj.* 冰河形成的；極冷的
- **glacier** [`glesɪɚ] *n.* 冰河

deglaciation [ˌdiglesɪ`eʃən] *n.* 冰消期、冰河消退

Due to the global warming, both the Arctic and Antarctica are suffering from deglaciation.

因全球暖化的關係，南北極正遭受到冰河消退的現象。

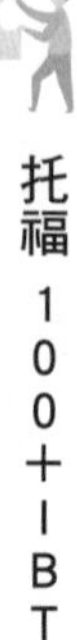

167 mari

海

源自於拉丁文「大海」、「海洋」的意思。

- **submarine** [`sʌbmərin] *n.* 潛水艇
- **maritime** [`mærɪtaɪm] *adj.* 海事的；沿海的
- **marine** [mə`rin] *adj.* 海洋的、海運的、航海的
- **marina** [mə`rinə] *n.* 小港口、娛樂用小船塢

submarine [`sʌbmərin] *n.* 潛水艇

Currently, only seven countries have the technology to develop nuclear submarines.

目前全球只有七個國家有發展核能潛水艇的技術。

168 ante-, anti-, anci

前

源自於拉丁文，有「之前」、「在…前面」的意思。

- **anterior** [æn`tɪərɪɚ] *adj.* 前部的、向前的、先前的
- **anticipate** [æn`tɪsɪpet] *v.* 預期、期盼、預見（anti 先前，cip 擁有, -ate 動詞結尾）
- **antenna** [æn`tɛnə] *n.* 觸角、天線（複數：antennae）
- **ancient** [`enʃənt] *adj.* 古老的、古代的

anterior [æn`tɪərɪɚ] *adj.* 前部的、向前的、先前的

According to scientists, the anterior part of the brain is mainly responsible for receiving information from other parts of the body.

根據科學家的解釋，腦部前端主要負責接收來自身體其他部位的各種訊息。

UNIT 15

空間方位與程度

Pre-Under ▶MP3 015

169 pre-

前

源自於拉丁文，在時間或空間上「之前」的意思。

- **preface** [ˋprɛfəs] *n.* 前言、序幕
- **prejudice** [ˋprɛdʒʊdɪs] *n.* 偏見（judice-審理，先於審斷的意見即偏見）
- **prehistoric** [prɪhɪˋstɔrɪk] *adj.* 史前的
- **premature** [ˌpriməˋtjʊr] *adj.* 過早的、不成熟的

preface [ˋprɛfəs] *n.* 前言、序幕

The author states in the preface that all the main characters in this historical fiction are real people.

作者在前言中說明，這本歷史小說中的主角都是真有其人。

170 pro-

前

源自古希臘文，也有「之前、從前」或「在…前面」的意思。

- **proceed** [prəˋsid] *adj.* 繼續進行、接著做；前進
- **pronoun** [ˋpronaʊn] *n.* 代名詞
- **propel** [prəˋpɛl] *v.* 推動、推進（pel-由拉丁文「驅使」演化而來）
- **prospective** [prəˋspɛktɪv] *adj.* 潛在的、預期的（spect-看）

proceed [prəˋsid] *adj.* 繼續進行、接著做；前進

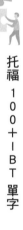

During the group climbing competition, no one can proceed alone and leave the wounded team member behind.
團體登山競賽中，沒有人能丟下自己受傷的隊友獨自前進。

171 **fore-** 前 源自於德語系字首，有「前面」或「預先」的意思。	▪ **forecast** [ˋfɔrkæst] *v. n.* 預報、預測 ▪ **forecourt** [ˋfɔrkɔrt] *n.* 前院；（網球場）前場 ▪ **foregoing** [ˋfɔrgoɪŋ] *adj.* 上述的、前面提及的 ▪ **foremost** [ˋfɔrmost] *adv.* 領先的、最重要的、最佳的

forecast [ˋfɔrkæst] *v. n.* 預報、預測

One famous financial magazine released an economic forecast of Asian countries for the next half year.
某一著名財經雜誌發表了一則亞洲國家下半年的經濟預測。

172 **post-** 後 源自於拉丁文「之後」、「後面」或「晚」的意思。	▪ **posterior** [pɑˋstɪərɪɚ] *adj.* 後部的、尾端的；稍晚的 ▪ **postdoctoral** [postˋdɑktərəl] *adj.* 博士後的 ▪ **postscript** [ˋpostskrɪpt] *n.* 附筆、附言、補充說明（簡寫成 ps） ▪ **post-war** [postˋwɔr] *adj.* （二次世界大戰）戰後的

posterior [pɑˋstɪərɪɚ] *adj.* 後部的、尾端的；稍晚的

Since the construction date is posterior to the announcement, the new policy can be applied to the building.
既然建造日期是在公布政策之後，那新政策可適用於這棟建築上。

173 **retro-** 後 源自於拉丁文「後面」、「背後」或「倒退」的意思。	▪ **retroact** [ˌrɛtro`ækt] *v.* 追溯既往 ▪ **retroflex** [`rɛtroflɛks] *adj.* 翻轉的；捲舌音的 ▪ **retrogress** [ˌrɛtro`grɛs] *v.* 倒退、衰退 ▪ **retrospective** [rɛtro`spɛktɪv] *adj.* 回顧的、追溯以往的

retroact [ˌrɛtro`ækt] *v.* 追溯既往

The policy does not retroact the case that happened before the announcement day.

這項政策不追溯公告日期以前的案件。

174 **over** 上 源自古德文「在…之上」、「超過」的意思。	▪ **overlap** [ovɚ`læp] *v.* 交疊、部分重疊、有共通處 ▪ **oversee** [ovɚ`si] *v.* 監督、監察 ▪ **overturn** [ovɚ`tɝn] *v.* 打翻、弄倒、顛覆 ▪ **overwhelming** [ovɚ`wɛlmɪŋ] *adj.* 難以抵擋的、大量的、巨大的

overlap [ovɚ`læp] *v.* 交疊、部分重疊、有共通處

We decided to revise our team project again because part of the topic overlaps with the other team.

我們決定要重新修改我們的小組報告，因為我們部分的主題和別組重複。

175 **super**

上

源自於拉丁文，over 的原形，也有「在…之上」、「超過」的意思。

- **superficial** [ˌsupɚˋfɪʃəl] *adj.* 膚淺的
- **superintendent** [supɚɪnˋtɛndənt] *n.* 主管、負責人
- **superiority** [suˌpɪrɪˋɔrətɪ] *n.* 優勢、優越性
- **superstition** [ˌsupɚˋstɪʃən] *n.* 迷信

superficial [ˌsupɚˋfɪʃəl] *adj.* 膚淺的

Superficial knowledge about other cultures can easily cause misunderstandings.

對其他文化淺薄的認知容易導致誤會。

176 **sur-**

上

源自於拉丁文，和 super 同源，「在…之上、上面」的意思。

- **surmount** [sɚˋmaʊnt] *v.* 在…頂端、聳立於…；解決、克服
- **surname** [ˋsɝnem] *n.* 姓氏 *v.* 冠姓；給…起別名、稱號
- **surrender** [səˋrɛndɚ] *v.* 屈服、投降、放棄
- **surround** [səˋraʊnd] *v.* 包圍、圍繞（原拉丁文義為「淹沒」）

surmount [sɚˋmaʊnt] *v.* 在…頂端、聳立於…；解決、克服

Although he had seen pyramids dozens of times in photos, he was still in awe when facing the real ones surmounting among the desert.

雖然他在照片中看過好幾次金字塔，然而當他面對沙漠中矗立的真正金字塔時，仍感到敬畏。

de-

下

源自拉丁文「往下」、「遠離」的意思。

- **degenerate** [dɪ`dʒɛnərət] *v.* 衰退、品質下降 *adj.* 下降的、退化的
- **descent** [dɪ`sɛnt] *n.* 下沉、下降；墮落
- **deteriorate** [dɪ`tɪərɪəret] *v.* 惡化、變壞
- **deviate** [`divɪet] *v.* 脫離、違背（via-方向、道路）

degenerate [dɪ`dʒɛnərət] *v.* 衰退、品質下降 *adj.* 下降的、退化的

A gourmet found the quality and taste of the food of his favorite restaurant is degenerating.

一位美食家發現，他最喜愛的餐廳的食物品質和口味正在下降中。

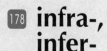

infra-, infer-

下

源自於拉丁文「在…之下」、「下面」的意思。

- **infracostal** [ɪnfrə`kastəl] *adj.* 肋骨下方的
- **infrasonic** [ˌɪnfrə`sanɪk] *adj.* 低音頻的
- **infrastructure** [`ɪnfrəˌstrʌktʃɚ] *n.* 基礎建設
- **inferior** [ɪn`fɪərɪɚ] *adj.* 差的、低層級的

infracostal [ɪnfrə`kastəl] *adj.* 肋骨下方的

The article compares the difference of supercostal and infracostal approaches of the treatment of upper ureteral stones.

這篇文章比較從肋骨上方和下方治療上輸尿管結石的不同。

179 hypo-

下

源自於希臘文「底下」、「在…之下」的意思。

- **hypocenter** [`haɪposɛntɚ] *n.* 震源
- **hypocrisy** [hɪ`pakrəsɪ] *n.* 偽善、虛偽（源自希臘文「判斷之下」，衍生為「假裝」的意思）
- **hypothesis** [haɪ`paθəsɪs] *n.* 假說、假設（thesis-放置，原指「基礎」的意思）

hypocenter [`haɪposɛntɚ] *n.* 震源

Earthquakes with shallow hypocenters could cause serious damage.
淺源的地震有可能會造成嚴重損害。

180 under

下

源自於古德文「在…之下」的意思。

- **undermine** [ʌndɚ`maɪn] *v.* 損害…基礎、削弱信心或權力
- **undergo** [ʌndɚ`go] *v.* 經歷
- **undergraduate** [ʌndɚ`grædjʊət] *n.* 大學生（graduate-研究生）
- **underneath** [ʌndɚ`niθ] *adv. prep.* 在…底下、下面

undermine [ʌndɚ`maɪn] *v.* 損害…基礎、削弱信心或權力

Constant raining undermined the bridge piers, and the bridge finally broke due to a lack of support.
連日降雨掏空橋墩，而橋樑終因失去支撐而斷裂。

UNIT 16 空間方位與程度

Sub-Mini ▶MP3 016

181 **sub-**

下

源自於拉丁文「在…之下」、「底下」的意思。

- **subsidize** [ˋsʌbsɪdaɪz] *v.* 給予津貼、資助
- **subtle** [ˋsʌtəl] *adj.* 隱約的、微妙的、細微的、不易察覺的
- **subsequent** [ˋsʌbsɪkwənt] *adj.* 隨後的、接著的
- **subordinate** [səˋbɔrdɪnət] *adj.* 從屬的、次要的 *n.* 下屬 *v.* 使從屬於

subsidize [ˋsʌbsɪdaɪz] *v.* 給予津貼、資助

Some students planned a program of fundraising, wishing to subsidize children in remote villages for education.

一些學生擬定了一個募款計畫，希望能資助偏鄉小孩的教育。

182 **intra-**

內

源自於希臘文「內部」或「裡面」的意思。

- **intracellular** [ˌɪntrəˋsɛljʊlɚ] *adj.* 細胞內部的
- **intramural** [ˌɪntrəˋmjʊrəl] *adj.* 內部的、學校內的
- **intranet** [ˋɪntrənɛt] *n.* 內聯網、局域網
- **intrapersonal** [ˌɪntrəˋpɝsənəl] *adj.* 內省的、自我意識的

intracellular [ˌɪntrə`sɛljʊlɚ] *adj.* 細胞內部的

Most life operational reactions occur within intracellular organelles.
大部分生命的運作反應都發生在細胞內部的胞器。

183 **endo-**
內
源自於希臘文「內部」、「內層」等意思。

- **endocardial** [ˌɛndo`kardɪəl] *adj.* 心臟內部的
- **endocrine** [`ɛndokraɪn] *n.* 內分泌
- **endogenous** [ɛn`dadʒɪnəs] *adj.* 源自內部的、內生的

endocardial [ˌɛndo`kardɪəl] *adj.* 心臟內部的

The doctor suggest he install endocardial artificial vessel; otherwise, there is a very high rate for myocardial infarction.
醫生建議他安裝心臟內人工血管，否則會有很高的心肌梗塞發生率。

184 **exo-**
外
源自於希臘文「外部」、「外側」的意思。

- **exocarp** [`ɛksokarp] *n.* 外果皮
- **exodus** [`ɛksədəs] *n.* （大批人）離開、退出；出埃及記
- **exogamy** [ɪk`sagəmɪ] *n.* 異族通婚
- **exotic** [ɪg`zatɪk] *adj.* 異國的

exocarp [`ɛksokarp] *n.* 外果皮

Exocarps usually contain a rich nutritional value, and experts suggest we not peel fruits such as apples.
外果皮通常含有豐富的營養價值，專家也建議我們不要將水果如蘋果削皮。

185 **extra-**

外

源自於拉丁文「外面」、「外在」等意思。

- **extractive** [ɪk`stræktɪv] *adj.* 萃取的、提取的
- **extraneous** [ɪk`strenɪəs] *adj.* 外來的、無關的
- **extracurricular** [ɛkstrəkə`rɪkjʊlɚ] *adj.* 課外的、業餘的
- **extravagant** [ɪk`strævəgənt] *adj.* 奢侈的、浪費的、過度的

extractive [ɪk`stræktɪv] *adj.* 萃取的、提取的

Extractive technique has become a very important part within food industry.

萃取技術已成為食品產業中重要的一環。

186 **inter**

中間

源自於拉丁文「在…之間」或「裡面」的意思。

- **interaction** [ɪntɚ`ækʃən] *n.* 互動、交流、相互作用
- **interim** [`ɪntərɪm] *n.* 過渡時期；暫時、中間時間 *adj.* 過渡的
- **interruption** [ɪntɚ`rʌpʃən] *n.* 打斷、中止
- **intervene** [ɪntɚ`vin] *v.* 干涉、干預

interaction [ɪntɚ`ækʃən] *n.* 互動、交流、相互作用

From the way of their interaction, you can judge that they just met each other.

從他們互動模式來看，他們不過是剛認識而已。

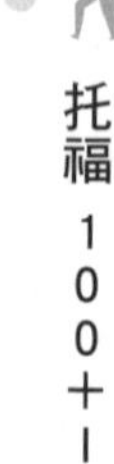

187 **meso**
中間

源自於希臘文「中間」、「介於…之間」的意思。

- **mesophyll** [`mɛsofɪl] *n.* 葉肉（phyll-希臘文「葉子」的意思）
- **Mesoamerica** [ˌmɛsoə`mɛrɪkə] *n.* 中美洲
- **mesolithic** [ˌmɛso`lɪθɪk] *adj.* 中石器時期的
- **mesosphere** [`mɛsəsfɪɚ] *n.* 中氣層

mesophyll [`mɛsofɪl] *n.* 葉肉（phyll-希臘文「葉子」的意思）

Mesophyll is a place for photosynthesis as well as a place for water storage.
葉肉是光合作用的場所，也是水分儲存的地方。

188 **circum-**
周圍

源自於拉丁文「圓內」的意思，衍生為「周圍、附近」之意。

- **circumambulate** [ˌsɚkəm`æmbjʊlet] *v.* 繞行
- **circumference** [sɚ`kʌmfərəns] *n.* 圓周、周長
- **circumfluent** [sɚ`kʌmflʊənt] *adj.* 環流的、週流的
- **circumscribe** [`sɝkəmskraɪb] *v.* 畫外接圓；限制、約束

circumambulate [ˌsɚkəm`æmbjʊlet] *v.* 繞行

During the ritual, believers circumambulated the fire in the center and heard the priest reciting.
儀式中，信眾們繞火而行，並聽著祭司念誦。

189 peri

周圍

源自於希臘文「附近」、「接近」的意思。

- **periarterial** [ˌpɛrɪɑr`tɛrɪəl] *adj.* 動脈周邊的（artery-動脈）
- **perigee** [`pɛrɪdʒi] *n.* 近地點（gee-地球）
- **perihelion** [ˌpɛrɪ`hilɪən] *n.* 近日點（helion-拉丁文「太陽」的意思）
- **perilune** [`pɛrɪlun] *n.* 近月點（luna-拉丁文「月亮」的意思）

periarterial [ˌpɛrɪɑr`tɛrɪəl] *adj.* 動脈周邊的（artery-動脈）

Periarterial fat can easily accumulate, but difficult to remove.
動脈周邊的脂肪容易堆積但不易去除。

190 macro-

大

希臘文「巨大」、「放大」或「極長」的意思。

- **macrobiotic** [ˌmækrobaɪ`ɑtɪk] *adj.* 健康的（食物）
- **macrocosm** [`mækrokɑzəm] *n.* 宏觀世界、宇宙
- **macroeconomic** [ˌmækroikə`nɑmɪk] *adj.* 整體經濟學的
- **macroscopic** [ˌmækro`skɑpɪk] *adj.* 宏觀的、肉眼可見的

macrobiotic [ˌmækrobaɪ`ɑtɪk] *adj.* 健康的（食物）（bio-生命，原指「長壽」的意思）

Macrobiotic diet is the key for health and longevity.
養生的飲食是健康和長壽的關鍵。

191 **mega-**
大

源自於希臘文「龐大」、「巨大」或「有力」的意思。

- **megabyte** [ˋmɛgəbaɪt] *n.* 百萬位元組（簡稱 MB）
- **megahertz** [ˋmɛgəhɝts] *n.* 赫兆（簡稱 MHz）
- **megalopolis** [ˌmɛgəˋlɑpəlɪs] *n.* 大都市
- **megaphone** [ˋmɛgəfon] *n.* 擴音器、大聲公

megabyte [ˋmɛgəbaɪt] *n.* 百萬位元組（簡稱 MB）

Memory cards with few megabytes are already not enough in this digitalized world.
只有幾 MB 的記憶卡在這個數位化的時代已經不敷使用了。

192 **mini-**
小

源自於拉丁文「小的」或「少量」的意思。

- **minibus** [ˋmɪnɪbʌs] *n.* 小巴士
- **miniature** [ˋmɪnɪtʃɚ] *adj.* 微小的、小型的 *n.* 微型畫
- **minimal** [ˋmɪnɪməl] *adj.* 極小的、極少的
- **minimize** [ˋmɪnɪmaɪz] *v.* 降到最低、減到最少；輕描淡寫、淡化

minibus [ˋmɪnɪbʌs] *n.* 小巴士

Since the road lead to the village is narrow, there is only one minibus that carries villagers to the city at the foot of the mountain.
因為到村落的路窄，因此僅有一輛小巴士載村民來回山腳下的城市。

UNIT 17

空間方位與程度

Micro-Demi ▶ MP3 017

193 micro-

小

源自於希臘文「極小」、「微小」的意思。

- **microbe** [`maɪkrob] *n.* 微生物、細菌
- **microbiology** [ˌmaɪkrobaɪ`ɑlədʒɪ] *n.* 微生物學
- **microchip** [`maɪkrotʃɪp] *n.* 晶片、積體電路片
- **microphone** [`maɪkrəfon] *n.* 麥克風

microbe [`maɪkrob] *n.* 微生物、細菌

Unlike microbes which can survive on their own, viruses are parasites that need hosts.

不像微生物能自己維生，病毒是寄生生物，需要宿主寄生。

194 multi-

多

源自於拉丁文「許多」的意思。

- **multicultural** [mʌltɪ`kʌltʃərəl] *adj.* 多元文化的
- **multifarious** [ˌmʌltɪ`fɛrɪəs] *adj.* 各式各樣的、多種類的
- **multinational** [mʌltɪ`næʃənəl] *adj.* 多國經營的、跨國的
- **multitude** [`mʌltɪtjud] *n.* 許多；大眾

multicultural [mʌltɪ`kʌltʃərəl] *adj.* 多元文化的

Taiwan is a multicultural society, but sadly sometimes we do not know how to react to its diversity.
台灣是個多元文化的社會，只可惜有時候我們不知道要如何面對其多元性。

195 poly-
多

源自於希臘文「多樣」、「豐富」或「大量」的意思。

- **polyamory** [ˌpalɪˋæmərɪ] *n.* 一夫多妻制
- **polychromatic** [ˌpalɪkrəˋmætɪk] *adj.* 多色彩的
- **polyester** [ˌpalɪˋɛstɚ] *n.* 聚酯纖維
- **polygon** [ˋpalɪgən] *n.* 多邊形

polyamory [ˌpalɪˋæmərɪ] *n.* 一夫多妻制

While some lambaste polyamory, others consider it an alternative lifestyle.
當有些人嚴厲撻伐一夫多妻制，有些人則認為那是另一種生活方式罷了。

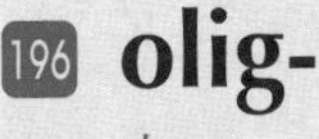

196 olig-
少

源自於希臘文「少量」、「極少」的意思。

- **oligarchy** [ˋɔlɪgarkɪ] *n.* 寡頭團體、寡頭政治國家
- **oligarchic** [ˋɔlɪgarkɪk] *adj.* 主張寡頭政治的
- **oligopsony** [ɔlɪˋgapsənɪ] *n.* 商品採購壟斷
- **oligotrophy** [ˌɔlɪˋgatrəfɪ] *n.* 營養貧乏

oligarchy [ˋɔlɪgarkɪ] *n.* 寡頭團體、寡頭政治國家

Myanmar is transforming from an oligarchy to a democracy.
緬甸正從一個寡頭政治國家轉型成為一個民主國家。

197 under-

少

源自於古德文「偏少」、「不足」的意思。

- **undercapitalized** [ʌndɚ`kæpɪtəlaIzd] *adj.* 投資不足的
- **underdeveloped** [ʌndɚdɪ`vɛləpt] *adj.* 不發達的、低開發的
- **underage** [`ʌndɚ,edʒ] *adj.* 未成年的、未達法定年齡的
- **underestimate** [ʌndɚ`ɛstɪmet] *v.* 低估、輕視

undercapitalized [ʌndɚ`kæpɪtəlaIzd] *adj.* 投資不足的

Cultural and sport business and activities are often undercapitalized because of their uncertain ROI.

由於投資報酬率不穩定，文化和運動事業與活動常常投資不足。

198 bene

好

源自於拉丁文「好的」、「善良的」。

- **benefactor** [`bɛnɪfæktɚ] *n.* 贊助人、捐助者
- **beneficent** [bɪ`nɛfɪsənt] *adj.* 行善的、慈善的
- **beneficial** [bɛnɪ`fɪʃəl] *adj.* 有益的、有利的
- **benevolent** [bɪ`nɛvələnt] *adj.* 仁慈的、有愛心的

benefactor [`bɛnɪfæktɚ] *n.* 贊助人、捐助者

The team of documentary received a sponsorship from an anonymous benefactor when they faced the shortage of funds.

當紀錄片劇組面臨資金短缺時，他們收到來自一位無名贊助者的資助。

199 eu-

好

源自於希臘文「好的」、「正常的」或「令人愉悅的」意思。

- **euphemism** [ˋjufəmɪzəm] *n.* 委婉說法、婉辭（phem-說話）
- **euphoric** [juˋfɑrɪk] *adj.* 狂喜的、亢奮的
- **eupeptic** [juˋpɛptɪk] *adj.* 有助消化的；愉快的
- **eulogy** [ˋjulədʒɪ] *n.* 頌詞、頌文；悼詞

euphemism [ˋjufəmɪzəm] *n.* 委婉說法、婉辭（phem-說話）

This composition contains too much euphemism and does not express the thesis clearly.

這篇文章用了太多婉辭，沒有清楚表達主旨。

200 mal-

壞

拉丁文「壞的」、「糟的」或「邪惡的」、「錯誤的」意思。

- **maladjusted** [ˌmæləˋdʒʌstɪd] *adj.* 適應不良的、不適應社會環境的
- **maladroit** [ˌmæləˋdrɔɪt] *adj.* 不靈活的、笨拙的
- **malady** [ˋmælədɪ] *n.* 疾病；問題、弊病、沉痾
- **malefactor** [ˋmælɪˌfæktɚ] *n.* 壞人、罪犯

maladjusted [ˌmæləˋdʒʌstɪd] *adj.* 適應不良的、不適應社會環境的

The tutor established a studio, especially for maladjusted children.

輔導老師成立一個工作坊幫助適應不良的兒童。

201 mis-

壞

源自於上古英文「壞的」、「錯誤的」意思。

- **misbehavior** [mɪsbɪˋhevjɚ] *v.* 失禮、行為不當
- **mischievous** [ˋmɪstʃɪvəs] *adj.* 愛惡作劇的、搗蛋的；惡意的、有害的
- **misfortune** [mɪsˋfɔrtʃun] *n.* 不幸、厄運、災難
- **mistaken** [mɪˋstekən] *adj.* 錯誤的、弄錯的

misbehavior [mɪsbɪˋhevjɚ] *v.* 失禮、行為不當

The counselors believe that there are always reasons for teenagers' misbehavior and that what they need is love.

輔導員相信青少年行為不當背後總會有一個原因，而他們需要的是關愛。

202 omni-

全

源自於拉丁文「全部」、「所有」的意思。

- **omnibus** [ˋɑmnɪbəs] *n.* 選集；公車 *adj.* 綜合性的，多項的
- **omnifarious** [ˏɑmnɪˋfɛrɪəs] *adj.* 多方面的、五花八門的
- **omnipresent** [ɑmnɪˋprɛzənt] *adj.* 無所不在的、遍及各地的
- **omniscient** [ɑmˋnɪsɪənt] *adj.* 全知的、無所不知的

omnibus [ˋɑmnɪbəs] *n.* 選集；公車 *adj.* 綜合性的，多項的

The students were asked to read some omnibuses of proses and poems during the summer vacation.

學生們被要求暑假期間閱讀廣泛的散文與詩集。

203 **pan-**

全

源自於希臘文「所有」、「完全」或「全部」的意思。

- **pandect** [ˋpændɛkt] *n.* 法令全書
- **pandemic** [pænˋdɛmɪk] *adj.* 大規模流行的、廣泛擴及的
- **panorama** [pænəˋramə] *n.* 全景；全貌、概要
- **pantheism** [ˋpænθiɪzəm] *n.* 泛神論

pandect [ˋpændɛkt] *n.* 法令全書

The law publishing company is very proud of their refined hardcover pandect series during the book fair.

在書展上，法律出版社為他們的精裝法令全書系列感到驕傲。

204 **demi-**

半

源自於拉丁文「一半」的意思。

- **demigod** [ˋdɛmɪgad] *n.* 半人半神；被神化的名人
- **demilune** [ˋdɛmɪlun] *n.* 半月形
- **demi-pension** [ˏdɛmɪˋpenʃən] *n.* 兩餐制旅館
- **demirelief** [ˏdɛmɪrɛˋlif] *n.* 半浮雕

demigod [ˋdɛmɪgad] *n.* 半人半神；被神化的名人

Some fans already view their idol as a demigod and cannot accept the news of his errors.

有些歌迷已將他們的偶像神化，無法接受他犯錯的消息。

UNIT 18

空間方位與程度

Hemi-Ag ▶MP3 018

205 hemi-

半

源自於希臘文「一半」的意思。

- **hemicrania** [hɛmɪ`krenɪə] *n.* 偏頭痛（crain-拉丁文「頭蓋骨」）
- **hemicycle** [`hɛmɪsaɪkəl] *n.* 半圓形
- **hemisphere** [`hɛmɪsfɪɚ] *n.* 半球
- **hemiplegia** [ˌhɛmɪ`plidʒə] *n.* 半身癱瘓

hemicrania [hɛmɪ`krenɪə] *n.* 偏頭痛（crain-拉丁文「頭蓋骨」）

In the winter, she has to wear a bonnet in windy days; otherwise, she will suffer from the hemicrania for the whole night.
冬天時她必須在風大時戴頂毛帽，否則整晚她就會偏頭痛。

206 semi-

半

源自於拉丁文「一半」、「部分」的意思。

- **semiconductor** [ˌsɛmɪkən`dʌktɚ] *n.* 半導體
- **semicolon** [ˌsɛmɪ`kolən] *n.* 分號
- **semi-final** [sɛmɪ`faɪnəl] *n.* 準決賽
- **semirigid** [sɛmɪ`rɪdʒɪd] *adj.* 半硬質的

semiconductor [ˌsɛmɪkən`dʌktɚ] *n.* 半導體

Taiwan is called a kingdom of semiconductors; however, we should think of our next step to move into innovation business.

台灣被稱為是半導體王國，不過我們應該想想下一步往創新產業的發展。

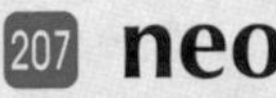

207 neo-

新

源自於希臘文，有「新穎的」、「新生的」或「年輕的」含意。

- **neologism** [nɪˋɑlədʒɪzəm] *n.* 新詞彙
- **neoclassical** [nioˋklæsɪkəl] *adj.* 新古典主義的
- **neon** [ˋniɑn] *n.* 氖氣；霓虹燈（源自希臘文「新東西」的意思）

neologism [nɪˋɑlədʒɪzəm] *n.* 新詞彙

To encourage handwriting and admiration of the beauty of Chinese characters, a cultural foundation holds a neologism creating competition with a high premium.

為了鼓勵手寫體和欣賞漢字的美麗，一個文化基金會舉辦了一個高額獎金的新詞彙創作比賽。

208 paleo-

舊

源自於希臘文，有「原本的」、「古老的」等意思。

- **Paleolithic** [ˌpælɪoˋlɪθɪk] *adj.* 舊石器時代的
- **paleocene** [ˋpælɪosin] *n.* 古新世（紀）
- **paleoclimate** [ˋpælɪoˌklaɪmət] *n.* 古氣候學
- **paleoanthropology** [ˌpælɪoænθrəˋpɑlədʒɪ] *n.* 古人類學

Paleolithic [ˌpælɪoˋlɪθɪk] *adj.* 舊石器時代的

In the Paleolithic period, human beings began to know how to use stone as tools or weapons.

在舊石器時代，人類開始知道如何使用石頭當作器具或武器。

209 sur-

超

源自於拉丁文，和 super 同源，「在…之上」、「超過」的意思。

- **surveillance** [sə`veləns] *n.* 監視、盯哨（veill-拉丁文，看）
- **surreal** [sə`rɪəl] *adj.* 超現實的、離奇的
- **surplus** [`sɝpləs] *n.* 剩餘、多餘 *adj.* 多餘的、過多的
- **surpass** [sə`pæs] *v.* 勝過、優於、超過

surveillance [sə`veləns] *n.* 監視、盯哨（veill-拉丁文，看）

The rock music festival is included in the surveillance of the police due to the past history of violence and drug deals.

搖滾音樂節因為之前暴力和毒品買賣的紀錄，被警方列入監視名單中。

210 ultra-

超

源自於拉丁文「超越」、「另一側」或「極致」的意思。

- **ultraviolet** [ʌltrə`vaɪələt] *n. adj.* 紫外線（的）
- **ultra vires** [ˌʌltrə`vaɪriz] *adj. adv.* 超越權限的（地）
- **ultra-high frequency** [ˌʌltrə haɪ `frikwənsɪ] *n.* 超高頻
- **ultraist** [`ʌltrəɪst] *n.* 極端主義者

ultraviolet [ʌltrə`vaɪələt] *n. adj.* 紫外線（的）

In a modern building where large pieces of glass window are preferred, a layer of anti-ultraviolet film is needed.

現代建築偏好使用大片玻璃窗，因此需要一層抗紫外線貼膜。

211 **meta-** 超 源自於希臘文「之後」、「超越」或是「改變」的意思。	▪ **metabolic** [mɛtə`bɑlɪk] *adj.* 新陳代謝的（原指「改變」的意思） ▪ **metaphor** [`mɛtəfɚ] *n.* 暗喻、隱喻（希臘文「轉換」的意思） ▪ **metafiction** [`mɛtəfɪkʃən] *n.* 後設小說 ▪ **metagalaxy** [`mɛtə͵gæləksɪ] *n.* 總星系

metabolic [mɛtə`bɑlɪk] *adj.* 新陳代謝的（原指「改變」的意思）

Progeria is a genetic disease which causes a metabolic disorder of the cells.

早老症是一項基因疾病，會造成細胞不正常代謝。

212 **hyper-** 超 源自於希臘文「超越」、「在…之上」、「異於一般」的意思。	▪ **hyperacidity** [͵haɪpɚə`sɪdətɪ] *n.* 胃酸過多 ▪ **hyperbaric** [͵haɪpɚ`bærɪk] *adj.* 高壓的 ▪ **hyperlink** [`haɪpɚlɪŋk] *n.* 超連結 ▪ **hyperopia** [͵haɪpɚ`opɪə] *n.* 遠視

hyperacidity [͵haɪpɚə`sɪdətɪ] *n.* 胃酸過多

The reasons of hyperacidity vary from person to person, but regular and proper meals can usually prevent its occurrence.

胃酸過多的原因因人而異，但規律和正常的飲食可避免這樣的情形發生。

213 ac-

加強

拉丁字首　的變形，有「向…」、「靠近」或「面對」等加強的意思。

- **accelerate** [ək`sɛləret] *v.* 加速、加快、促進
- **accumulate** [ə`kjumjʊlet] *v.* 累積、逐漸增加
- **accede** [æk`sid] *v.* 同意、允許；登基；就任
- **acquire** [ə`kwaɪɚ] *v.* 學習；獲得、購得

accelerate [ək`sɛləret] *v.* 加速、加快、促進

The drunken driver was afraid of sobriety test, so when he saw the police car, he simply accelerated his car and ran away.

酒醉的駕駛害怕被酒測，因此當他看到警車時他便加速逃逸。

214 ad-

加強

源自於拉丁文「向…」、「靠近」或「面對」等加強的意思。

- **addicted** [ə`dɪktɪd] *adj.* 成癮的、沉溺的、入迷的
- **adhere** [əd`hɪɚ] *v.* 依附、附著；堅持、擁護
- **adjacent** [ə`dʒesənt] *adj.* 鄰近的、比鄰的
- **advent** [`ædvənt] *n.* 來臨、到來

addicted [ə`dɪktɪd] *adj.* 成癮的、沉溺的、入迷的

After an accident caused him to lose his job, he did not know how to seek help and was addicted to alcohol.

遭遇一場意外並失掉工作以後，他不知道要如何尋求幫助，且開始酗酒。

215 af-

加強

拉丁字首 的變形，有「向…」、「靠近」或「面對」等加強的意思。

- **affectionate** [ə`fɛkʃənət] *adj.* 表示愛的、充滿感情的
- **affiliate** [ə`fɪlɪet] *v.* 使併入、隸屬 *n.* 隸屬機構
- **affirm** [ə`fɝm] *v.* 證實、確認；聲明
- **afflict** [ə`flɪkt] *v.* 折磨、使痛苦

affectionate [ə`fɛkʃənət] *adj.* 表示愛的、充滿感情的

The boy left home for his dream, and he always remembered the affectionate kiss from his mother when he faced difficulties.

男孩為夢想離家，每當面對困難時，總會想起母親充滿關愛的吻。

216 ag-

加強

拉丁字首 的變形，有「向…」、「靠近」或「面對」等加強的意思。

- **agglutinate** [ə`glutɪnet] *v.* 黏著、凝集、接合
- **aggradation** [ˌægrə`deʃən] *n.* 沉積
- **aggrandize** [ə`grændaɪz] *v.* 強化、增加；誇大、吹捧
- **aggrieved** [ə`grivd] *adj.* 憤憤不平的、受到委屈的

agglutinate [ə`glutɪnet] *v.* 黏著、凝集、接合

My grandpa asked me to find adhesive to agglutinate his dentures.

我爺爺要我去為他找可以黏合假牙的黏著劑。

UNIT

19 空間方位與程度

Ap-Vice　▶ MP3 019

217 ap-

加強

拉丁字首　的變形，有「向…」、「靠近」或「面對」等加強的意思。

- **appall** [əˋpɔl] *v.* 使震驚、驚駭
- **apparatus** [ˌæpəˋretəs] *n.* （全套）設備、儀器；組織、機構
- **applicable** [əˋplɪkəbəl] *adj.* 適用的、生效的
- **apprehension** [æprɪˋhɛnʃən] *n.* 憂慮、擔心、忐忑

---

appall [əˋpɔl] *v.* 使震驚、驚駭

When she first stepped into this African school, she was appalled by the sadness in children's eyes.

當她第一次踏進非洲小學時，她對小孩眼中的憂傷感到震驚。

 218 as-

加強

拉丁字首 ad 的變形，有「向…」、「靠近」或「面對」等加強的意思。

- **ascertain** [ˌæsɚˋten] *v.* 弄清楚、查明、確定
- **assert** [əˋsɝt] *v.* 堅持、表現堅定；肯定地說；主張
- **assignment** [əˋsaɪnmənt] *n.* 任務；功課
- **assumption** [əˋsʌmpʃən] *n.* 假定、假設

ascertain [ˌæsɚ`ten] *v.* 弄清楚、查明、確定

Some life questions, such as "what is the meaning of life?" need not to ascertain in a short period but a lifetime to answer.

有些人生的問題如「人生的意義是什麼？」不需要短時間內去弄清楚，這種問題是要用一生來慢慢回答的。

219 **com-**

加強

源自於拉丁文「一起」、「增強」等加強的意思。

- **commodity** [kə`mɑdətɪ] *n.* 商品、貨物
- **communal** [`kɑmjʊnəl] *adj.* 共有的、公共的、集體的
- **communicative** [kə`mjunɪkətɪv] *adj.* 健談的；表達的、溝通的
- **competence** [`kɑmpɪtəns] *n.* 能力、才幹

commodity [kə`mɑdətɪ] *n.* 商品、貨物（modity-原「測量」之義，與 com 合起來為「獲益」的意思）

Rare earth elements are commodities that are more valuable than most people regard.

稀土金屬是比一般人認為還要更有價值的商品。

220 **con-**

加強

拉丁字首 com 的變形，有「一起」、「增強」等加強的意思。

- **conceal** [kən`sil] *v.* 隱藏、隱匿
- **congregate** [`kɑŋgrɪget] *v.* 聚集、集合
- **contractor** [kən`træktɚ] *n.* 承辦者、承包商
- **constellation** [ˌkɑnstə`leʃən] *n.* 星座

conceal [kən`sil] *v.* 隱藏、隱匿

She could not conceal her surprise when the seemingly young guy revealed his age.
那位看起來年輕的男子透露他的年紀時，她無法隱藏她的驚訝。

221 **en-**
加強

源自於希臘文「靠近」、「啟蒙」或「造成」等加強的意思。

- **enact** [ɪ`nækt] *v.* 實行；制定
- **energize** [`ɛnədʒaɪz] *v.* 始有活力、激勵
- **enthusiasm** [ɪn`θuzɪæzəm] *n.* 熱忱、熱情；熱衷的事物或活動
- **enzyme** [`ɛnzaɪm] *n.* 酶

enact [ɪ`nækt] *v.* 實行；制定

The student association pressured the university to enact the new student benefit policy.
學生會向學校施壓，希望促成新學生利益規定實行。

222 **col-**
共同

源自於拉丁文，有「一起」、「共同」的意思。

- **collaboration** [kəlæbə`reʃn] *n.* 合作
- **collected** [kə`lɛktɪd] *adj.* 收集成冊的；鎮定的、泰然自若的
- **collective** [kə`lɛktɪv] *adj.* 集體的、共同的
- **collector** [kə`lɛktɚ] *n.* 收藏家；剪票員、收款者

collaboration [kəlæbə`reʃn] *n.* 合作

The local government holds a great cultural festival in collaboration with several foundations.
當地政府與幾個基金會合作舉辦了一場盛大的文化節。

223 **sym-**

共同

源自於希臘文「一起」、「融合」或「相似」的意思。

- **symmetrical** [sɪˋmɛtrɪkəl] *adj.* 對稱的
- **symbolic** [sɪmˋbɑlɪk] *adj.* 象徵（性）的
- **symmetry** [ˋsɪmətrɪ] *n.* 對稱
- **sympathy** [ˋsɪmpəθɪ] *n.* 同理心、理解；支持（性）

symmetrical [sɪˋmɛtrɪkəl] *adj.* 對稱的

According to the nature rule, nothing is the same, so there is no perfect symmetrical face.

根據大自然的法則，沒有東西是完全一樣的，因此也沒有完全對稱的臉。

224 **syn-**

共同

與 sym 同源，希臘文「一起」、「融合」或「相似」的意思。

- **synchronize** [ˋsɪŋkrənaɪz] *v.* 使同步、使同時發生
- **synchronous** [ˋsɪŋkrənəs] *adj.* 同時發生的、同時存在的
- **syndicate** [ˋsɪndɪkət] *n.* 聯合組織 *v.* 組成聯合組織
- **syndrome** [ˋsɪndrom] *n.* 併發症、綜合症、症候群

synchronize [ˋsɪŋkrənaɪz] *v.* 使同步、使同時發生

The first lesson of dancing a two-person dance is to synchronize with your partner.

跳雙人舞的第一課就是和你的舞伴同步。

225 iso-

相等

源自於希臘字首「同等」、「相同」的意思。

- **isobar** [`aɪsobɑr] *n.* 等壓線
- **isochromatic** [ˌaɪsokrə`mætɪk] *adj.* 同色的、等色的
- **isosceles** [aɪ`sɑsɪliz] *adj.* 等腰的
- **isotope** [`aɪsətop] *n.* 同位素

isobar [`aɪsobɑr] *n.* 等壓線

The weather forecast predicts that tomorrow will be a very windy day since isobars on the weather chart are very close to each other.

天氣預報預估明天風會很大，因為天氣圖上的等壓線十分密集。

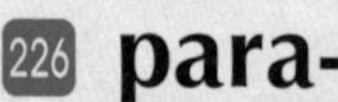

226 para-

旁邊

源自於希臘文「一旁」、「旁邊」或「超越」。

- **paradigm** [`pærədaɪm] *n.* 範例、典範
- **parallel** [`pærəlɛl] *adj.* 平行的；類似的 *adv.* 平行地 *n.* 平行線
- **paralyze** [`pærəlaɪz] *v.* 癱瘓、使喪失活動能力（原指半邊行動不便的意思）

paralyze [`pærəlaɪz] *v.* 癱瘓、使喪失活動能力（原指半邊行動不便的意思）

Fear can paralyze a person's mobility, so the training of a quick reaction is essential for outdoor survival.

恐懼會癱瘓人的行動能力，因此野外求生時快速反應訓練是必要的。

227 **quasi-**

次要

源自於拉丁文「相似」、「彷彿」的意思，通常翻譯為「準…」。

- **quasicrystal** [ˋkwezaɪkrɪstəl] *adj.* 準晶體
- **quasi-contract** [ˌkwezaɪˋkɑntrækt] *n.* 準契約
- **quasi-science** [ˌkwezaɪˋsaɪns] *n.* 準科學
- **quasi-stellar** [ˌkwezaɪˋstɛlɚ] *adj.* 類星體的

quasicrystal [ˋkwezaɪkrɪstəl] *adj.* 準晶體

The structure of quasicrystal was first known by mathematicians and then was first discovered by a physician in 2011.

準晶體的結構先被數學家了解，然後到 2011 年才由一名物理學家發現。

228 **vice-**

次要的

源自於拉丁文「次要」的意思，通常用在指稱職位「副…」上。

- **vice-admiral** [ˌvaɪsˋædmərəl] *n.* 海軍中將
- **vice-chancellor** [ˌvaɪˋtʃɑnsəlɚ] *n.* 大學副校長
- **vice-president** [ˌvaɪsˋprɛsədənt] *n.* 副總統、副總裁、副董事
- **vicegerent** [vaɪsˋdʒɪrənt] *adj.* 代理的 *n.* 代理人

vice-admiral [ˌvaɪsˋædmərəl] *n.* 海軍中將

The retired vice-admiral liked to talk about his life and journey in the U.S Navy to his grandchildren.

退休的海軍中將喜歡跟他的孫子講他在美國海軍的生活和旅程。

UNIT 20 空間方位與程度－反對

Dia-Anti ▶MP3 020

229 **dia-**

穿越

源自於希臘文「穿越」、「分離」或「跨越」的意思。

- **diabetes** [daɪə`bitiz] *n.* 糖尿病
- **diagnose** [`daɪəgnoz] *v.* 診斷（dia-分開，gnosis-知道、指認）
- **diagonal** [daɪ`ægənəl] *adj.* 斜線的、對角線的 *n.* 對角線
- **diameter** [daɪ`æmɪtɚ] *n.* 直徑

diabetes [daɪə`bitiz] *n.* 糖尿病（diabetes mellitus 的簡稱，希臘／拉丁文中 diabetes- 穿越，mellitus- 甜味）

There are two types of diabetes: while most people suffer from this illness in older ages, some have innate malfunction of their cells.

糖尿病有兩種型態：大部分的人在老年時才會因此病所苦，然有些人則是因先天細胞功能不全。

230 **a-**

否定

源自於希臘文「沒有」、「缺乏」等否定的意思。

- **abyss** [ə`bɪs] *n.* 深淵；絕境（byss-底部）
- **amoral** [e`mɔrəl] *adj.* 無道德觀的
- **amorphous** [ə`mɔrfəs] *adj.* 無固定形狀的；無清楚架構的
- **apathetic** [æpə`θɛtɪk] *adj.* 不關心的、沒興趣的、無動於衷的

abyss [ə`bɪs] *n.* 深淵；絕境（byss-底部）

Humans built artificial abysses because of the mining industry.
人們因礦業發展建造了人工的深淵。

231 an-
否定

與 a- 同源，希臘文「沒有」、「缺乏」等否定的意思。

- **anasthesia** [͵ænɪs`θizɪə] *n.* 麻醉狀態（asthesia-感覺）
- **analgesic** [͵ænəl`dʒizɪk] *n.* 止痛劑 *adj.* 止痛的
- **anarchic** [ə`nɑrkɪk] *adj.* 不守秩序的；無政府狀態的
- **anemia** [ə`nimɪə] *n.* 貧血

anasthesia [͵ænɪs`θizɪə] *n.* 麻醉狀態（asthesia-感覺）

The dentist assured the patient that it would be partly anasthesia during the tooth extraction, so she would not feel any pain.
牙醫師向病人保證拔牙時會局部麻醉，所以她不會感到任何疼痛。

232 de-
否定

源自於拉丁文「去除」、「反轉」等否定的意思。

- **defect** [`difɛkt] *n.* 缺陷、缺點
- **deficient** [dɪ`fɪʃənt] *adj.* 缺乏的、不足的
- **deprive** [dɪ`praɪv] *v.* 剝奪、搶走
- **detach** [dɪ`tætʃt] *v.* 分離的、獨立的

defect [`difɛkt] *n.* 缺陷、缺點

The software company abandoned the old version of antivirus software due to its countless defects.
軟體公司放棄舊版的防毒軟體，因為它有太多缺點了。

233 dis-

否定

拉丁文「否定」或「負面」意思的字首。

- **disability** [dɪsə`bɪlətɪ] *n.* 殘疾、缺陷
- **disagreement** [dɪsə`grimənt] *n.* 意見不合、紛歧
- **disbelief** [dɪsbɪ`lif] *n.* 不相信、懷疑
- **disgrace** [dɪs`gres] *n.* 不光彩的行為、恥辱 *v.* 使…蒙羞

disability [dɪsə`bɪlətɪ] *n.* 殘疾、缺陷

Although she suffered from a learning disability, she still finished Master's degree.

雖然她有學習障礙，但她仍完成了碩士學位。

234 in-

否定

源自於拉丁文，有「不是」、「非」等否定的意思。

- **inaccurate** [ɪn`ækjʊrət] *adj.* 不精確的
- **inactive** [ɪn`æktɪv] *adj.* 不活動的、不活躍的
- **indisposed** [ɪndɪ`spozd] *adj.* 不舒服的；不願意的
- **inexpensive** [ɪnɪk`spɛnsɪv] *adj.* 不貴的、便宜的

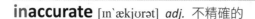

inaccurate [ɪn`ækjʊrət] *adj.* 不精確的

The estimated data was wildly inaccurate when the result came out.

預估的資料在結果出來後發現非常的不精確。

235 il-

否定

與 in- 同源，有「不是」、「非」等否定的意思，置於開頭的單字前。

- **illegible** [ɪ`lɛdʒɪbəl] *adj.* 不可讀的、難辨認的
- **illegitimate** [ˌɪlɪ`dʒɪtɪmət] *adj.* 非法的；私生的
- **illiterate** [ɪ`lɪtərət] *adj.* 不識字的；所知甚少的、外行的
- **illogical** [ɪ`lɑdʒɪkəl] *adj.* 不合邏輯的

illegible [ɪ`lɛdʒɪbəl] *adj.* 不可讀的、難辨認的

The letter has been thrown into a washing machine, and the words on it became very illegible.

這封信被丟入洗衣機裡，而上面的字跡變得難以辨認。

236 im-

否定

與 in- 同源，有「不是」、「非」等否定的意思，置於開頭的單字前。

- **imbalanced** [ɪm`bælənst] *adj.* 不均衡的、失調的
- **immature** [ˌɪmə`tjʊɚ] *adj.* 不成熟的、沒經驗的、未發育的
- **immovable** [ɪ`muvəbəl] *adj.* 不可移動的、堅定不移的
- **immune** [ɪ`mjun] *adj.* 免疫的；不受影響的；豁免的、免除的

imbalanced [ɪm`bælənst] *adj.* 不均衡的、失調的

The negotiation between the two countries did not go very well due to their imbalanced power.

因為兩國之間不對等的權力，他們之間的談判不是很順利。

237 ir-

否定

與 in- 同源，有「不是」、「非」等否定的意思，置於開頭的單字前。

- **irregular** [ɪ`rɛgjʊlɚ] *adj.* 不規則的、不合常規的、不正常的
- **irrelevant** [ɪ`rɛlɪvənt] *adj.* 不相關的
- **irresistible** [ɪrɪ`zɪstəbəl] *adj.* 無法抗拒的、不可抵擋的
- **irrespective** [ɪrɪ`spɛktɪv] *adj.* 不考慮、不論

irregular [ɪ`rɛgjʊlɚ] *adj.* 不規則的、不合常規的、不正常的

They challenged to put a hundred irregular pieces of porcelain together on the wall and made a picture out of them.

他們挑戰將一百片不規則的磁磚拼起來並做成一幅畫。

238 non-

否定

源自於拉丁文「沒有」、「不是」的否定意思。

- **non-alcoholic** [nɑnælkə`hɔlɪk] *adj.* 不含酒精的
- **noncommittal** [nɑnkə`mɪtəl] *adj.* 不表態的、含糊其辭的
- **non-flammable** [nɑn`flæməbəl] *adj.* 不易燃的
- **non-violent** [nɑn`vaɪələnt] *adj.* 非暴力的

non-alcoholic [nɑnælkə`hɔlɪk] *adj.* 不含酒精的

Pregnant women should drink non-alcoholic and non-caffeine beverages.

懷孕婦女應飲用不含酒精、不含咖啡因的飲料。

239 neg-

否定

源自於拉丁文「不是」、「否定」等意思。

- **negation** [nɪˋgeʃən] *n.* 否定
- **negative** [ˋnɛgətɪv] *adj.* 否定的、拒絕的
- **neglect** [nɪˋglɛkt] *v.* 疏忽、忽略、忽視
- **negligent** [ˋnɛglɪdʒənt] *adj.* 疏忽的、失職的

negation [nɪˋgeʃən] *n.* 否定

We need a result before the end of this week, no matter if it is confirmation or negation.

我們這週結束前需要一個答案，無論是肯定還是否定。

240 anti-

反對

源自於希臘文「反對」、「相反」等對立的意思。

- **antibiotic** [ˌæntɪbaɪˋɑtɪk] *n.* 抗生素
- **antibody** [ˋæntɪbɑdɪ] *n.* 抗體
- **anticlimax** [æntɪˋklaɪmæks] *n.* 反高潮、掃興的結尾
- **antidote** [ˋæntɪdot] *n.* 解毒劑；緩解方法、對抗手段

antibiotic [ˌæntɪbaɪˋɑtɪk] *n.* 抗生素

If you are taking a course of antibiotics, you should comply with the doctor's prescription and do not stop during the course.

若你正在接受抗生素療程，你應遵守醫生的指示且不得於療程中中斷。

UNIT 21

否定－除去、取消

Contra-Un ▶MP3 021

241 contra-

相反

拉丁文「相反」、「相對」或「衝突」的意思。

- **contradict** [kɑntrə`dɪkt] *v.* 反駁、否定；與…矛盾、牴觸
- **contradictory** [kɑntrə`dɪktərɪ] *adj.* 對立的、相互矛盾的
- **contrary** [`kɑntrərɪ] *adj.* 相反的、對立的 *n.* 相反、對立面
- **contrast** [`kɑntræst] *adj.* 差異、對比、對照

contradict [kɑntrə`dɪkt] *v.* 反駁、否定；與…矛盾、牴觸

In the actress' short statement, she contradicted herself four times.
在女演員簡短的聲明中，她自我矛盾了四次。

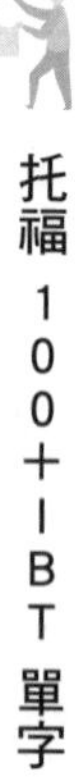

242 counter-

反對

和 contra- 同源，有「相反」、「反對」或「對抗」的意思。

- **counteract** [kaʊntɚ`ækt] *v.* 抵銷、減少、對抗
- **counterbalance** [`kaʊntɚ͵bæləns] *v. n.* （使）平衡、彌補
- **counterclockwise** [kaʊntɚ`klɑkwaɪz] *adj. adv.* 逆時鐘方向的（地）
- **counterpart** [`kaʊntɚpɑrt] *n.* 相對應者

counteract [kaʊntə`ækt] *v.* 抵銷、減少、對抗

Airbags and seat belts are proved able to counteract the striking force from the accident.

安全氣囊與安全帶證明可以減少事故發生時帶來的撞擊力。

243 **re-**

往回

源自於拉丁文「向後」、「往回」或「重複」的意思。

- **reciprocal** [rɪ`sɪprəkəl] *adj.* 回報的；互補的；倒數的
- **reclaim** [rɪ`klem] *v.* 取回、拿回、收回
- **refund** [rɪ`fʌnd] *v.* 退款、退還
- **rejection** [rɪ`dʒɛkʃən] *n.* 拒絕

reciprocal [rɪ`sɪprəkəl] *adj.* 回報的；互補的；倒數的

She believes that doing real charity means not expecting any reciprocal benefits.

她相信做真正的慈善就是不求任何回報。

244 **em-**

使成為

源自於希臘文，使名詞變成動作的字首。

- **embark** [ɪm`bɑrk] *v.* 登船
- **embed** [ɪm`bɛd] *v.* 鑲嵌、嵌入
- **embrace** [ɪm`bres] *v.* 擁抱；欣然接受、採納；包括
- **emphasis** [`ɛmfəsɪs] *n.* 強調、重視

embark [ɪm`bɑrk] *v.* 登船

After the end of World War II, my grandmother's fiancé embarked for Japan and then lost contact afterwards.

二戰之後我奶奶的未婚夫登船回到日本，之後就失去聯繫了。

245 **en-**

使成為

與 in- 同源，使名詞變成動作的字首，有「提供」的意涵。

- **enlarge** [ɪn`lɑrdʒ] *v.* 放大
- **enlighten** [ɪn`laɪtən] *v.* 啟發、啟蒙、開導
- **enrich** [ɪn`rɪtʃ] *v.* 使豐富、充實；使…富有
- **ensue** [ɪn`sju] *v.* 接著發生

enlarge [ɪn`lɑrdʒ] *v.* 放大

My father showed me an ordinary photo, but when he enlarged it, I saw an amazing hidden surprise!

我父親給我看一張平凡的照片，但當他將照片放大後我看到了驚人的隱

246 **in-**

使成為

源自於拉丁文，原指「向內的」，後衍生為「促使」、「成為」等意思。

- **inaugurate** [ɪ`nɔgjʊret] *v.* 正式就職；啟用；開創、開始
- **incentive** [ɪn`sɛntɪv] *n.* 激勵、鼓勵
- **induce** [ɪn`djus] *v.* 誘使、勸說；導致
- **inflict** [ɪn`flɪkt] *v.* 使遭受、承受

incentive [ɪn`sɛntɪv] *n.* 激勵、鼓勵

According to a survey, convenience and inexpensive prices are the main incentives for taking public transportation.

根據一則調查，便利性和便宜的價格是搭乘大眾交通工具的主要激勵原因。

247 im-

使成為

與 in- 同源，原指「向內的」，後衍生為「促使」、「成為」等意思。

- **imminent** [`ɪmɪnənt] *adj.* 即將來臨的
- **impart** [ɪm`pɑrt] *v.* 傳授、告知；賦予
- **imperative** [ɪm`pɛrətɪv] *adj.* 緊急迫切的、十分重要的
- **impulse** [`ɪmpʌls] *n.* 強烈慾望、心血來潮、一時興起

imminent [`ɪmɪnənt] *adj.* 即將來臨的

An imminent political storm is at the corner, but some just cannot see the omen.

一場政治風暴即將來臨，但就是有些人無法看見預兆。

248 ex-

使成為

源自於希臘文「外面的」，後衍生為「完成」、「完全」等意思。

- **excerpt** [ɛk`sɝpt] *v. n.* 摘錄、節錄
- **execute** [`ɛksɪkjut] *v.* 履行、實行、執行
- **expedition** [ɛkspɪ`dɪʃən] *n.* 遠征、探險、考察
- **extort** [ɪk`stɔrt] *v.* 勒索、敲詐

extort [ɪk`stɔrt] *v.* 勒索、敲詐

An anonymous person attempted to extort money from the agency of the actor, seemingly wishing to damage his reputation.

一位匿名人士試圖向演員的經紀公司勒索，似乎想要毀壞他的名聲。

249 de-

去除

源自於拉丁文「遠離」，在此衍生為「去除」、「消失」的意思。

- **default** [dɪ`fɔlt] *n.* 預設值、既定結果；違約、拖欠 *v.* 默認、預設為…；違約
- **deter** [dɪ`tɝ] *v.* 嚇阻、威懾；使不敢、使斷念
- **devalue** [dɪ`vælju] *v.* 貶值；輕視、貶低
- **devastating** [`dɛvəstetɪŋ] *adj.* 毀滅性的；驚人的、令人震撼的

default [dɪ`fɔlt] *n.* 預設值、既定結果；違約、拖欠 *v.* 默認、預設為…；違約

The repairer explained that his phone which got a virus is repairable, but it will be revert to default settings.

修理師告訴他中毒的手機修得好，但會被還原到預設狀態。

250 dis-

去除

源自於拉丁文，「分開」、「去除」等意思。

- **discomfort** [dɪs`kʌmfɚt] *n.* 不適、不安
- **dissipate** [`dɪsə,pet] *v.* 逐漸消失、逐漸浪費
- **distil** [dɪ`stɪl] *v.* 蒸餾；濃縮
- **distract** [dɪ`strakt] *v.* 使分心

discomfort [dɪs`kʌmfɚt] *n.* 不適、不安

A study implies that violent pictures in movies may cause discomfort to young children.

一項研究暗示電影中暴力的畫面可能會造成幼兒感到不安。

251 out-

去除

源自於古英文，原有「外面」的意思，亦衍生為「消除」、「去除」之意。

- **outage** [`aʊtɪdʒ] *n.* 停電期間
- **outgas** [aʊt`gæs] *v.* 除氣、釋出氣體
- **outlaw** [`aʊtlɔ] *n.* 不法之徒 *v.* 使成為非法、禁止
- **outwash** [`aʊtwɑʃ] *n.* 冰川沖刷、外洗平原

outwash [`aʊtwɑʃ] *n.* 冰川沖刷、外洗平原

Our tour guide brought us to a hill and showed us the outwash and moraine left by the glacier in the last century.

我們導遊帶我們到一座山丘上，看上世紀冰川留下來的外洗平原和冰磧石。

252 un-

消除

源自希臘文 anti-，有「移除」、「消除」或「開放」等意思。

- **unpack** [ʌn`pæk] *v.* 打開（行李）；解釋、説明
- **uncover** [ʌn`kʌvɚ] *v.* 揭露、揭開、發掘
- **undo** [ʌn`du] *v.* 解開、大開；消除、抵銷
- **unload** [ʌn`lod] *v.* 去除、卸下、取出

unpack [ʌn`pæk] *v.* 打開（行李）；解釋、説明

They were so tired because of today's travel that they did not want to unpack their luggage after they laid down on the bed.

他們因今日的行程感到十分的疲憊，因此當他們當躺到床上後就不想打開行李。

UNIT 22

名詞字尾

Ain-Ator ▶MP3 022

253 -ain

人

源自於拉丁文，代表「與…相關的人」。

- **chaplain** [`tʃæplɪn] *n.* 特遣牧師，於非宗教場所服務的牧師
- **captain** [`kæptɪn] *n.* 機長、船長、隊長；上校、上尉
- **swain** [sweɪn] *n.* （文學中）年輕的戀人或追求者
- **villain** [`vɪlən] *n.* 反派

chaplain [`tʃæplɪn] *n.* 特遣牧師，於非宗教場所服務的牧師

After finishing his study of theology in the university, he is considering becoming a prison chaplain in the future.

自大學神學系畢業後，他考慮在未來當監獄牧師。

254 -aire

人

源自於拉丁文，指有某中特質的人，通常加在來自法文的單字字尾。

- **concessionaire** [kən͵sɛʃə`nɛr] *n.* 特許經銷商
- **commissionaire** [kə͵mɪʃə`nɛr] *n.* 看門員、門口警衛
- **legionnaire** [͵lidʒə`nɛr] *n.* 軍團
- **millionaire** [mɪljə`nɛr] *n.* 百萬富翁

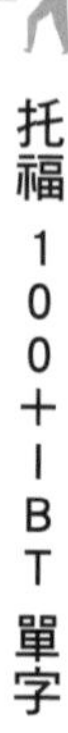

concessionaire [kən͵sɛʃə`nɛr] *n.* 特許經銷商

The watchdog group emphasizes that BOT should not allow certain concessionaires to gain illegal profits.

監督團體強調政府民間合作案不應允許讓特許經銷商獲得不法利益。

255 -ian

人

演化自拉丁文字尾 -an，指專家或特殊的人物。

- **barbarian** [bɑr`bɛrɪən] *n.* 野蠻人；無教化的人
- **comedian** [kə`midɪən] *n.* 喜劇演員
- **lesbian** [`lɛzbɪən] *n.* 女同性戀者
- **statistician** [stætɪ`stɪʃən] *n.* 統計學家、統計員

barbarian [bɑr`bɛrɪən] *n.* 野蠻人；無教化的人

You cannot call them barbarians merely because they have a different culture from you.

你不能因為他們的文化和你的不同就叫他們野蠻人。

256 -ant, -ent

人

源自於拉丁文，意思為「…的人」。

- **attendant** [ə`tɛndənt] *n.* 服務員、侍者
- **defendant** [dɪ`fɛndənt] *n.* 被告人
- **correspondent** [kɔrɪ`spɑndənt] *n.* 通訊記者、通信人
- **tyrant** [`taɪrənt] *n.* 暴君、專橫的人

attendant [ə`tɛndənt] *n.* 服務員、侍者

With his fluent English and charming smile, he successfully became a flight attendant.

憑著他流利的英文和迷人的笑容，他成功地成為一名空服員。

257 -ar, -or

人

源自於拉丁文「與…相關的人」的字尾。

- **administrator** [əd`mɪnɪstretə] *n.* 行政人員
- **bachelor** [`bætʃələ] *n.* 單身漢；學士
- **counselor** [`kaʊnsələ] *n.* 顧問、律師；輔導員
- **vicar** [`vɪkə] *n.* 教區（堂）牧師

administrator [əd`mɪnɪstretə] *n.* 行政人員

The conductor was annoyed that she needed approval of the administrator every time she chose performing pieces.

指揮很不高興每次她選擇的表演曲目都要經過行政人員同意。

258 -er

人

源自於古英文的字尾，廣泛用於職業人員或其他帶有特別特質的人。

- **retailer** [`ritelə] *n.* 零售商
- **shareholder** [`ʃɛrholdə] *n.* 股票持有人、股東
- **toddler** [`tɑdlə] *n.* 初學走路的幼兒
- **taxpayer** [`tækspeə] *n.* 納稅人

retailer [`ritelə] *n.* 零售商

As the biggest book retailer in the country, the company provides multiple services to include more customers.

身為全國最大的零售商，該公司提供多元服務以吸引更多客戶。

259 -ard

人

源自於古法文，代表有某種習慣或特性的人。

- **coward** [`kaʊɚd] *n.* 膽小鬼、懦夫
- **drunkard** [`drʌŋkɚd] *n.* 酗酒者、酒鬼
- **steward** [`stjuɚd] *n.* 服務員；負責人、管家
- **wizard** [`wɪzɚd] *n.* 巫師

coward [`kaʊɚd] *n.* 膽小鬼、懦夫

She was deemed a coward in schooldays due to her cautiousness and prudence.

她的小心謹慎使她在學生時期被視為一個膽小鬼。

260 -arian

人

源自於拉丁文，出現於 -ary 結尾變成的名詞中。

- **humanitarian** [hjʊˌmænɪ`tɛrɪən] *n.* 人道主義者
- **librarian** [laɪ`brɛrɪən] *n.* 圖書館員
- **vegetarian** [vɛdʒɪ`tɛrɪən] *n.* 素食者
- **veterinarian** [ˌvɛtərɪ`nɛrɪən] *n.* 獸醫

humanitarian [hjʊˌmænɪ`tɛrɪən] *n.* 人道主義者

She does not consider herself a humanitarian because she thinks that everyone has the right and power to be involved.

她不認為她自己是一名人道主義者，因為她認為每個人都有權、有力量能參與這件事。

261 -ary

人

源自於拉丁文，意指「…樣的人」。

- **adversary** [`ædvəsərɪ] *n.* 對手、敵手
- **judiciary** [dʒʊ`dɪʃərɪ] *n.* 法官（總稱）、審判官
- **luminary** [`lumɪnərɪ] *n.* 專家、著名學者
- **missionary** [`mɪʃənərɪ] *n.* 傳教士

adversary [`ædvəsərɪ] *n.* 對手、敵手

Jim cannot believe that his friend from school's archery club is his adversary in this contest.

吉姆不敢相信他之前學校箭術社的朋友是當天比賽的對手。

262 -ast

人

源自於希臘文的字尾，通常改變自 -ize 動詞，「…的人」。

- **iconoclast** [aɪ`kɑnəklæst] *n.* 反對偶像崇拜者、批評某價值者
- **encomiast** [ɛn`komɪæst] *n.* 阿諛者、讚美者
- **enthusiast** [ɪn`θjuzɪæst] *n.* 熱衷於…者、愛好者
- **gymnast** [`dʒɪmnæst] *n.* 體操運動員

iconoclast [aɪ`kɑnəklæst] *n.* 反對偶像崇拜者、批評某價值者

Many priceless ancient books and buildings were destroyed by iconoclasts during the Cultural Revolution.

在文化大革命中有許多無價的古老典籍和建築被反舊習者破壞。

263 -ate

人

源自拉丁文，有「做…事的人」或是和官方有關者。

- **advocate** [`ædvəkət] *n.* 支持者、擁護者
- **consulate** [`kɑnsjʊlət] *n.* 領事館、領事
- **delegate** [`dɛlɪgət] *n.* 代表
- **inmate** [`ɪnmet] *n.* 囚犯；病人

inmate [`ɪnmet] *n.* 囚犯；病人

The prison makes money by letting inmates involve in the handicraft production.

這間監獄讓囚犯參與手工藝製作而賺錢。

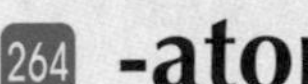

264 -ator

者

拉丁字尾，將 -ate 動詞改變成名詞的結尾。

- **creator** [kri`etɚ] *n.* 創造者、創作者
- **dictator** [dɪk`tetɚ] *n.* 獨裁者、獨斷專行者
- **legislator** [`lɛdʒɪsletɚ] *n.* 立法者
- **negotiator** [nɪ`goʃɪetɚ] *n.* 談判者、談判專家

negotiator [nɪ`goʃɪetɚ] *n.* 談判者、談判專家

The police found the negotiator to convince the kidnapper to release the hostages.

警方找到談判專家說服綁匪釋放人質。

UNIT
23 名詞字尾

Ee-Trix ▶MP3 023

265 -ee

者

拉丁字尾，代表接受某種動作的人。

- **examinee** [ɪgzæmɪ`ni] *n.* 受試者、考生
- **nominee** [nɑmɪ`ni] *n.* 被提名者
- **referee** [rɛfə`ri] *n.* 裁判；仲裁者；推薦者
- **trainee** [tre`ni] *n.* 受訓者、實習生

examinee [ɪgzæmɪ`ni] *n.* 受試者、考生

Do not worry. The university has already prepared an alternative plan for examinees who are intervened by severe weather.

別擔心，大學已經為被惡劣天氣阻撓的考生準備好備案了。

266 -eer

人

源自於拉丁文，代表「做…的人」。

- **pioneer** [paɪə`nɪɚ] *n.* 先鋒、創始人、開拓者
- **profiteer** [prɑfɪ`tɪɚ] *n.* 奸商、投機商
- **overseer** [`ovɚsɪɚ] *n.* 工頭、監工
- **volunteer** [ˌvɑlən`tɪɚ] *n.* 志願者、志工

pioneer [paɪə`nɪɚ] *n.* 先鋒、創始人、開拓者

Apple computers were the pioneer of the personal computer.

蘋果電腦是個人電腦的先鋒。

267 -el

人

代表「…人」的意思，由南歐語系如法、義大利文演變而來的詞語。

- **colonel** [ˋkɝnəl] *n.* （陸、空軍）上校
- **infidel** [ˋɪnfɪdəl] *n.* 異教徒
- **minstrel** [ˋmɪnstrəl] *n.* （中世紀的）吟遊歌手
- **personnel** [pɝsəˋnɛl] *n.* 人事、員工

colonel [ˋkɝnəl] *n.* （陸、空軍）上校

The army held a grand and solemn funeral for the colonel who died in the line of duty.

軍方為殉職的上校舉辦一場隆重且莊嚴的喪禮。

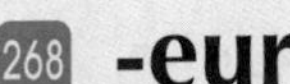

268 -eur

人

源自於法文，由特定動詞轉化為名詞，「…人」的意思。

- **entrepreneur** [͵ɑntrəprəˋnɝ] *n.* 企業家、創業家
- **flaneur** [flɑˋnɝ] *n.* 漫遊者
- **masseur** [mæˋsɝ] *n.* 按摩師
- **voyeur** [vwɑˋjɝ] *n.* 偷窺者

voyeur [vwɑˋjɝ] *n.* 偷窺者

The voyeur of the female public toilet was caught on the spot by two tourists.

女用公共廁所的偷窺者被兩名旅客當場逮到。

269 -ist

人

源自於希臘文，指「從事或參與…的人」。

- **activist** [`æktɪvɪst] *n.* 積極分子、行動分子
- **columnist** [`kaləmnɪst] *n.* 專欄作家
- **environmentalist** [ɪn͵vaɪrən`mɛntəlɪst] *n.* 環境保護主義者
- **pharmacist** [`farməsɪst] *n.* 藥劑師

pharmacist [`farməsɪst] *n.* 藥劑師

It is better to ask pharmacists' suggestion even if you are purchasing non-prescription medicine.

即使你是買非處方用藥，仍最好詢問藥劑師的意見。

270 -logist

學者

源自於希臘文，指某特別領域的學者。

- **ecologist** [ɪ`kalədʒɪst] *n.* 生態學家
- **meteorologist** [͵mitɪə`ralədʒɪst] *n.* 氣象學家
- **psychologist** [saɪ`kalədʒɪst] *n.* 心理學家
- **sociologist** [sosi`alədʒɪst] *n.* 社會學家

sociologist [sosi`alədʒɪst] *n.* 社會學家

Sociologists study the problem that most people ignore and lead the public to think of a better solution.

社會學家研究大部分人不關心的問題，並引領大眾思考更好的解決方法。

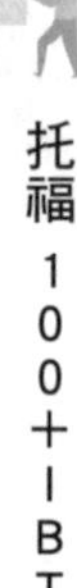

271 **-nik**

者

源自斯拉夫語系，指特定政治、文化等狀態或信仰相關的支持者或響應者。

- **beatnik** [`bitnɪk] *n.* （五、六〇年代）「垮掉的一代」成員
- **computernik** [kəm`pjutɚnɪk] *n.* 電腦迷
- **peacenik** [`pisnɪk] *n.* 反戰分子
- **refusenik** [rɪ`fjuznɪk] *n.* 被拒移民者

beatnik [`bitnɪk] *n.* （五、六〇年代）「垮掉的一代」成員

He was a beatnik who wore loose clothes and had long hair to express his dissatisfaction to mainstream values.

他過去曾是垮掉一代的成員，他們穿寬鬆的衣物並留著長髮，以示他們對主流價值的不滿。

272 **-ster**

人

源自於古英文，指有特殊職業或習慣的人。

- **gamester** [`gemstɚ] *n.* 賭徒 gangster [`gæŋstɚ] *n.* 歹徒；犯罪集團成員
- **trickster** [`trɪkstɚ] *n.* 騙子、狡猾的人
- **youngster** [`jʌŋstɚ] *n.* 少年

gamester [`gemstɚ] *n.* 賭徒

Someone ironically commented that businessmen are legal gamesters who either earn a fortune or lose everything.

有人諷刺地批評說，商人就是合法的職業賭徒，要不賺大筆、要不失去所有。

273 -enne

女…

源自於法文中的陰性名詞，代表「女性的…」，在英文中已越來越少見。

- **comedienne** [kə͵midɪˋɛn] *n.* 女喜劇演員
- **doyenne** [dɔɪˋɛn] *n.* 女前輩、女老專家
- **equestrienne** [ɪ͵kwɛstrɪˋɛn] *n.* 女騎手表演者
- **tragedienne** [trə͵dʒidɪˋɛn] *n.* 女悲劇演員

comedienne [kə͵midɪˋɛn] *n.* 女喜劇演員

Comediennes are still not very common nowadays because girls are still expected to act like a lady.

女喜劇演員至今仍不多見，因為小女孩仍被期望表現得像淑女。

274 -ess

女…

從希臘文演變而來的陰性字尾，代表特定女性身分。

- **duchess** [ˋdʌtʃəs] *n.* 公爵夫人、女公爵
- **goddess** [ˋgɑdɪs] *n.* 女神
- **governess** [ˋgʌvɚnəs] *n.* 家庭女教師
- **hostess** [ˋhostəs] *n.* 女主人

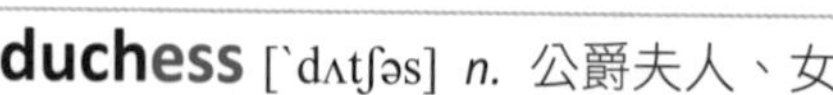

duchess [ˋdʌtʃəs] *n.* 公爵夫人、女公爵

Kate Middleton married Prince William in 2011 and became Duchess of Cambridge.

凱特・密道頓於 2011 年嫁給威廉王子而成為劍橋公爵夫人。

275 -ress

女…

與 -ess 同源，從希臘文演變而來的陰性字尾，代表特定女性身分。

- **actress** [`æktrəs] *n.* 女演員
- **laundress** [`lɔndrəs] *n.* 洗衣婦
- **mistress** [`mɪstrəs] *n.* 女主人；情婦

actress [`æktrəs] *n.* 女演員

The girl wanted to be an actress with intelligence, not merely a beautiful face.

女孩想成為一個有智慧的女演員，而不只是空有外在美。

276 -trix

女性的

源自於拉丁文，代表「女性的」、「陰性的」等意思。

- **aviatrix** [ˌevɪ`etrɪks] *n.* （舊）女飛行員
- **dominatrix** [ˌdɑmɪ`netrɪks] *n.* 母夜叉
- **executrix** [ɪg`zɛkjutrɪks] *n.* 女遺囑執行人
- **testatrix** [tɛ`stetrɪks] *n.* 女遺囑人

aviatrix [ˌevɪ`etrɪks] *n.* （舊）女飛行員

Amelia Earhart was one of the best pilots in the twentieth century and was the first aviatrix who crossed the Atlantic Ocean alone.

愛蜜莉・艾爾哈特是二十世紀最優秀的飛行員之一，也是第一位獨自橫跨大西洋的女飛行員。

名詞字尾

Ade-Faction ▶MP3 024

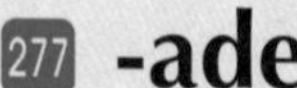

277 -ade

做…事的過程

源自於拉丁文，指完成的動作、特定材料做成的物品或做某事的過程。

- **arcade** [ɑr`ked] *n.* 拱廊；拱廊商店街
- **brigade** [brɪ`ged] *n.* 軍旅；隊、幫、派
- **crusade** [kru`sed] *n.* 十字軍；（為理想而奮鬥的）運動
- **parade** [pə`red] *n.* 遊行；一系列事務、一隊人

arcade [ɑr`ked] *n.* 拱廊；拱廊商店街

Ten years after graduation the artist found what she reminisced about is the arcade circulating the garden in the department building. 畢業十年後，藝術家發現她最懷念的是環繞系館花園的拱廊。

278 -ant

帶有…特質

源自於拉丁文，將動詞轉為形容詞或名詞，指帶有…特質的事物。

- **contaminant** [kən`tæmɪnənt] *n.* 汙染物
- **covenant** [`kʌvənənt] *n.* 契約、協定、承諾
- **remnant** [`rɛmnənt] *n.* 殘餘、剩餘部分；零頭、零料
- **toxicant** [`tɑksɪkənt] *n.* 有毒物質

contaminant [kən`tæmɪnənt] *n.* 汙染物

The islanders firmly expressed their dissatisfaction of living near nuclear contaminants.
島嶼居民嚴正表達他們住在核電汙染物附近的不滿。

279 **-ar**
和…有關、有…天性

源自於拉丁文，指和…有關或有…天性的事物。

- **altar** [`ɔltɚ] *n.* 聖壇、祭壇
- **cellar** [`sɛlɚ] *n.* 地下室、地窖
- **seminar** [`sɛmɪnɑr] *n.* 研討會、專題討論會
- **pillar** [`pɪlɚ] *n.* 柱子

altar [`ɔltɚ] *n.* 聖壇、祭壇

The pyramids belonging to the Maya civilization are believed to be ancient altars of rituals.
馬雅文明中的金字塔據信是祭典儀式的祭壇。

280 **-ary**
與…有關、帶有…特色

拉丁字尾，與…有關或帶有…特色的事物或地點。

- **boundary** [`baʊndərɪ] *n.* 分界線、邊界、界限
- **documentary** [dɑkjʊ`mɛntərɪ] *n.* 紀錄片
- **obituary** [o`bɪtʃʊərɪ] *n.* 訃聞
- **sanctuary** [`sæŋktjʊərɪ] *n.* 保護、庇護所、避難所；保護區

boundary [`baʊndərɪ] *n.* 分界線、邊界、界限

As an island country, there are no country boundary problems but issues of territorial waters.
一個海島型國家沒有國土邊界問題，但有海域的議題。

281 **-ator**

動詞轉做名詞字尾

源自於拉丁文，將動詞轉換成名詞的字尾。

- **equator** [ɪ`kwetɚ] *n.* 赤道
- **indicator** [`ɪndɪketɚ] *n.* 指標
- **motivator** [`motɪvetɚ] __________ *n.* 動力、激發因素
- **radiator** [`redɪetɚ] *n.* 散熱器、冷卻器

equator [ɪ`kwetɚ] *n.* 赤道

The weather around the equator is steadier than many parts of the earth.

赤道附近的天氣比地球上很多地方來得穩定。

282 **-cle**

某一動作結果、某種方法

源自於古法文，代表某一動作的結果或某種方法。

- **miracle** [`mɪrəkəl] *n.* 奇蹟
- **obstacle** [`ɑbstəkəl] *n.* 阻礙
- **oracle** [ɔrəkəl] *n.* 神諭；神使、聖人
- **spectacle** [`spɛtəkəl] *n.* 奇觀、（壯麗的）景象、場面

miracle [`mɪrəkəl] *n.* 奇蹟

Her total recovery from breast cancer without medical treatment was regarded as a miracle.

她不靠醫療而完全從乳癌康復被視為一個奇蹟。

283 -ette

小

源自於法文，表示「小的⋯」。

- **barrette** [bæ`rɛt] *n.* 小髮夾
- **cigarette** [sɪgə`rɛt] *n.* 香菸（cigar-雪茄）
- **kitchenette** [kɪtʃɪ`nɛt] *n.* 小廚房
- **palette** [`pælɪt] *n.* 調色板

barrette [bæ`rɛt] *n.* 小髮夾

The little girl was very excited and happy to receive her first barrette as her birthday gift.

小女孩很高興且興奮收到她第一個小髮夾作為生日禮物。

284 -arium

某特定場所

源自於希臘文，依據前面字根的意思代表某特定場所。

- **aquarium** [ə`kwɛrɪəm] *n.* 水族箱；水族館
- **planetarium** [ˌplænɪ`tɛrɪəm] *n.* 天文館
- **sanitarium** [ˌsænɪ`tɛrɪəm] *n.* 療養院
- **solarium** [sə`lɛrɪəm] *n.* 日光浴室

aquarium [ə`kwɛrɪəm] *n.* 水族箱；水族館

The little boy's wonder of the ocean started from the day when his parents brought him to visit an aquarium on his ninth birthday.

小男孩對海洋的好奇始於他父母在他九歲生日當天，帶他去參觀水族館的那日起。

285 -orium

…的地方

源自於拉丁文，指「…的地方」。

- **auditorium** [ɔdɪ`tɔrɪəm] *n.* 聽眾席、觀眾席；（美）音樂廳、禮堂
- **crematorium** [͵krɛmə`tɔrɪəm] *n.* 火葬場
- **emporium** [ɛm`pɔrɪəm] *n.* 商場；大百貨商店

auditorium [ɔdɪ`tɔrɪəm] *n.* 聽眾席、觀眾席；（美）音樂廳、禮堂

Smoking and eating are forbidden in the auditorium of this theater.
在這家劇院的觀眾席禁止抽菸和吃東西。

286 -age

某種狀態、功能；動作的結果

拉丁文字尾，表示某種狀態、功能或是動作的結果。

- **beverage** [`bɛvərɪdʒ] *n.* 飲料（bever = 拉丁文 bibere-喝）
- **coverage** [`kʌvərɪdʒ] *n.* 涵蓋、涉及；新聞報導；保險
- **dosage** [`dosɪdʒ] *n.* 劑量
- **footage** [`fʊtɪdʒ] *n.* 片段、一段影片；鏡頭

beverage [`bɛvərɪdʒ] *n.* 飲料（bever = 拉丁文 bibere-喝）

The cross-country trains provide various hot and cold beverages but do not include alcoholic ones.
跨縣市的長途火車提供各種冷熱飲，但不包含酒精飲料。

287 **-cy**

一種狀態、情況

源自拉丁文，代表一種狀態、情況或是行為結果。

- **bureaucracy** [ˌbjʊˋrɑkrəsɪ] *n.* 官僚體制、官僚作風
- **conspiracy** [kənˋspɪrəsɪ] *n.* 密謀、陰謀
- **discrepancy** [dɪsˋkrɛpənsɪ] *n.* 不一致、出入、差異
- **intimacy** [ˋɪntəməsɪ] *n.* 親密、密切關係

bureaucracy [ˌbjʊˋrɑkrəsɪ] *n.* 官僚體制、官僚作風

The artist was very disappointed by the inefficiency of bureaucracy and withdrew from the public art project.

那位藝術家對官僚體制的低效率感到不滿，而退出公共藝術計畫。

288 **-faction**

使…成為

源自於拉丁文，有「使…成為」、「致使」、「形成」等意思。

- **benefaction** [ˌbɛnɪˋfækʃən] *n.* 捐助、恩惠、施捨
- **faction** [ˋfækʃən] *n.* 派別、小集團
- **liquefaction** [lɪkwɪˋfækʃən] *n.* 液化（作用）
- **olfaction** [ɑlˋfækʃən] *n.* 嗅覺

olfaction [ɑlˋfækʃən] *n.* 嗅覺

The article published by a neurobiologist points out the difficulty of olfaction study.

由一位神經生物學家發表的文章點出嗅覺研究的困難。

UNIT 25

名詞字尾—形容詞字尾

Ment-Form ▶ MP3 025

289 -ment

某動作、方法或結果

源自於拉丁文，表示某動作、方法或結果。

- **contentment** [kən`tɛntmənt] *n.* 滿足、滿意
- **engagement** [ɪn`gedʒmənt] *n.* 訂婚；約定、安排；參與
- **harassment** [hə`ræsmənt] *n.* 騷擾行為
- **testament** [`tɛstəmənt] *n.* 證明；遺囑

contentment [kən`tɛntmənt] *n.* 滿足、滿意

He found the contentment of a simple life in the countryside with a person understanding him is very precious.

他發現和一個懂他的人在鄉間簡單生活所帶來的滿足是非常珍貴的。

-ness

名詞字尾，代表狀態、品質

將形容詞轉為名詞的字尾，代表一種狀態或品質。

- **consciousness** [`kɑnʃəsnɪs] *n.* 意識、感覺、知覺、神智（清醒）
- **illness** [`ɪlnəs] *n.* 疾病、生病
- **thickness** [`θɪknəs] *n.* 厚度；厚、粗；一層…
- **weakness** [`wiknəs] *n.* 軟弱；缺點、弱點

consciousness [`kɑnʃəsnɪs] *n.* 意識、感覺、知覺、神智（清醒）

After the car accident, he lost consciousness for three days.
車禍之後，他失去意識三天。

291 **-tion** 名詞字尾，某狀態或動作 將動詞轉為名詞的拉丁詞尾，代表某狀態或動作。	▪ **adaptation** [ædəp`teʃən] *n.* 適應；改編 ▪ **conservation** [kɑnsɚ`veʃən] *n.* 保育；保護、節約 ▪ **intonation** [ɪntə`neʃən] *n.* 聲調、語調；音準 ▪ **meditation** [mɛdɪ`teʃən] *n.* 沉思、冥想、深思

adaptation [ædəp`teʃən] *n.* 適應；改編

The chief editor announced the next project is a series of adaptations of classic adult fiction for children.
主編宣布下一個計劃是一系列為兒童改編經典的成人小說。

292 **-sion** 名詞字尾，表示狀況與行動 將動詞轉為名詞的拉丁詞尾，也是表示狀況與行動。	▪ **collision** [kə`lɪʒən] *n.* 碰撞、相撞；牴觸、衝突 ▪ **confession** [kən`fɛʃən] *n.* 坦白、承認、招認；（宗教）懺悔 ▪ **illusion** [ɪ`luʒən] *n.* 幻想、幻覺；錯覺、假象 ▪ **provision** [prə`vɪʒən] *n.* 供給、提供、準備；糧食、物資

collision [kə`lɪʒən] *n.* 碰撞、相撞；牴觸、衝突

He did not expect that there would be collisions of opinions on marketing between his company and the co-operator.
他沒料到他公司和合作者之間在行銷方面會有意見衝突。

293 -ure

動作、結果或狀態

源自於拉丁文，代表動作、結果或狀態的詞尾。

- **expenditure** [ɪk`spɛndɪtʃɚ] *n.* 全部支出、花費、耗費
- **fixture** [`fɪkstʃɚ] *n.* 固定裝置、設備；固定成員
- **posture** [`pastʃɚ] *n.* 姿勢、儀態；立場、態度
- **torture** [`tɔrtʃɚ] *n.* 折磨、煎熬；虐待、拷打

expenditure [ɪk`spɛndɪtʃɚ] *n.* 全部支出、花費、耗費

The old artist was happy to know that the government's annual expenditure on art education and subsidy increased gradually.

老藝術家很高興得知政府在藝術教育和補助上的支出逐漸增加。

294 -dom

表示身分或狀態

抽象和集合名詞字尾，表示身分或狀態。

- **boredom** [`bɔrdəm] *n.* 無聊、乏味
- **chiefdom** [`tʃifdəm] *n.* 領導、首領地位
- **freedom** [`fridəm] *n.* 自由
- **wisdom** [`wɪzdəm] *n.* 智慧

boredom [`bɔrdəm] *n.* 無聊、乏味

The teenagers told the police that they joined brawls simply out of boredom.

青少年告訴警察他們參與鬥毆僅出於無聊。

295 -hood

身分同質性

源自於古英文的字尾，表示一群人的身分同質性。

- **adulthood** [`ædʌlthʊd] *n.* 成年（身分）
- **brotherhood** [`brʌðəhʊd] *n.* 兄弟情誼；同手足的友誼；同道
- 會 **childhood** [`tʃaɪldhʊd] *n.* 童年、孩童時代
- **motherhood** [`mʌðəhʊd] *n.* 母親身分

adulthood [`ædʌlthʊd] *n.* 成年（身分）

She felt that her adulthood began the first time she left home at 20 for a new life.

她二十歲第一次離家過生活時，覺得自己正式開始了她的成年時期。

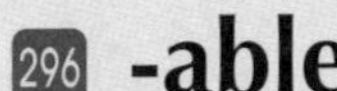

296 -able

可以…的

拉丁字尾，表示「可以…的」或是「能夠…的」的意思。

- **amiable** [`emɪəbəl] *adj.* 和藹可親的、友好的（ami-朋友）
- **notable** [`notəbəl] *adj.* 顯著的、值得注意的
- **liable** [`laɪəbəl] *adj.* 承擔（法律）責任的；非常可能會發生的
- **vulnerable** [`vʌlnərəbəl] *adj.* 易受傷害的、脆弱的、易受攻擊的

amiable [`emɪəbəl] *adj.* 和藹可親的、友好的（ami-朋友）

She enjoys the amiable atmosphere in her working environment where colleagues help each other.

她很享受工作環境中友好的氣氛，同事們互相幫助。

297 -ible

可以…的

與 -able 同源，表示「可以…的」或是「能夠…的」的意思。

- **accessible** [ək`sɛsəbəl] *adj.* 可接近的、能進入的、易使用的
- **eligible** [`ɛlɪdʒəbəl] *adj.* 有…資格的、具備條件的
- **negligible** [`nɛglɪdʒəbəl] *adj.* 微不足道的、可忽略的
- **plausible** [`plɔzəbəl] *adj.* 看似可行的、貌似有理的

accessible [ək`sɛsəbəl] *adj.* 可接近的、能進入的、易使用的

According to a designer's observation, many buildings in Taiwan still do not have an accessible entrance for the disabled.

根據一位設計師的觀察，臺灣許多建築仍沒有給身障者的易使用入口。

298 -aceous

和…有關

拉丁字尾，指「和…有關」、「有…特性或天性」的意思。

- **carbonaceous** [ˌkɑrbə`neʃəs] *adj.* 含炭的、炭質的
- **crustaceous** [krʌ`steʃəs] *adj.* 外殼的；甲殼類的
- **curvaceous** [kɚ`veʃəs] *adj.* 身材曲線優美的
- **herbaceous** [hɚ`beʃəs] *adj.* 草本的

carbonaceous [ˌkɑrbə`neʃəs] *adj.* 含炭的、炭質的

The carbonaceous rock formation was found but the exploitation kept delayed due to environmental issues.

已發現含炭的岩層，但因環境問題遲遲沒有開採。

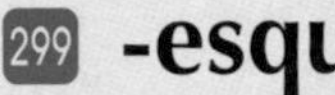

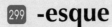

299 -esque

有…特性的

來自法文的詞尾，將名詞轉為形容詞，表示「有…特性的」、「像…的」等意思。

- **grotesque** [gro`tɛsk] *adj.* 怪異的、荒誕的、奇形怪狀的
- **gigantesque** [dʒaɪ`gæn,tɛsk] *adj.* 像巨人的、龐大的
- **Romanesque** [,romə`nɛsk] *adj.* 羅馬式的
- **statuesque** [,stætʃʊ`ɛsk] *adj.* 像雕像的；高挑優雅的

grotesque [gro`tɛsk] *adj.* 怪異的、荒誕的、奇形怪狀的

During a masquerade, people wore grotesque masks walking around and some children were scared.

化裝舞會中，人們戴著奇怪的面具，而有些小孩因此被嚇到了。

300 -form

有…形狀的

源自於拉丁文，表示「有…形狀的」之意。

- **aliform** [`elɪfɔrm] *adj.* 翼狀的
- **cordiform** [`kordə,form] *adj.* 心型的
- **cruciform** [`krusɪfɔrm] *adj.* 十字形的
- **fungiform** [`fʌŋdʒɪfɔrm] *adj.* 蕈狀的

aliform [`elɪfɔrm] *adj.* 翼狀的

They put an aliform decoration on the Christmas tree as a new modelling this year.

他們在聖誕樹上放上一個翼狀的裝飾品，做為今年的造型。

UNIT

26 形容詞字尾

Ine-Ate ▶ MP3 026

301 **-ine**

與…相似

源自於希臘文，表示「與…相似」、「像…的」或「有…特質」的意思。

- **crystalline** [`krɪstəlaɪn] *adj.* 水晶般晶瑩剔透的
- **divine** [dɪ`vaɪn] *adj.* 神的、如神一般的
- **feline** [`filaɪn] *adj.* 貓科的
- **pristine** [`prɪstin] *adj.* 嶄新的、狀態良好的；原始的、純樸的

crystalline [`krɪstəlaɪn] *adj.* 水晶般晶瑩剔透的

He likes the crystalline laugh of his girlfriend and likes to make her laugh.

他喜歡他女友水晶般的笑聲，也喜歡逗她笑。

302 **-ish**

像是…

古英文字尾，指「像是…、接近…」或「有…傾向」之意。

- **lavish** [`lævɪʃ] *adj.* 奢華的；慷慨大方的
- **reddish** [`rɛdɪʃ] *adj.* 略帶紅色的、淡紅色的
- **snobbish** [`snɑbɪʃ] *adj.* 勢利的、愛虛榮的
- **stylish** [`staɪlɪʃ] *adj.* 時髦的、精緻優雅的

lavish [`lævɪʃ] *adj.* 奢華的；慷慨大方的

She was impressed by the lavish party with gorgeous food, but she still felt the emptiness in this event.
她對這場有美味食物的奢華派對印象深刻，但她仍感覺得到其中的空虛。

303 -like

像…一樣

源自於古英文，表示「像…一樣」的意思。

- **childlike** [ˋtʃaɪldlaɪk] *adj.* 孩子般的、純真無邪的
- **dreamlike** [ˋdrimlaɪk] *adj.* 夢幻的、如夢般的
- **ladylike** [ˋledɪlaɪk] *adj.* 淑女般的、端莊的
- **lifelike** [ˋlaɪflaɪk] *adj.* 逼真的

childlike [ˋtʃaɪldlaɪk] *adj.* 孩子般的、純真無邪的

His childlike quality does not disappear even though he has already passed his 40th birthday.
即使他已年過四十，仍保有那股孩子般的特質。

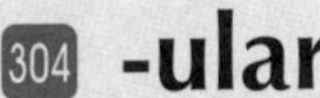

304 -ular

像…的

拉丁字尾，有「像…的」之意，多用在形狀。

- **circular** [ˋsɝkjʊlɚ] *adj.* 圓形的、環形的
- **globular** [ˋglɑbjʊlɚ] *adj.* 球狀的
- **rectangular** [rɛkˋtæŋgjʊlɚ] *adj.* 矩形的、長方形的
- **tubular** [ˋtjubjʊlɚ] *adj.* 管狀的

globular [ˋglɑbjʊlɚ] *adj.* 球狀的

Near a big window hangs a globular campanula she bought from her last trip.
大窗戶旁掛著一個她上次旅行買回來的球形風鈴。

305 -y

有…特質的

源自於希臘文，代表「有…特質的」之意。

- **furry** [`fɝɪ] *adj.* 毛茸茸的
- **gloomy** [`glumɪ] *adj.* 黑暗的；沮喪的、憂愁的
- **rocky** [`rɑkɪ] *adj.* 多岩石的；崎嶇的
- **sandy** [`sændɪ] *adj.* 含沙的

furry [`fɝɪ] *adj.* 毛茸茸的

The little girl has no resistance to any furry cute animal or toy.
小女孩對毛茸茸可愛的小動物或玩具完全沒有抵抗力。

306 -ful

充滿…

源自於古英文，代表「充滿…」的意思。

- **disgraceful** [dɪs`gresfʊl] *adj.* 不光彩的、可恥的
- **fearful** [`fɪɚfʊl] *adj.* 害怕的、擔心恐懼的
- **fruitful** [`frutfʊl] *adj.* 結許多果實的；很有成果的
- **playful** [`plefʊl] *adj.* 有趣的、玩樂心態的、逗著玩的

disgraceful [dɪs`gresfʊl] *adj.* 不光彩的、可恥的

Some old doctors still think that it is disgraceful if their grandchildren do not become a doctor as well.
有些老醫生還是認為他的孫子們不當醫生是很不光彩的。

-ous

充滿…特質的

拉丁字尾，表示「充滿…特質的」之意。

- **ambiguous** [æm`bɪgjʊəs] *adj.* 含糊不清的、模稜兩可的
- **fabulous** [`fæbjʊləs] *adj.* 極好的、絕佳的；虛構的
- **glamorous** [`glæmərəs] *adj.* 迷人的、有魅力的、令人嚮往的
- **notorious** [no`torɪəs] *adj.* 惡名昭彰的

ambiguous [æm`bɪgjʊəs] *adj.* 含糊不清的、模稜兩可的

She is tired of his ambiguous reasons he gave for his travelling all the time.

她已經受不了他每次出去旅行總是給她含糊不清的原因。

-olent, -ulent

充滿…、非常…

源自於拉丁文，表示「充滿…」或「非常…」的意思。

- **feculent** [`fɛkjʊlənt] *adj.* 骯髒的、不潔淨的
- **insolent** [`ɪnsələnt] *adj.* 傲慢無禮的
- **opulent** [`ɑpjʊlənt] *adj.* 奢侈的、豪華的
- **turbulent** [`tɝbjʊlənt] *adj.* 動盪的、混亂的；湍急的、洶湧的

feculent [`fɛkjʊlənt] *adj.* 骯髒的、不潔淨的

My brother walked the dog after a heavy rain, so its feculent feet made a mess in the entrance of the apartment.

我弟弟在一場大雨後去遛狗，所以小狗髒髒的腳在公寓門前弄得一團亂。

309 -acious

有…傾向

源自於拉丁文，代表「有…傾向」、「和…有關」的意思。

- **audacious** [ɔ`deʃəs] *adj.* 大膽的；魯莽的、放肆的
- **capacious** [kə`peʃəs] *adj.* 內部空間大的
- **gracious** [`greʃəs] *adj.* 親切的、有禮貌的、和藹的
- **spacious** [`speʃəs] *adj.* 寬敞的、大空間的

audacious [ɔ`deʃəs] *adj.* 大膽的；魯莽的、放肆的

The newly elected major's audacious policies raised many discussions.

新出任市長大膽的政策引起大眾議論紛紛。

310 -aneous

帶有…性質

拉丁複合式字尾，有「帶有…性質」的意思。

- **instantaneous** [ˌɪnstən`tenɪəs] *adj.* 立即的、瞬間的
- **miscellaneous** [ˌmɪsə`lenɪəs] *adj.* 各式各樣的、混雜的
- **simultaneous** [ˌsɪməl`tenɪəs] *adj.* 同時的
- **spontaneous** [spɑn`tenɪəs] *adj.* 自發的

miscellaneous [ˌmɪsə`lenɪəs] *adj.* 各式各樣的、混雜的

The price's party was full of miscellaneous people from all around the world.

王子的派對裏頭有來自世界各地各種各樣的賓客。

311 **-ar**

和…有關

源自於拉丁文，表示「和…有關」、「有…特性的」。

- **linear** [ˋlɪnɪɚ] *adj.* 直的、線性的
- **muscular** [ˋmʌskjʊlɚ] *adj.* 肌肉的；肌肉發達的、強壯的
- **polar** [ˋpolɚ] *adj.* 兩極的
- **spectacular** [spɛkˋtækjʊlɚ] *adj.* 壯觀的、驚人的；巨大的

linear [ˋlɪnɪɚ] *adj.* 直的、線性的

Not many dances have only linear movements, so a dancer has to be cautious of the direction of each movement.

很少有舞蹈只有直線前進的舞步，因此一名舞者要隨時注意每一步的方向。

312 **-ate**

擁有…特性

拉丁文字尾，代表「擁有…特性」的意思。

- **fortunate** [ˋfɔrtʃənət] *adj.* 幸運的
- **intricate** [ˋɪntrɪkət] *adj.* 錯綜複雜的、難以理解的
- **literate** [ˋlɪtərət] *adj.* 識字的；通曉…的
- **ultimate** [ˋʌltɪmət] *adj.* 最終的、最基礎的、最佳的

intricate [ˋɪntrɪkət] *adj.* 錯綜複雜的、難以理解的

My local friend led me to explore the intricate lanes of the old town in their capital.

我當地的朋友帶我去探索他們首都舊城裡錯綜複雜的巷弄。

UNIT 27 形容詞字尾

Ary-Stic ▶ MP3 027

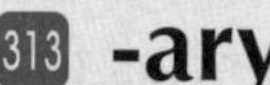

313 -ary

和…有關

拉丁字尾，表示「和…有關」、「有…特性」的意思。

- **arbitrary** [`ɑrbətrərɪ] *adj.* 任意的、隨機的、隨心所欲的；武斷的
- **customary** [`kʌstəmərɪ] *adj.* 慣常的；傳統習俗的
- **disciplinary** [`dɪsəplɪnərɪ] *adj.* 有紀律的
- **unnecessary** [ʌn`nɛsəsərɪ] *adj.* 不需要的、多餘的

arbitrary [`ɑrbətrərɪ] *adj.* 任意的、隨機的、隨心所欲的；武斷的

The choice of representative of each class is arbitrary, so every pupil has to prepare for the possible speech.

每個班級代表是隨機選取的，因此每個學童都要準備可能要上台演講。

314 -ent

和…動作有關

拉丁形容詞字尾，表示「和…動作有關」的意思。

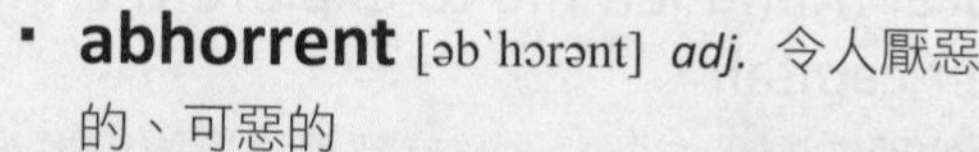

- **abhorrent** [əb`hɔrənt] *adj.* 令人厭惡的、可惡的
- **coherent** [ko`hɪrənt] *adj.* 前後一致的、有條理的、連貫的
- **insentient** [ɪn`sɛnʃənt] *adj.* 無情的、無知覺的
- **reminiscent** [rɛmɪ`nɪsənt] *adj.* 使人想起…的；使回憶起的

abhorrent [əb`hɔrənt] *adj.* 令人厭惡的、可惡的

After coming back from studying aboard, he found the abhorrent racism was so common in his native country.
一趟留學之旅回來後，他發現令他深惡痛絕的種族主義竟在他的家鄉如此常見。

315 **-eous** 有…性質 源自於拉丁文，表示「有…性質」的意思。	▪ **erroneous** [ɪ`ronɪəs] *adj.* 錯誤的、不正確的 ▪ **gorgeous** [`gɔrdʒəs] *adj.* 極其動人的、令人愉悅的 ▪ **homogeneous** [͵hɑmo`dʒinɪəs] *adj.* 同質的、類似的、同類的 ▪ **outrageous** [aʊt`redʒəs] *adj.* 駭人的、令人震驚的、無法接受的

erroneous [ɪ`ronɪəs] *adj.* 錯誤的、不正確的

Insufficient information may lead to an erroneous assumption.
不足的資訊會導致錯誤的設想。

316 **-ial** 和…有關 拉丁字尾，代表「和…有關」、「有…特性」、「與…類似」的意思。	▪ **colloquial** [kə`lokwɪəl] *adj.* 口語的、非正式的 ▪ **crucial** [`kruʃəl] *adj.* 關鍵的、決定性的 ▪ **martial** [`mɑrʃəl] *adj.* 戰爭的、武打的 ▪ **trivial** [`trɪvɪəl] *adj.* 瑣碎的、微不足到的；容易解決的

colloquial [kə`lokwɪəl] *adj.* 口語的、非正式的

Living with local people can learn some colloquial phrases and words.
和當地人一起住會學到很多口語上的字詞。

317 -ic

與…相關的

古希臘字尾，表示「與…相關的」、「有…類似特質的」。

- **allergic** [ə`lɝdʒɪk] *adj.* 過敏（性）的；對…極反感的
- **Arctic** [`ɑrktɪk] *adj.* 北極的
- **ceramic** [sɪ`ræmɪk] *adj.* 瓷的
- **ecstatic** [ɪk`stætɪk] *adj.* 狂喜的、欣喜若狂的

ecstatic [ɪk`stætɪk] *adj.* 狂喜的、欣喜若狂的

Ecstatic fans waited patiently in the airport, hoping to welcome their athletic hero.

欣喜若狂的粉絲們在機場耐心守候，希望能迎接他們的運動英雄。

318 -ical

與…有關

源自於拉丁文，將名詞轉為形容的字尾，表示「與…有關」、「有…特性」或「由…組成的」。

- **periodical** [pɪrɪ`ɑdɪkəl] *adj.* 定期的、間歇的、時而發生的
- **skeptical** [`skɛptɪkəl] *adj.* 持懷疑態度的
- **theoretical** [θɪə`rɛtɪkəl] *adj.* 理論上的
- **vertical** [`vɝtɪkəl] *adj.* 垂直的、豎立的

periodical [pɪrɪ`ɑdɪkəl] *adj.* 定期的、間歇的、時而發生的

There will be periodical review of each staff's working performance in one year.

每年中都會有定期對員工工作表現的審查。

319 -ior

與…有關

拉丁字尾，表示「與…有關」的意思。

- **interior** [ɪn`tɪərɪɚ] *adj.* 內部的
- **prior** [`praɪɚ] *adj.* 事先的、在…之前的
- **superior** [su`pɪərɪɚ] *adj.* 優越的、好於平均的
- **ulterior** [ʌl`tɪrɪɚ] *adj.* 不可告人的

ulterior [ʌl`tɪrɪɚ] *adj.* 不可告人的

His weird question must have an ulterior motive behind it.

他奇怪的問題背後一定有不可告人的動機。

320 -ive

有…特性

源自於拉丁文，表示「有…特性」或「有…傾向」的意思。

- **comprehensive** [kɑmprɪ`hɛnsɪv] *adj.* 全面的、綜合的
- **distinctive** [dɪ`stɪŋktɪv] *adj.* 與眾不同的、獨特的
- **massive** [`mæsɪv] *adj.* 巨大的、大量的
- **subjective** [səb`dʒɛktɪv] *adj.* 主觀的

comprehensive [kɑmprɪ`hɛnsɪv] *adj.* 全面的、綜合的

The cram school promises to offer a comprehensive course package for students.

補習班答應會提供一個綜合的學習課程給學生。

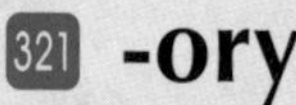

321 -ory

和…有關

拉丁字尾，表示「和…有關」、「與…相似」的意思。

- **compulsory** [kəm`pʌlsərɪ] *adj.* 必須的、強制的
- **contradictory** [kɑntrə`dɪktərɪ] *adj.* 對立的、相互矛盾的
- **obligatory** [ə`blɪgətorɪ] *adj.* 有義務的、強制性的
- **statutory** [`stætʃʊtorɪ] *adj.* 法定的

statutory [`stætʃʊtorɪ] *adj.* 法定的

Farmers wish that there will be statutory control prices for seasonal fruits; otherwise, they sometimes cannot earn much from what they grow.

農民希望當季水果有法定規定價格，否則有時他們根本賺不了錢。

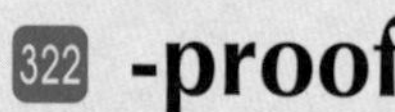

322 -proof

防…的

源自於古英文，表示「不受…的」、「防…的」之意。

- **burglarproof** [`bɝglɚ,pruf] *adj.* 防小偷的
- **childproof** [`tʃaɪldpruf] *adj.* 防兒童使用的
- **fireproof** [`faɪrpruf] *adj.* 防火的
- **waterproof** [`wɑtɚpruf] *adj.* 防水的

burglarproof [`bɝglɚ,pruf] *adj.* 防小偷的

Modern houses and offices are often equipped with burglarproof devices at the entrance.

現代住家或公司大都於入口有防小偷裝置。

323 -some

有…特色的

古英文字尾，表示「有…特色的」、「有…傾向的」。

- **awesome** [ˋɔsəm] *adj.* 令人驚嘆的、令人敬畏的
- **lonesome** [ˋlonsəm] *adj.* 孤獨的、寂寞的
- **quarrelsome** [ˋkwɔrəlsəm] *adj.* 愛爭吵的
- **wholesome** [ˋholsəm] *adj.* 有益的

wholesome [ˋholsəm] *adj.* 有益的

With much more correct ideas, people now take in wholesome food more often.

現在人們有更多正確的觀念，所以更常攝取有益的健康食品。

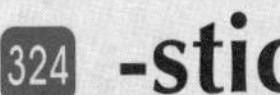

324 -stic

和…有關

古希臘字尾，表示「和…有關」的意思。

- **drastic** [ˋdræstɪk] *adj.* 嚴厲的、猛烈的
- **majestic** [məˋdʒɛstɪk] *adj.* 雄偉的、壯麗的
- **optimistic** [ɑptəˋmɪstɪk] *adj.* 樂觀的
- **realistic** [rɪəˋlɪstɪk] *adj.* 現實的、實事求是的

majestic [məˋdʒɛstɪk] *adj.* 雄偉的、壯麗的

They could not believe that there are such majestic mountains and rivers in this small place.

他們無法相信這麼小的地方有如此雄偉的山川。

增加推測文意的能力，拿到超乎水平的成績

不用每個單字都懂，許多關鍵考點其實能靠上下文就能推測出答案，增加推測文意能力能無形中翻轉考試結果，最終表現出超乎水平的英語實力。

PART 02

・語境記憶・

01 UNIT 精選必考字彙❶

Vocabulary in Context

❶ The newly elected administration has launched an aggressive ________________ for federal counterterrorism in hopes of solidifying national security.
Planning is in the closest meaning to this word.
A. transaction B. prejudice
C. strategy D. disconnection

❷ The research findings about hypnosis healing remain inconclusive and ________________; therefore, the curing method still has a long way to go.
Debatable is in the closest meaning to this word.
A. potential B. anxious
C. magnificent D. controversial

❸ Animal rights groups ________________ to take more drastic measures unless the cosmetic manufactures stopped inhumane animal tests.
Announced is in the closest meaning to this word.
A. claimed B. unraveled
C. surrendered D. liberated

❹ The Internet ________________ among adolescents brought about serious academic and personality problems and has gradually aroused social attention.
Dependence is in the closest meaning to this word.

A. governance　　B. addiction
C. retreat　　D. provocation

❶ 新上任的內閣已經推動積極的國家反恐策略，為的是希望鞏固國家安全。
Planning 的意思最接近於這個字。
A. 交易　　B. 偏見
C. 策略　　D. 中斷

❷ 有關於催眠治療的研究發現依舊是未定且有爭議的；因此，這種治療方式仍有待努力。
Debatable 的意思最接近於這個字。
A. 有潛力的　　B. 焦慮的
C. 壯麗的　　D. 有爭議的

❸ 動物權益團體宣稱，除非化妝品製造廠商停止不人道的動物實驗，否則將採取更激烈的手段，。
Announced 的意思最接近於這個字。
A. 宣稱　　B. 闡明
C. 投降　　D. 解放

❹ 青少年的網路成癮導致嚴重的課業及人格問題，並且逐漸地引發社會關切。
Dependence 的意思最接近於這個字。
A. 管理　　B. 上癮
C. 撤退　　D. 挑釁

答案 ❶ C　❷ D　❸ A　❹ B

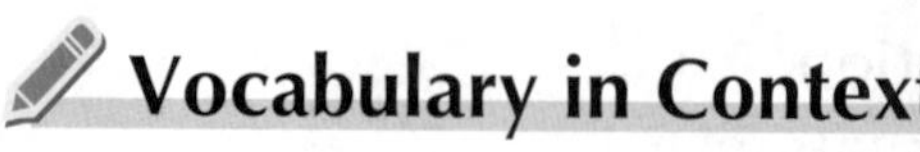

Vocabulary in Context

❺ Thanks to the decreased costs of 3D printers, the technology of the three- dimensional printing has recently gained ________________ among different fields of industry.
Prevalence is in the closest meaning to this word.
A. richness B. popularity
C. manipulation D. capability

❻ The financial institution posted an advertisement to offer jobs for business school graduates with ________________ consciousness and abilities.
Creative is in the closest meaning to this word.
A. rigid B. innovative
C. optional D. retrospective

❼ Young generations should be taught from their early childhood to practice the 3R ________________ – Reduce, Reuse, and Recycle to protect and sustain the earth.
Regulations is in the closest meaning to this word.
A. Groups B. Facilities
C. Principles D. Restrictions

❽ Mr. Banks is a lawyer ________________ in criminal laws and is dedicated to defending against criminal charges.
Professionalized is in the closest meaning to this word.
A. franchised B. managed
C. abolished D. specialized

❺ 幸虧有 3D 立體印刷機的降價，3D 立體印刷科技近日在各個不同產業領域受到歡迎。
Prevalence 的意思最接近於這個字。

A. 財富　　B. 受歡迎
C. 操弄　　D. 能力

❻ 這家經融機構刊登職缺廣告來徵求具創新意識及能力的商學院畢業生。
Creative 的意思最接近於這個字。

A. 僵化的　　B. 創新的
C. 可選擇的　　D. 回顧的

❼ 年輕世代應從小被教導力行 3R 原則 — 減量、重複使用，以及回收，以保護並延續地球。
Regulations 的意思最接近於這個字。

A. 團體　　B. 設施
C. 原則　　D. 限制

❽ 班克斯先生是一名專精於刑事訴訟法的律師，並致力於刑事訴訟的辯護。
Professionalized 的意思最接近於這個字。

A. 加盟　　B. 設法
C. 廢除　　D. 專攻

答案 ❺ B　❻ B　❼ C　❽ D

Vocabulary in Context

❾ The dazzling northern lights, also called "the aurora borealis," display one of nature's greatest spectacles, and are ________________ to only certain regions in Canada, Scotland, Norway, and Sweden.
Special is in the closest meaning to this word.
A. unique B. conceptual
C. practical D. invisible

❿ After surviving the horrible plane crash, Pamela came to realize the value of life and was ________________ to social charity causes.
Changed is in the closest meaning to this word.
A. emigrated B. navigated
C. improved D. converted

⓫ The refined merchandise exhibited in the Trade Fair last month was ________________ by Morrison Company and has received great numbers of orders since then.
Produced is in the closest meaning to this word.
A. approached B. combined
C. manufactured D. rejected

⓬ The rich and renowned CEO remained modest and was ________________ about charitable affairs by donating millions of dollars each year.
Zealous is in the closest meaning to this word.
A. violent B. indifferent
C. popular D. enthusiastic

❾ 炫目的極北之光，又稱為「北極光」，展現大自然絕佳的奇觀之一，並且是加拿大、蘇格蘭、挪威，及瑞典特定地區獨具的景觀。

Special 的意思最接近於這個字。

A. 獨特的　　B. 概念的
C. 實際的　　D. 隱形的

❿ 潘蜜拉在可怕的墜機事件倖存後，領悟到生命的可貴，並轉而致力於社會慈善工作。

Changed 的意思最接近於這個字。

A. 移民　　B. 航行
C. 改善　　D. 轉變

⓫ 上個月在貿易展展示的優質商品是由莫里森公司所製造的，並從那時起接獲大量的訂單。

Produced 的意思最接近於這個字。

A. 接近　　B. 結合
C. 製造　　D. 排斥

⓬ 這位富有且著名的執行長依舊保持謙遜的態度，並且熱心於每年捐贈數百萬元贊助慈善事業。

Zealous 的意思最接近於這個字。

A. 暴力的　　B. 冷淡的
C. 受歡迎的　　D. 熱忱的

答案 ❾ A　❿ D　⓫ C　⓬ D

02 UNIT 精選必考字彙❷

Vocabulary in Context

❶ It is ________________ that producing books in hard copy format may bring several million tons of harmful CO2 into the atmosphere, so E-books are definitely here to stay.
Calculated is in the closest meaning to this word.
A. rebelled B. estimated
C. undertaken D. humiliated

❷ According to neuroscientists, ________________ 20 percent of short-term memory can be improved by regular physical exercise, especially to the elderly.
Roughly is in the closest meaning to this word.
A. recently B. approximately
C. perpetually D. ironically

❸ With ________________ pop music superstars creating extraordinary performances, Korean pop music trend has prevailed worldwide.
Talented is in the closest meaning to this word.
A. mandatory B. economical
C. renewable D. versatile

❹ Music, with its functions of offering soothing feelings and full relaxation, remains a ________________ language for

all times.
General is in the closest meaning to this word.

A. separate　　B. constructive
C. defiant　　D. universal

❶ 據估計，製造硬皮書籍可能將數百萬公噸有害的二氧化碳氣體帶入大氣層，所以電子書當然應該普遍推廣。
Calculated 的意思最接近於這個字。

A. 反叛　　B. 估計
C. 從事　　D. 羞辱

❷ 根據神經科學家的說法，將近百分之二十短暫的記憶可以經由規律的體能運動得到改善，尤其是對老年人而言。
Roughly 的意思最接近於這個字。

A. 近來　　B. 將近
C. 永久地　　D. 諷刺地

❸ 有著多才多藝流行音樂超級巨星創造傑出的表演，韓國流行音樂的潮流遍及全世界。
Talented 的意思最接近於這個字。

A. 命令的　　B. 節約的
C. 可更新的　　D. 多才多藝的

❹ 音樂，具有提供舒緩情緒及全面放鬆的功用，一直以來是一個世界性的語言。
General 的意思最接近於這個字。

A. 分隔的　　B. 積極的
C. 違抗的　　D. 全世界的

答案    
❶B　❷B　❸D　❹D

Vocabulary in Context

❺ Some extreme-sports enthusiasts are capable of achieving difficult and challenging extreme tasks with ________________ perfection.

Unbelievable is in the closest meaning to this word.

A. synthetic B. luxurious

C. incredible D. thorny

❻ Due to wide ________________ of public opinion, the political figure caught in a dilemma had a hard time getting away from the scandal.

Changes is in the closest meaning to this word.

A. variations B. solitude

C. approaches D. isolation

❼ The company has recently renewed the computer software, and is working on tests to make sure the new system will be ________________ with the existing apparatus.

Agreeable is in the closest meaning to this word.

A. sympathetic B. experimental

C. compatible D. interruptible

❽ Martin has lived in comfort and luxury ever since he made successful ________________ investments and piled up a considerable fortune.

Pecuniary is in the closest meaning to this word.

A. financial B. profound

C. superstitious D. awkward

❺ 有些極限運動的愛好者有能力以令人難以置信的完美方式達成艱困且具挑戰性的極限任務。

Unbelievable 的意思最接近於這個字。

A. 綜合的　B. 奢華的

C. 令人難以置信的　D. 棘手的

❻ 由於輿論的眾説紛紜，這位深陷進退兩難困境的政治人物很難從醜聞中脱身。

Changes 的意思最接近於這個字。

A. 變化　B. 孤獨

C. 方法　D. 隔離

❼ 這家公司最近更新了電腦軟體，並正在測試以確保新的系統與現有的裝置相容。

Agreeable 的意思最接近於這個字。

A. 同情的　B. 實驗的

C. 相容的　D. 可中斷的

❽ 馬汀自從金融投資成功且積聚可觀的財富後，一直過著舒適奢華的生活。

Pecuniary 的意思最接近於這個字。

A. 金融的　B. 深奧的

C. 迷信的　D. 笨拙的

答案 ❺ C ❻ A ❼ C ❽ A

Vocabulary in Context

⑨ Most volunteers are delighted to help needy people, for they can not only learn useful skills to prepare them for work but mainly ________________ great pleasure from doing it.
Obtain is in the closest meaning to this word.

A. justify　　B. abandon
C. multiply　　D. derive

⑩ It's predictable that the confrontation will persistently go on since the management and the ________________ failed to reach any satisfactory agreement.
Workers is in the closest meaning to this word.

A. executives　　B. individuals
C. employees　　D. retailers

⑪ Mrs. Newman planned to move to the countryside, following her doctor's advice that the rural environment might lead to the ________________ of her health.
Recovery is in the closest meaning to this word.

A. stimulation　　B. contribution
C. restoration　　D. introduction

⑫ Given that dust storms have been ________________ in huge amounts with greater forces, scientists all over the world are working on the causes and the solutions.
Created is in the closest meaning to this word.

A. accompanied　　B. produced
C. summoned　　D. degenerated

❾ 大多數的志工樂於幫助貧困的人，目的不僅在於學習職場技能，主要是能從中得到極大的樂趣。
Obtain 的意思最接近於這個字。

A. 辯護　B. 拋棄
C. 成倍增加　D. 獲得

❿ 由於管理階層和員工無法達成任何滿意的共識，雙方將會持續地抗爭是可預期的
Workers 的意思最接近於這個字。

A. 主管　B. 個人
C. 員工　D. 零售商

⓫ 遵循醫生所提出關於鄉村環境有助於恢復健康的勸告，紐曼太太計畫搬到鄉下去居住。
Recovery 的意思最接近於這個字。

A. 刺激　B. 貢獻
C. 復原　D. 介紹

⓬ 考慮到沙塵暴以更強的威力大量地成形中，世界各地的科學家正努力於探討成因及解決之道。
Created 的意思最接近於這個字。

A. 陪伴　B. 生產
C. 召喚　D. 衰退

答案 ❾ D　❿ C　⓫ C　⓬ B

03 UNIT 精選必考字彙❸

Vocabulary in Context

❶ During the process of brainstorming, several __________________ solutions to the thorny problem were eventually worked out.
Useful is in the closest meaning to this word.
A. practical B. rectangular
C. superficial D. competitive

❷ The sudden collapse of the bridge during the rush hour was the major cause of the severe __________________ to the commuters and passers-by.
Damage is in the closest meaning to this word.
A. continuity B. illnesses
C. magnitude D. injuries

❸ Cathy had a hard time writing her thesis, for her professor requested that she should __________________ her argument with more exact and innovative points of view.
Strengthen is in the closest meaning to this word.
A. reinforce B. correspond
C. meditate D. familiarize

❹ Luke __________________ on the idea that people should protect rare and extinct animals, and he constantly sponsored campaigns of the kind.

Held is in the closest meaning to this word.

A. commenced　　B. fastened
C. negotiated　　D. ridiculed

❶ 腦力激盪的過程中，數種解決這個棘手問題的實用方案終於被激盪出來。

Useful 的意思最接近於這個字。

A. 實用的　　B. 矩形的
C. 膚淺的　　D. 競爭的

❷ 在交通尖峰期間，橋梁突然的倒塌是造成通勤族和行人嚴重傷害的主因。

Damage 的意思最接近於這個字。

A. 持續　　B. 疾病
C. 強度　　D. 傷害

❸ 凱西寫論文寫得很辛苦，因為她的教授要求她應該使用更確切且更創新的觀點來加強論證。

Strengthen 的意思最接近於這個字。

A. 加強　　B. 通信
C. 沉思　　D. 熟悉

❹ 路克堅持於人們應該保護稀有瀕臨絕種動物的想法，並且時常贊助此種類型的活動。

Held 的意思最接近於這個字。

A. 開始　　B. 堅持
C. 協商　　D. 揶揄

答案 ❶A　❷D　❸A　❹B

Vocabulary in Context

❺ The private art gallery, seemingly a building of small scale, had an ________________ large collection of Oriental and Western paintings.
Surprisingly is in the closest meaning to this word.
A. eventually B. amazingly
C. inevitably D. automatically

❻ The company aimed at recruiting new staff members familiar with international trade and fluent with Japanese, since the Japanese market ________________ 40% of its revenue.
Occupied is in the closest meaning to this word.
A. prescribed B. explored
C. accounted for D. restrained

❼ It's amazing that nowadays consumers can ________________ almost anything through shopping websites on the Internet.
Buy is in the closest meaning to this word.
A. purchase B. adopt
C. rehearse D. coordinate

❽ Electronic products ________________ from Japan have always received great welcome because they tend to be functional and durable.
Introduced is in the closest meaning to this word.
A. imported B. settled
C. appreciated D. vaccinated

❺ 這間私人經營的藝術畫廊，表面上似乎是座小規模的建築，卻有著驚人數量東西方畫作的收藏。

Surprisingly 的意思最接近於這個字。

A. 最終地　B. 驚人地

C. 無可避免地　D. 自動地

❻ 由於日本市場佔了公司收入的百分之四十，這家公司的目標是招募熟悉國際貿易以及精通日語的新職員。

Occupied 的意思最接近於這個字。

A. 開藥方　B. 探索

C. 佔…　D. 限制

❼ 今日而言，消費者能夠透過網際網路的購物網站購買得到幾乎任何東西是很驚人的。

Buy 的意思最接近於這個字。

A. 購買　B. 採用

C. 預演　D. 協調

❽ 從日本進口的電子產品一向大受歡迎，因為他們的產品既實用又耐用。

Introduced 的意思最接近於這個字。

A. 進口　B. 定居

C. 欣賞　D. 接種疫苗

答案 ❺B ❻C ❼A ❽A

Vocabulary in Context

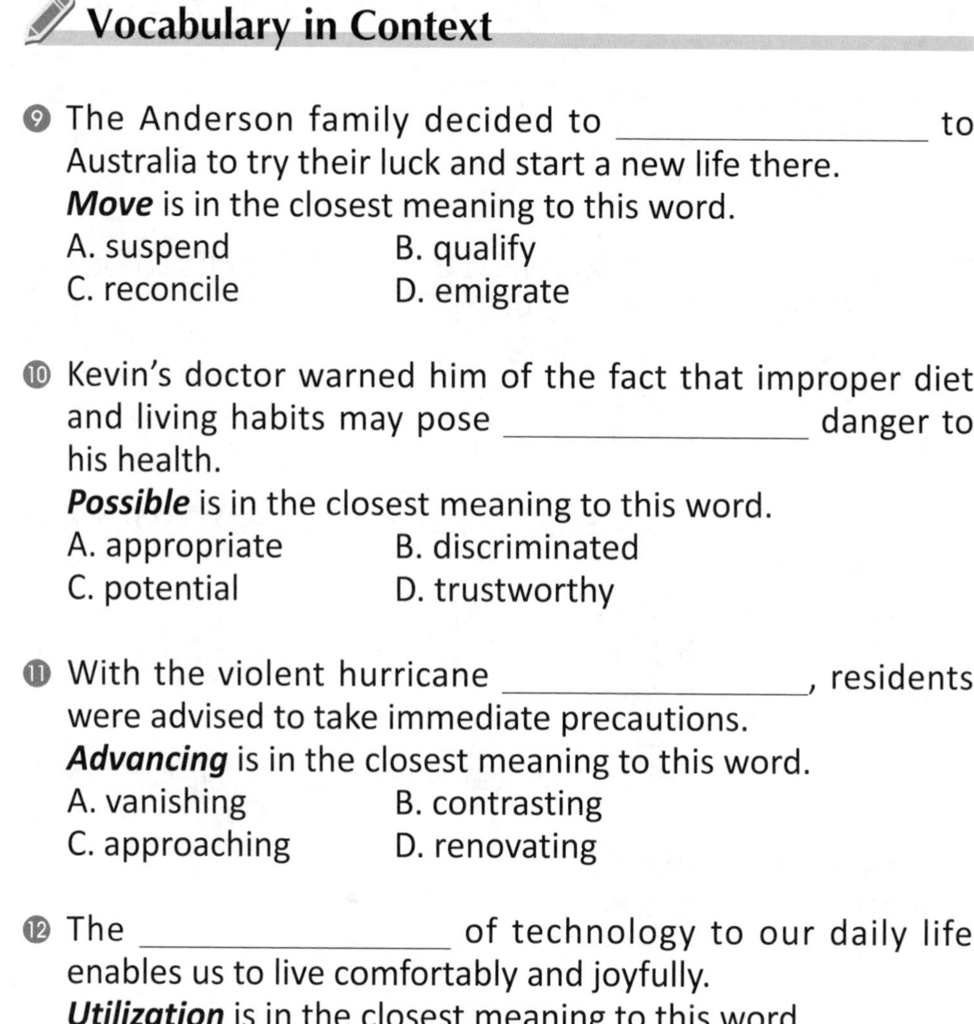

⑨ The Anderson family decided to ________________ to Australia to try their luck and start a new life there.
Move is in the closest meaning to this word.
A. suspend B. qualify
C. reconcile D. emigrate

⑩ Kevin's doctor warned him of the fact that improper diet and living habits may pose ________________ danger to his health.
Possible is in the closest meaning to this word.
A. appropriate B. discriminated
C. potential D. trustworthy

⑪ With the violent hurricane ________________, residents were advised to take immediate precautions.
Advancing is in the closest meaning to this word.
A. vanishing B. contrasting
C. approaching D. renovating

⑫ The ________________ of technology to our daily life enables us to live comfortably and joyfully.
Utilization is in the closest meaning to this word.
A. glamour B. sophistication
C. monotony D. application

❾ 安德森一家人決定移民到澳洲去謀求發展並試圖在那裡展開新生活。

Move 的意思最接近於這個字。

A. 懸掛　　B. 合格

C. 妥協　　D. 移民

❿ 凱文的醫生警告他不適當的飲食以及生活習慣可能對他的健康造成潛在的危險。

Possible 的意思最接近於這個字。

A. 適當的　　B. 歧視的

C. 潛在的D. 值得信賴的

⓫ 隨著猛烈颶風的逼近，居民被建議採取立即的預防措施。

Advancing 的意思最接近於這個字。

A. 消失　　B. 對照

C. 接近　　D. 整修

⓬ 把科技運用於我們的日常生活中促使我們能夠過著舒適及享受的生活。

Utilization 的意思最接近於這個字。

A. 魅力　　B. 世故

C. 單調　　D. 應用

答案 ❾ D　❿ C　⓫ C　⓬ D

精選必考字彙④

Vocabulary in Context

❶ Irene had better watch out for those of her gossip friends who may once in a while ________________ rumors about her.
Scatter is in the closest meaning to this word.
A. decorate　　B. spread
C. pacify　　D. experience

❷ At the present time, scientists spare no efforts to find resources of the alternative energy to substitute for the fossil fuels ________________ by industry.
Exhausted is in the closest meaning to this word.
A. occurred　　B. consumed
C. represented　　D. prospered

❸ After most of its safety ________________ failed to meet the standards, the mall was seriously penalized, and had to make immediate improvement.
Examination is in the closest meaning to this word.
A. motivation　　B. inspections
C. purification　　D. concessions

❹ Compared with others, people tortured by depression ________________ need more care and attention, for they don't easily reveal their emotional problems.
Comparatively is in the closest meaning to this word.

A. viciously　　B. competently
C. relatively　　D. punctually

❶ 艾琳最好要小心她那群偶爾會散播有關於她謠言的八卦朋友。
Scatter 的意思最接近於這個字。
A. 裝飾　　B. 散播
C. 平和　　D. 經歷

❷ 目前來說，科學家們不遺餘力地尋找替代能源的資源來取代工業所消耗的化石燃料。
Exhausted 的意思最接近於這個字。
A. 發生　　B. 消耗
C. 代表　　D. 繁榮

❸ 在大部分的安全檢驗無法符合標準之後，這個大賣場被嚴厲地處罰，並且必須做立即的改善。
Examination 的意思最接近於這個字。
A. 動機　　B. 檢查
C. 淨化　　D. 讓步

❹ 和一般人比較起來，為憂鬱症所苦的人相對地需要更多的關心和注意，因為他們不輕易地透露他們的情緒問題。
Comparatively 的意思最接近於這個字。
A. 邪惡地　　B. 勝任地
C. 相對地　　D. 準時地

答案 ❶ B　❷ B　❸ B　❹ C

Vocabulary in Context

❺ To keep healthy, one should be careful not to consume too much the food that ________________ additives, such as preservatives, coloring, or artificial flavorings.
Includes is in the closest meaning to this word.

A. contains B. digests
C. huddles D. transforms

❻ The manager informed the factory that they might ________________ or even cancel the original ordes if the goods shipped in continued to be in poor quality.
Reduce is in the closest meaning to this word.

A. resolve B. approve
C. withhold D. decrease

❼ To make both ends meet, Roy had no choice but to take several part-time jobs to ________________ additional income.
Produce is in the closest meaning to this word.

A. despise B. supervise
C. generate D. overlook

❽ The magician's ________________ performances attracted full attention of the audience and won him long and loud applause.
Wonderful is in the closest meaning to this word.

A. marvelous B. exclusive
C. reckless D. feasible

❺ 為了維持健康，人們應該小心不要吃太多含有添加物的食物，例如：防腐劑、色素，或者人工調味料。
Includes 的意思最接近於這個字。
A. 包含　　B. 消化
C. 蜷縮　　D. 轉變

❻ 經理通知工廠，假使進貨的商品仍舊品質不良的話，他們會減少或甚至取消原有的訂單。
Reduce 的意思最接近於這個字。
A. 下定決心　　B. 贊同
C. 阻擋　　D. 減少

❼ 為了收支均衡，羅伊不得不兼職數份兼差的工作來賺取額外的收入。
Produce 的意思最接近於這個字。
A. 鄙視　　B. 監督
C. 產生　　D. 忽略

❽ 魔術師奇妙的表演吸引全場觀眾的目光，並且為自己贏得許久響亮的喝采聲。
Wonderful 的意思最接近於這個字。
A. 奇妙的　　B. 獨家的
C. 粗率的　　D. 可行的

答案 ❺A ❻D ❼C ❽A

Vocabulary in Context

❾ People who ________________ from a migraine headache can relieve the pain effectively by all forms of relaxation, a lot of water-drinking, or keeping away from noises and bright lights.

Torture is in the closest meaning to this word.

A. guarantee B. suffer
C. proceed D. investigate

❿ Mr. Cosby had a serious cold and coughed a lot; thus, he could hardly ________________ anything because of the painful throat.

Gulp is in the closest meaning to this word.

A. fumble B. console
C. swallow D. nominate

⓫ The movie adapted from a novel was disappointing to the moviegoers because they could hardly find any ________________ between the two.

Correspondence is in the closest meaning to this word.

A. insistence B. metabolism
C. integrity D. consistency

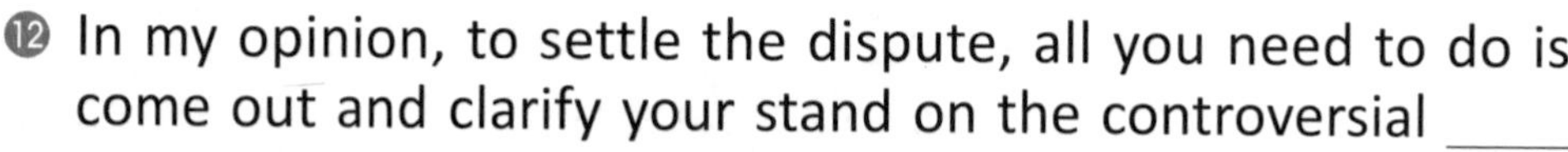

⓬ In my opinion, to settle the dispute, all you need to do is come out and clarify your stand on the controversial ________________.

Problem is in the closest meaning to this word.

A. vacancy B. issue
C. revision D. diagnosis

❾ 罹患偏頭痛的人可以藉由各種放鬆的方式，喝大量的水，或遠離噪音及亮光來有效地紓緩疼痛。
Torture 的意思最接近於這個字。

A. 保證　　B. 受苦
C. 行進　　D. 調查

❿ 寇斯比先生由於嚴重的感冒加上咳嗽咳得厲害，以致於喉嚨疼痛而無法吞嚥任何東西。
Gulp 的意思最接近於這個字。

A. 摸索　　B. 安慰
C. 吞嚥　　D. 提名

⓫ 這部由小說改編的電影讓電影觀賞者感到失望，因為他們幾乎找不出兩者間情節相符之處。
Correspondence 的意思最接近於這個字。

A. 堅持　　B. 新陳代謝
C. 廉潔　　D. 一致性

⓬ 依我之見，為了解決紛爭，你所必須做的是出面並澄清你對於這個具有爭議性議題的立場。
Problem 的意思最接近於這個字。

A. 空缺　　B. 議題
C. 修訂　　D. 診斷

答案 ❾ B　❿ C　⓫ D　⓬ B

精選必考字彙❺

Vocabulary in Context

❶ After a long separation from each other since senior high, Julie had a surprising and pleasant ________________ with Alex.
Meeting is in the closest meaning to this word.
A. machinery B. encounter
C. reputation D. assortment

❷ It is imperative that we humans put emphasis on ecological ________________ and set up as many wildlife reserves as we can.
Protection is in the closest meaning to this word.
A. authority B. frustration
C. tranquility D. preservation

❸ As an optimistic and diligent college graduate, James is willing to explore a new working field and take up ________________ tasks.
Confronting is in the closest meaning to this word.
A. challenging B. stubborn
C. prompt D. easy-going

❹ The world surrounding us is a seriously ________________ one, and we must take precautions to cope with the global ecological crisis.

Polluted is in the closest meaning to this word.

A. released　　　　B. outdated
C. contaminated　　D. engaged

❶ 自從高中彼此分開一段長時間後，茱莉和艾力克斯有一次驚喜且愉快的邂逅。
Meeting 的意思最接近於這個字。
A. 機械　　　B. 偶遇
C. 名譽　　　D. 分類

❷ 我們人類現在急需要做的是重視生態保育並且盡可能多設置野生動物保護區。
Protection 的意思最接近於這個字。
A. 權威　　　B. 挫折
C. 寧靜　　　D. 保存

❸ 身為一名樂觀且勤奮的大學畢業生，詹姆斯很樂意去探索新的工作領域並承擔具挑戰性的任務。
Confronting 的意思最接近於這個字。
A. 挑戰的　　B. 固執的
C. 快速的　　D. 隨和的

❹ 環繞在我們周遭的是一個嚴重污染的世界，我們必須採取預防措施來對抗全球的生態危機。
Polluted 的意思最接近於這個字。
A. 釋放的　　B. 過時的
C. 汙染的　　D. 忙於…的

❶ B　❷ D　❸ A　❹ C

Vocabulary in Context

❺ Scientists are ______________ robots with multiple functions to provide services that can meet varied needs of all the users.
Producing is in the closest meaning to this word.
A. developing B. objecting
C. hallmarking D. perishing

❻ The applicant's additional language skills and working experience definitely ______________ the chance of being employed.
Add is in the closest meaning to this word.
A. abbreviate B. increase
C. occupy D. withstand

❼ To ______________ the risk of clogged arteries and heart attacks, one had better get away from trans fats, which may cause the rise of cholesterol in the blood.
Decrease is in the closest meaning to this word.
A. reduce B. accumulate
C. conclude D. utilize

❽ Jason's bossy character and his wish to ______________ over others make him the least popular person among all.
Control is in the closest meaning to this word.
A. dominate B. accommodate
C. prevent D. segregate

❺ 科學家正在研發具多重功用的機器人以提供服務來滿足所有使用者各種不同的需求。

Producing 的意思最接近於這個字。

A. 發展　　B. 反對

C. 標記　　D. 滅亡

❻ 這名應徵者額外的語言技能和工作經驗必定可以使他增加被僱用的機會。

Add 的意思最接近於這個字。

A. 縮寫　　B. 增加

C. 佔據　　D. 抵抗

❼ 為了降低動脈堵塞及心臟病發生的風險，人們最好遠離會導致血液中膽固醇提高的反式脂肪。

Decrease 的意思最接近於這個字。

A. 減少　　B. 累積

C. 下結論　　D. 利用

❽ 傑森愛指使人的個性以及總是喜歡控制別人的作風，使他成為所有人當中最不受歡迎的一個。

Control 的意思最接近於這個字。

A. 統治　　B. 容納

C. 預防　　D. 隔離

答案 ❺A ❻B ❼A ❽A

Vocabulary in Context

❾ Due to the continuous bad selling condition, the company ________________ that a certain percentage of the staff members had to be laid off.
Announced is in the closest meaning to this word.
A. cultivated B. migrated
C. declared D. submitted

❿ The poor financial management of Mr. Smith's enterprise was responsible for his unfortunate ________________ in the end.
Failure is in the closest meaning to this word.
A. achievement B. recommendation
C. innocence D. bankruptcy

⓫ It's essential for every global villager to keep it in mind that we all should undertake the ________________ to protect the environment for our future generations.
Duty is in the closest meaning to this word.
A. structure B. obligation
C. hospitality D. irrigation

⓬ Dr. Martin Luther King Jr.'s ________________ of non-violence in struggling against racial discrimination and segregation won him the utmost respect from the world.
Maintenance is in the closest meaning to this word.
A. shortcoming B. opportunity
C. probation D. advocacy

❾ 由於不良的銷售狀況持續地發生，這家公司宣佈特定比例的職員必須被裁員。
Announced 的意思最接近於這個字。
A. 培養　B. 遷徙
C. 宣佈　D. 投降

❿ 企業不良的財政營運狀況導致史密斯先生最終不幸面臨破產。
Failure 的意思最接近於這個字。
A. 成就　B. 推薦
C. 無辜　D. 破產

⓫ 每位地球村的居民必定要謹記在心：我們都應該為後代子孫承擔起保護環境的義務。
Duty 的意思最接近於這個字。
A. 結構　B. 義務
C. 好客　D. 灌溉

⓬ 馬丁・路德・金恩博士在對抗種族歧視和隔離政策所倡導非暴力的方式為他贏得世人最崇高的敬意。
Maintenance 的意思最接近於這個字。
A. 缺點　B. 機會
C. 緩刑　D. 倡導

答案 ❾ C　❿ D　⓫ B　⓬ D

06 UNIT 精選必考字彙❻

Vocabulary in Context

❶. Jeremy Lin ________________ himself as a humble and prominent Asian American NBA player.
Differentiates is in the closest meaning to this word.
A. laments B. distinguishes
C. installs D. tolerates

❷ To reduce the impact of global warming on humans, researches and scientists all over the world are developing alternative energy ________________.
Assets is in the closest meaning to this word.
A. equipment B. resources
C. prosecution D. assurances

❸ The reckless truck driver, talking on the cell phone while driving, wasn't ________________ of the approaching car and got crashed.
Conscious is in the closest meaning to this word.
A. iconic B. silent
C. aware D. complacent

❹ All those present were bothered by the intruder, who both inappropriately dressed himself and rudely behaved on the solemn ________________.
Circumstance is in the closest meaning to this word.

A. calamity　　B. suburb
C. occasion　　D. moderation

❶ 林書豪以身為一名謙遜且傑出的美籍亞裔 NBA 球員獨樹一格。
Differentiates 的意思最接近於這個字。
A. 哀嘆　　B. 顯出特色
C. 安裝　　D. 忍受

❷ 為了要減少全球暖化對人類所造成的衝擊，世界各地的研究學者和科學家正在研發替代能源。
Assets 的意思最接近於這個字。
A. 設備　　B. 資源
C. 起訴　　D. 保證

❸ 這位粗心的卡車司機邊開車邊講手機，沒有意識到前來的車輛而撞車。
Conscious 的意思最接近於這個字。
A. 圖像的　　B. 沉默的
C. 有意識的　　D. 自滿的

❹ 所有出席這個莊重場合的人皆受到這位穿著不合宜且行為粗魯的入侵者的干擾。
Circumstance 的意思最接近於這個字。
A. 災難　　B. 郊區
C. 場合　　D. 適度

答案 ❶ B　❷ B　❸ C　❹ C

Vocabulary in Context

❺ To fill the growing ________________ for their merchandise, the workers of the factory were required to work overtime.

Need is in the closest meaning to this word.

A. discount　　B. notification
C. demand　　D. nomination

❻ Though careful with the budget, with the soaring high living costs, Michael's expenses invariably ________________ his income every month.

Surpassed is in the closest meaning to this word.

A. exceeded　　B. subsidized
C. conquered　　D. immigrated

❼ Alexander Bell had a highly ________________ mind. After making many years of experiments, in 1876, his "talking machine," the telephone, finally came out and changed people's lives.

Creative is in the closest meaning to this word.

A. cooperative　　B. disastrous
C. inventive　　D. reliable

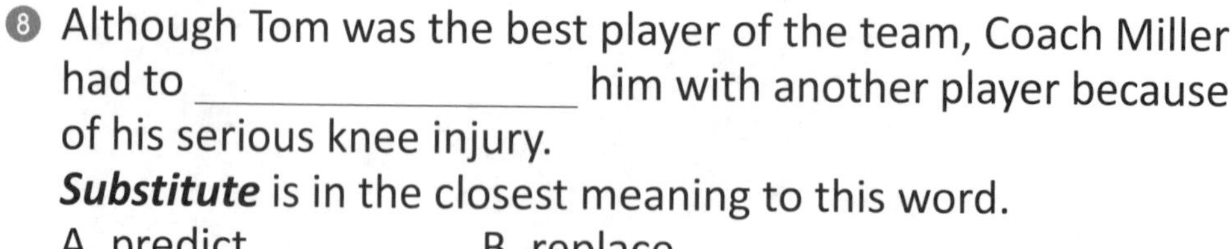

❽ Although Tom was the best player of the team, Coach Miller had to ________________ him with another player because of his serious knee injury.

Substitute is in the closest meaning to this word.

A. predict　　B. replace
C. litter　　D. conflict

❺ 為了要應付他們商品數量逐漸增加的需求，工廠員工被要求加班。
Need 的意思最接近於這個字。

A. 打折　　B. 通知
C. 需求　　D. 提名

❻ 雖然小心翼翼地做預算，但隨著生活費用的高升，麥可每個月必定入不敷出。
Surpassed 的意思最接近於這個字。

A. 超過　　B. 補助
C. 征服　　D. 遷入

❼ 亞歷山大・貝爾擁有高度發明的創意。經過多年實驗之後，在 1876 年，他那部"會講話的機器"，也就是電話，終於問世並且改變了人類的生活。
Creative 的意思最接近於這個字。

A. 合作的　　B. 毀滅的
C. 發明的　　D. 可靠的

❽ 儘管湯姆是球隊中最好的球員，由於他的膝蓋嚴重受傷，米勒教練不得不以另一名球員取代他。
Substitute 的意思最接近於這個字。

A. 預測　　B. 取代
C. 亂丟　　D. 衝突

答案 ❺ C ❻ A ❼ C ❽ B

Vocabulary in Context

❾ On Christmas, every household decorates their Christmas trees and the house will be ________________ with the twinkling lights, adding warmth and joy to the atmosphere. ***Bright*** is in the closest meaning to this word.

A. confident　　B. stressful
C. brilliant　　D. panoramic

❿ As soon as the renowned company posted an advertisement of a position for a manager, a large number of qualified jobseekers ________________ for the job.
Administered is in the closest meaning to this word.

A. applied　　B. disobeyed
C. monitored　　D. transferred

⓫ In different countries, all kinds of hand gestures ________________ varied hints; thus, to avoid offending others, tourists had better look into them first.
Express is in the closest meaning to this word.

A. admire　　B. stimulate
C. convey　　D. reconfirm

⓬ It still remains a mystery that just how certain people possessing the special ability to generate electricity should have the ________________ power.
Unusual is in the closest meaning to this word.

A. harmful　　B. unemployed
C. classical　　D. extraordinary

❾ 耶誕節時，每個家庭裝飾耶誕樹，房子因閃閃發亮的燈飾而明亮，增添了溫馨歡樂的氣氛。
Bright 的意思最接近於這個字。
A. 自信的　　B. 有壓力的
C. 明亮的　　D. 全景的

❿ 這間聲譽卓越的公司一張貼徵求經理職位的廣告，大批符合資格的求職者前來申請這個工作。
Administered 的意思最接近於這個字。
A. 申請　　B. 反抗
C. 監督　　D. 移轉

⓫ 在不同的國家中，各種手勢傳達不同的暗示；因此，為了避免冒犯他人，觀光客最好事先做了解。
Express 的意思最接近於這個字。
A. 仰慕　　B. 刺激
C. 傳達　　D. 再確定

⓬ 某些擁有產生電力能力的人士究竟是如何能夠具有此特殊的本領依舊是一個謎。
Unusual 的意思最接近於這個字。
A. 傷害的　　B. 失業的
C. 經典的　　D. 非凡的

答案 ❾ C　❿ A　⓫ C　⓬ D

07 UNIT 精選必考字彙❼

Vocabulary in Context

❶ When writing his doctoral thesis, Frank made good use of the ________________ facilities in the school library and finally got graduated with honors.
Obtainable is in the closest meaning to this word.
A. chaotic　　B. available
C. religious　　D. paradoxical

❷ In ________________, when asking someone for help while you travel in Europe, you may speak English. However, the local people will be much pleasant if you ask in their language.
Common is in the closest meaning to this word.
A. general　　B. memory
C. advance　　D. circulation

❸. We are fortunate to live in an era of convenience and information. Through the far-reaching Internet, we can easily get ________________ with the world.
Linked is in the closest meaning to this word.
A. connected　　B. delayed
C. submerged　　D. organized

❹ Online shoppers always find themselves get attracted by the dazzling ________________ advertisements and increase the unnecessary spending.

Mercantile is in the closest meaning to this word.

A. vulnerable　　B. idiomatic
C. commercial　　D. reluctant

❶ 法蘭克在寫博士論文時，善用學校圖書館裡可利用的設備，並在最後以優異的成績畢業。

Obtainable 的意思最接近於這個字。

A. 混亂的　　B. 可利用的
C. 宗教的　　D. 自相矛盾的

❷ 一般而言，在歐洲旅遊時，你可以使用英語向他人請求幫助。然而，假使你使用他們的語言，當地人會更樂於提供協助。

Common 的意思最接近於這個字。

A. 一般　　B. 記憶
C. 預先　　D. 循環

❸ 我們很幸運地生活在一個資訊便利的時代。經由無遠弗屆的網際網路，我們可以很輕易地和世界接軌。

Linked 的意思最接近於這個字。

A. 連結的　　B. 延遲的
C. 淹沒的　　D. 組織的

❹ 線上購物者發現自己經常會被炫目的商業廣告所吸引而增加不必要的消費。

Mercantile 的意思最接近於這個字。

A. 易受傷的　　B. 慣用語的
C. 商業的　　D. 不情願的

答案 ❶B　❷A　❸A　❹C

Vocabulary in Context

❺ Though the Dutch painter, Vincent Van Gogh, had a miserable life all his life, he was ________________ one of the most talented and the most influential artists in the world.
Thought is in the closest meaning to this word.
A. dismissed B. reflected
C. considered D. nurtured

❻ According to medical researches, nuts are very ________________ at lowering cholesterol levels and preventing heart and blood vessel diseases.
Effectual is in the closest meaning to this word.
A. redundant B. nimble
C. compassionate D. effective

❼ DNA was ________________ by a German scientist, Friedrich Miescher, in 1869. From the information in DNA, a lot about a human's family, health, and personality can be revealed.
Found is in the closest meaning to this word.
A. discovered B. preferred
C. notified D. interviewed

❽ Pablo Picasso, probably the most important painter of the 20th century, ________________ an enviable reputation for his outstanding artistic ability.
Obtained is in the closest meaning to this word.
A. compensated B. forbade
C. acquired D. subordinated

❺ 雖然荷蘭畫家，文森・梵谷，這一生命運多舛，他仍被視為全世界最具天分且最具影響力的藝術家之一。
Thought 的意思最接近於這個字。

A. 解散　　B. 反射
C. 認為　　D. 養育

❻ 根據醫學研究，堅果在降低膽固醇以及預防心血管疾病方面非常有效果。
Effectual 的意思最接近於這個字。

A. 多餘的　　B. 敏捷的
C. 同情的　　D. 有效的

❼ DNA 是由德國科學家，弗雷德里希・米歇爾，在 1869 年所發現的。從 DNA 所呈現的訊息，可以充分了解一個人的家族血緣、健康狀況，以及人格特質。
Found 的意思最接近於這個字。

A. 發現　　B. 寧願
C. 通知　　D. 面試

❽ 巴布羅・畢卡索可說是 20 世紀最重要的畫家，他以他傑出的藝術才能獲得令人仰慕的聲譽。
Obtained 的意思最接近於這個字。

A. 賠償　　B. 禁止
C. 獲得　　D. 居次要地位

答案 ❺ C　❻ D　❼ A　❽ C

Vocabulary in Context

❾ With a strong ______________ for childcare, Rebecca has devoted herself to teaching in a kindergarten and has done a great job.
Enthusiasm is in the closest meaning to this word.
A. complaint B. passion
C. tradition D. service

❿ Mark made up his mind to be a doctor and worked hard for it. No hardness could stop him from ______________ his goal.
Seeking is in the closest meaning to this word.
A. regretting B. pursuing
C. commemorating D. integrating

⓫ This brand of laptop has been selling well for it's ______________, portable, and easy to operate.
Cheap is in the closest meaning to this word.
A. ambiguous B. weighty
C. dialectic D. inexpensive

⓬ You can of course contact a travel agency to make travel arrangements for you; one ______________ to this is that you and your family can organize your own trip.
Choice is in the closest meaning to this word.
A. recipe B. seclusion
C. alternative D. depreciation

❾ 蕾貝嘉對於照顧兒童有著強烈的熱忱，她一直致力於幼稚園的教學並且勝任稱職。
Enthusiasm 的意思最接近於這個字。

A. 抱怨　　B. 熱情
C. 傳統　　D. 服務

❿ 馬克下定決心並致力於成為一名醫生。沒有任何困難可以阻止他追求他的目標。
Seeking 的意思最接近於這個字。

A. 後悔　　B. 追求
C. 紀念　　D. 融合

⓫ 這個品牌的筆電銷路一向不錯，因為它價格便宜、便於攜帶，並且易於操作。
Cheap 的意思最接近於這個字。

A. 模稜兩可的　　B. 沉重的
C. 方言的　　D. 便宜的

⓬ 你當然可以接洽旅行社為你做旅遊行程的安排；此外的另一選擇是你可以和你的家人共同籌畫你們自己的行程。
Choice 的意思最接近於這個字。

A. 食譜　　B. 隱居
C. 可供選擇的事物　　D. 貶值

答案 ❾ B　❿ B　⓫ D　⓬ C

08 UNIT 精選必考字彙❽

Vocabulary in Context

❶ The most ________________ trip for the happy couple was the trip to Europe for their 10th Wedding Anniversary.
Memorable is in the closest meaning to this word.
A. routine B. unforgettable
C. constant D. subsequent

❷ It's hard to ________________ what life would be like if there were no water and electricity in the world.
Fancy is in the closest meaning to this word.
A. nourish B. unlock
C. imagine D. dismantle

❸ Scientists have found that the music that Mozart composed and ________________ has a miraculous healing and calming effect to its listeners.
Played is in the closest meaning to this word.
A. performed B. exchanged
C. desolated D. necessitated

❹ Dealing with ________________ from all sources is no easy task; however, to gain true happiness, it's worth making the efforts.
Stress is in the closest meaning to this word.
A. ecstasy B. morality
C. pressure D. transport

❶ 對這對幸福的夫婦來說，最難忘的旅遊是歡慶十周年結婚紀念前往歐洲的那趟旅遊。
Memorable 的意思最接近於這個字。

A. 例行的　　B. 難忘的
C. 時常的　　D. 隨後的

❷ 很難想像世界上假使沒有水和電，生活將會是什麼樣子。
Fancy 的意思最接近於這個字。

A. 提供養分　　B. 解開
C. 想像　　D. 拆除

❸ 科學家發現莫札特所創造和演奏的樂曲對於聽眾具有奇蹟般治療和鎮定的效果。
Played 的意思最接近於這個字。

A. 演奏　　B. 交換
C. 使荒涼　　D. 需要

❹ 處理各種壓力不是件簡單的事；然而，為了獲得真正的快樂，努力是值得的。
Stress 的意思最接近於這個字。

A. 狂喜　　B. 道德
C. 壓力　　D. 運輸

答案 ❶B ❷C ❸A ❹C

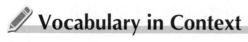

Vocabulary in Context

5 The serial killer's bold and ________________ murdering finally resulted in his being arrested and sentenced.
Ceaseless is in the closest meaning to this word.
A. worthwhile B. continuous
C. tropical D. contemporary

6 The methods of mass production and mass markets were first provided by the Industrial ________________ in the 18th century, which in turn contributed to the development of international business.
Revolt is in the closest meaning to this word.
A. Fair B. Cooperation
C. Engineering D. Revolution

7 Richard was the "Workaholic" in his office because he always kept himself busy and was fully ________________ in his work.
Occupied is in the closest meaning to this word.
A. engaged B. condensed
C. signified D. underwent

8 The Dinosaur Park in Canada has always been a ________________ and popular tourist spot, where visitors can appreciate all kinds of dinosaur fossils.
Renowned is in the closest meaning to this word.
A. famous B. delicious
C. notorious D. subconscious

❺ 這名連續殺人犯大膽且持續地犯案，終究導致他被逮捕並判刑。
Ceaseless 的意思最接近於這個字。

A. 值得做的　B. 持續的
C. 熱帶的　D. 當代的

❻ 18 世紀的工業革命提供大規模生產的方式以及市場，進而促成國際商業的發展。
Revolt 的意思最接近於這個字。

A. 展覽會　B. 合作
C. 工程學　D. 革命

❼ 理察是他辦公室裡的“工作狂”，因為他總是十分忙碌並且全神貫注於他的工作。
Occupied 的意思最接近於這個字。

A. 從事　B. 濃縮
C. 表示　D. 經歷

❽ 加拿大的恐龍公園一向是著名並且受歡迎的觀光景點，訪客在這裡可以欣賞到各式各樣的恐龍化石。
Renowned 的意思最接近於這個字。

A. 著名的　B. 美味的
C. 惡名昭彰的　D. 潛意識的

答案 ❺ B ❻ D ❼ A ❽ A

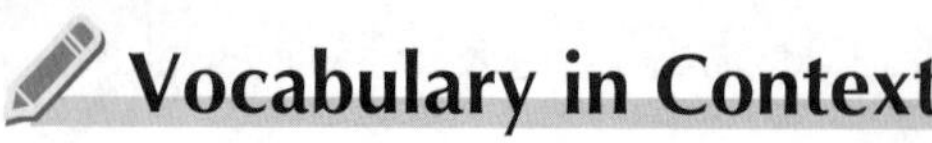

Vocabulary in Context

❾ Fanny studied and researched diligently and finally got ________________ to her ideal graduate school.
Consented is in the closest meaning to this word.

A. admitted B. immigrated
C. perplexed D. resembled

❿ It took Philip one whole month to ________________ the long novel into one with only three chapters.
Shorten is in the closest meaning to this word.

A. wander B. condense
C. solicit D. forecast

⓫ Owing to the ________________ resources, we must do our utmost to come up with practical measures for sustainable development.
Restricted is in the closest meaning to this word.

A. swift B. limited
C. marginal D. radioactive

⓬ ________________, with the company of a new pet dog, Raymond recovered from the depression and the guiltiness of losing his old dog.
Progressively is in the closest meaning to this word.

A. Splendidly B. Previously
C. Attractively D. Gradually

❾ 芬妮十分勤勉地讀書及做研究，最終錄取並進入她理想的研究所。
Consented 的意思最接近於這個字。

A. 錄取　　B. 移民
C. 困惑　　D. 相似

❿ 菲力普花了整整一個月的時間把一本長篇小說濃縮成只有三個章節。
Shorten 的意思最接近於這個字。

A. 徘徊　　B. 濃縮
C. 請求　　D. 預測

⓫ 由於資源有限，我們必須盡最大的努力提出可供持續發展的實際措施。
Restricted 的意思最接近於這個字。

A. 迅速的　　B. 有限的
C. 邊緣的　　D. 放射性的

⓬ 逐漸地，有著新寵物狗的陪伴，雷蒙從失去原有的狗所引發的憂鬱和愧疚中恢復過來。
Progressively 的意思最接近於這個字。

A. 華麗地　　B. 先前地
C. 吸引人地　　D. 逐漸地

答案 ❾ A　❿ B　⓫ B　⓬ D

09 UNIT 精選必考字彙9

Vocabulary in Context

❶ In the action movie, the superheroes, with each of whom equipped with combating skills, finally won the victory with ________________ forces.
Supreme is in the closest meaning to this word.
A. temporary B. dominant
C. seasonal D. fundamental

❷ Undoubtedly, it is the parents that should strictly regulate their children not to watch TV programs that are too ________________ in violence.
Lifelike is in the closest meaning to this word.
A. realistic B. amiable
C. conventional D. luxuriant

❸ After transferring to the new company, Lucy could pleasantly work in a much more ________________ and efficient way.
Adjustable is in the closest meaning to this word.
A. agricultural B. uncertain
C. flexible D. legitimate

❹ As a safety policy against terroism, all passengers are ________________ to undergo and pass the strict security check at the airport.

Demanded is in the closest meaning to this word.

A. compiled　　B. required
C. worshipped　　D. overestimated

❶ 在這部動作片中，超級英雄們各個身懷絕技，最終以絕佳優勢贏得勝利。

Supreme 的意思最接近於這個字。

A. 暫時的　　B. 優勢的
C. 季節的　　D. 基本的

❷ 無疑地，父母親應該嚴格規範孩童不要觀看過於暴力寫實的電視節目。

Lifelike 的意思最接近於這個字。

A. 寫實的　　B. 和藹的
C. 傳統的　　D. 繁茂的

❸ 露西在轉任到新公司後，可以很愉快地以更加彈性而且有效率的方式工作。

Adjustable 的意思最接近於這個字。

A. 農業的　　B. 不確定的
C. 彈性的　　D. 合法正當的

❹ 基於對抗恐怖主義的安全政策，所有的乘客被要求接受並且通過機場嚴格的安全檢查。

Demanded 的意思最接近於這個字。

A. 編纂　　B. 要求
C. 崇拜　　D. 高估

答案 ❶B ❷A ❸C ❹B

Vocabulary in Context

❺ What the general public expects from the government is a ________________ economic development that it is supposed to achieve.
Steady is in the closest meaning to this word.
A. changeable B. alcoholic
C. stable D. waterproof

❻ A lot of celebrities dressed up and attended the party tonight to support the charity campaign that was ________________ by the association.
Started is in the closest meaning to this word.
A. amplified B. prolonged
C. launched D. twinkled

❼ The news reporter purchased the newest laptop computer ________________ for the purpose of covering instant news.
Particularly is in the closest meaning to this word.
A. affectionately B. narrowly
C. gloriously D. specifically

❽ Doctors warned people against the long ________________ to the burning sunlight, which might easily cause skin cancer.
Uncovering is in the closest meaning to this word.
A. reliability B. dedication
C. exposure D. negligence

❺ 一般民眾對於政府的期許是一個理當由它所達成穩定的經濟發展。
Steady 的意思最接近於這個字。

A. 易變的　　B. 含酒精的
C. 穩定的　　D. 防水的

❻ 許多名流盛裝出席今晚的宴會來支持由協會所發起的慈善活動。
Started 的意思最接近於這個字。

A. 放大　　B. 延長
C. 發起　　D. 閃爍

❼ 這名新聞記者為了採訪即時新聞特地購買了最新型的筆記型電腦。
Particularly 的意思最接近於這個字。

A. 關愛地　　B. 狹隘地
C. 輝煌地　　D. 特別地

❽ 醫生警告人們不要長時間曝曬在熾熱的陽光下，因為這樣容易罹患皮膚癌。
Uncovering 的意思最接近於這個字。

A. 可靠　　B. 奉獻
C. 曝曬　　D. 輕忽

答案 ❺C ❻C ❼D ❽C

Vocabulary in Context

❾ President Barack Obama, the first African-American president, has been admired worldwide for his ________________ achievements in both domestic and foreign affairs.
Prominent is in the closest meaning to this word.
A. conceited B. identical
C. short-sighted D. outstanding

❿ It's amazing and puzzling how the ancient Egyptians could have had the ability to ________________ the Great Pyramids of Giza.
Build is in the closest meaning to this word.
A. construct B. whisper
C. predict D. intervene

⓫ Oliver is at present a resident doctor in the hospital his father ________________ and plans to take over his father's business in the future.
Founded is in the closest meaning to this word.
A. appealed B. established
C. smuggled D. broadcast

⓬ Patrick has been under ________________ pressure recently as he has to make immediate decision on whether to work in the hometown or to accept the challenging position overseas.
Forceful is in the closest meaning to this word.
A. reputable B. climatic
C. intense D. merciful

⑨ 巴拉克・歐巴馬總統是首位非裔美籍的總統，以他在內政及外交方面傑出的成就為世人所崇拜。
Prominent 的意思最接近於這個字。

A. 自負的　B. 相同的
C. 短視的　D. 傑出的

⑩ 人們對於古代埃及人竟然有能力建造吉薩的大金塔感到驚奇而且困惑。
Build 的意思最接近於這個字。

A. 建造　B. 耳語
C. 預測　D. 干預

⑩ 奧利佛目前在他父親所建立的醫院裡擔任住院醫師，並且計劃在未來接管父親的事業。
Founded 的意思最接近於這個字。

A. 吸引　B. 建立
C. 走私　D. 轉播

⑫ 派翠克最近身處於極大的壓力之下，因為他必須要盡快決定留在家鄉工作或是接受國外具挑戰性的職務。
Forceful 的意思最接近於這個字。

A. 聲譽好的　B. 氣候的
C. 強烈的　D. 仁慈的

答案 ⑨ D　⑩ A　⑪ B　⑫ C

精選必考字彙⑩

Vocabulary in Context

❶ The ancient Machu Picchu used to be a summer resort for Incan emperors and their ________ family.
Royal is in the closest meaning to this word.
A. abusive B. tempting
C. imperial D. contemplating

❷ All the students unwillingly ________ the cancellation of the field trip because of the approaching typhoon.
Accepted is in the closest meaning to this word.
A. deserted B. received
C. symbolized D. prolonged

❸ The publicity campaign did much to ________ the new product, promoting its unexpected big sale.
Advertise is in the closest meaning to this word.
A. anticipate B. retire
C. depopulate D. popularize

❹ Donald adopted practical and clever marketing ________ and earned great profits for his company.
Skills is in the closest meaning to this word.
A. balances B. supposition
C. techniques D. coincidence

❶ 馬丘比丘古城過去曾經是印加國王和他們的皇室家族避暑的地點。
Royal 的意思最接近於這個字。

A. 虐待的　B. 誘人的
C. 皇室的　D. 深思的

❷ 由於颱風即將來臨，所有的學生不情願地接受戶外教學的取消。
Accepted 的意思最接近於這個字。

A. 遺棄　B. 接受
C. 象徵　D. 延長

❸ 這項宣傳活動對於提升新產品的知名度有很大的幫助，促成了意想不到的大賣。
Advertise 的意思最接近於這個字。

A. 預期　B. 退休
C. 減少人口　D. 受歡迎

❹ 唐納採用實際而且靈活的行銷技巧為他的公司賺取大量的利潤。
Skills 的意思最接近於這個字。

A. 均衡　B. 猜測
C. 技巧　D. 巧合

答案 ❶C ❷B ❸D ❹C

Vocabulary in Context

❺ Besides the strict enforcement of laws against drunk driving, our government should conduct public education to alert people to the dangers of drunk driving to ____________________ their safety.
Assure is in the closest meaning to this word.

A. ensure B. overload
C. switch D. undermine

❻ The candidate suffered a serious setback when the newsweekly ____________________ a series of disgraceful scandals about his family.
Uncovered is in the closest meaning to this word.

A. flourished B. paraded
C. revealed D. discouraged

❼ It was irresponsible of Miss Hope to make the serious ____________________ against Carl that he had stolen her cell phone before she had any positive proof.
Charge is in the closest meaning to this word.

A. occupation B. harassment
C. inhabitant D. accusation

❽ Since the merchandise of his company has superior quality and famous branding, Sam could easily achieve successful sales and ____________________.
Advancement is in the closest meaning to this word.

A. treatment B. promotion
C. convenience D. depiction

❺ 除了取締酒駕法律嚴格的執行，我們的政府應該實施大眾教育使民眾警覺酒駕的危險以確保自身的安全。
Assure 的意思最接近於這個字。

A. 確保　　B. 超載
C. 轉換　　D. 破壞

❻ 當新聞週刊揭露一連串有關於他的家族丟臉的醜聞時，這名候選人遭受嚴重的挫折。
Uncovered 的意思最接近於這個字。

A. 茂盛　　B. 遊行
C. 揭露　　D. 氣餒

❼ 霍普老師非常不負責任，因為她在還沒有任何證據之前就嚴正地指控卡爾偷竊她的手機。
Charge 的意思最接近於這個字。

A. 職業　　B. 騷擾
C. 居民　　D. 指控

❽ 由於山姆公司的商品具有優異的品質以及著名的品牌，他可以輕易地達成成功的販售及促銷。
Advancement 的意思最接近於這個字。

A. 治療　　B. 促銷
C. 便利　　D. 描繪

答案 ❺A ❻C ❼D ❽B

Vocabulary in Context

❾ Due to her thoughtful personality and language capability, Lydia was fully qualified as a competent flight ________________.

Stewardess is in the closest meaning to this word.

A. rebel B. detective

C. attendant D. principal

❿ Mother Teresa's lifelong devotion to the welfare of people and the advocacy of humanity won worldwide ________________ and was awarded the Nobel Peace Prize in 1979.

Acknowledgement is in the closest meaning to this word.

A. trifle B. permanence

C. appointment D. recognition

⓫ It was naïve of Anna to ________________ that everyone would support her proposal wholeheartedly.

Suppose is in the closest meaning to this word.

A. assume B. compose

C. renovate D. overwhelm

⓬ His making a scene of trifles in the middle of the party ________________ not only himself but his family present on the scene.

Disgraced is in the closest meaning to this word.

A. amused B. insulted

C. dedicated D. reproached

❾ 由於她善解人意的個性及語言的能力，莉迪亞有充分的資格成為勝任的空服員。
Stewardess 的意思最接近於這個字。
A. 反叛者　B. 偵探
C. 服務員　D. 校長

❿ 德蕾莎修女因一生奉獻於人類的福祉以及人道主義的倡導而贏得世人的讚譽，並且在 1979 年獲頒諾貝爾和平獎。
Acknowledgement 的意思最接近於這個字。
A. 瑣事　B. 永久
C. 任命　D. 讚譽

⓫ 安娜過於天真地認為每個人都會全心地支持她的提案。
Suppose 的意思最接近於這個字。
A. 假定　B. 組成
C. 整修　D. 壓倒

⓬ 他在宴會中為小事大吵大鬧，不僅侮辱自己也使得在場的家人蒙羞。
Disgraced 的意思最接近於這個字。
A. 取悅　B. 侮辱
C. 致力　D. 責備

答案 ❾ C　❿ D　⓫ A　⓬ B

精選必考字彙⑪

Vocabulary in Context

❶ Little did we expect that the minor misunderstanding between the couple should have ________________ caused them to break up.
Unexpectedly is in the closest meaning to this word.
A. gracefully B. luxuriously
C. abundantly D. dramatically

❷ It was a ________________ belief in the past that after the appearance of a comet, which was regarded as an omen, great disasters and tragedies might occur.
General is in the closest meaning to this word.
A. common B. solitary
C. passionate D. luminous

❸ Those naughty students were insistently requested to make ________________ of their misbehavior, or they might receive a severe punishment.
Alteration is in the closest meaning to this word.
A. efficiency B. mistakes
C. separation D. corrections

❹ People all over the world used to view the United States as a land of golden ________________ and tried their luck by emigrating there.
Chance is in the closest meaning to this word.

A. warehouse B. opportunity
C. remedy D. derivation

❶ 我們一點都沒料到這對情侶間小小的誤會竟然會戲劇性地導致他們分手。
Unexpectedly 的意思最接近於這個字。
A. 優雅地 B. 奢華地
C. 豐富地 D. 戲劇性地

❷ 在過去，人們普遍地相信在被視為是凶兆的彗星出現後，巨大的災難和悲劇可能會發生。
General 的意思最接近於這個字。
A. 普遍的 B. 孤單的
C. 熱情的 D. 發光的

❸ 那些頑皮的學生一再地被要求改正他們不良的行為，否則他們可能將得接受嚴厲的處分。
Alteration 的意思最接近於這個字。
A. 效率 B. 錯誤
C. 分開 D. 修正

❹ 在過去，世界各地的人們把美國視為是一個充滿絕佳機會的國度因而移民到那裏去開創契機。
Chance 的意思最接近於這個字。
A. 倉庫 B. 機會
C. 治療藥方 D. 起源

答案 ❶D ❷A ❸D ❹B

Vocabulary in Context

❺ Carlos bought an apartment near the MRT station as he considered it ________________ and time-saving for him to commute by MRT.
Handy is in the closest meaning to this word.

A. convenient B. slight
C. annoying D. theoretical

❻ According to TV reports, the sending out of the ________________ gas and fumes of the factory might be the cause of the serious sickness of the residents.
Poisonous is in the closest meaning to this word.

A. harmless B. spacious
C. toxic D. architectural

❼ In America, young people will often move out and live an ________________ life when they turn eighteen or go to college.
Autonomous is in the closest meaning to this word.

A. anxious B. energetic
C. undermined D. independent

❽ ________________, the speedy passenger ship hit on an iceberg and got crashed, resulting in heavy casualties.
Unluckily is in the closest meaning to this word.

A. Gratefully B. Collectively
C. Unfortunately D. Mutually

❺ 卡洛斯在捷運站附近買了一間公寓，因為他認為坐捷運通勤既方便又節省時間。
Handy 的意思最接近於這個字。
A. 便利的　B. 輕微的
C. 煩人的　D. 理論的

❻ 根據電視新聞報導，這座工廠排放出的有毒氣體和煙霧可能是導致居民罹患嚴重疾病的主因。
Poisonous 的意思最接近於這個字。
A. 無害的　B. 寬敞的
C. 有毒的　D. 建築的

❼ 在美國，當年輕人到了十八歲或是上大學的時候，他們經常會搬離家庭並且過著獨立的生活。
Autonomous 的意思最接近於這個字。
A. 焦慮的　B. 有活力的
C. 破壞的　D. 獨立的

❽ 很不幸地，疾馳而行的客輪撞上冰山撞毀，因而導致慘重的傷亡。
Unluckily 的意思最接近於這個字。
A. 感激地　B. 集體地
C. 不幸地　D. 相互地

答案 ❺ A ❻ C ❼ D ❽ C

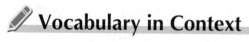

Vocabulary in Context

❾ The method of trial and ________________ helped Mrs. Cooper a lot in her raising the three children.
Mistake is in the closest meaning to this word.
A. error B. contract
C. refund D. notification

❿ Owing to economic recession, Mr. Norman's company met with the dramatic plunge in ________________ and finally went bankrupt.
Earnings is in the closest meaning to this word.
A. beverage B. profits
C. equality D. findings

⓫ The American singer and song writer, Bob Dylan, gained ________________ prestige by winning the 2016 Nobel Prize in Literature for his achievements in creating new poetic expressions within the great American song tradition.
Global is in the closest meaning to this word.
A. obscure B. functional
C. tribal D. international

⓬ Traveling a lot can be of great ________________ to young people in broadening their horizons.
Advantage is in the closest meaning to this word.
A. morale B. ailment
C. benefit D. regularity

❾ 「嘗試錯誤」的方法在庫柏太太撫育三個孩子方面有極大的幫助。
Mistake 的意思最接近於這個字。

A. 錯誤　　B. 合約
C. 退款　　D. 通知

❿ 由於經濟不景氣，諾曼先生的公司遭逢利潤銳減的窘境，最終宣告破產。
Earnings 的意思最接近於這個字。

A. 飲料　　B. 利潤
C. 平等　　D. 發現

⓫ 美國歌手兼作曲家，巴比・狄倫，由於在偉大的美國歌曲傳統中注入創新詩意表達的成就而獲頒 2016 年諾貝爾文學獎，並因此贏得國際盛讚。
Global 的意思最接近於這個字。

A. 模糊的　　B. 功能的
C. 部落的　　D. 國際的

⓬ 經常旅遊對於年輕人拓展視野具有很大的益處。
Advantage 的意思最接近於這個字。

A. 士氣　　B. 疾病
C. 利益　　D. 規則性

答案 ❾ A ❿ B ⓫ D ⓬ C

12 UNIT 精選必考字彙⑫

Vocabulary in Context

❶ Andrew had a natural talent for learning and playing all kinds of musical ________________, and he formed a rock band of his own when entering college.
Devices is in the closest meaning to this word.
A. animation B. gestures
C. substitute D. instruments

❷ Due to the reddish coloring from the iron oxide on its ________________, Mars is often referred to as the "Red Planet".
Exterior is in the closest meaning to this word.
A. surface B. galaxy
C. carpet D. maintenance

❸ The corporation planned to establish chain stores all over the world and made great efforts to look for superior and ________________ store managers.
Trustworthy is in the closest meaning to this word.
A. absent-minded B. sanitary
C. reliable D. descriptive

❹ To achieve immortality and enjoy the afterlife, the ancient Egyptian pharaohs were mummified after their death to ________________ their bodies from decaying.

Stop is in the closest meaning to this word.

A. abandon　　B. prevent

C. celebrate　　D. stipulate

❶ 安德魯有學習和演奏各種樂器的天份，一上大學他就組了一支他自己的搖滾樂團。

Devices 的意思最接近於這個字。

A. 動畫　　B. 手勢

C. 替代品　　D. 儀器

❷ 由於來自於星球表面的氧化鐵而形成紅色色澤，火星經常被稱為"紅色星球"。

Exterior 的意思最接近於這個字。

A. 表面　　B. 銀河

C. 地毯　　D. 維修

❸ 這家公司計畫在全世界建立連鎖店，因而努力尋找優秀且可靠的分店經理。

Trustworthy 的意思最接近於這個字。

A. 心不在焉的　　B. 衛生的

C. 可信賴的　　D. 描述的

❹ 為了追求不朽以及享受來生，古埃及法老在死後被製作成木乃伊以防止遺體腐化。

Stop 的意思最接近於這個字。

A. 遺棄　　B. 防止

C. 慶祝　　D. 規定

答案 ❶ D　❷ A　❸ C　❹ B

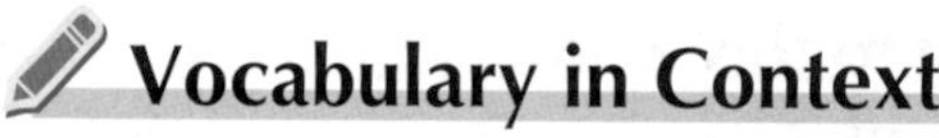

Vocabulary in Context

⑤ The factory was forced to slow down its manufacturing speed after parts of its ________________ apparatus went wrong.
Machine-operated is in the closest meaning to this word.
A. artistic B. symbolic
C. mechanical D. therapeutic

⑥ What is great about Bill Gates is that he is not only a successful ________________ but a person dedicated to his ideals of making the world better by working for charitable causes.
Businessman is in the closest meaning to this word.
A. critic B. narrator
C. publisher D. entrepreneur

⑦ In the class reunion, we could hardly ________________ Henry, who has changed a lot in appearance over the past ten years.
Identify is in the closest meaning to this word.
A. coax B. recognize
C. inspect D. enlighten

⑧ It's rather a pity that man ________________ little what he has but craves much for what he doesn't own.
Values is in the closest meaning to this word.
A. explains B. mingles
C. tolerates D. appreciates

❺ 這座工廠在它部份的機械設備出狀況後，被迫放慢製造的速度。
Machine-operated 的意思最接近於這個字。

A. 藝術的　　B. 象徵的
C. 機械的　　D. 有療效的

❻ 比爾蓋茲了不起的地方在於他不僅是一名成功的企業家，並且是一名致力於藉由從事慈善事業而使得這個世界更美好的理念的人。
Businessman 的意思最接近於這個字。

A. 評論家　　B. 敘事者
C. 出版商　　D. 企業家

❼ 在同學會中，我們幾乎認不出亨利了，因為他的外表在過去十年來改變很多。
Identify 的意思最接近於這個字。

A. 哄騙　　B. 認得
C. 檢查　　D. 啟蒙

❽ 人們不珍惜他們所擁有的反而去過度渴望他們所沒有的東西是件令人相當遺憾的事。
Values 的意思最接近於這個字。

A. 說明　　B. 混和
C. 忍受　　D. 賞識

答案 ❺C ❻D ❼B ❽D

Vocabulary in Context

❾ The notorious mayor, who committed bribery and embezzlement, finally handed in his ________________ and was put in jail.
Quitting is in the closest meaning to this word.
A. thesis B. measurement
C. resignation D. disapproval

❿ To ________________ a higher level of education is vital to your getting better employment and fairer salaries in the future.
Receive is in the closest meaning to this word.
A. obtain B. promise
C. inquire D. exaggerate

⓫ Talking too loudly on a cell phone may cause disturbance to people around you, ________________ in a cinema.
Particularly is in the closest meaning to this word.
A. especially B. consequently
C. potentially D. righteously

⓬ To achieve the sustainability of the earth and humans, it's essential that we cherish and conserve the ________________ natural ecosystems.
Undeveloped is in the closest meaning to this word.
A. doubtful B. unexploited
C. refundable D. communicative

⑨ 因犯下賄賂及盜用公款罪行而聲名狼藉的市長最後的結局是遞交辭呈並且被關入監獄裡。

Quitting 的意思最接近於這個字。

A. 論文　　B. 測量

C. 辭職　　D. 不贊同

⑩ 獲得較高學位對於日後你要取得較佳的工作及較高的薪水是很關鍵的。

Receive 的意思最接近於這個字。

A. 獲得　　B. 允諾

C. 詢問　　D. 誇大

⑫ 手機講太大聲可能會對你週遭的人造成困擾，尤其是在電影院裡的時候。

Particularly 的意思最接近於這個字。

A. 尤其　　B. 結果

C. 潛在地　　D. 正直地

⑫ 為了要達成地球和人類永續的生存，我們必須要珍惜並保護未開發的自然生態系統。

Undeveloped 的意思最接近於這個字。

A. 可疑的　　B. 未開發的

C. 可退款的　　D. 溝通的

答案 ⑨ C　⑩ A　⑪ A　⑫ B

13 UNIT

精選必考字彙⑬

Vocabulary in Context

❶ Mr. Goodman enjoyed collecting the __________ Chinese art and antiques; he even opened an antique shop for his hobby.
Old is in the closest meaning to this word.
A. optimistic B. venomous
C. ancient D. supernatural

❷ At the embarrassing moment, Anthony had a hard time finding __________ words to express his apology.
Proper is in the closest meaning to this word.
A. fragrant B. suitable
C. proficient D. antisocial

❸ In __________ days, making proper health management is essential since health is the foundation of success and happiness.
Contemporary is in the closest meaning to this word.
A. modern B. justifiable
C. attractive D. prehistoric

❹ As long as you make the __________, the department store counter will consent to allow a full refund of the amount paid.
Demand is in the closest meaning to this word.

A. ancestor　　B. flare
C. performance　　D. request

❶ 古德曼先生喜愛收集古代中國藝術品和古董；他甚至因為這項嗜好開了一家古董店。
Old 的意思最接近於這個字。
A. 樂觀的　　B. 有毒的
C. 古代的　　D. 超自然的

❷ 在尷尬的那一瞬間，安東尼找不出貼切的話來表達他的歉意。
Proper 的意思最接近於這個字。
A. 芳香的　　B. 適合的
C. 精通的　　D. 反社會的

❸ 就今日來說，由於健康是成功以及快樂的基礎，做好適當的健康管理是必要的。
Contemporary 的意思最接近於這個字。
A. 現代的　　B. 有理由的
C. 吸引人的　　D. 史前的

❹ 只要你提出要求，百貨公司櫃台會同意給予退還全部的付款。
Demand 的意思最接近於這個字。
A. 祖先　　B. 閃光
C. 表演　　D. 要求

答案 ❶ C　❷ B　 A　❹ D

Vocabulary in Context

❺ It's ________________ for people to yearn for longevity and scientists have been working on ways of lengthening mankind's life span.
Normal is in the closest meaning to this word.

A. natural　　B. sociable
C. impulsive　　D. legitimate

❻ The painful bothering and torments to celebrities and the ________________ are the endless pursuit and photographing of the paparazzi.
Nobles is in the closest meaning to this word.

A. guardians　　B. minority
C. royalty　　D. artists

❼ The brutal man committed serious crimes out of impulse; ________________, he was sentenced to life imprisonment and was deprived of his civil rights.
Consequently is in the closest meaning to this word.

A. firstly　　B. however
C. previously　　D. therefore

❽ It's generally believed that during the fourth century B.C., Alexander the Great ________________ the arrival of perfume in Greece.
Presented is in the closest meaning to this word.

A. wrinkled　　B. meditated
C. radiated　　D. introduced

❺ 人們渴望長壽是很自然的，而科學家正致力於尋找延長人類壽命的方法。
Normal 的意思最接近於這個字。
A. 自然的　B. 擅長交際的
C. 衝動的　D. 合法的

❻ 名流和皇室成員痛苦的困擾及折磨在於狗仔隊永無止盡的跟蹤和拍照。
Nobles 的意思最接近於這個字。
A. 監護人　B. 少數民族
C. 皇室成員　D. 藝術家

❼ 這個殘暴的人因衝動犯下嚴重的罪行；因此，他被判處終身監禁並且被剝奪公民權。
Consequently 的意思最接近於這個字。
A. 首先　B. 然而
C. 先前地　D. 因此

❽ 一般人相信在西元前第四世紀期間，亞歷山大大帝把香水引進至希臘。
Presented 的意思最接近於這個字。
A. 弄皺　B. 沉思
C. 輻射　D. 介紹

答案 ❺A　❻C　❼D　❽D

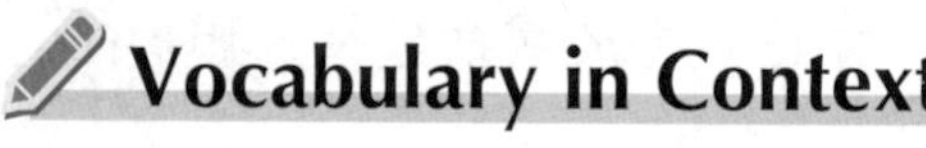

Vocabulary in Context

❾ The extraordinary director, Ang Lee, has won himself an international ________________ for his amazingly unique ways of directing films.
Fame is in the closest meaning to this word.
A. conservation B. heritage
C. reputation D. program

❿ Out of pity, Rick ________________ the old man who seemed to have lost his way to the police station and helped him return home.
Escorted is in the closest meaning to this word.
A. distorted B. accompanied
C. idolized D. supervised

⓫ Recently, a team of scientists, teachers, and students went on an ________________ to explore some of the wonders of the Amazon Rainforest.
Journey is in the closest meaning to this word.
A. expedition B. orchestra
C. isolation D. unemployment

⓬ The board of directors announced several measures to minimize the problem to a more ________________ level.
Controllable is in the closest meaning to this word.
A. opposing B. diplomatic
C. casual D. manageable

❾ 卓越的李安導演因其令人驚嘆獨特的導演方式而贏得國際聲譽。
Fame 的意思最接近於這個字。

A. 保存　　B. 遺產
C. 聲望　　D. 節目

❿ 出自於同情，瑞克陪伴那位似乎迷路的老先生到警局並協助他返家。
Escorted 的意思最接近於這個字。

A. 扭曲　　B. 伴隨
C. 崇拜　　D. 監督

⓫ 最近，一支由科學家、教師，以及學生組成的隊伍進行遠征去探索亞馬遜河熱帶雨林區的一些奇景。
Journey 的意思最接近於這個字。

A. 遠征　　B. 管弦樂隊
C. 孤立　　D. 失業

⓬ 董事會宣佈數項措施來把問題降低到比較能應付的程度。
Controllable 的意思最接近於這個字。

A. 對立的　　B. 外交的
C. 隨意的　　D. 可處理的

答案 ❾ C　❿ B　⓫ A　⓬ D

14 UNIT 精選必考字彙⑭

Vocabulary in Context

❶ The admirable NBA basketball players are not only ____________ in their basketball skills but passionate and generous in supporting charity work.
Well-trained is in the closest meaning to this word.

A. different B. antisocial
C. territorial D. professional

❷ Though separated far apart, Melissa still maintained regular ____________ with her best friend these years.
Letter-writing is in the closest meaning to this word.

A. landscape B. poverty
C. correspondence D. temptation

❸ Her elaborate presentation and smooth use of the powerpoint slides gave the ____________ that she was well-prepared and organized.
Feeling is in the closest meaning to this word.

A. cultivation B. impression
C. possession D. reservation

❹ Due to the ____________ serious delays of shipment, the company decided to ask for compensation or even a full refund.
Many is in the closest meaning to this word.

A. numerous B. logical
C. scarce D. observant

❶ 令人欽佩的 NBA 籃球球星不僅專業於他們的籃球技巧，並且熱情慷慨地支持慈善工作。
Well-trained 的意思最接近於這個字。
A. 不同的 B. 反社會的
C. 領土的 D. 專業的

❷ 儘管相隔遙遠，梅莉莎這些年來仍然持續地和她最要好的朋友保持定期的通信。
Letter-writing 的意思最接近於這個字。
A. 風景 B. 貧窮
C. 通信 D. 誘惑

❸ 她詳盡的報告以及流暢的簡報運用給予人們她事前準備充分並且條理分明的印象。
Feeling 的意思最接近於這個字。
A. 栽培 B. 印象
C. 擁有 D. 預約

❹ 由於多次貨物運送的嚴重延遲，這家公司決定要求索賠或甚至全額退款。
Many 的意思最接近於這個字。
A. 許多的 B. 合邏輯的
C. 稀少的 D. 善於觀察的

答案 ❶ D ❷ C ❸ B ❹ A

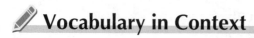

Vocabulary in Context

❺ Ralph got fired this month because his performance failed to reach the required ________________; however, he planned to start all over again.
Criteria is in the closest meaning to this word.
A. publication B. standard
C. expansion D. trademark

❻ As soon as Steven got his year-end bonus, he purchased a highly functional digital camera that could adjust ________________.
Spontaneously is in the closest meaning to this word.
A. constructively B. gradually
C. irrelevantly D. automatically

❼ The ________________ cars shown in the International Car Fair attracted lots of car fans all over the world to appreciate.
Antique is in the closest meaning to this word.
A. pointed B. accurate
C. vintage D. sympathetic

❽ Owing to generation gap, modern parents find it more and more difficult to ________________ with their children.
Link is in the closest meaning to this word.
A. bewilder B. exempt
C. project D. communicate

❺ 勞夫由於表現未達到要求的標準而在這個月遭到解雇；然而，他計畫全部重新開始。

Criteria 的意思最接近於這個字。

A. 出版　　B. 標準
C. 擴張　　D. 商標

❻ 史蒂芬一拿到年終獎金就去購買具有自動調節功能高度實用的數位相機。

Spontaneously 的意思最接近於這個字。

A. 建設性地　　B. 逐漸地
C. 無關地　　D. 自動地

❼ 國際車展中陳列展示的古董車吸引許多世界各地的車迷慕名前來觀賞。

Antique 的意思最接近於這個字。

A. 尖銳的　　B. 正確的
C. 古董的　　D. 同情的

❽ 由於代溝，現代的父母覺得越來越難和他們的孩子溝通。

Link 的意思最接近於這個字。

A. 困惑　　B. 免除
C. 投射　　D. 溝通

答案 ❺B　❻D　❼C　❽D

Vocabulary in Context

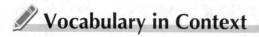

⑨ The ________________ expressions the professor used made it easier for the students to comprehend the difficult theories.
Condensed is in the closest meaning to this word.
A. simplified B. arbitrary
C. desolate D. nominal

⑩ The real estate prices brought up by rich investors recently have become hardly ________________, especially to young people with low income.
Buyable is in the closest meaning to this word.
A. radical B. affordable
C. unified D. economical

⑪ The police tried to find the true murderer by ________________ the suspects one by one through investigation.
Excluding is in the closest meaning to this word.
A. deceiving B. standardizing
C. overlapping D. eliminating

⑫ The heavy casualties on the superhighway last weekend resulted from the serious chain ________________ among seven cars, accompanied by terrifying car-burning afterward.
Smashing is in the closest meaning to this word.
A. exception B. participation
C. collision D. reconciliation

❾ 這位教授所使用簡化的解釋用語讓學生比較容易理解困難的理論。
Condensed 的意思最接近於這個字。

A. 簡化的　　B. 獨斷的
C. 荒涼的　　D. 名義上的

❿ 近日由富有的投資者所帶動提高的房地產價格超出人們所能負擔，尤其是對低薪的年輕人而言。
Buyable 的意思最接近於這個字。

A. 徹底的　　B. 負擔得起的
C. 統一的　　D. 節約的

⓫ 警方經由調查一一排除嫌疑犯試著去找出真正的兇手。
Excluding 的意思最接近於這個字。

A. 欺騙　　B. 標準化
C. 重疊　　D. 排除

⓬ 上週末在高速公路上的慘重傷亡肇因於七部車嚴重的連環追撞，伴隨著後續恐怖的火燒車意外。
Smashing 的意思最接近於這個字。

A. 例外　　B. 參加
C. 碰撞　　D. 和解

答案 ❾ A　❿ B　⓫ D　⓬ C

15 UNIT 精選必考字彙⑮

Vocabulary in Context

❶ The team going on the journey of exploration into the Brazilian tropical jungles ________________ of professors, researchers, and scientists.
Included is in the closest meaning to this word.
A. consisted　　B. scattered
C. worshipped　　D. prohibited

❷ The sample was observed carefully under ________________ of 1,000 times their actual size through the powerful microscope.
Enlargement is in the closest meaning to this word.
A. projection　　B. exclusion
C. destruction　　D. magnification

❸ According to archaeologists, the ________________ of the Stonehenge in Southern England was originally to serve as an observatory and an astronomical calendar.
Building is in the closest meaning to this word.
A. disillusion　　B. prevalence
C. construction　　D. significance

❹ After working in the company for ten years, Joseph decided to quit the job owing to the ________________ of his enduring the heavy workload.

Limitation is in the closest meaning to this word.

A. serenity B. extremity

C. charity D. regularity

❶ 這支前往巴西熱帶叢林考察的隊伍是由教授、研究人員，以及科學家所組成的。

Included 的意思最接近於這個字。

A. 組成 B. 分散

C. 崇拜 D. 禁止

❷ 這份樣本是透過放大 1000 倍於實物的高倍率顯微鏡加以仔細觀察的。

Enlargement 的意思最接近於這個字。

A. 投射 B. 排除

C. 毀壞 D. 放大

❸ 根據考古學家的説法，建造英國南方巨石陣原先的目的是用作天文觀測台以及天文曆法的功用。

Building 的意思最接近於這個字。

A. 幻滅 B. 流行

C. 建造 D. 意義

❹ 約瑟夫在這家公司工作十年後決定要辭職，因為他對於沉重工作負擔的忍耐已經到極限了。

Limitation 的意思最接近於這個字。

A. 寧靜 B. 極端

C. 慈善 D. 規則性

答案 ❶ A ❷ D ❸ C ❹ B

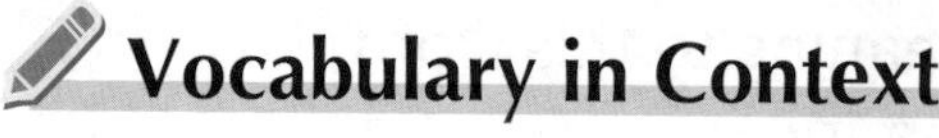

Vocabulary in Context

❺ With his smooth body language, the salesman successfully __________ the operation of the kitchen appliances.

Displayed is in the closest meaning to this word.

A. cultivated B. smuggled
C. proclaimed D. demonstrated

❻ It's odd that some people should be able to make accurate __________ about the future happening. They even claimed to have seen those incidents in person in their dreams.

Forecasts is in the closest meaning to this word.

A. expeditions B. temptation
C. predictions D. generation

❼ The distant __________ of the Pluto at the furthest reaches of the sun has always aroused astronomers' curiosity and interests to know more about it.

Revolving is in the closest meaning to this word.

A. deposit B. rotation
C. milestone D. obstacle

❽ Galileo was a famous Italian astronomer. He used his telescope to make __________ of the moon and the Jupiter, and then made great theories.

Watching is in the closest meaning to this word.

A. actions B. decisions
C. selections D. observations

❺ 這名銷售員運用流暢的肢體語言成功地示範廚房用具的操作方式。
Displayed 的意思最接近於這個字。

A. 耕作　　B. 走私
C. 宣佈　　D. 示範

❻ 很奇怪的是有些人竟然能夠對於未來即將發生的事做準確的預測。他們甚至宣稱在他們的夢境中親眼目睹那些事件。
Forecasts 的意思最接近於這個字。

A. 探險　　B. 誘惑
C. 預測　　D. 產生

❼ 冥王星在距離太陽最遙遠地方的旋轉一向引起天文學者的好奇以及興趣而想作進一步的了解。
Revolving 的意思最接近於這個字。

A. 存款　　B. 旋轉
C. 里程碑　　D. 障礙

❽ 伽利略是著名的義大利天文學家。他曾使用望遠鏡對月亮及木星作觀測，因而提出重要的理論。
Watching 的意思最接近於這個字。

A. 行動　　B. 決定
C. 挑選　　D. 觀察

答案 ❺ D　❻ C　❼ B　❽ D

Vocabulary in Context

❾ Though astronomers and scientists have been trying to make it real for humans to ________________ to Mars, the biggest challenge lies in how to get people to and from the planet.
Move is in the closest meaning to this word.
A. express　　B. immigrate
C. provoke　　D. transplant

❿ When asked about the political scandal, the former minister refused to ________________ and walked away in haste.
Remark is in the closest meaning to this word.
A. comment　　B. expire
C. idolize　　D. rehearse

⓫ Ashley doesn't like to follow trends in her dressing. She has her unique and ________________ styles, which makes her distinctive from others.
Creative is in the closest meaning to this word.
A. dedicated　　B. original
C. righteous　　D. potential

⓬ Mr. Hamilton was respected for both of his ________________ character and boundless enthusiasm in helping others.
Honest is in the closest meaning to this word.
A. mobile　　B. deceptive
C. upright　　D. controversial

❾ 雖然天文學者及科學家一直試圖要把人類移民火星的夢想付諸實現，然而最大的挑戰在於如何讓人們在火星間來回。
Move 的意思最接近於這個字。

A. 表達　　B. 移民
C. 激怒　　D. 移植

❿ 當被問及政治醜聞的時候，這名前部長拒絕作評論並且倉促離去。
Remark 的意思最接近於這個字。

A. 評論　　B. 過期
C. 崇拜　　D. 排演

⓫ 艾旭麗在服裝穿著方面不喜歡趕流行。她有她自己獨特且原創的穿衣風格，而就是這一點使得她與眾不同。
Creative 的意思最接近於這個字。

A. 奉獻的　　B. 有創意的
C. 正直的　　D. 潛在的

⓬ 漢彌頓先生以他正直的品格以及助人的高度熱忱受到大家的敬重。
Honest 的意思最接近於這個字。

A. 移動的　　B. 欺騙的
C. 正直的　　D. 有爭議的

答案 ❾ B ❿ A ⓫ B ⓬ C

16 UNIT 精選必考字彙⑯

Vocabulary in Context

❶. The tragic sinking of the British luxury liner *Titanic* in 1912 resulted in the heavy casualties of 1,500 deaths out of around 2,500 ________________.
Riders is in the closest meaning to this word.
A. documents B. inhabitants
C. passengers D. villagers

❷ The famous American jazz musician, Louis Armstrong, was not only a popular entertainer but an innovative jazz composer, who greatly ________________ and influenced the young music generations.
Encouraged is in the closest meaning to this word.
A. judged B. delayed
C. inspired D. intensified

❸ Groups of animal lovers held protests to show their disapproval of scientists and labs ________________ on animals.
Testing is in the closest meaning to this word.
A. implying B. opposing
C. testifying D. experimenting

❹ It bothered Barney a lot that his wife had been such a shopaholic that their debts were worsened to a hardly ________________ level.

Manageable is in the closest meaning to this word.

A. academic B. controllable

C. volcanic D. responsible

❶ 在 1912 年，英國豪華郵輪鐵達尼號的不幸沉沒導致大約 2500 名乘客中有1500 名死亡的重大死傷。

Riders 的意思最接近於這個字。

A. 文件 B. 居民

C. 乘客 D. 村民

❷ 美國著名的爵士音樂家路易斯・阿姆斯壯，不僅是一名受歡迎的藝人，並且是一名創新的爵士樂作曲家，他大大地鼓舞以及影響年輕的音樂世代。

Encouraged 的意思最接近於這個字。

A. 批判 B. 延遲

C. 鼓舞 D. 加強

❸ 愛護動物團體為了表明不贊成科學家及實驗室利用動物做實驗而進行抗議。

Testing 的意思最接近於這個字。

A. 暗示 B. 反對

C. 證實 D. 實驗

❹ 巴尼十分困擾於他的妻子是如此糟糕的購物狂以至於他們的債務已經嚴重到無法應付的程度了。

Manageable 的意思最接近於這個字。

A. 學術的 B. 控制的

C. 火山的 D. 負責的

答案 ❶C ❷C ❸D ❹B

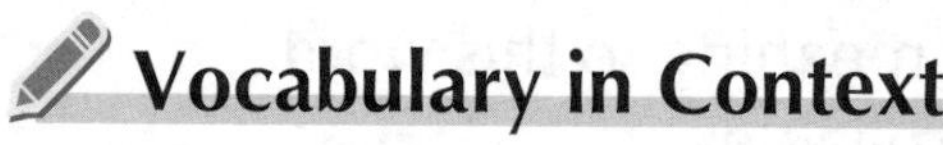

5 With the economic recession getting worse, currency inflation has continued and the unemployment rate has ________________ to 20%, which in turn triggered social problems.
Towered is in the closest meaning to this word.
A. soared B. animated
C. dwelt D. modified

6 The holy water in a small town in France is famed for creating magical curing powers and has yearly attracted lots of pilgrims and tourists all over the world to witness the ________________.
Wonder is in the closest meaning to this word.
A. reform B. miracle
C. portrait D. civilization

7 The American industrialist, Henry Ford, was a ________________ in auto industry, who mass produced cars affordable to average people with the assembly-line technique.
Forerunner is in the closest meaning to this word.
A. victim B. critic
C. pioneer D. delinquent

8 Nancy's ________________ reaction was to accept Warner's invitation, but after careful consideration, she decided to decline it to avoid misunderstanding.
Beginning is in the closest meaning to this word.
A. initial B. negative
C. component D. hypothetical

❺ 隨著經濟不景氣日益嚴重，目前通貨膨脹持續不斷，失業率高升至百分之二十，進而引發社會問題。
Towered 的意思最接近於這個字。
A. 高升　B. 動畫
C. 居住　D. 修改

❻ 法國一座小鎮裡的聖水以創造神奇的治療功效而著名，每年吸引許多世界各地的朝聖者及觀光客來見證這一個奇蹟。
Wonder 的意思最接近於這個字。
A. 改革　B. 奇蹟
C. 肖像畫　D. 文明

❼ 美國工業家亨利・福特是汽車工業的先驅，他利用生產線的技術大量製造一般民眾負擔得起的汽車。
Forerunner 的意思最接近於這個字。
A. 受害者　B. 評論家
C. 先驅　D. 青少年罪犯

❽ 南西起初的反應是接受了華納的邀請，但是經過仔細考慮後決定予以婉拒以避免誤會。
Beginning 的意思最接近於這個字。
A. 最初的　B. 否定的
C. 組成的　D. 假設的

答案 ❺A ❻B ❼C ❽A

Vocabulary in Context

❾ The ________________ drop in temperature these days has brought about great damage to crops and the farmed fish.
Sudden is in the closest meaning to this word.
A. charming B. dramatic
C. relevant D. overcrowded

❿ We all should make every ________________ to strengthen our environmental awareness and work out measures to cope with global warming.
Effort is in the closest meaning to this word.
A. endeavor B. impression
C. operation D. revenge

⓫ On hot summer days, children and adults alike find the ________________ to eating refreshing ice cream too hard to break down.
Refusal is in the closest meaning to this word.
A. mishap B. benefit
C. illusion D. resistance

⓬ The successful writing of the magic adventures of Harry Potter by J. K. Rowling aroused the ________________ of readers all over the world.
Fantasy is in the closest meaning to this word.
A. extinction B. legislation
C. imagination D. relaxation

❾ 近日氣溫的驟降導致農作物和養殖魚場的重大損傷。
Sudden 的意思最接近於這個字。

A. 迷人的　　B. 戲劇性的
C. 相關的　　D. 過度擁擠的

❿ 我們都應該努力加強環保意識並且制定對抗全球暖化的對策。
Effort 的意思最接近於這個字。

A. 努力　　B. 印象
C. 操作　　D. 復仇

⓫ 在炎熱的夏日裡，小孩和大人都認為清涼冰淇淋的誘惑太難以抗拒了。
Refusal 的意思最接近於這個字。

A. 不幸　　B. 利益
C. 幻覺　　D. 抗拒

⓬ J. K. 羅琳成功撰寫的哈利波特魔法冒險激發全世界讀者的想像力。
Fantasy 的意思最接近於這個字。

A. 滅絕　　B. 立法
C. 想像　　D. 放鬆

答案 ❾ B　❿ A　⓫ D　⓬ C

精選必考字彙⑰

Vocabulary in Context

❶. Albert Einstein, the 1921 Nobel Prize winner in physics, made great ________________ to the world by his Theory of Relativity, which changed mankind's understanding of science.
Service is in the closest meaning to this word.
A. explanations B. breakthrough
C. contributions D. steadiness

❷ The entire country is going through an economic ________________ and is filled with an atmosphere of uncertainty and anxiety.
Recession is in the closest meaning to this word.
A. famine B. depression
C. observance D. assertion

❸ Though Mr. Cook's health had notably ________________, he remained optimistic and lighthearted for fear that his family might be sad.
Weakened is in the closest meaning to this word.
A. declined B. survived
C. kidnapped D. economized

❹ The extraordinary new Hollywood actress ________________ her position as the most promising future star by her

excellent performing skills and high popularity with movie fans.
Secured is in the closest meaning to this word.
A. ruined B. portrayed
C. gossiped D. consolidated

❶ 艾伯特・愛因斯坦是 1921 年諾貝爾物理學獎得主，他以改變人類對科學了解的相對論對世界做出極大的貢獻。*Service* 的意思最接近於這個字。
A. 解釋 B. 突破
C. 貢獻 D. 穩定

❷ 這整個國家正經歷經濟蕭條的情境，並充塞著不確定和焦慮的氛圍。*Recession* 的意思最接近於這個字。
A. 饑荒 B. 不景氣
C. 遵守 D. 聲稱

❸ 雖然庫克先生的健康狀況明顯惡化，但他依然保持樂觀輕鬆的態度，以免他的家人悲傷。*Weakened* 的意思最接近於這個字。
A. 衰退 B. 倖存
C. 綁架 D. 節省

❹ 卓越不凡的好萊塢新興女星以她精湛的演技以及超高的人氣鞏固最有前途明日巨星的地位。*Secured* 的意思最接近於這個字。
A. 毀壞 B. 描繪
C. 閒聊 D. 鞏固

答案 ❶ C ❷ B ❸ A ❹ D

Vocabulary in Context

❺ After going through the serious ______________ conditions in the airplane last year, Mrs. Spencer claimed to avoid taking any airplanes because of the strong fear of flights.
Violent is in the closest meaning to this word.
A. flexible B. elementary
C. obscure D. turbulent

❻ Eco-minded car drivers are encouraged to purchase cars equipped with lower ______________ of CO2 and hybrid engines so as to support global green revolution.
Discharge is in the closest meaning to this word.
A. emissions B. priorities
C. resources D. masterpieces

❼ According to medical researches, second-hand smoking is closely ______________ with lung cancer.
Connected is in the closest meaning to this word.
A. endangered B. undergone
C. overtaken D. associated

❽ Sean's family and friends shared the joy and honor with him because through constant diligence and ______________, his dream of entering an ideal college eventually came true.
Perseverance is in the closest meaning to this word.
A. allergy B. persistence
C. declaration D. sentiment

❺ 去年在飛機上經歷過嚴重猛烈氣流的狀況後，史班塞太太因為對於飛行強烈的恐懼而聲稱將避免搭乘飛機。
Violent 的意思最接近於這個字。
A. 有彈性的　　B. 基礎的
C. 不清楚的　　D. 猛烈的

❻ 具有環保觀念的駕駛被鼓勵去購買配備有二氧化碳低排放量以及油電混合引擎的汽車以支持地球的綠色革命。
Discharge 的意思最接近於這個字。
A. 排放　　B. 優先
C. 資源　　D. 傑作

❼ 根據醫學研究，二手煙與肺癌有密切的關係。
Connected 的意思最接近於這個字。
A. 危及　　B. 經歷
C. 趕上　　D. 聯想

❽ 尚恩的家人和朋友與他共享喜悅和榮耀，因為經由持續不斷的努力和堅持，他終於實現了進入理想大學的夢想。
Perseverance 的意思最接近於這個字。
A. 過敏　　B. 堅持
C. 宣佈　　D. 感情

答案 ❺ D　❻ A　❼ D　❽ B

Vocabulary in Context

❾ After five years of hard-working, Eddie was ________________ promoted to the managerial position, and all of his colleagues agreed that he deserved the advancement.
Finally is in the closest meaning to this word.
A. largely B. systematically
C. eventually D. simultaneously

❿ It is taken for granted that you will be seriously punished if you violate the traffic ________________ by driving in the wrong direction.
Rules is in the closest meaning to this word.
A. donations B. regulations
C. solutions D. quotations

⓫ With lots of photos and signatures of movie stars hung on the wall, the famous restaurant was ________________ as a dining place frequented by celebrities and movie stars.
Characterized is in the closest meaning to this word.
A. featured B. refused
C. prohibited D. allocated

⓬ Myron was ________________ as the leader of the project team and was fully dedicated to the realization of his new ideas.
Appointed is in the closest meaning to this word.
A. analyzed B. ornamented
C. designated D. reproached

❾ 經過五年的努力之後，艾迪終於被擢升到經理的職位，他所有的同事都一致認為這份升遷是他應得的。
Finally 的意思最接近於這個字。

A. 主要地　　B. 系統地
C. 最終地　　D. 同時地

❿ 你因逆向行駛違反交通規則而被嚴厲處罰是件理所當然的事。
Rules 的意思最接近於這個字。

A. 捐贈　　B. 規則
C. 解決方案　　D. 引語

⓫ 這家著名的餐廳牆上掛著許多電影明星的照片和簽名，它最大的特色在於它是名流和電影明星經常光顧的用餐地點。
Characterized 的意思最接近於這個字。

A. 特色　　B. 拒絕
C. 禁止　　D. 分配

⓬ 麥倫被指派去擔任專案小組的領導人並努力執行他的新點子。
Appointed 的意思最接近於這個字。

A. 分析　　B. 裝飾
C. 指派　　D. 責備

答案 ❾ C　❿ B　⓫ A　⓬ C

主題式記憶拓展知識面，提高答陌生主題應對能力

新托福主題廣泛，大多是我們不熟悉的主題，熟悉各樣的主題能有效提升答陌生主題時的解題速度跟應對能力，並從中累積許多高階單字，在閱讀跟寫作中都無往不利。

PART

03

·主題式記憶·
·神秘事件·

The Loch Ness Monster

尼斯湖水怪

1 MP3 028

The Loch Ness Monster is an aquatic creature said to live in Loch Ness, a lake in the Scottish Highlands. The earliest mention of "Nessie," another name for it, can be dated back to AD 565. The modern legends of the Monster have started since 1933. However, it became famous only when the so-called "Surgeon's Photograph," taken by a London doctor, Robert Wilson, was published in 1934. The picture was the first photo that clearly captured a dinosaur-like creature with a long "head and neck."

尼斯湖水怪據説是住在蘇格蘭高地尼斯湖的海洋生物。小尼斯，它的另一個名字，最早被提及的時間可追溯到西元 565 年。水怪現代的傳説則從 1933 年開始。然而，它是在由倫敦醫生羅勃．威爾遜所拍攝所謂的「外科醫生的照片」在 1934 年出版後才出名的。這個照片是第一張很清晰地顯示出具有長的頭部和頸部像恐龍般生物的照片。

字彙加油站

aquatic *adj.* 水生的；水棲的	surgeon *n.* 外科醫生

2 MP3 029

Specialized and amateur investigators kept launching expeditions, using sonar and underwater photography to search in the deep lake and tried to explore the truth about it. Over the years, a variety of explanations have been made to account for sightings of the Monster. The giant long-necked creature could probably be an eel, a bird, an elephant, or a resident animal. Nevertheless, nothing conclusive was found. The famous 1934 photo was later proven to be fake, and most scientists claimed it was impossible for a dinosaur-like creature to have survived for millions of years. With the complicated formations of the water areas there, till today, scientists still can't be sure if the monster actually exists.

專業和業餘的調查學者，不停地發動探險，並使用聲納和海底攝影術到深湖去搜尋它。多年以來，有各式各樣的説明來解説被目擊到的水怪。這隻巨大的長頸生物很可能是鰻魚、鳥、大象，或是當地的生物，然而，沒有得到具體的證實。後來，1934 年著名的照片被證實是假造的，而大部分的科學家們宣稱像恐龍般的生物要存活數百萬年是不可能的。由於尼斯湖地形複雜，直到今日，科學家們仍舊無法確定水怪是否存在。

字彙加油站

amateur *adj.* 業餘的；外行的	investigator *n.* 調查者；研究者
launch *v.* 開辦；發起	expedition *n.* 遠征；探險
conclusive *adj.* 決定性的；最終的	survive *v.* 由……生還；活下來

02 UNIT

Horrible Haunted Houses

恐怖鬼屋

1 MP3 030

Creepy ghost stories can be a way for children to be well-behaved and intrigued. In fact, haunted houses are terrifying to most people, the old and the young alike. In America, some modern buildings and ancient houses have a reputation for being haunted by evil spirits. Paranormal activities are constantly reported, which may include sounds of footsteps, or door-slamming, strange blood dripping down the wall, sudden appearances and mischievous behaviors of ghosts, or even brutal killing scenes.

驚悚鬼故事可以是個讓小孩安分守己且存有好奇心的方式。事實上，對大部分人來說，老年人和年輕人都一樣，鬼屋是很恐怖的。在美國，一些現代建築物及古老的房子因為被邪靈纏繞而聲名大噪。超自然活動經常被報導，包括腳步聲、開門聲、奇異的血漬沿著牆壁滴下來、鬼魂突然地出現和惡作劇，或甚至有殘酷的殺戮場景。

字彙加油站

paranormal *adj.* 超自然的	mischievous *adj.* 調皮的；淘氣的

2 MP3 031

All these are told to be made by previous ghost-house owners too obsessed to leave or victims trying to get revenge. The haunted houses usually have special family, regional, or historical backgrounds. Originally, they might be built right on or close to a cemetery, battlegrounds, or crime scenes. The reasons they were haunted could be the locations where a mass murder, battle conflicts, or suicides happened. Therefore, the wandering spirits may include mistreated slaves, witches with great grievance, ghost soldiers, or serial-killing victims. The horrible spirits and the supernatural occurrences make people afraid and wish to keep them away, for the mysterious power is way beyond humans' understanding and control.

這些都是由不願離去的前任鬼屋屋主或試圖復仇的受害者所製造出來的。鬼屋通常有著特殊家庭、區域或是歷史的背景。起初，它們可能是在公墓、戰場或是犯罪現場的正上方或者是附近被建造出來的。它們被鬼纏身的理由可能是集體謀殺、戰場上衝突或自殺事發之地。因此，鬼屋的遊魂可能是被虐待的奴隸、心懷怨恨的女巫、士兵或是連續殺人案的受害者。可怕的鬼魂和超自然事件令人們畏懼並且希望能夠離它們遠遠地，因為這股神祕的力量遠超過人們的理解及掌控。

字彙加油站

obsess *v.* 著迷；煩擾	revenge *n.* 報仇；報復
originally *adv.* 起初地；原來地	

03 UNIT The Swarming Locusts
蝗蟲過境

1 MP3 032

Locusts are mysterious and powerful destructors capable of endangering human beings' livelihood by causing great crop losses. Within a short period of time, the estimated billions of locusts gather in cohesive groups and swarm over and down the vast areas of farming lands at high speeds. They feed and rest on the ground, and then move on when the whole vegetation is exhausted. With food shortage being one of the global crises, the destructive locusts can be an important contributing factor to plaguing all plants, vegetables, and crops. 蝗蟲是神秘且有強大力量的毀滅者，牠們能使農作物蒙受重大損害而危及到人類的生計。在極短的時間內，據估計有數十億成群的蝗蟲以高速蜂擁於廣大農田上方。牠們停留在農地上覓食，然後當所有的作物被吃光了之後，就繼續向前走。食物短缺已是全球危機之一，具毀滅性的蝗蟲，可能是禍及所有的植物、蔬菜和農作物重要的主因。

字彙加油站

endanger *v.* 危及；使遭到危險	livelihood *n.* 生活；生計

2 MP3 033

Therefore, human beings take preventive measures for locust control, such as spreading pesticides, or eating them as food, since they are high in protein. According to researchers, the possible factors for them to fly in great swarms may be their habitual behavior and a certain locust pheromone, which makes them attracted to each other and fly cohesively. Due to having a strong sense of direction induced by the sun, the swarming locusts can fly a great distance. The puzzle of how they have their own such unusual power still needs to be solved. Hopefully, with more secrets unraveled, human beings can have an excellent locust control to lessen the impact they bring to the world.

因此，人類採取蝗蟲管制的預防措施，譬如噴灑殺蟲劑，或因為蝗蟲富含蛋白質而把牠們當作食物來食用。根據研究學者的說法，蝗蟲會群飛的可能因素是由於牠們的自然習性，以及因為具有特定的蝗蟲費洛蒙導致牠們彼此吸引，並且群飛。由於藉由太陽所引導出強烈的方向感，牠們能夠做長距離的飛行。牠們是如何能夠擁有如此不尋常能力的謎，仍有待揭曉。但願隨著越多祕密的揭曉，人類可以做絕佳的蝗蟲管控來減緩牠們帶給世人的衝擊。

字彙加油站

protein *n.* 蛋白質	pheromone *n.* 費洛蒙；外荷爾蒙
unravel *v.* 闡明；解開	

04 UNIT The Yeti
大雪怪

1 MP3 034

The Yeti, also known as the Abominable Snowman, is a mysterious human-like beast spotted in the beautifully bleak and frozen Himalayan regions of Nepal and Tibet. Since the 19th century, the Yeti has been mentioned by the indigenous Himalayan people, and the Sherpa guides along with mountain climbers from all over the world. Till the present day, a large number of reports and accounts sighting the Yeti have been released.

大雪怪，又被稱為喜馬拉雅山雪人，是在美麗荒涼冰凍的尼泊爾和西藏喜馬拉雅山區被發現神秘似人的野獸。自從 19 世紀以來，大雪怪一直被當地的喜馬拉雅人和西藏導遊連同來自世界各地的登山客所提及。到目前為止，有關目擊大雪怪大量的報導和文獻已被公諸於世。

字彙加油站

abominable *adj.* 令人憎惡的；極其討厭的	indigenous *adj.* 土著的；本地的

2 MP3 035

Most of them described the Yeti as a tall, big, and fearful creature, weighing 200 to 400 pounds and covered with long, dark fur. It walked upright, roared fiercely, carried a large stone as a weapon, and always left big footprints on the snowy ground. However, some of the seemingly convincing accounts and photos were later suspected as untrue and unreliable evidence from hoaxers with a view to boosting the tourism in the poor region. In fact, the Yeti is probably only an indigenous gorilla or bear. Since there is little physical evidence concerning it, the scientific community generally regards the Yeti merely as a legend.

大部分的報導及文獻把大雪怪描述為重 200~400 磅，全身覆蓋著長且黑的毛髮，高大且嚇人的生物。它直立行走，大聲怒吼，隨身帶著一顆巨大的石塊作為武器，並且總是在雪地上留下巨大的足跡。但是，有些表面上看似可信的文章和照片，後來被懷疑是來自於欺騙者不實且不可靠的證據，目的是要振興當地窮困地區的觀光業。事實上，大雪怪很可能只是當地的一隻大猩猩或者是一頭熊。由於有關於大雪怪的實質證據非常少，科學界一般只把大雪怪視為一個傳奇罷了。

字彙加油站

hoaxer *n.* 騙子	tourism *n.* 觀光；旅遊業
community *n.* 社區；團體	

05 UNIT

Mermaids
美人魚

1 MP3 036

Images of surpassing beauty and strong determination will flash into one's mind when mermaids are mentioned. They are mysterious marine figures taking the form of a female human above the waist and the tail of a fish below. Mermaids are rich in symbolism in all kinds of depictions about them. In fact, when reading British folklore, you will be surprised to find that they have been deemed as unlucky omens.

當美人魚被提及的時候，絕佳的美貌和堅定意志的形象會在人們的心中浮現。它們是神祕的海洋生物，腰部以上是女性的外貌，腰部以下則呈現魚尾的樣貌。美人魚在各式各樣有關於它們的描述中有豐富的意象。事實上，當閱讀英國民間故事時，你會很驚訝於發現它們一向被視為不吉利的象徵。

字彙加油站

surpassing *adj.* 出眾的；非凡的	omen *n.* 預兆；預告

2 MP3 037

Although mermaids have been linked to bring disasters, tragic death, and terrible misfortunes, they do get praised for granting people's wishes. Among the fascinating legendary works, Hans Anderson's fairy tale, The Little Mermaid, published in 1873, enjoys the greatest popularity. In the tale, the Mermaid bravely pursues her true love at the cost of her life. Though she fails eventually and ends up dissolving into foam, the tragic yet romantic love story has greatly touched and inspired readers worldwide. In 1913, a statue of the Little Mermaid was set up in Copenhagen, Denmark. Till today, countless fans go to visit her and admire her persistence in seeking eternal love and at the same time, lament over her tragic doom.

儘管美人魚一直與帶來災難、悲劇性的死亡和可怕的厄運，她們也因為實現人們願望而受到讚美。在所有令人嚮往的傳奇性作品當中，漢斯．安徒生 1873 年出版的童話故事，「小美人魚」，最受到歡迎。故事當中，小美人魚在犧牲自己性命的代價下，勇敢追求它的真愛。雖然終究失敗並幻化成泡沫，這悲劇卻浪漫的愛情故事大大地感動且啟發全世界的讀者。在 1913 年，以安徒生童話故事為基礎，小美人魚的雕像在丹麥哥本哈根被設立。至今，無數的美人魚迷會去拜訪它，仰慕它尋求永恆真愛的毅力並且同時感慨它悲劇般的命運。

字彙加油站

fascinating *adj.* 迷人的；極好的	lament *v.* 悲痛；痛惜

06
UNIT

Crop Circles
麥田圈

1 MP3 038

Each year, when the first crops ripen, crop circle enthusiasts, including researchers, artists, and tourists can't wait to visit the crop fields in England to appreciate and research into the diverse and mysterious crop circles. Since the first crop circles were sighted and reported in England in the 17th century, they have aroused worldwide attention. Recently, the refined and complicated designs of the flattened crop formations have increased in size and amount attracting even more public interest.

每一年，當第一批農作物成熟時，麥田圈的狂熱分子，包括研究者、藝術家，以及觀光客，等不及要到英國去探望麥田來欣賞並且研究多變化而且神秘的麥田圈。自從 17 世紀第一批麥田圈在英國被發現並被報導之後，他們已經引起全世界的矚目。最近，精緻而且複雜的平坦麥田圈的圖案，在大小和數量上大大地增加，並且引起更多民眾的興趣。

字彙加油站

diverse *adj.* 多種多樣的；多變化的	arouse *v.* 喚起；使奮發

2 MP3 039

As to the causes of crop circles, it is still open to dispute. In the 1960s, many reports of UFO sightings described farmers' witnessing saucer-shaped crafts, implying that the crop circles were made by aliens overnight. In the meantime, scientists doing research have come up with all kinds of scientific theories about the phenomena without good evidence. However, in 1991, Bower and Chorley made headline claims that they, inspired by the extraterrestrial explanations, made all the circles during the 1978-1991 with simple tools. Whether all the amazing crop circles were created by a natural phenomenon or by human hands still puzzles the world.

至於麥田圈形成的原因，目前仍是眾說紛紜。在 1960 年代，許多目擊不明飛行物體的報導，描述農夫親眼目睹到飛碟外觀的太空船，暗示著麥田圈是在一夜之間被外星人所製造出來的。在此同時，做研究的科學家們有提出各種關於此現象的科學理論，卻沒有實質的證據。然而，在 1991 年，鮑爾和柯里做出頭條新聞的宣稱說，他們受到外星人說法的啟發，用簡單的工具在 1978 到 1991 年之間創造出所有的圈圈。所有驚人的麥田圈究竟是由自然現象還是藉由人類之手所創造來的仍舊困惑著整個世界。

字彙加油站

dispute *n.* 爭論；爭執	phenomenon *n.* 現象；稀有的事
extraterrestrial *adj.* 地球外的；外星球的	amazing *adj.* 驚奇的；驚人的

Whales' Mass Suicide
鯨魚集體自殺

MP3 040

Once in a while, there are reports about suicidal behaviors of animals. Among them, cases of whales' mass suicidal behaviors are the most alarming and tragic. It is supposed that as the largest creature in the ocean, whales' lives aren't easily threatened by other marine life. However, quite a few cases have been reported recently. Groups of whales, about 100 whales or so, would swim on shore together, get stranded on the beach and die due to lack of water.

偶爾，我們會聽聞到有關於動物自殺行為的報導。這些報導中，鯨魚集體自殺的行為是最令人震驚且最悲慘的。一般人認為，身為海洋中最巨大的生物，鯨魚的生命並不容易被其他海洋生物所威脅。然而，最近有相當多的個案被報導出來。將近一百條的成群鯨魚會集體游上岸，在沙灘上擱淺並因缺乏水分而死亡。

字彙加油站

threaten *v.* 威脅；恐嚇	strand *v.* 擱淺；處於困境

2 MP3 041

With such weight and body shape, whales, once on shore, are hard to be rescued, and die eventually. Researchers have given several possible reasons for the causes. One is the leading whales' losing their sense of hearing and misleading the direction. Another is that they want to save their partners. Others may include their getting diseases from certain parasites, being terrified by violent thunderstorms, or simply their being influenced by the power of magnetic fields. All these uncertain factors may need to be studied and verified. Hopefully, after realizing the reasons, human beings will offer help to save their lives.

鯨魚有著極重的重量和龐大的體型，一旦上岸便難以拯救，終究會死亡。研究學者們對於這樣的現象提出數項可能的解釋。一個原因是說領頭的鯨魚失去了聽覺，所以誤導方向，另一個原因是牠們想要拯救牠們的夥伴。還有其他可能的原因是有某些寄生蟲導致鯨魚罹患疾病，另或被強烈的暴風雨所嚇到，或是僅僅是因為被磁場的力量所影響。這些不確定的因素也許有待研究與釐清。但願人們在了解原因後能夠提供幫助以拯救牠們的生命。

字彙加油站

rescue *v.* 援救；挽救	disease *n.* 疾病
magnetic *adj.* 磁鐵的；有磁性的	verify *v.* 核對；證實

08 UNIT Vampires
吸血鬼

1 MP3 042

A vampire is a mysterious being who feeds on the blood of living creatures to sustain its life. Since the early 19th century, frightful vampires roaming streets at midnight have been recorded in legends. They were depicted as pale-faced evils in a black cape, obsessed with drinking blood. They feared the sunlight, so they came out after midnight and went back to their coffin before dawn. They drank fresh blood from human victims for immortality.

吸血鬼是一種神祕的生物，它仰賴生物的血液來延續生命。自從 19 世紀早期以來，嚇人的吸血鬼在傳說中就有被描述到半夜在街頭遊走。它們被描述成蒼白、邪惡、吸血，並且穿著黑色的斗篷。它們畏懼陽光，所以在午夜後才出來，並在天亮之前回到棺木中。它們為了求得永生，吸取來自人類受害者身上的鮮血。

字彙加油站

roam *v.* 漫步；漫遊	immortality *n.* 不朽；不滅

2 MP3 043

According to vampire hunters, the best time to permanently end a vampire's life is in the daytime. And the best way to kill it is to penetrate its heart by a sharpened stick. Besides, by holding garlic and crosses in hand, one can also keep vampires away. In the past, among all the vampire figures created in fictional stories, Count Dracula was probably the most famous of all time. However, nowadays, the vampires in the recently released Twilight movie series seem to be more widely known and the vampires in the movies tend to be comparatively powerful. Garlic, holy crosses, and sunlight can harm them no more. Vampire stories are so prevalent that these mysterious creatures occupy the hearts of millions of viewers today.

根據吸血鬼獵人的說法，永遠終止吸血鬼生命最好的時機是在白天，而殺死它最好的辦法是利用銳利的木棍插入其心臟。此外，藉由手中握著蒜頭以及十字架，人們可以使得吸血鬼遠離。在過去，在所有創造出來的吸血鬼人物之中，德古拉伯爵很可能是所有時期以來最著名的。但是，今日來說，在最近放映的「暮光之城」電影系列中的吸血鬼似乎更有名，力量也更為強大。蒜頭、神聖十字架以及陽光皆再也無法傷害它們。吸血鬼故事是如此流行以至於這些神秘的生物在百萬觀眾中仍佔有一席之地。

字彙加油站

sharpen *v.* 削尖；使尖銳	twilight *n.* 薄暮；暮光

Human Electricity Generators
人體發電機

MP3 044

Human electricity generators refer to people who possess the special ability to generate electricity. They are by far the most extraordinary and the most amazing people to the general public. Some seem to have higher voltage of electricity than normal people and can suddenly send off strong electric currents. They were said to electrify the fish in the tank to death or damage electric appliances, and the electricity from them was so powerful that it even once knocked down people nearby.

人體發電機指的是某些擁有特殊能力可以產生電的人。就一般大眾而言，他們是最獨特而且是最驚人的。他們之中有些人似乎比一般正常人擁有更高的電量並且能突然發送強烈的電流。他們曾經被傳聞電死水族箱中的魚，損壞電器設備，而且他們身上散發出的電流是如此的強烈以至於附近的人遭電擊而暈倒。

字彙加油站

voltage *n.* 電壓；伏特數

2 MP3 045

However, one interesting thing about them is that they could easily light a bulb or a flashlight, which is considered supernatural power when performed in a show or at a competition. On the other hand, some extraordinary people can touch high voltage of electricity with their bare hands without being shocked by electricity. Among all ordinary people, they can endure high voltage of electric currents the best. Probably it's because they have rougher or drier skin than others, functioning as an insulating mechanism. And, according to scientists, that is why some people could escape from being hurt though stricken by some violent lightning. As to the true reasons why the human electricity generators can have such extraordinary power, it still calls for scientists' persistent working to find out. 然而，有一件有趣的事是他們可以輕易地點燃燈泡或手電筒，而這種能力在表演場或競賽場中被視為是一種超能力。從另一方面來說，有些具有超能力的人可以直接用手去觸摸高壓電而不會被電到。在所有平常人中，他們最能忍受高電壓的電流。那或許是因為他們比別人擁有更粗糙或更乾燥的皮膚以充當絕緣的作用。根據科學家的說法，那也是有些人縱使被雷電擊中仍然可以免於受到傷害的原因。至於為什麼人體發電機能夠擁有如此超能力的真實原因，仍有待科學家持續努力地去尋找。

字彙加油站

flashlight *n.* 手電筒	persistent *adj.* 執著的；堅持不懈的

10 UNIT

Ghost Ships
幽靈船

MP3 046

For centuries, ghost ships, spotted constantly in vast oceans, are heated subjects for adventurous explorers to discover and make research into. Ghost ships, also named "Phantom Ships," are ships drifting endlessly in the enormous ocean with no passengers or crew aboard, who might be previously missing or killed for unknown reasons. The possible causes, according to researchers, could be bad weather, malfunction of the mechanism, getting lost in the sea, or some human-caused reasons, such as piracy, mutiny, murdering.

許多世紀以來，經常在廣大海域被發現到的幽靈船提供熱門的話題給富冒險精神的探險家去發現並研究。鬼船又名幽靈船，是無止盡地在廣大海域上漂流的船隻，船上並沒有乘客或是船員，他們很可能是因不知名的原因而失蹤或被謀殺。根據研究學者的說法，可能的原因是不良的天候、機械故障、在海上迷失方向，或者是其他人為的因素，例如海盜、叛艦、謀殺。

字彙加油站

malfunction *n.* 失常；出現故障	mutiny *n.* 反叛；叛亂

2 MP3 047

Some even attribute the tragic occurrences to alien abductions, which of course need to be proven. For the past few hundred years, ghost ships have attracted the world's attention, a phenomenon created by literary fictions and horror films. Those artistic works portray the mystically unknown causes of the ship's getting lost in the sea and crew members disappearing overnight. The mysterious settings and tragic happenings truly catch readers' and the audience's eye. With the unanswered questions related to those abandoned and forgotten ships, ghost ships remain the center of focus of public attention.

有些人甚至把這些悲劇的發生歸因於外星人綁架，然而這一點當然有待證實。過去數百年來，由於文學小說以及恐怖電影的推波助瀾之下，幽靈船吸引了世人的注意。那些藝術作品描述在一夜之間，船隻以及船員神秘失蹤的可能原因。這些神秘的背景和悲慘的事件，確實吸引了讀者及觀眾的注意。在解決那些遭遺棄且遭人遺忘船隻的事件前，幽靈船仍是眾人矚目的焦點。

字彙加油站

literary *adj.* 文學的；文藝的	abandon *v.* 遺棄；捨棄
attribute *v.* 歸因於……	

The Mothman
天蛾人

1 MP3 048

The Mothman is a moth-like creature, about seven feet tall with large flying wings and glowing red eyes. It first appeared in the Point Pleasant Area, West Virginia, from 1966 to 1977. In November, 1966, different witnesses separately claimed to have seen the huge, gray, human-like creature, saying that it attempted to fly close to them and chase after them. Frightened by the evil-looking monster, local residents were in great panic.

天蛾人是一個長得像飛蛾的生物，大約七英尺高，有著巨大的飛行翅膀及閃閃發亮的紅眼睛。它是從 1966 到 1977 年間，在西維吉尼亞州的歡樂城附近首度出現。在 1966 年 11 月，不同的目擊者分別宣稱曾經看過這隻巨大灰白色似人類的生物，提及它企圖飛近他們並追逐他們。受到邪惡長相怪物的驚嚇，當地居民極度地恐慌。

字彙加油站

attempt *v.* 企圖；嘗試	resident *n.* 居民；住戶

2 MP3 049

People deem the Mothman as a byproduct of experiment failure by the government or a mutation resulting from chemical waste of an industrial plant, and it has been linked to aliens for its bizarre look. With its bizarre, transformed looks, it was even believed to be a kind of alien from outer space, since the places where it was witnessed were also famous for sighting UFOs. In addition, it was an omen of bad luck, for some people making contact with it died for unknown reasons. Also, in December, 1967, right after it appeared, the Silver Bridge suddenly collapsed, and 46 people tragically died. These unexplained incidents triggered people's firm belief that it brought about disasters. Therefore, when watching the exciting and horrifying movie, the Mothman , we can't help wondering about the true identity and the myth about it. 人們認為天蛾人是政府實驗失敗的副產品或工業工廠化學廢棄物的突變，而且它因奇異的外貌一直被認為與外星人有關連。此外，因為有些和它做過接觸的人們因不明原因身亡導致它被視為一個厄運的徵兆。在 1967 年 12 月，就在它出現後，銀橋（Silver Bridge）突然塌陷造成 46 人死亡的悲劇。這些無法解說的事件，導致人們堅信天蛾人會帶來災難。因此，當我們觀賞刺激嚇人的天蛾人電影時，我們不得不懷疑有關天蛾人的真實身分及傳說。

字彙加油站

collapse *v.* 倒塌；崩潰

trigger *v.* 發動；引起

Kappa, the Japanese River Child
日本河童

1 MP3 050

A kappa in Japanese folklore is an elf in the water. The name is a combination of “kawa,” meaning “river,” and “wappa,” meaning “child.” According to legend, the river child resembles the giant amphibian, the salamander. It lives in the ponds and rivers, about the size of a child with a beak, a turtle-like shell and webbed hands and feet. It has scaly skin with different colors. In addition, there is a bowl-like plate on the top of its head.

「河童」在日本民間傳說中是水中的精靈。這個名字是由表示「河流」的 kawa 以及表示「孩童」的 wappa 所結合而成的。根據傳說，河童類似於巨大的兩棲生物─蠑螈。祂居住在池塘和河流中，體型和孩童類似，身上有著鳥嘴、龜殼以及有蹼的手和腳。祂的鱗皮可以有各種不同的顏色。此外，祂的頭頂有著碗狀的托盤。

字彙加油站

combination *n.* 結合；聯合	resemble *v.* 相像；類似

2 MP3 051

If the plate were full of water, it would be powerful. However, if the plate ever dried out, the Kappa would lose its power and might even die. The Kappa sometimes acts as if it were a cute little troublemaker, hiding under the river surface and playing tricks on people who fall in the river. But it also has a bad reputation for killing horses, cows, kidnapping children, and suffocating people who fall into the water. And that is why the Kappa has long been used to warn children of the potential danger from the river. However, the Kappa isn't always bad. It is sometimes helpful and brings good fortune to the local people. Some Japanese shrines worship it as the River God. So, the mysterious Kappa surely has a great influence on the Japanese culture. 假使這個托盤是滿水狀態時，祂便會力大無窮。相反地，假使這個托盤乾涸了，河童便會失去力量，甚至死亡。河童有時表現地宛如只是一個俏皮的小麻煩製造者，祂會躲在河裡捉弄落入河中的人。但是，祂也具有不好的名聲是因為祂會殺死馬和牛、綁架孩童，並且會將墜入水中的人們悶死。這也就是為什麼「河童」長久以來被用來警告孩童要去注意潛伏在河流中的危險。但事實上，河童並不總是那麼糟糕，有時祂也樂於助人，並且會為當地人帶來好運，有些日本寺廟將它尊奉為「河神」。所以神秘的河童確實為日本文化帶來極大的影響。

字彙加油站

kidnap *v.* 劫持；綁架

suffocate *v.* 窒息；悶死

Reincarnation
輪迴轉世

1 MP3 052

Reincarnation is the natural process of birth, death, and rebirth. A human being's soul or spirit, after death, can begin a new life in a new body. In Buddhism, we human beings are the true masters of our own fate. What you did yesterday makes what you are today. If you did good deeds in the previous life, you would enjoy the fruitful taste in this life. On the contrary, if you were immoral then, you would suffer now.

輪迴轉世是出生，死亡而再生的過程。人類的靈魂或鬼魂在死亡後能夠藉由一個新的軀體開始一個新的生命。就佛教而言，我們人類是我們自己命運的真實主宰者。昨天你的所作所為造就今日的你，如果你前世做好事，今生你將享受美果。相反地，假使你當時不道德，你現在將會受折磨。

字彙加油站

immoral *adj.* 不道德的；邪惡的

2 MP3 053

Seeing life from this point of view, we should think that it is high time that we worked hard to discipline ourselves and performed charities to have a better life in both this life and the next life. The notions of reincarnation in religion may differ from culture to culture, while most scientists and researchers hold skeptical attitudes towards them. Those who oppose hold the idea that ordinary people do not remember previous lives and it is impossible for them to survive death and enter another body. Nevertheless, with more and more cases of reincarnation reported all over the world, they have started to accept the possibility of its existence. For the future to come, reincarnation will still remain a magical mystery that needs to be explored.

從這個角度看人生，我們應該想到我們早就該努力規範自己並且做善事，好讓我們今生與來生都會有一個比較好的人生。宗教轉世輪迴的觀念可能因文化而異，然而大部分科學家和調查員對轉世輪迴抱持著懷疑的態度。反對者認為一般人不記得前世，他們也不可能規避死亡並且進入另一個軀體。然而，隨著全世界有越來越多關於輪迴轉世的報導，他們也開始接受輪迴轉世確實存在的可能性。就未來的歲月來說，輪迴轉世將持續保持是需要被探索的魔幻之謎。

字彙加油站

discipline *v.* 訓練；有紀律	existence *n.* 存在；生存

Pica Eating Disorder
異食癖

MP3 054

When it's time to enjoy a great meal, people think of delicious fish, meat, vegetables, and fruits. However, to people suffering from Pica, they will have a totally different menu. Pica is an abnormal craving or appetite for nonfood substances, such as soil, clay, glass, or metal. In fact, eating soil in certain African regions that lack sufficient food is a common practice. To people there, especially to pregnant women, the underground soil is rich in different minerals, from which they can supplement nutrition.

享受大餐時，人們會想到美味的魚，肉，蔬菜，和水果。然而，對罹患異食癖的人來説，他們菜單上的菜色卻是大大的不同。異食癖是對非食物的物質，譬如像土壤，黏土，玻璃，或金屬，產生一種不正常的熱愛或食慾。事實上，在某些缺乏足夠糧食的非洲地區，吃土壤是司空見慣的。對那裡的人來説，地下土壤富含礦物質，他們，尤其是孕婦，可以從地下土壤補充營養。

字彙加油站

abnormal *adj.* 不正常的；反常的

supplement *v.* 補充；補給

2 MP3 055

However, medically speaking, a Pica patient may get seriously sick because of lead-poisoning, malnutrition, parasite infection, intestinal obstruction, or tearing in the stomach. Some Pica patients may have certain mental disorders, while others may simply want to relieve the stress from their family or the society. As for the healing solutions, besides taking medication, psychological treatments, family guidance, and reinforcement of social communication skills are recommended. Though it's hard to imagine eating odd stuff, from dirt, glass, to even bikes, or TV sets, most of them claim that they will feel sick if forbidden to eat the non-food they like.

但是就醫學而言，有異食癖的病患可能會因為鉛中毒、營養不足、寄生蟲感染、腸阻塞、或腸胃撕裂而病重。某些異食癖病患也許有特定的精神異常狀況，而有些可能只是想要舒緩來自於家庭或社會的壓力。至於治療的解決方法，除了吃藥之外，心理治療、家庭指導以及社交溝通技能的強化是被推薦的。雖然人們很難想像去吃像泥土、玻璃，甚至是腳踏車或電視機這樣古怪的東西，大部分異食癖患者卻宣稱，假使他們被禁止吃他們喜愛吃的非食物，他們反而會生病。

字彙加油站

malnutrition *n.* 營養不良；營養失調

psychological *adj.* 心理學的；精神的

15 UNIT The Elephants' Graveyard
大象墓園

MP3 056

In Africa, there's a legendary myth that when elephants get old and sense their upcoming death, they would walk a long distance to the "Elephants' Graveyard" and die there alone. However, till now, we still haven't had the slightest idea about where the burial grounds are. Elephant tusks can be made into ivories that are highly valuable, so greedy hunters are always searching for the graveyard. To them, they must be full of precious ivory tusks. Strange to say, their wishful thinking has never been fulfilled.

在非洲，有一個流傳的神秘說法：當大象年紀大了，並且意識到即將死亡，牠們會單獨走很長一段路去到「大象墓園」，並且獨自在那兒死亡。但是至今我們仍不知「大象墓園」在那裡。大象的牙齒可以製造成高價值的象牙，所以貪婪的獵人一直在搜尋墓園。對他們來說，墓園裡必定充滿著珍貴的象牙。說也奇怪，他們的心願從來沒有實現過。

字彙加油站

legendary *adj.* 傳奇的；傳說的	ivory *n.* 象牙；象牙製品

2 MP3 057

Most hunters and explorers had difficulty finding it, though some local tribal chiefs claimed to have seen one. In fact, whether the graveyard exits or not still remains doubtful. Besides, the causes of elephants' death vary. Researchers maintain that some seemingly tusk-piled locations cannot be sure to be the graveyard where elephants choose to complete the process of death, for water floods may have resulted in the accumulation of large piles of the tusks. And, great numbers of elephants may have died there shortly after some great food or water shortage. Besides, other natural disasters may have caused their death, too. Still another supposition is that cruel and notorious poachers might deliberately trap and kill them to get ivory tusks.

雖然曾有當地土著酋長宣稱曾經看過墓園，大部分的獵人和探險家找不到它。事實上，墓園是否真的存在仍令人懷疑。此外，大象死亡的原因不一。研究學者們主張，某些看起來似乎堆滿了象牙的地方無法確定就是大象選擇結束生命過程的墓園，因為大洪水可能導致大量的象牙成堆地累積。而且，在某個重大的食物或飲水短缺之後不久，大量的大象有可能死於墓園內。此外，其他天然災害也有可能導致牠們的死亡。另一個假設是說，殘忍且聲名狼藉的盜獵者有可能蓄意地設陷阱捕殺牠們取得象牙。

字彙加油站

accumulation *n.* 累積；積聚	poacher *n.* 偷獵者；盜獵者

Disaster-Predicting Dreams
災難預知夢

1 MP3 058

Most of us spend about one third of our lives sleeping, and what we dream about while sleeping can have great significance. It's a long known mystery that some people claim to have disaster-predicting dreams. They seem to have a special sixth sense and, without having related knowledge in advance, can have dreams predicting future incidents, either natural disasters or human-caused accidents. Natural disasters may include floods, earthquakes, tornadoes, tsunamis, or hurricanes, such as the devastating Hurricane Katrina. 我們大多數人一生中有三分之一的時間在睡覺，而睡覺時作的夢具有極大的意義。這是一個人們長久以來聽聞的現象，即有些人宣稱能夠預先夢見災難。他們似乎擁有特別的第六感，事前並不知道任何相關的訊息，但是竟然能夠作預告未來事件的夢，不管是天然災害，或者是人為的意外事故。天然災害可能包含有水災、地震、龍捲風、海嘯，或者是颶風，譬如像極具災難性的卡翠納颶風。

字彙加油站

significance *n.* 意義；重要	devastating *adj.* 毀滅性的；驚人的

2 MP3 059

On the other hand, dreams predicting human-caused accidents maybe about shooting incidents, plane crashes, or shipwrecks, such as the tragic sinking of the dubbed "Unsinkable" Titanic. From researchers' point of view, what these predictors claimed can hardly be real. In their opinion, these foretold disaster dreams are nothing but responses to events in the dreamers' personal life, and the dreams may probably be just coincidences. However, with the vivid, detailed, and exact descriptions of those dreamers, we can't help wondering how the disasters they dream about can actually happen in the real world. Therefore, we believe there is still a long way to go to explore humans' subconscious minds and dreams. 另一方面，預見人為意外事件的夢境則可能是槍擊事件、飛機墜機，或者是船難，譬如像號稱「永不沉沒」的鐵達尼號悲慘沉沒的事件。從研究學者的觀點來說，預測者所宣稱的夢境不可能是真實的。依他們之見，這些預知災難的夢境只是作夢者個人生活事件的反應，可能只是巧合罷了。但是，隨著那些作夢者生動詳細而且確切的描述，我們不得不納悶他們夢到的災難如何能夠確切地在真實事件中發生。所以，我們相信探索人類潛意識的心靈和夢境仍然有長遠的路要走。

字彙加油站

shipwreck *n.* 海難；船舶失事	coincidence *n.* 巧合；巧事
vivid *adj.* 清晰的；生動的	subconscious *adj.* 潛意識的

17 UNIT The Mysterious Holy Water
神秘聖水

1 MP3 060

Inside the sanctuary at Lourdes, France, is a famous place of pilgrimage providing holy water that creates miracle cures. It's said that the holy water never stopped springing out and possessed curing effects for illnesses. In fact, the discovery of the holy water was full of mythical origins. During the 19th century, a poor girl named Bernadette Soubirous accidentally found a cave and met a smiling noble lady, whom the townspeople thought to be the Virgin Mary later.

在法國盧德的聖殿裡，有一處提供奇蹟療效聖水而著名的朝聖地。當地居民從未想到這聖水竟帶給他們極大的改變。據說這聖水從不停止噴湧出來，並有療病的效果。事實上，聖水的發現充滿神秘的起源。在 19 世紀期間，有一個叫做 Bernadette Soubirous 的貧窮女孩，無意間發現一個洞穴並且遇見一位面帶微笑的高貴女士，這位女士後來被居民認為是聖母瑪利亞。

字彙加油站

accidentally *adv.* 意外地；偶然地

Bernadette followed Mary's instructions and dug a well. People who drank water from there found their symptoms alleviated or cured. The church was built for appreciation for the Virgin Mary and since then holy water became famous. The pious Catholic pilgrims and tourists would visit the place either to get their illnesses cured or to witness the miracle. After lining up for hours, they would usually light up candles, say prayers, drink the holy water, and bathe in it for curing or purification. However, where the endless holy water comes from and why it has such great healing properties are still mysteries to the world.

Bernadette 遵從瑪莉的指示挖了井。從那裡飲用井水的人發現症狀減輕或痊癒了。人們為了感謝聖母瑪利亞建造的教堂，從那時候起，聖水也變有名了。虔誠的天主教朝聖者以及觀光客會來參觀這個地方，也許是要為自己治療疾病，或者是要見證奇蹟。在排隊排上好幾個小時後，他們一般會點燃蠟燭祈禱，喝聖水，並浸泡在聖水中來取得治療或淨化的作用。然而，永無止盡的聖水來自於何處，以及它為何具有如此大的治療功效，對世人來說仍舊是謎。

字彙加油站

pious *adj.* 虔誠的；敬神的	purification *n.* 洗淨；淨化

Pythons That Swallow Large Animals

蟒蛇吞巨物

1 MP3 062

Although non-venomous, pythons are fierce and brutal predators. Pythons attack whatever they see when hungry. Horrifying incidents as such are frequently reported worldwide, especially in Africa and Australia. Some ferocious pythons can swallow huge-sized animals, such as sheep, deer, and cows. They also eat alligators, kangaroos, and even young children. Once hungry, little do they hesitate to ambush and swallow the animal they spot even though they are huge.

雖然無毒性，蟒蛇是凶猛殘暴的掠食者。當飢餓時蟒蛇攻擊任何看到的東西。像這樣恐怖的事件，經常在全世界被報導，尤其是在非洲和澳洲。有些兇猛的蟒蛇，能夠吞下像綿羊、鹿，和牛這樣大型的動物。牠們也吃鱷魚、袋鼠，甚至是孩童。一旦餓了，牠們毫不遲疑於突襲並且吞嚥牠們所看見的動物，儘管牠們體型龐大。

字彙加油站

ferocious *adj.* 兇猛的；殘忍的	hesitate *v.* 猶豫；有疑慮

2 MP3 063

With a certain unique method, they consume the innocent creature. First, they constrict it to death, and then gorge it in just one bite. In one or two gulps, the poor victim is devoured. Once the pythons begin to devour, seldom do they stop. Afterwards, though painful with a swollen stomach, they can digest the prey with their special feeding mechanism. In South Africa, no sooner had a ten-year-old boy run fast to get away from a python that moved silently than he got swallowed and consumed within minutes. How terrible! So, next time, when planning to keep a python as a pet, one may as well give it a second thought!

牠們會用獨特的方式把無辜的生物吞噬。首先，牠們把牠絞死，接著一口咬住，可憐的受害者一兩口就被吞下肚了。一旦蟒蛇開始吞噬，牠們很少稍作停留。稍後，雖然因腫脹的肚子而感到痛苦，牠們會以特殊的餵食機制來消化獵物。在南非，有一個 10 歲大的小男孩一快跑以逃離無聲無息且快速前行的蟒蛇，卻馬上就被吞噬而且幾分鐘內就被吃進肚了。真可怕！所以，下一次，當人們計畫要養蟒蛇做寵物時，最好能三思！

字彙加油站

consume *v.* 吃完；耗費	devour *v.* 吃光；吞沒
swollen *adj.* 膨脹的；誇大的	

19 UNIT The Mysterious Bermuda Triangle

神秘的百慕達三角

1 MP3 064

Within the Bermuda Islands, the Bermuda Triangle is a region bounded by Florida, Bermuda, and Puerto Rico in the Atlantic Ocean. Ever since the American reporter, Edward Jones, first published the article about the ship missing incident in the Bermuda Triangle in 1950, it has been misted with a mysterious veil. Dozens of ships and planes, due to the alleged supernatural powers, have disappeared for no reason, which made the region haunted and extremely mysterious, and was thus even nicknamed "Devil's Triangle." 身處於百慕達群島裡，百慕達三角是大西洋中由佛羅里達、百慕達和波多黎各所形成的一個區域。自從美國記者，愛德華・瓊斯在 1950 年首度出版了有關於在百慕達三角船隻失蹤事件的文章後，這個地方就被一層神秘的面紗所籠罩著。成打的船隻和飛機，由於傳說中的超自然力量，無緣無故地失蹤了，使得這個區域鬼影幢幢，且相當地神秘，甚至因此得到「魔鬼三角」的綽號。

字彙加油站

bound *v.* 與……接界；限制	disappear *v.* 消失；不見

2 MP3 065

Scientists and specialists tried to investigate and analyze the possible reasons for the mishaps, among which, the missing of the US navy bombers, Flight 19, in 1945 and the passenger-carrying aircraft, Star Tiger, in 1948 were the most notable. Possible factors might be human errors in violent weather, influences of the Mexican Gulf stream, compass deviations due to the physical magnetic power, and so on. Nevertheless, with all these scientific explanations, the Bermuda Triangle remains mysterious because of the prevalent legends of fake and exaggerations made by people awed by the tragic and mystical incidents. Still, the mystery is absolutely worth our efforts to solve.

科學家和專家們試圖去調查並分析這些不幸事件發生的可能原因。在這些不幸事件當中，1945 年的美國海軍轟炸機“19 號機隊”，以及 1948 年的民航客機「星虎號」的失蹤案件最為著名。結論指出，失蹤的可能的原因，包含劇烈天候狀況下人為的疏失、墨西哥海灣洋流的影響、物理磁力導致羅盤的變化，…等等。但是，即使有這些科學的說明，人們對這些悲劇且神秘的事件仍深感敬畏而捏造出廣泛流傳的杜撰且誇張的傳說，使得百慕達三角依舊是充滿神祕的。儘管如此，這謎題絕對值得我們努力去解開。

字彙加油站

deviation *n.* 偏差	prevalent *adj.* 流行的；普遍的

Alien Abduction
外星人綁架案

1 MP3 066

Quite a few cases of alien abduction have been heard about in America during the 20th century. Theories concerning the high intelligence of aliens are a lot, from creating highly evolved civilization on earth to making contact with earth people. However, the most horrible are the reported cases of abduction done by them. Since the appearance of UFOs in the 1940s', aliens have been heard to kidnap humans for unknown reasons, probably for research, experiments, or even reproduction.

20 世紀時，在美國有傳聞相當多的外星人綁架事件。有關於高智慧外星人的理論相當多，從創造地球高度演化文明直到跟地球人做接觸。但是，最可怕的是報導傳聞由它們所做的綁架案件。自從 1940 年代幽浮出現之後，傳說外星人為了一些不知名的理由綁架人類，很可能是要做研究、做實驗，或者是繁殖。

字彙加油站

abduction *n.* 綁架；劫持	experiment *n.* 實驗；試驗

2 MP3 067

The first widely publicized case was the Betty and Barney Hill Abduction in 1961. After being attacked by some UFO at night, Mr. and Mrs. Hill seemed to have missed a large span of time and couldn't recall anything. And then, they painfully suffered from mental disorder until a hypnotherapist cured them of their sickness through hypnosis. As they remembered, the short, gray aliens, with arms and legs, and a small mouth but no nose, looked quite different from humans. The Hills were then terrified and were made some experiments on. Other similar victims were also convinced that they were kidnapped by aliens. Nevertheless, some of the alleged happenings were later proved merely deceptive. but there's no knowing the true motives behind alien abduction.

第一宗廣為宣稱的案子是 1961 年貝蒂和巴尼・希爾夫婦的綁架案。某一個夜晚在被幽浮攻擊過後，希爾夫婦似乎有一大段時間的記憶是空白的，而且他們無法回憶起任何事情。然而，之後，他們痛苦地蒙受精神失調的疾病，一直到有一位催眠治療師透過催眠術治癒了他們的疾病。在他們的記憶中，矮小、灰色、有手腳、小嘴巴，但是沒有鼻子的外星人，看起來和人類大不相同。希爾夫婦在當時感到害怕，同時外星人有在他們身上做了些實驗。其他類似的受害者也相信他們自己曾被外星人綁架。然而，事後有些據稱的事件被證實只是詐騙。但是外星人綁架人類背後的動機無從得知。

字彙加油站

publicize *v.* 宣傳；公佈	motive *n.* 動機；目的

21 UNIT The Mystery of UFOs
幽浮之謎

1 MP3 068

For centuries, people have believed we are not alone in the universe. Aliens taking the UFO, short for Unidentified Flying Objects, often visit us on earth. Many sightings of UFOs were reported worldwide, and a great percentage of Americans claim to have either witnessed or made contact with them. Among those incidents, the 1947 Rosewell Incident was the most noticeable, in which a flying saucer supposedly crashed in New Mexico. However, the US Air Force tried to cover up the whole incident.

數個世紀以來，人們相信我們在宇宙中並不是孤單的。乘坐幽浮（不明飛行物體的簡稱）的外星人經常到地球來探望我們。全世界都有許多看見幽浮的報導。極大比例的美國人宣稱曾經目擊或者是跟外星人接觸過。這些事件中，1947 年羅斯威爾事件是最引人注目的。在這事件中，有一部飛碟據説在新墨西哥州墜毀。但是，美國空軍試圖遮掩整個事件。

字彙加油站

unidentified *adj.* 未辨別出的	noticeable *adj.* 顯著的

2 MP3 069

The US government was believed to not only take over the wreckage of the spaceship but examine the four or five aliens' dead bodies recovered from the site. Afterwards, the army tried to hide the truth from the public in panic to lessen the impact by announcing the seemingly crashed aircraft was only a weather balloon. Still, sightings of UFOs were reported one after another by both military pilots and civilians. Terrified people might take them for real, while skeptical investigators regard them only as people's imaginations, hoaxes or misinterpretation of known objects, such as balloons, meteors, or solar reflections. Nevertheless, it's hard to rule out the possibility of extraterrestrial phenomena, which still remains an unsolved mystery.

一般人相信美國政府不僅接收了太空船的殘骸，同時檢驗了在失事現場所找尋到的 4~5 具外星人屍體。稍後，軍方藉由宣布看起來似乎是墜毀的太空船只是一個觀測天氣的氣球來遮掩事實以減緩民眾的恐慌。然而，軍方的飛行員和一般百姓接而連三地通報目睹到幽浮。驚慌的民眾可能信以為真，但是懷疑的調查人員僅把它們視為人們的想像、欺騙，或是對於已知的物件，譬如像氣球、流星，或是太陽反射的誤解。然而，要排除外星人現象的可能性是很困難的，而這也將保持是一個未解的謎。

字彙加油站

misinterpretation *n.* 誤解；誤釋　reflection *n.* 反射；反映

22

UNIT

The Suicide Forest

自殺森林

1 MP3 070

Aokigahara, a forest situated in the northwest base of Mt. Fuji, is a well-known suicide location. Each year, the forest attracts not only tourists to appreciate its natural beauty but people determined to end their lives there. Since 1960, after the publication of a popular novel describing the main character's suicide there, even more people ended their lives there. It has become a common but horrible trend. In fact, entering the dense black forest with the sunlight blocked makes hikers afraid.

位於富士山西北山腳下的青木原是一個知名的自殺地點。每一年，這座森林吸引的不僅是要欣賞它天然美景的觀光客，也吸引了執意要在此地結束生命的民眾。1960 年以來，就在一本描述主角在此地自殺的暢銷小說出版後，更多人去到青木原結束生命。這已經成為一個普遍且可怕的流行趨勢。事實上，健行者進入這座被陽光遮蔽的茂密黑森林時，會感到害怕。

字彙加油站

determined *adj.* 堅定的；決然的

2 MP3 071

Due to the magnetic iron deposits in the volcanic soil, compasses cannot work and hikers will easily get lost. Furthermore, the forest allegedly used to be a place, in ancient times, where the sick and the old were abandoned, so it's full of vengeful spirits. That's why the forest seems to be veiled in black mystery of grievance, sadness, and death, which might trigger travelers' desire to commit suicide there. With the worsening global economy, the suicide cases have increased rapidly. Therefore, the signs advising hikers that they should cherish their lives and should not commit suicide there are even put up at the entrance of the forest. The mystery of the suicide forest truly needs to be solved before the happening of more tragedies.

由於火山土壤含磁鐵的沉積物，使得羅盤無法作用而常導致健行者迷失方向。此外，據稱這座森林在古代是一個患病者和老年者被遺棄的地方，所以森林充滿著怨恨的冤魂。這也是為何這座森林似乎是籠罩在怨恨、悲傷和死亡的黑色神秘之中，因而可能引發旅客想在此地自殺的念頭。隨著全球經濟惡化，自殺事件快速地增加。因此，勸導登山者應該要珍惜生命，不應該自殺的標語，甚至被設立於森林入口處。自殺森林之謎在更多的悲劇發生之前確實應該被解開。

字彙加油站

volcanic *adj.* 火山的；爆裂的	grievance *n.* 不滿；怨言

23 UNIT The Nasca Lines

納斯卡線

1 MP3 072

The Nasca Lines are a series of straight lines cut into the surface of the Nasca Desert in southeastern Peru. Covering 450 square kilometers, the Nasca Lines have been called the biggest drawing ever created. They consist of thousands of geometric shapes and hundreds of complex figures from both the natural world and the human imagination. They include the hummingbird, spider, pelican, lizard, monkeys, plants and human figures. Scholars believe that the Lines were created by the Nasca culture between 500 BC and 500 AD. 納斯卡線是一系列被雕刻於祕魯東南方納斯卡沙漠的直線。納斯卡線面積有 450 平方公里，號稱是有史以來最大的一幅畫作。它們有上千個幾何圖形以及上百個來自於自然界和人類想像複雜的圖案。它們包含有蜂鳥、蜘蛛、鵜鶘、蜥蜴、猿猴、植物，以及人類的圖騰。學者們相信納斯卡線是在西元前 500 年至西元 500 年之間被納斯卡文化創造出來的。

字彙加油站

complex *adj.* 複雜的；難懂的	scholar *n.* 學者；有學問的人

2 MP3 073

The complexity of the Lines proves that the remarkable Nascan people used to have highly developed surveying skills. Besides, the designed patterns can be clearly identified only from the sky, which shows Nascan Indians could fly in the sky, probably in balloons. It's also very likely that aliens with high intelligence from outer space might have instructed them to accomplish the masterpiece. Other speculations are that the Lines might have functioned for religious purposes, or for water irrigation, since water is vital but rare in the desert. And surprisingly, the Lines are even believed to have been used as landing areas for alien spaceships. All in all, the mystery of Nasca Lines still calls for the archaeologists nowadays to explore.

納斯卡線的複雜度證實了不起的納斯卡人過去曾有高度發展的測量技能。此外，這些設計圖案僅能夠從高處清楚的被看見，這表示納斯卡印地安人可能當時能夠乘坐氣球在空中飛行。因此，來自於外太空具有高度智慧的外星人可能當時曾指導他們完成這幅巨作。其他的推測則是納斯卡線可能是有著宗教的目的或者是因為沙漠地區水很重要但缺乏而做為水源灌溉的用途。令人驚訝的是，納斯卡線一度被認為是給外星人太空船降落的地點。總而言之，納斯卡線之謎仍有待今日的考古學家來探索。

字彙加油站

remarkable *adj.* 非凡的；卓超的	irrigation *n.* 灌溉；沖洗

The Dinosaur Park

恐龍公園

MP3 074

The Dinosaur Park, located near Brooks, in the Province of Alberta, Canada, has always been a popular tourist attraction. After its grand opening in 1955, the park has become well known for both being given the honor of UNESCO World Heritage Site in 1979 and one of the most abundant dinosaur fossil locations in the world. About forty dinosaur species have been discovered there, which attracts floods of researchers and dinosaur lovers.

位於加拿大艾伯塔省布魯克斯附近的恐龍公園一向是熱門的觀光景點。在 1955 年盛大開幕後，這座公園因為在 1979 年獲頒「聯合國教育科學暨文化組織」認定為世界遺產的殊榮以及號稱為全世界恐龍化石蘊藏量最大的地點之一而著名。在那兒曾發現大約有 40 種的恐龍品種，因而吸引大量研究者及恐龍愛好者前來。

字彙加油站

abundant *adj.* 豐富的；充足的

2 MP3 075

Inside the Park Center, visitors can enjoy appreciating the exhibits about dinosaurs, fossils, the geological structures and the natural history of the park. In addition, it has unique scenery, and diverse formations of landscape. Dinosaur experts can find different kinds of plant and dinosaur fossils there and usually the discoveries made will be shipped to museums worldwide for scientific analysis and exhibition. When dinosaur fans stroll in the park feeling sorry for the extinction of the dinosaurs, they can't help wondering what had exactly happened sixty-five million years ago. Why should the dinosaurs, once the master of the world, though probably got killed either by the hit of an asteroid or comet, or by the sudden freezing cold climate, completely disappear from the earth?

在公園中心內，訪客可以欣賞到恐龍、化石、地質情況，以及公園天然歷史等的展覽。此外，它有獨特的風景以及多變化的地質景觀。恐龍專家們可以在那兒找到各種不同的植物及恐龍的化石，而且一般在那兒的發現會被運送到全世界的博物館做科學分析以及展覽。當恐龍迷在公園漫步，為恐龍的滅絕感到遺憾時，他們不得不懷疑 6500 萬年前究竟發生了什麼事，為什麼一度是世界主宰者的恐龍，雖然很可能喪命於小流星或慧星的衝擊，或全球氣候的驟降，竟然會完全地從地球消失了？

字彙加油站

exhibition *n.* 展覽；展示會

extinction *n.* 滅絕；消滅

The Amazing Dead Sea
神奇的死海

1 MP3 076

The Dead Sea is a salt lake located between Jordan and Israel. Being about 400 meters deep, it is the deepest landlocked lake with the highest concentration of salt in the world. The high salinity prevents any life forms from surviving in the lake, the reason for its being called a "Dead" Sea. However, one thing interesting about it is that the high salinity of it enables people to float on the surface without worrying about sinking down, and many vacationers look forward to doing that. Isn't that amazing?

死海是位於約旦和以色列間的鹹水湖。死海大約四百公尺深，是全世界鹽度最高且最深的內陸湖。高鹽度使得所有的生物都無法在湖裡生存，所以它被稱為「死」海。然而有趣的是，死海的高鹽度可以讓人們無憂於下沉而在海面上漂浮，許多遊客也很期盼於這麼做。那不是很神奇嗎？

字彙加油站

landlocked *adj.* 內陸的；閉合水域的	concentration *n.* 專心；濃度

2 MP3 077

Nowadays, the Dead Sea has become a popular health resort. Tourists can visit some purely historic spots, enjoy the breathtaking natural scenery, and enjoy the seawater in the bathing areas. In addition, visitors come here for its unique products of both healing properties, such as beauty cosmetics. The composition of the salts and minerals in the water can be used to cure people of chronic diseases, such as arthritis and the deposits of the black mud from the sea can be materials for cosmetic products. With these amazing characteristics, no wonder it has become such a popular tourist attraction. Will the mysterious "Dead Sea" cease "living" one day? The answer definitely is "No!"

今日而言，死海已成為一個受歡迎的健康度假中心。觀光客可以參觀正統的歷史景點，享受令人屏息的天然美景，並且享受浸泡區的海水此外，訪客是為了具治療藥效及美妝品的獨特產品而來到這裡。海水中鹽及礦物質的合成物能用來治療人們，譬如像關節炎的慢性疾病，而且來自大海黑泥的沉澱物可作為製造化妝品的材料。有這些驚人的特色，難怪它成為如此受歡迎的觀光景點。神秘的死海有一天將停止「生存」嗎？答案是「絕對不可能」！

字彙加油站

resort *n.* 休閒度假之處；名勝	healing *adj.* 有治療功用的；康復中的
chronic *adj.* 慢性的；長期的	characteristic *n.* 特徵；特色

26 UNIT Area 51

51 區

1 MP3 078

The famous US Air Force facility, commonly known as Area 51, is located in Nevada, the western United States. It is estimated that probably the main purpose of the large military airfield is to test and develop experimental aircraft and weapons systems. Nevertheless, what is done there is in fact a generally held secret from the public, which adds a certain mysterious atmosphere to the area. One of the most common rumors has it that inside the base, there are crashed alien spacecrafts.

美國著名的空軍機構，51 區，位於美國西部內華達州。根據估測，這一個巨大的軍用航空站可能主要目的是用來測試及發展實驗飛機和武器系統。然而事實上，在那裡所做的事一般是隱瞞不為大眾所知的，這樣的作法為這個區域增添了神祕的氣氛。最常聽見的謠傳之一是，在這個基地裡有墜毀的外星人太空船。

字彙加油站

atmosphere *n.* 大氣層；氣氛	manufacture *n.* 製造；虛構

2 MP3 079

And, also, the researches of the manufacture of the alien aircraft and the aliens, both living and dead, are done there. Therefore, Area 51 has always attracted UFO fans all over the world and they all hope to visit the public areas surrounding it. It was not until July, 2013 that the US government officially acknowledged the existence of the restricted area, Area 51. Nowadays, many people still doubt whether aliens and UFO aircraft are truly placed in Area 51. However, one thing can be sure is that the mysterious site offers military and UFO fans a lotof topics to talk about.

此外，這裡也進行著有關於外星人太空船的製造以及活著的或死了的外星人的研究。所以，51 區一向吸引世界各地的幽浮迷，他們同時也盼望能參觀它附近的公共場所。一直到 2013 年 7 月，美國政府才正式承認 51 禁區的存在。今日來說，許多人仍懷疑 51 區內是否真的有外星人和幽浮太空船。但是，有一點可以確定的是這個神秘基地提供軍事和幽浮迷許多可以討論的話題。

字彙加油站

acknowledge *v.* 承認；致意	restricted *adj.* 有限的；受限制的

27 UNIT

The Valley of Death

死亡谷

1 MP3 080

One of the most horrible valleys of death in the world is in Kamchatka, Russia. No vegetation, no birds, and no animals could ever survive there. The valley lies in the western slope of Kikhpinych Volcano in Kamchatka, ranging about 2,000 meters long, 100 to 300 meters wide. It has crooked, rough, uneven surfaces and formations, and also it has allegedly poisonous volcanic gases. In addition, the valley was rumored to have been a mystic zone like hell and was dubbed the "Valley of Death".

全世界最恐怖的死亡谷之一，是在俄羅斯的堪姆恰特卡。在那裡，從未有任何的植物、鳥類，或動物可以存活。這座山谷位於堪姆恰特卡，奇克皮查火山的西面山坡上，橫跨 2,000 公尺長，100~300 公尺寬。它有蜿蜒、粗糙，不均衡的表面及構造，而且據說含有劇毒的火山瓦斯氣體。此外，據謠傳這座山谷是地獄般的神秘區域，並有「死亡之谷」的稱號。

字彙加油站

vegetation *n.* 植物；草木	crooked *adj.* 彎曲的；欺詐的

It was once filled with dead bodies and skeletons of various living things, such as birds, foxes, wolves, bears, and other unknown victims. Some of the animals were witnessed to suddenly fall down in pain and die. Reports had it that over the years, at least 30 innocent people were found dead there. Researchers held the theory that the poisonous volcanic gases consisting of carbon dioxide, hydrogen sulfide and highly toxic cyanides might be the cause of the death of these living things. Therefore, to be on the safe side, tourists and lovers of extreme trips had better be careful when planning to explore the valley, for no one knows for sure what might happen there next.

這裡一度充滿著各式各樣生物的死屍和骷髏，譬如像鳥、狐狸、狼、熊，以及其他不知名的受害者。有些動物曾被目擊突然痛苦倒地並死亡。據報導，多年以來，至少曾有 30 名無辜民眾被發現在此喪命。研究學者認為，包含有二氧化碳、硫化氫，和有高度劇毒氰化物的毒火山氣體，可能是導致這些生物死亡的原因。因此，為了安全起見，觀光客及熱愛極限旅遊者計劃要到此山谷探險時，最好小心一點，因為沒有人確定那裡接下來會發生什麼事。

字彙加油站

innocent *adj.* 無罪的；清白的	toxic *adj.* 有毒的；毒性的

28 UNIT Black Holes
黑洞

1 MP3 082

A black hole is a region in space with gravitational effects so strong that nothing, including light, can escape from it. Once dying stars burn up all their energy, with nothing to counter their gravity, they begin to collapse under their own weight. Soon the stars get so small and dense that they form black holes. In accordance with Einstein's Theory of Relativity, a black hole, due to its massive gravitational influence, distorts space and time of the neighborhood.

黑洞在太空是一個有著如此強烈重力效果的區域，以至於包括光在內，沒有任何一樣東西能夠逃離它。垂死的恆星一旦燃盡它所有的能量，沒有任何東西能和它的重力抗衡，它們就開始在自己的重量下瓦解。很快地，恆星變得如此的小，而且密度大，以至於就此形成黑洞。符合於愛因斯坦的相對論，由於它本身巨大的重力影響，黑洞扭曲在它附近的空間和時間。

字彙加油站

gravitational *adj.* 萬有引力的；重力的

distort *v.* 扭曲；曲解

2 MP3 083

The theories of black holes were first proposed by scientists during the mid-eighteenth century. And in 1974, Professor Stephen Hawking maintained that black holes would eventually evaporate over time. While this theory, known as "Hawking Radiation," still needs time to be verified, black holes create mysterious and dangerous images in ordinary people's minds. Usually the closer we get to a black hole, the slower time runs. Whatever gets pulled into a black hole can never escape. However, it is only when objects get too close to the black hole that the stronger gravitational force will become apparent and pull objects in. With so much mystery of black holes in our Milky Way Galaxy, the astronomical phenomenon leaves us endless space of enchantment and imagination.

黑洞理論是在 18 世紀中期首度由科學家所提出來的。然後在 1974 年，史蒂芬・霍金教授主張黑洞隨著時間終將蒸發。這個所謂「霍金輻射」的理論仍需要時間來證實之餘，黑洞在一般人的心目中創造出神秘且危險的形象。一般說來，我們越接近黑洞，時間進行的越緩慢。任何被拉進黑洞中的物件便永遠無法逃脫。然而唯有當物件太靠近黑洞時，才會導致較強烈的重力變得明顯並且把物件拉進去。我們的銀河系中竟存在著如此神秘的黑洞，這種天文現象留給我們無限神往及想像的空間。

字彙加油站

verify *v.* 證明；證實

enchantment *n.* 魅力；著迷

29 UNIT The Mysterious Pluto

神秘的冥王星

1 MP3 084

Pluto, as the planet in the solar system that is furthest from the sun, remains mysterious all the time. In 1930, an American research assistant, Clyde Tombaugh, aged 24, found Pluto. Meanwhile, an eleven-year-old girl Venetia Burney named it Pluto, the Roman god of the Underworld due to the similar images of the Underworld and the planet. The previous one is far away from the earth; the latter rotates at the furthest reaches of the sun.

身為太陽系中離太陽最遠的行星，冥王星向來保持著神祕的形象。在 1930 年時，一名 24 歲的美國研究助理，克萊德・湯博，發現了冥王星，同時，11 歲大的女孩，薇妮第・伯納以羅馬地獄神之名為其命名為冥王星。如此命名的源由在於兩者擁有同樣的形象。前者離人世間相當遠，後者則於離太陽最遙遠的地方旋轉著。

字彙加油站

rotate *v.* 旋轉；轉動

Besides, Pluto was the smallest and the last, the ninth, planet to be discovered. Pluto is believed to have a thick methane atmosphere about a few kilometers deep and is covered with frost and ice. During the 1970s, astronomers discovered that both Pluto and its satellite, Charon completed a revolution about six to seven days by themselves and the two have almost the same size, so sometimes astronomers refer to them as double planets. Though deemed as an official planet for 76 years, Pluto was renamed a "Dwarf Planet" in 2006, due to the new discovery that it is merely the brightest member of the Kuiper Belt, a mass of objects that orbit the sun beyond Neptune. In spite of all these, the small, dark, and distant Dwarf Planet, Pluto, arouses our curiosity and interests. 此外冥王星是最小顆，同時是最後一顆，也就是第九顆被發現的行星。據了解，冥王星擁有約幾公里深濃密的沼氣大氣層，並且被霜和冰所覆蓋著。在 1970 年代，天文學家發現冥王星和它的衛星，查倫，完成一趟旋轉週期需要 6~7 天左右，而且這兩顆行星有著幾乎相同的大小，所以有時候天文學家稱呼它們為雙行星。冥王星雖然被視為一顆正式的行星長達 76 年，但是在 2006 年它被重新命名為「矮行星」，因為最新發現到它只是古柏帶，也就是在海王星外環繞太陽軌道運轉的一群行星體中最亮的成員。儘管如此，冥王星這顆渺小、黑暗而且遙遠的「矮行星」激發了我們的好奇心以及興趣。

字彙加油站

methane *n.* 甲烷；沼氣	satellite *n.* 衛星；人造衛星

The Oregon Vortex
奧勒岡漩渦

MP3 086

Unlike ordinary water vortexes fast spinning and pulling things into its center, the Oregon Vortex exists on land, and is a popular roadside touring spot located in Gold Hill, Oregon. Since its opening in 1930, it has attracted huge numbers of visitors. From the outside, tourists can see a small house that is not located horizontally on the surface; it slightly tilts. When getting close to the house of mystery, they can feel a great force pulling them inside.

不同於一般快速旋轉且拉扯物件進入其中心的水底漩渦，奧勒岡漩渦存在於地面上，並且是位於奧勒岡黃金山丘的一個熱門路邊觀光景點。自從 1930 年開幕以來，它吸引了眾多的訪客。從外表，觀光客看見的不是水平地座落在地面上的小房子；它有點傾斜。當他們接近神秘之屋時，可以感受到有一股把他們拉進去的巨大力量。

字彙加油站

ordinary *adj.* 普通的；平凡的	horizontally *adv.* 地平地；水平地

2 MP3 087

Inside the house, the floating things, such as pieces of paper, will become spiral-shaped flying all over. What's even more interesting is that the Vortex seems to be a spherical field of force. When a person stands inside the house, he cannot stand erect. He is, on the contrary, always in a position that inclines toward magnetic north. And if another person goes away from him towards the south, he becomes taller. According to scientists, this situation is only an optical illusion. What truly happens is due to the gravity in this area being so powerful that it turns into an electromagnetic force, and thus creates the oddly unusual phenomena. However, in the past, these situations were referred to as paranormal phenomena.

在屋內，飄動的東西，譬如像紙張，會形成螺旋狀四處飛揚。更有趣的是，這個漩渦近似於一個球狀的力場。當一個人站立在屋內時，他無法站直。相反地，他總是站立於傾向磁鐵北方的位置。假使另一個人，朝向南方離他遙遠地站立著，他則變得比較高。根據科學家的說法，這樣的情境只是視覺上的錯覺罷了。真正發生的原因是，這個地方的重力是如此的強大以至於形成一種電磁力，因此創造出這種古怪不尋常的現象。然而，在過去，這種現象被視為超自然現象。

字彙加油站

spherical *adj.* 球面的；圓的	illusion *n.* 錯覺；幻想

31 UNIT The Zone of Silence
沉寂之區

1 MP3 088

The Zone of Silence refers to a desert area near Durango, northern Mexico. Since the 1930s, the Zone has been noted for its horrible weather, all kinds of strange ancient fossils, and falling meteorites. Above all, alleged sayings have it that there must be a strong magnetic field underground which causes magnetic disturbances, for all the radio signals, communications equipment would fail to work there for some unknown reasons.

沉寂之區指的是墨西哥北部靠近都蘭哥的一個沙漠區域。自從 1930 年代以來，這個區域一直以它惡劣的天氣、各式各樣奇特的古代化石，以及掉落的隕石著名。尤其是，據傳聞這個區域必定存在有導致磁力干擾的強烈地下磁場。因為所有的收音機訊號和通訊設備在那裡會因不知明原因而無法運作。

字彙加油站

fossil *n.* 化石；守舊的事物	disturbance *n.* 干擾；打擾

2 MP3 089

The frequent malfunction of any type of communications: no television, radio, short wave, microwave, or satellite signals seems to be prevalent in this Zone. A perfect silence seems to prevail over this dark and silent Zone. According to scientists and investigators, there may be some unusual magnetic properties associated with either the minerals in the soil containing chalk, or with the contamination from the meteorites, thus a strong magnetic field is created. Another theory is that the underground magnetic field might have been the place where the aliens store their abundant energy, for there have been not only frequent reports of aliens and UFO sightings but also other unusual phenomena mainly caused by the unusual magnetic properties.

任何一種通訊常見的作用不良的情形，譬如像沒有電視、收音機、短波、微波，或是衛星訊息似乎可以盛行於這個區域。全然的死寂似乎籠罩在這黑暗且沉寂的區域。根據科學家和調查員的說法，這裡也許存在著某些不尋常的磁場特性，有可能是跟包含有白堊土壤中的礦物質有關，或是跟來自於隕石的汙染物有關，因此製造出一個強烈的磁場。另外一個理論是說，地底下的磁場可能是外星人儲存它們大量能源的地方，因為那裡不僅有目擊外星人與幽浮的報導，還有其他主要是因不尋常的磁場特質所導致不尋常的現象。

字彙加油站

prevalent *adj.* 盛行的；普遍的	chalk *n.* 白堊；粉筆

Halley's Comet

哈雷彗星

MP3 090

Though comets are rarely seen in the sky, they are important heavenly bodies of the solar system. Among them, Halley's Comet is probably the most famous. Every 75 to 76 years, this short-period comet is clearly visible to the naked eye from earth. The early track of it could be dated back as far as 240 BC when the ancient Chinese astronomers kept records of its appearances. However, in 1705, an English astronomer, Edmund Halley, first concluded the comet's regular and periodic appearances.

雖然彗星在天空中很罕見，它們卻是太陽系中重要的天體。在所有的彗星之中，哈雷彗星很可能是最著名的。每隔 75~76 年間，這顆短周期彗星可以從地球很清楚地用肉眼看見。哈雷彗星軌跡的追蹤最早可以追溯到西元前 240 年，當時古代的中國天文學者記載下它的出現。然而，在 1705 年，英國天文學家，艾德蒙・哈雷，首度推斷哈雷彗星規律且定期的出現。

字彙加油站

visible *adj.* 可看見的；清晰的

2 MP3 091

and it was thus named after him. In 1986, the year of its previous perihelion passage, through space probes of several different countries, Halley's Comet was observed in detail for the first time. The structure of its nucleus, the mechanism of coma and tail formation were further observed and confirmed. According to astronomers, Halley's Comet is probably composed of water, carbon dioxide, ammonia, dust, etc., like a "dirty snowball," because a small portion of it is icy. In addition, Halley's Comet has long been thought to be an omen and has been awed by the general public, for after its appearances, great disasters and unfavorable changes might take place. Nevertheless, we still look forward to the coming of 2016 when Halley's Comet is predicted to reappear. 由此哈雷彗星因他而命名。在 1986 年，也就是上一次最靠近太陽的那一年，透過數個不同國家的太空探測器，哈雷彗星首度仔細地被觀測。哈雷彗星彗核的結構，彗髮的構造，以及彗尾的形成，進一步地被觀察並確認。根據天文學家的説法，它很可能是由水、二氧化碳、氨、塵埃…等等所組成，宛如一顆「骯髒雪球」，而且它有一小部分是冰凍的。此外哈雷彗星長久以來被視為一種惡兆，同時被大眾所敬畏著，因為它的出現後重大災難以及不利的變動可能發生。然而，我們仍舊期盼 2016 年的到來，也就是預測哈雷彗星會再度出現的那一年。

字彙加油站

perihelion *n.* 近日點；最高點

unfavorable *adj.* 不利的；不吉利的

33 UNIT The Red Planet 紅色星球

MP3 092

Mars is often referred to as the "Red Planet" because of its reddish coloring, resulting from the iron oxide on its surface. The Greeks and Romans named the planet after the God of War, Mars. Astronomers have long been interested in it, and from space probes, more and more interesting discoveries were shown to the world. In 1976 and 2001 separately, photographs of a human face drew worldwide attention. People interested in extraterrestrial life maintained that aliens created the "Face."

火星由於表面上的氧化鐵，使得它有著紅色的外表，常被稱為「紅色星球」。希臘羅馬人依戰神之名替它命名為火星。天文學家長久以來對它擁有高度興趣，經由太空探測，有越來越多有趣的發現呈現給世人。分別在 1976 和 2001 年，一張人臉的照片吸引全世界的矚目。對外星生物有興趣的人們主張是外星人創造了這一張人臉。

字彙加油站

reddish *adj.* 帶紅色的；淡紅的	separately *adv.* 個別地；分別地

2 MP3 093

However, scientists explained that the "Face" was likely only an optical illusion. Mars is similar to the earth in several ways, such as its geological formations, rotational periods, seasonal cycles, and so on. What's more, it is the closest planet to Earth, and what intrigues scientists is the assumed presence of liquid water on the planet's surface. Evidence shows that in the past, liquid water once existed on Mars, which will be vital for the future possibility of humans' immigrating and surviving there. Till today, there are still ongoing assessments and research of a possible future living on Mars. Whether humans will carry out the wishes of building a space colony there or not still needs time and effort.

然而科學家解釋這張臉很可能只是一種視覺上的錯覺罷了。火星在某些方面類似於地球，譬如它的地質構造、轉動週期、季節循環…等等。再者，它是最靠近地球的行星，而令科學家感到興奮的是，火星表面有可能存在液態水。證據顯示，在過去，液態水曾經存在於火星，而這點對未來人類移居並生存於火星的可能性是很關鍵的。直到今日，目前還有許多對未來住在火星可能性的評估和研究正在進行著。人類是否將會實現在那裡建築太空殖民地的心願仍需要時間和努力。

字彙加油站

rotational *adj.* 旋轉的；輪流的	intrigue *v.* 激起好奇心；使迷惑

34 UNIT Mahatma Gandhi
聖雄甘地

1 MP3 094

Mohandas Karamchand Gandhi was the spiritual leader of the Indian National Liberation Movement opposing the British rule. To fight for the rights of the Indian people in South Asia and the independence from British government, Gandhi preached the concept of nonviolent civil disobedience and noncooperation instead of a violent protest or actual combat. His ideals and practices inspired a huge crowd of faithful followers, and he was highly honored as "Mahatma," meaning a respectable holy person.

莫罕達斯・卡蘭默肯・甘地是對抗英國統治，印度民族解放運動的精神領袖。為了爭取南亞印度人的權益和脫離英國政府而獨立，甘地倡導以非暴力的不合作運動來取代暴力的抗議或實質的戰鬥。他的理念和做法激勵了大批忠誠的追隨者，而他被高度地推崇為「聖雄」，表示是一名備受敬重的聖人。

字彙加油站

spiritual *adj.* 精神上的；心靈的	combat *n.* 戰鬥；格鬥

2 MP3 095

Throughout his life, he dedicated himself to eliminating poverty, promoting women's rights, building religious and ethnic harmony, and achieving autonomy. In 1947, they finally won the independence granted by Britain. However, some religious extremists have long opposed Gandhi's doctrine of nonviolence and his being too gentle and moderate to the Muslims. On 30 January 1948, Nathuram Godse, a Hindu nationalist, assassinated Gandhi by firing three bullets into his chest at a close distance, and was tried and executed in 1949. Nevertheless, prior to Gandhi's death, there had been five unsuccessful assassination attempts. The mystery lies in the doubts that the Indian police and government should have made better precautions against the possible assassination, but unfortunately, they failed to.

終其一生，他致力於消弭貧窮，提升婦女權益，建立宗教和種族和諧，並且努力取得自治。在 1947 年，他們終於得到英國認可的獨立。然而，某些宗教極端份子，長久以來反對甘地非暴力的論說以及他對回教徒太過於溫和容忍的態度。在 1948 年 1 月 30 日，那順拉姆・戈德塞，一名印度國家主義者，近距離對甘地的胸部射擊三發子彈，暗殺了甘地。在 1949 年，戈德塞被審判並執行死刑。但是在甘地身亡前，已有過五次未成功的暗殺意圖。人民懷疑的是印度警方和政府原先應做好預防暗殺可能性的措施，但是不幸地他們並沒有這麼做。

字彙加油站

doctrine *n.* 信條；教義

execute *v.* 執行；處死

The Attack on Pearl Harbor
偷襲珍珠港

1 MP3 096

During World War Two, due to President Roosevelt's oil embargo, Japan had chosen to start a war against the US, for it was entirely dependent on imported oil. Therefore, on the 7 of December, 1941, Japanese aircraft attacked Pearl Harbor in Hawaii, where the American naval base lay. The severe destruction included 18 warships and 300 aircraft destroyed, and heavy casualties: 2,451 US personnel killed, 1,282 injured.

二次大戰期間，由於羅斯福總統石油禁運的政策，日本選擇對美國開戰，因為日本非常依賴進口石油。因此在 1941 年 12 月 7 日，日本飛機對美國海軍基地所在地夏威夷的珍珠港進行偷襲轟炸。嚴重的損失包含有 18 艘戰艦、300 架飛機毀損，以及 2,451 美國人員死亡，1,282 人受傷的重大傷亡。

字彙加油站

embargo *n.* 禁運；禁止買賣	casualty *n.* 傷亡人員；受害人

Different from the previous attitude of Isolationism toward the War, Americans were overwhelmed with shock and fury; patriotism was thus aroused. With the support of most Americans, President Franklin D. Roosevelt declared war on Japan the day after the raid. America's involvement in the War brought total defeat of the Axis powers represented by Japan, Germany, and Italy, and eventually led the Allies to victory. Though Roosevelt described the date of the Raid as "a date that will live in infamy", it was theorized that the US was warned of the Japanese attack in advance. However, Roosevelt seemed to have deliberately ignored the warning and have allowed it to happen to get a legitimate reason for declaring a war on Japan, since before that, most public and political opinions had been against America's entry into the War. In this way, the attack on Pearl Harbor drew America into the War and changed the course of history.

不同於先前對於二次世界大戰採取「孤立主義」的態度，美國人飽受重大的震撼及憤怒，因而激發起愛國心。有大部分美國人的支持，富蘭克林・羅斯福總統在偷襲日的第二天對日本宣戰。美國的參戰導致軸心國，日本、德國和義大利全面挫敗，最終將同盟國帶往勝利之路。雖然羅斯福總統把偷襲日描述成「蒙羞日」，人們推論美國先前已被警告日本即將來襲。但是，羅斯福總統似乎是蓄意忽視這個警告，並且默許它發生以取得一個名正言順的理由來對日本宣戰，因為在此之前，多數的美國民意和政界人士皆反對美國參戰。如此一來，偷襲珍珠港使得美國參戰，並且改變歷史軌跡。

36
UNIT

The Assassination of John F. Kennedy

約翰・甘迺迪遇刺

MP3 098

John Fitzgerald Kennedy was elected the 35th president of the US in November, 1960. The promising young president was expected to accomplish great achievements during his presidency. However, on the 22nd of November, 1963, he was assassinated by Lee Harvey Oswald in Dallas, Texas. Oswald was arrested and charged with the assassination. Unexpectedly, two days later, Oswald was shot and killed by Jack Ruby, a Dallas nightclub owner.

約翰・費茲傑羅・甘迺迪在 1960 年 11 月獲選為美國第 35 屆總統。這位前途被看好的年輕總統，原來被預期在他總統任內能夠成就偉大成就。但是，在 1963 年 11 月 22 日時，他在德州達拉斯被李・哈維・奧斯華所暗殺。奧斯華被逮捕並以暗殺罪名起訴。出乎意料地，兩天後，奧斯華被達拉斯夜總會老闆，傑克・盧比槍殺身亡。

字彙加油站

arrest *v.* 逮捕；拘留

2 MP3 099

The JFK assassination was one of the world's most shocking moments, and a majority of Americans believed that there was a conspiracy behind. In fact, numerous conspiracy theories have been put forth since then, even to the US Vice President Lyndon Johnson. To find out the true murderer, the US government set up the Warren Commission on the 29th of November, 1963 to investigate the assassination. And in 1964, the Warren Report was released asserting that there was no conspiracy, and Oswald acted alone. However, the US government was believed to have intentionally covered up crucial information. Besides, the complete "Warren Report" is now held back by the US government and scheduled to be released publicly only after 2038 when the mystery might be unraveled then. 甘迺迪遇刺是令世人最震驚的時刻之一，而大多數美國人相信背後存在著一個重大的陰謀。事實上，從那時起數種陰謀論被提出甚至是副總統林登・強生。為了找出真正的兇手美國政府在 1963 年 11 月 29 日設立「華倫委員會」來調查這起刺殺案件。在 1964 年，「華倫報告」公布並宣稱沒有陰謀奧斯華是獨自犯案。但是人們相信美國政府蓄意掩蓋關鍵的情資。此外，完整的「華倫報告」目前被美國政府所扣留，預計在 2038 年之後才會公諸於世，屆時也許會揭曉這起神秘遇刺案。

字彙加油站

intentionally *adv.* 有意地；故意地

schedule *v.* 計劃；預定

37 UNIT The Derinkuyu Underground City
土耳其地下城

1 MP3 100

In history, Turkey has been at the center of several empires and a bridge between the Eastern and Western cultures. Among Turkey's many naturally formed tourists' attractions, the Derinkuyu Underground City is an amazing mystery to the world. With caves built in the soft volcanic rock, it is located in the Cappadocia region, where the world's most exquisite collection of underground cities and villages were found. It was discovered in 1963 by accident when a man renovated his home finding a stone passageway behind a wall. 歷史上土耳其一向是帝國的重鎮且是東西文化的橋樑。在土耳其眾多天然形成的觀光景點之中，代林庫悠地下城對全世界來說是一個神奇之謎。有著建築在柔軟火山岩中的山洞，地下城位於卡帕多西亞高原中，這座高原中有著全世界最雅緻的地下城市及村莊。它是在 1963 年無意中被發現的，當時有一個整修房子的人在一面牆後方發現一座石製的通道。

字彙加油站

exquisite *adj.* 精緻的；製作精良的	renovate *v.* 整修；更新

It is a collection of long tunnels and lots of rooms stretching around 60 meters below the surface. Researchers speculated that with about 4,000 years of history, it might have been used for two purposes. One was to function as an agricultural space for storing and transporting food and produce. Furthermore, it was once capable of housing up to around 20,000 people. So, the other function was to create a hiding place. According to historians, in case of attacks, a great part of the Turkish population would take refuge in these underground chambers to escape persecution. However, just exactly by whom, how, and when the underground structures were built still need further research.

它集結了往地底下延伸約 60 公尺的漫長隧道和大量的房間。研究學者推測，它具有 4000 年的歷史，很可能具有兩種作用。一個是充當儲存及輸送食物和農產品的農業處所。此外，它一度曾經能夠容納高達兩萬人。所以，另一個功用是創造一個隱藏的處所。根據歷史學家的說法，萬一遭逢攻擊，極大比例的土耳其人會在地下房間避難以遠離迫害。然而，究竟這些地下城的結構是由誰建造的，如何建造的，及何時建造的，仍須進一步研究。

字彙加油站

persecution *n.* 迫害；困擾	underground *adj,* 地下的

The Berlin Wall
柏林圍牆

1 MP3 102

On 13 August 1961, the Berlin Wall was constructed to close the border between East and West Berlin. The Wall was used as a way of preventing East Germans from entering West Germany. Nevertheless, many East German defectors kept trying to escape across the Wall to West Berlin, only to be shot relentlessly by border guards as traitors. On 9 November 1989, the East Germans could put up with the Wall no more and it was finally brought down, allowing the crowds to rush to the other side.

在 1961 年 8 月 13 日，柏林圍牆被築起以關閉東西柏林間的邊境。這座牆被用來做為阻擋東德人進入西德的一個方式。然而，許多東德叛逃者不斷地嘗試跨越過圍牆逃到西柏林，最終是被邊境守衛視同叛徒無情地射殺。在 1989 年 11 月 9 日，東德人再也無法忍受這座圍牆而它終於被拆除，允許群眾衝向另外一端。

字彙加油站

defector *n.* 叛離者；背叛者

relentlessly *adv.* 無情地；殘酷地

2 MP3 103

The fall of the Berlin Wall symbolized the end of the tyrannical communism and also the end of the Cold War starting from the end of World War Two. According to historians, the mystery of building the Wall lay in the subtle reactions of the American President John F. Kennedy. He got increasingly concerned about a coming war after Nikita Khrushchev, the Soviet Union leader, warned him to remove western forces. Therefore, when Kennedy heard of the construction of the Wall, to the public, he condemned it as a physical representation of the Communist Iron Curtain. However, he didn't take any concrete action. Instead, it's said that he actually felt relieved. He was reported to have said that a wall should be a lot better than a war and that ended the Berlin Crisis. 柏林圍牆的倒塌象徵暴虐共產主義的結束，並且是從二次大戰末開始冷戰的結束。根據歷史學家的說法，柏林圍牆建築之謎在於美國總統約翰甘迺迪微妙的反應。他在前蘇聯領袖，尼克塔・赫魯雪夫警告他要撤除西方武力後，逐漸地警戒到即將有戰爭的來臨。因此，當甘迺迪聽聞柏林圍牆的建築時，表面上，他譴責柏林圍牆是一種共產主義鐵幕實質的表徵。然而，他並沒有採取任何具體的行動。相反地，據說他事實上感覺鬆了一口氣。據報導，他曾說，一道圍牆應該比一場戰爭好太多了，而那也終止了柏林危機。

字彙加油站

tyrannical *adj.* 暴虐的；專制君主的	subtle *adj.* 微妙的；詭秘的

Easter Island
復活島

MP3 104

Easter Island is a tiny Polynesian island in the southeastern Pacific Ocean. It has become famous since the eighteenth century when European explorers arrived at this remote island and discovered Moai, the Easter Island Heads. According to archaeologists, the Heads were probably built sometime between 1,000 and 1,100 AD though the Island's earliest civilization might have started as early as 400 AD. Along the Pacific Ocean, the Island was lined with hundreds of god-like statues carved from volcanic rock.

復活島是位於太平洋東南方一座小的波里尼西亞島。它從 18 世紀以來變得出名了，當時歐洲探險家到達這座遙遠的島嶼並且發現摩埃，也就是復活島頭像。根據考古學家的說法，雖然這座島最早的文化可能是從西元 400 年開始的，這些頭像可能是在西元 1,000 至 1,100 年之間某時刻建造的。沿著太平洋，復活島佈滿著數百尊由火山岩雕刻出來神一般的雕像。

字彙加油站

statue *n.* 雕像；塑像

2 MP3 105

Each huge statue wore a crown, had very long ears, and weighed up to 14 tons, facing inland, away from the sea. They were believed to have represented the tribe's ancestors, probably the status symbols of the powerful chiefs. However, the legend had it that sometime during the late seventeenth century, the tribe that built the statues was completely destroyed in a fatal battle, and the tragedy brought ghostly air to the Island and the inhabitants. In fact, not only the legendary tribe's tragic doom but also the exact purpose of building the huge sculptures and how they were mounted into place till today still puzzle the world a lot. Before the puzzles are finally solved, the majestic Easter Island Moai will always be a great mystery.

每一尊巨大的雕像戴著皇冠，有著非常長的耳朵，重達 14 公噸，遠遠地離海而面向島內。人們相信它們代表著部落的祖先，極可能是很大權勢酋長地位的象徵。然而，有傳聞說 17 世紀末期的某個時刻，建造這些雕像的部落，在一次致命的戰役當中全數被殲滅了，而這個悲劇帶給復活島和當地居民一股鬼魅般的氣氛。事實上，不僅是傳說中部落悲慘的命運，建造巨型雕像確切的目的，以及它們是如何被搬移定位，迄今也仍令世人十分地困惑。在謎底最終揭曉前，宏偉的復活島摩埃雕像將永遠是一個謎。

字彙加油站

weigh *v.* 重達；重壓	majestic *adj.* 雄偉的；崇高的

40 UNIT

The Fall of A Kungfu King

功夫之王的殞落

1 MP3 106

Bruce Lee, though he died young, had made great contributions to Chinese Kungfu. He is considered one of the most influential martial artists of all time. Skilled in Chinese martial arts, Lee taught Kungfu, wrote books, and acted in popular Chinese Kungfu movies. Through his unique Kungfu movies, Lee's self-discipline, diligence and excellence in martial arts techniques finally won him world recognition as a Kungfu king. In fact, not only Lee himself but the special and fantastic Chinese martial arts were seen and admired by the world. 李小龍，雖然英年早逝，對中國功夫有極大的貢獻。他被視為有史以來最具有影響力的功夫大師之一。李小龍的中國武術精湛，他傳授功夫，撰寫書籍，並且在受歡迎的中國功夫電影裡演戲。透過他獨特的功夫電影，李小龍的自律、勤勉，以及功夫武術的精湛，終於為他贏得全世界公認的功夫大師的美譽。事實上，不僅李小龍本人，特殊且奇妙的中國武術也被世人看見及仰慕。

字彙加油站

diligence *n.* 勤勉；勤奮	recognition *n.* 確認；表彰

However, Lee's sudden death in 1973 shocked the world and the causes of his death have remained mysterious since then. The official reports stated that he died from brain swelling due to a serious allergic reaction to Equagesic, a painkiller for headaches, and it was "a death by misadventure". Nevertheless, other speculations varied, which included being murdered by Chinese Triads, martial arts followers, or Italian Mafia, and so on. Among others, the most weird one was about Lee's family curse, which previously took his older brother's life, and after twenty years, accidentally in a gunshooting movie scene, took his son, Brandon's life. To Bruce's Kungfu fans, hopefully one day the mystery of Lee's death could be unraveled.

然而，李小龍 1973 的驟逝震撼整個世界，而從那時起，他的死因一直是十分地神秘。正式的報告陳述說他對一種治頭疼的止痛藥一艾奎杰希克，嚴重過敏，導致腦腫脹而死亡，而且這是一樁「意外死亡」。但是，各式各樣的揣測眾說紛紜，包含有兇手可能是中國三合會、武術的追隨者，或義大利的黑手黨等等。其中，最奇特的說法是有關於李小龍的家族詛咒。這個詛咒先前奪去他哥哥的生命，而 20 年後在一個槍枝射擊的電影場景中奪去他兒子布蘭登的生命。對李小龍的功夫影迷來說，期盼有一天李小龍的死亡之謎能夠被解開。

字彙加油站

swell *v.* 腫起；腫脹	allergic *adj.* 過敏的

Martin Luther King, Jr.
馬丁路德・金恩二世

1 MP3 108

Dr. Martin Luther King, Jr. was an important civil rights leader fighting for the equality of the African-Americans in the 1950s. He preached non-violence in marches, strikes, and demonstrations against racial discrimination and segregation. Owing to his sustained endeavors, he won worldwide recognition and was awarded the prestigious Nobel Peace Prize in 1964.

馬丁路德・金恩二世博士在 1950 年代是為非裔美國人爭取平等重要的人權領袖。他倡導在對抗種族歧視和隔離政策時舉行的遊行、罷工、和示威活動中使用非暴力。他堅持不懈的努力為他贏得全世界的肯定，並且在 1964 年獲頒聲譽卓越的諾貝爾和平獎。

字彙加油站

preach *v.* 講道；宣揚	segregation *n.* 分離；種族隔離

2 MP3 109

In his famous soul-touching speech, I Have a Dream, given in front of the Lincoln Memorial to huge crowds of whites and blacks, he told of a dream world where equality could be rooted in the American Dream and freed from racial prejudice. Nevertheless, on April 4, 1968, he was assassinated in Memphis, Tennessee. It was a racist and opponent of Dr. King's ideals, James Earl Ray that was responsible for the assassination. With sufficient and hard evidence, he was arrested and sentenced to 99 years in prison. However, until his death in prison on April 23, 1998, Ray had consistently maintained his innocence. Speculations had it that Ray could not have acted alone and should only be part of a larger conspiracy by the government, either directly or indirectly.

在林肯紀念堂前，他對成群的白人和黑人發表著名感人「我有一個夢想」的演説，並闡述一個根植於美國夢想並且免除種族偏見的平等美夢世界。但是，1968 年 4 月 4 日，他在田納西州曼菲斯被暗殺。這是由一名種族歧視，並且反對金恩博士理念的反對者，詹姆士・厄爾・雷所犯下的罪刑。由於有足夠且確鑿的證據，他被逮捕，並被宣判 99 年的徒刑。但是，直到 1998 年 4 月 23 日，雷在監獄死亡之前，不斷宣稱自己是無辜的。人們揣測雷不可能獨自犯案，而應該只是直接或間接地由政府所策劃大型陰謀中的一部份。

字彙加油站

prejudice *n.* 偏見；歧視

opponent *n.* 對手；反對者

The Great Pyramids of Giza
吉薩大金字塔

1 MP3 110

The Great Pyramids of Giza from ancient Egypt are the most impressive spectacles of human civilization and important Egyptian heritage. Guarded by the statue of the Sphinx, they were built as royal tombs for Pharaohs between 2,575 BC and 2,465 BC. Also, they probably served ritualistic purposes and astronomical functions as well. The largest of them held the record for the world's tallest structure for its height of 481 feet, with a base area around 570,000 square feet.

起源於古埃及的吉薩大金塔是人類文明最令人印象深刻的奇觀，並且是一項重要的埃及文化遺產。由人面獅身像所看守著，它們在西元前 2,575 年到西元前 2,465 年間被建為法老的皇室陵墓。它們同時可能有儀式上的目的以及天文上的作用。最大的一座金字塔以它 481 英尺的高度，以及 57 萬平方英尺的底座面積，具有全世界最高建築物的紀錄。

字彙加油站

impressive *adj.* 令人印象深刻的；令人欽佩的

ritualistic *adj.* 儀式的；慣例的

2 MP3 111

Inside the pyramids, there were elaborate corridors and huge chambers, with jewelry, stone blocks, and cutting tools found. Till today, amazing things about the Great Pyramids of Giza still puzzle the world a lot. It is estimated that it took at least 20 years to complete the construction of pyramids, and it required the labor of a hundred thousand workers moving 2.6 million blocks of stone into the site. People used to think that only the highly intelligent aliens from the outer space could have possibly created the huge and perfect pyramids. Otherwise, it would be impossible for the ancient Egyptians, supposedly with limited mathematical and astronomical knowledge, to have achieved the difficult task of making the exact measurements.

在金字塔內，有複雜的通道以及巨大的房間，連同珠寶、石塊以及切割工具。直至今日，有關於吉薩大金字塔驚人的狀況仍極度地困惑世人。據估計，完成這項建築至少花費 20 年，同時它需要十萬工人的勞力搬動 260 萬塊石塊到達建築地點。人們過去認為只有來自於外太空具有高度智慧的外星人才有可能創造出如此巨大而且完美的金字塔。否則，對於具有有限的數學和天文知識的古埃及人來說，是不可能去完成如此精準的測量。

字彙加油站

corridor *n.* 走廊；通道

mathematical *adj.* 數學上的；精確的

The Mysterious Death of Princess Diana

黛安娜王妃死亡之謎

1 MP3 112

In 1997, Princess Diana was killed in a tunnel car crash, and the world mourned her death. Or i g inal l y a nameles s kindergarten teacher, Diana's fairy-tale encounter and marriage with Prince Charles were envied and blessed. With her charm and elegance, she successfully caught the world's eye, which helped her a lot in her devotion to the good cause of charity. After the divorce, the paparazzi was still intrigued with Diana's private life. The chase led to her tragic death.

在 1997 年，黛安娜王妃喪命於隧道車禍中，世人均哀悼她的死亡。她原來是默默無名的幼稚園老師，而她與查爾斯王子童話般的邂逅與婚姻令眾人稱羨及祝福。藉由她的魅力和優雅，她成功地受到世人矚目，而大大有助於她奉獻於慈善工作的努力。離婚後，狗仔隊仍對於黛安娜王妃的私生活感到有興趣。狗仔隊的追逐導致了她的死亡。

字彙加油站

mourn *v.* 哀痛；哀悼	elegance *n.* 優雅；雅緻

2 MP3 113

In fact, Diana's mysterious death has been the center of whispers for years. It was speculated that Diana and her Egyptian boyfriend, Dodi Fayed, whom she was about to get engaged to as a mother-tobe, were murdered by agents sent by the British Royal Family. There was no chance that a Muslim could be the stepfather to the future British King, who might also have a possible half-Egyptian and half-Muslim sibling. Furthermore, Diana's death was so unacceptable to her fans that she was even said to have staged her own death for some privacy she wanted so much, only to go terribly wrong in the end. Hopefully, the mystery of the Princess's death could one day be clarified.

事實上，黛安娜王妃神秘的死亡，多年以來一直是人們耳語的焦點。據推測，黛安娜與她的埃及籍男友，道迪・菲德，懷有身孕並即將訂婚，卻雙雙被英國皇室特派員所謀殺。因為一名回教徒不可能是未來英國國王的繼父，而英國國王也不被允許有埃及和回教徒血統的手足。再者，黛安娜的死亡對她的支持者是如此地無法接受，以至於被謠傳說她為了取得渴望已久的隱私權自導自演車禍，沒想到最後釀成大禍。儘管如此，仍期盼未來黛安娜王妃死亡之謎終得以澄清。

字彙加油站

whisper *n.* 耳語；傳聞	engaged *adj.* 訂婚的

The Mysterious Stonehenge

神秘的巨石陣

1 MP3 114

Stonehenge is a prehistoric monument located in Salisbury Plain, Southern England. For centuries, archaeologists have been puzzled about the mysteries of how and why it was constructed. Built from around 3,100 BC to 1,100 BC, Stonehenge was composed of nearly 100 massive upright stones placed as an enclosure in a specific circular arrangement with each weighing up to 20 to 50 tons. How the ancient Neolithic builders moved huge stones remains a mystery.

巨石陣是位於英國南方，塞里斯貝瑞平原的史前遺跡。許多世紀以來，考古學家對於它如何並且為何被建造之謎感到困惑。巨石陣建築於約西元前 3,100 年到西元前 1,100 之間，是由將近 100 塊巨大直立的石塊以封閉且特別的圓形排列，每一個石塊重達 20 到 50 公噸。古代新石器時代的建築者如何能移動大石塊仍舊是個謎。

字彙加油站

enclosure *n.* 圈用地；圍場	Neolithic *adj.* 新石器時代的

2 MP3 115

On the one hand, the theory of the last ice-age glaciers' carrying them there was once raised. On the other hand, the stories of King Arthur were once associated with it. Legend had it that it was the wizard Merlin who flew the mighty stones into place with his magic powers. As for the purposes it served, opinions and theories varied. Some suggest that it was used as an observatory and an astronomical calendar to predict lunar and solar eclipses. Others believe that the ceremonial site held certain religious significance and was a memorial erected to honor their ancestors, and still others claim that it was constructed for burial rituals of royalty buried there.

一方面來說，上一個冰河時期的冰河把它們帶到那裏的理論曾經被提出，但是從未被證實。在另一方面，亞瑟王的故事曾經與它有關聯。據傳說，是梅林巫師用他的魔法將它們搬移到那裏的。至於它的功用，各方的意見和理論不一。有些人認為，它被用作天文觀測台以及天文曆法來預測月全蝕以及日全蝕，有些人相信，這個儀式的地點具有特定的宗教意義，並且此地是一個為了要推崇祖先所設立的紀念碑，而又有一些人宣稱，它是為了替埋葬於那裏的貴族舉行葬禮的儀式而被建造的。

字彙加油站

glacier *n.* 冰河	associate *v.* 聯想；有關聯
erect *v.* 豎立；建立	royalty *n.*（總稱）皇族（成員）

The Unsinkable Titanic

永不沉沒的鐵達尼號

MP3 116

The Titanic, dubbed “Unsinkable,” was the largest, the fastest, and the most luxurious ship ever built. Unfortunately, on the contrary, she submerged on her maiden voyage of sailing glory on April 14, 1912. In order to match up to the good fame of perfection, she sailed in the Atlantic Ocean at high speed, even during the dark midnight. Thus, only two days at sea and more than half way between England and the New York destination, she collided with a ghostly-looking iceberg.

號稱「永不沉沒」的鐵達尼號是有史以來最巨大、最快速，且最豪華的輪船。很不幸，相反地，她在 1912 年 4 月 14 日光榮的首航中沉沒了。為了要符合她完美的美名，她甚至在光線昏暗的夜半時分裡以高速疾馳於大西洋中。因此，在海上僅航行兩天，同時是從英國航行到目的地紐約的半途中，她與鬼魅般的冰山相撞。

字彙加油站

luxurious *adj.* 奢侈的；豪華的	submerge *v.* 淹沒；沉沒

2 MP3 117

Panic, fires on ship, and not providing enough lifeboats resulted in the heavy casualties of 1,500 deaths out of around 2,500 passengers. Over the years, legends surrounding the tragic happening prevailed. After careful examination and analysis, experts concluded that both the constructing materials and the compartment designing went wrong. Besides, the owners of the Titanic were too sure to equip enough lifeboats on board, being only one–fourth of her total passengers. In addition, the superstition of Titanic Mummy's Curse was the most prevalent cause of the tragedy. When the ship plunged, on board was a stone case with an Egyptian mummy inside, which allegedly would drown whoever made contact with it.

驚慌、船上的大火，以及救生艇提供不足導致大約 2,500 名乘客中，有 1,500 名死亡的重大死傷。多年來，環繞這個悲劇的傳說盛行。經過仔細的檢閱和分析，專家作結論說是建築材料和艙房的設計出了差錯。再者，鐵達尼號的船主，太有把握而沒有在船上配給足夠的救生艇，僅配備所有旅客四分之一的數量。此外，鐵達尼號木乃伊詛咒的迷信傳說是最盛行的沉船主因。當輪船下沉的時候，在船上有一個木乃伊石棺，據說凡是跟它接觸過的人都會溺斃。

字彙加油站

compartment *n.* 劃分；隔間	superstition *n.* 迷信；盲目恐懼
mummy *n.* 木乃伊；不腐屍體	

The Ancient Machu Picchu
馬丘比丘古城

MP3 118

Machu Picchu lies on an inaccessible ridge high above the Urubamba Valley in the Peruvian Andes. Used as a summer resort for Incan emperors, it was once discovered by the Spanish conquerors in the mid-15th century. And then, in 1911, it was the American explorer Hiram Bingham that discovered it accidentally and revealed the secrets of the ancient lost city to the world.

馬丘比丘位於祕魯安地斯山脈，很難到達的烏魯班巴山谷山脊上。它最早是印加國王的避暑勝地，一度曾經在 15 世紀中葉被西班牙征服者發現。然後在 1911 年，是美國探險家，海拉默・班漢姆，在無意中發現它，並且把這一座失落古城的秘密公諸於世。

字彙加油站

inaccessible *adj.* 難接近的；達不到的	conqueror *n.* 征服者；勝利者

2 MP3 119

It was built in the ancient Incan style, with three primary structures constructed with interlocking walls of smooth and polished stones by the ancient Incans, precisely fitting the stones together seamlessly. One mystery about Machu Picchu is how Incans could possibly move the heavy and huge stones, and place them in the site. Another mystery is the function of a peculiar giant rock situated on a raised platform towering above the plaza. It was believed to have been used for astronomical observations. Nowadays, Machu Picchu's superb preservation, excellent quality and its original architecture, and the breathtaking mountain scenery surrounding it have made itself Peru's most iconic sightseeing spot. Tourist trips to Peru won't be complete without visiting it.

馬丘比丘是以古印加風格所建立的，它具有三個主要的建築物，由古印加人利用平滑且拋光的石塊精準無縫地連結鑲嵌在牆面上而建造的。有關於馬丘比丘的一個謎是，印加人如何移動巨大沉重的石塊並且放置於建築的地點。另一個謎是，有一塊在廣場上端一塊突起的平台上奇特巨大石塊的用途。人們相信它有天文觀測的作用。今日來說，馬丘比丘絕佳的保存，原始建築的卓越品質，以及令人屏息的山景使它成為秘魯最具有代表性的觀光景點。它是觀光客來秘魯旅遊的必遊之處。

字彙加油站

primary *adj.* 首要的；主要的	interlock *v.* 連結；連扣
seamlessly *adv.* 無縫地	iconic *adj.* 圖像的；偶像的

The Mysterious Stone Spheres
神祕石球

1 MP3 120

The stone spheres of Costa Rica, first discovered in the Diquis Delta of Costa Rica during the 1930s, are a collection of over 300 almost perfect spherical balls. Ranging in size from a basketball to a compact car, most of them are sculpted from an igneous rock similar to granite. Probably created sometime between 200 BC and 1,600 BC, the mysterious balls, always point to the magnetic north, are arranged together in at least 20 stone balls in regular geometric patterns.

哥斯大黎加的石球，於 1930 年代在哥斯大黎加迪奎斯三角洲首度被發現，是一群超過三百顆幾近完美的球體。它們大多數有從一顆籃球到一部小車的大小，是由類似花崗岩的火成岩所雕刻而成的。這些神秘石球可能是在西元前 200 年到西元前 1,600 年之間被創造，它們經常指向磁鐵的北方，並以至少 20 顆球一起排列成規律的幾何圖案。

字彙加油站

collection *n.* 收集；積聚

geometric *adj.* 幾何的；幾何圖形的

The mysteriously smooth and perfectly spherical stones have long been regarded as symbols of tradition and ancient wisdom. However, the exact significance of the hand-made stone balls and the amazing skills employed to create such refined stone balls remain unsolved mysteries. According to archaeologists, probably they were created so as to serve certain ritualistic purposes, or simply to show status differences. Nevertheless, the tools the ancient Costa Ricans used and how some of the huge stone spheres could ever be moved around still remain unknown. Besides, the stones seem to have been arranged and made into certain large patterns, which might have some astronomical significance connected with aliens' spacecraft landing. 這些神秘、光滑而且幾近完美的石球長久以來被視為是傳統和古代智慧的象徵。但是，這些手工製石球的確切意義以及被用來創造如此優質石球的驚人技術，一直是難解之謎。根據考古學家的說法，它們被創造的目的是為了某些宗教目的，或只是為了表現不同的階級。然而，古代哥斯大黎加人使用的工具以及某些巨大石球如何被四處搬動，仍舊是無從知曉。此外，這些石球似乎被排列製作成特定大型的圖案，具有可能是與外星人駕駛的太空船降落有所連結的特殊含意。

字彙加油站

perfectly *adv.* 完美地；完全地	archaeologist *n.* 考古學家
arrange *v.* 排列；安排	astronomical *adj.* 天文的；天文學的

The Mausoleum of the Emperor Qin Shi Huang
秦始皇陵墓

MP3 122

The Mausoleum of Qin Shi Huang is a 76-meter-tall tomb complex located in Xi'an in northwest China's Shanxi Province. Since its accidental discovery in 1974, archaeologists have tried to unravel the mysteries not only of the overall planning and construction, but of the three tomb vaults where about 7,500 terracotta warriors and horses were excavated. Amazingly, each of them had unique outlooks and the real size of a soldier, around 2 meters in height.

秦始皇陵墓是位於中國北方陝西省西安 76 公尺高的陵墓建築。自從 1974 年，它意外地被發現後，考古學家試圖揭開它整體規畫建築的謎，以及從陵墓挖掘出 3 穴坑共約 7500 尊兵馬俑的謎。令人驚訝的是，每一尊兵馬俑都具有獨特的外貌，而且具有士兵真人的大小，大約 2 公尺的高度。

字彙加油站

mausoleum *n.* 陵墓	complex *n.* 綜合物；建築群
terracotta *n.* 赤陶；赤土	excavate *v.* 開鑿；發掘（古物）

2 MP3 123

Originally, the Mausoleum was made for Qin Shi Huang, who was the first emperor of the Qin Dynasty（221 BC- 207 BC）and also of China. He unified the warring China, the systems of laws and weights, and the Chinese written language. However, the dictatorial Emperor, to suppress opposition, ordered the burning of the books written by philosophers and the execution of the intellectual scholars. Besides, he had hundreds of thousands of slave laborers construct the Great Wall. Believing in immortality, he was obsessed with finding an elixir of life to stay alive forever and forced 700,000 laborers to build the Mausoleum. Furthermore, the 7,500 terracotta warriors were made and buried there for guarding and protecting him in the afterlife. After the excavation of the spectacular Mausoleum, it has drawn worldwide attention.

原先這座陵墓是為中國秦朝（西元前 221~西元前 207 年）第一位皇帝，秦始皇所建造的。他統一戰亂的中國，法律和度量衡的制度，以及中國文字。但是，這位獨裁的皇帝為了要鎮壓反對勢力，下令焚燒哲學家所著的書籍以及處死知識淵博的學者。此外，他命令數十萬的奴工建築萬里長城。他本身相信永生，所以著迷於尋找長生不老藥以獲得永生，並且強迫 70 萬勞工建立陵墓。再者，7500 尊兵馬俑被建造且埋葬於陵墓中，在來生時守衛並保護他。壯觀的陵墓被挖掘出來之後，引起全世界的矚目。

字彙加油站

dictatorial *adj.* 獨裁的；獨裁者的	elixir *n.* 長生不老藥；萬能藥

國家圖書館出版品預行編目(CIP)資料

新托福100+ iBT單字/ 倍斯特編輯部著.
-- 初版. -- 臺北市 : 倍斯特, 2018.6　面 ;
公分. --（考用英語系列 ; 9）
ISBN 978-986-96309-1-7（平裝附光碟）
1.托福單字 2.字彙

805.1894　　107007344

考用英語 009

新托福100+ iBT單字（附MP3）

初　　版　2018年6月
定　　價　新台幣429元

作　　者　倍斯特編輯部
出　　版　倍斯特出版事業有限公司
發 行 人　周瑞德
電　　話　886-2-2351-2007
傳　　真　886-2-2351-0887
地　　址　100 台北市中正區福州街1號10樓之2
E-mail　best.books.service@gmail.com
官　　網　www.bestbookstw.com
執行總監　齊心瑀
行銷經理　楊景輝
企劃編輯　陳韋佑
封面構成　高鍾琪
內頁構成　菩薩蠻數位文化有限公司
印　　製　大亞彩色印刷製版股份有限公司

港澳地區總經銷　泛華發行代理有限公司
地　　址　香港新界將軍澳工業邨駿昌街7號2樓
電　　話　852-2798-2323
傳　　真　852-2796-5471

Simply Learning, Simply Best!

Simply Learning, Simply Best!